CW01334991

LINDSAY BUROKER

STAR KINGDOM
HOME FRONT
BOOK SEVEN

Home Front

Star Kingdom, Book 7

by Lindsay Buroker

Copyright © Lindsay Buroker 2020

No part of this book may be reproduced, scanned, or distributed in any printed or electronic form without permission. Please do not participate in or encourage piracy of copyrighted materials in violation of the author's rights. Thank you for respecting the hard work of this author.

This is a work of fiction. Names, characters, places, and incidents either are the product of the author's imagination or are used fictitiously, and any resemblance to locales, events, business establishments, or actual persons—living or dead—is entirely coincidental.

ACKNOWLEDGMENTS

THANK YOU FOR FOLLOWING ALONG WITH MY STAR Kingdom series. This is the second to last novel (or the penultimate, if you enjoy vocabulary words), and I hope you'll find it a satisfying adventure!

Before you get rolling, please allow me to thank those who continue to help me get these books out: my editor, Shelley Holloway, my beta readers, Sarah Engelke, Rue Silver, and Cindy Wilkinson, and my cover artist, Jeff Brown. Also, thank you to Cyd, Gen, and Jenna for hunting for typos. Thanks, everyone!

CHAPTER 1

AS THE KINGDOM WARSHIP THE *OSPREY* SPED TOWARD Stardust Palace Station, Casmir paced in sickbay, contemplating how he was going to get his friends Bonita and Qin out of the brig on the *Chivalrous*.

He would have the help of his stalwart troops—Zee and a dozen other six-and-a-half-feet-tall tarry black crushers were in sickbay with him, alarming the crewmen with their presence. But Jorg also had crushers on board the *Chivalrous,* maybe more than Casmir had. All he knew for certain was that ten of Jorg's crushers had raided Bonita's ship to capture her and Qin.

For now, troop numbers were moot since Prince Jorg's ship was several hours ahead of the *Osprey*. Maybe a day ahead. The warship was towing Bonita's freighter, so it had taken them longer to get up to speed.

Even if the *Osprey* and the *Chivalrous* had been flying side by side, Casmir wouldn't have been able to convince Captain Ishii to force board the other vessel, not when it was commanded by Prince Jorg and they were all part of one big happy fleet. One big happy fleet that kidnapped each other's friends.

"Does anybody else have a headache?" Casmir muttered.

"Crushers do not get headaches," Zee informed him.

"I knew you were superior beings."

"Do you feel that a seizure is incipient? I am attempting to determine how to accurately predict episodes of your health condition. My medical files inform me that ictal headaches are associated with seizure activity and may occur before or after the event." Zee peered down at him. "Do you feel confused or forgetful? Are any parts of your body experiencing numbness or tingling?" Zee picked up Casmir's hand in his cool metal fingers and examined it, as if such numbness might be visible on the outside.

"No. Thank you for asking. I believe this is a royalty-induced headache."

"My medical files do not mention such things."

"Odd."

"Uhm, is your robot holding your hand, Professor?" A nurse carrying tubes of SkinFill paused to look over at them.

"Zee is trying to learn how to predict my seizures," Casmir said. "It disturbs him that canines can do this but that crushers—so far—cannot."

Judging by the look the nurse gave them as he continued past, he didn't find that any less weird.

As Casmir extricated his hand from Zee's examination, the coffee grinder in Kim's borrowed lab whirred.

"Shall we continue to discuss Incursion Plan B?" Zee stepped back and lifted an arm to include all of the crushers.

Casmir had been brainstorming with them on the private network that Zee had set up. The crushers were doing most of the brainstorming, since they'd been programmed to be experts on battle tactics, while he observed and worried.

"I'm concerned," Casmir said, "that any incursion would result in crusher deaths if you had to face your doppelgängers."

He also worried that taking action against Jorg would seal his fate and that he'd never be allowed to go home. But how could he do nothing when the prince had his friends? Jorg had said he was using Bonita and Qin to ensure compliance from Casmir, Sir Bjarke, and Asger. He'd also implied that he would kill Bonita and Qin if Casmir didn't capture Prince Dubashi and his lethal bioweapons before he escaped System Stymphalia and threatened the Kingdom.

"They are not doppelgängers," Zee said. "They are early-model crushers, smaller and inferior to a Z-6000."

Casmir decided not to point out that he'd built Zee in one night on a space station, kludging him together from the metals and existing medical nanites he'd been able to find. "They are smaller, but as diminutive guys around the cosmos tell the ladies, size isn't everything."

Maybe he should point that out in a video to Princess Oku. He hadn't sent her a message since he'd received that startling video from her with her father at her side. King Jager had been prompting her to speak in between promising Casmir her hand in marriage if he became an obedient slave and stopped working at cross-purposes with the crown.

HOME FRONT

Casmir wanted to let her know that he liked her but that he would never accept an arranged marriage in which she was a prize to be won, dangled by her father with blatant manipulation. But how could he do that when that message had made it clear that Royal Intelligence was monitoring their exchanges? He wasn't sure how, since he'd encrypted everything he'd sent, and his encryptions were known to flummox entire classes of graduate students, but he had to accept that they had no privacy.

"It is true that they have existed longer than we have, and may have more combat experience, but we have been personally shaped by our maker." Zee pointed a finger at Casmir's chest, and Casmir forced himself to focus on the more immediate problem. "We have learned to be clever and versatile and to understand human quirks."

"You think that will help in a battle?"

"We will not be flummoxed by sarcasm or humor, should we encounter human troops on the mission." Zee lowered his finger. "You have been calling our incursion Plan B. Are you brainstorming a Plan A?"

"I'd like to figure out a way to negotiate with Prince Jorg for Bonita and Qin's return," Casmir said.

A bleary-eyed doctor wandered past the group, giving the crushers a wide berth, and walked into Kim's laboratory. The smell of coffee was now wafting out of it.

Casmir wondered if Kim was, besides making coffee, learning anything more about the virus Dubashi had created. She'd disappeared into the lab earlier, talking about researching the possibility of vaccines in case they couldn't stop the bioweapon in time. Casmir didn't want to think about failing at that. They *had* to find a way to stop Dubashi. Casmir's to-do list was long and daunting.

The coffee grinder started up again.

"Crusher observations suggest that Prince Jorg is more erratic and delusional than typical for a human," Zee said. "According to Klinger's military psychology book on dealing with enemies using non-combat methods, any attempt to negotiate with him should play into his delusions."

"Probably true," Casmir said. "I'll keep that in mind."

The doctor walked out, holding a covered mug of coffee. Casmir watched in bemusement as two crewmen strode out with similar mugs.

"I told you she'd make mochas if we found chocolate syrup," one told the other.

"I didn't say she wouldn't, just that it would be hard to find. Do you think Ambassador Romano will miss that bar?"

"His secretary said he doesn't like chocolate and wouldn't."

"He's weird."

"Yeah."

"One moment, Zee." Casmir held up a finger, then walked to Kim's lab, curious as to why his aloof, privacy-preferring best friend had turned into a coffee barista. And also wondering if she could make him a hot chocolate. "Kim?"

When he poked his head in, he found her sipping from a mug and reading the results of some experiment off a wall display.

"Have you opened shop?" Casmir pointed at the portable espresso maker, grinder, and bag of beans she'd brought from Odin.

"Not officially."

"Unofficially?"

Her lips pressed together in disapproval. "Word got out that I have an espresso machine. The crew finds the coffee bulbs in the ship's stores as execrable as I do."

"Can you make me a hot chocolate?"

She frowned at him. "I'm studying outbreaks of the Orthobuliaviricetes virus over the last century and computer modeling the potential spread of the modified and far more deadly version that Scholar Sunflyer made, using estimates of virulence from the notes I found."

"But you made other people hot chocolates." Casmir smiled. He wasn't unconcerned about the virus, but he'd gotten the astroshaman leader Kyla Moonrazor to close off the wormhole gate leading out of System Stymphalia, so, at least for now, that threat couldn't get to Odin.

"Those were mochas. Espresso with chocolate syrup in it."

"Couldn't you make me the same thing without the espresso? I'm working on possible solutions to our problems, but my brain is tired. I think it needs sugar. Brains operate on sugar, you know."

"The brain operates on glucose, yes, but the human body can acquire glucose from any carbohydrate and can also, through a process called gluconeogenesis, convert it from protein. You don't *need* sugar."

"My brain is lazy. It doesn't want to convert anything. It—" A message appeared on Casmir's chip, and he grimaced. "Never mind. Captain Ishii wants me on the bridge." As he read on, he grimaced again. "He's expecting a comm from Prince Jorg."

"Will you get a chance to implement Plan A?"

He'd told Kim about his options earlier.

"I'll give it a shot." Casmir backed out of her lab and sent the rest of his thoughts to her chip. Zee joined him, leaving the rest of the crushers in sickbay. *I doubt he's going to negotiate with me. Regardless, I think we're going to need autonomy to implement any of our plans. I'll check on the repair status of Bonita's ship while I'm on the bridge.*

If we take it and leave the Osprey *again without permission...*

Casmir was flattered that she assumed he would be able to figure out a way to escape a Kingdom warship with a scruffy—and much slower—freighter, but maybe it would be better if he couldn't.

I know. I can kiss my arranged marriage to Oku goodbye. He'd also filled her in on that during their journey.

I was more concerned about neither of us ever being able to go home again.

I know, but we can't leave Bonita and Qin in Jorg's unstable hands. Casmir shuddered, remembering the video that Jorg had sent over of them beaten and battered in a brig cell on his ship. *And I doubt we'll be able to catch Dubashi if we're stuck doing it Jorg's way. Have you been in contact with Rache? I wonder if there's any chance he would taxi us around again.*

Casmir doubted they would be able to catch up with Dubashi even if they slipped away in the *Dragon,* but Rache's fast warship was another matter.

The last I heard, he wanted you to buy one of those mushroom-fiber purses for Jorg.

That wasn't going to be one of my negotiation tactics.

It was what Rache wanted in exchange for not attacking Jorg's ship while our friends are on board.

You shouldn't have to bribe a man not to blow up a ship, Kim.

Dubashi hired him to kill Jorg as well as Jager.

Casmir had already known that, but as he stepped into the lift and headed to the bridge, he rubbed his face, feeling newly distraught that his clone brother would happily assassinate a plethora of people. Even though he had no love for Jorg, Casmir didn't want to see his ship blown up. He *especially* didn't want to see it blown up with his friends in the brig.

I don't want him to assassinate anyone, Kim added, *but there's a cold analytical part of my mind that wonders if the removal of Jager and Jorg wouldn't solve some problems for our people.*

He shuddered again, horrified at even innocent musings that condoned murder. *It would create different problems—and possibly bring in a time of civil war and upheaval, since the Senate would not accept Oku as a leader and Finn is barely old enough to shave. Any upheaval would only make it easier for Dubashi to enact his plans to wipe out all humans on Odin and take over the planet for his own people. Did your models of virus spread show whether that's possible with the two rockets he got away with?*

After a grim pause, Kim admitted, *It's possible.*

I was afraid of that.

Casmir, not expecting trouble on Ishii's ship, stepped onto the bridge ahead of Zee. Two marines in combat armor with DEW-Tek rifles in their hands were positioned to either side of the door, and they reached for him.

"What?" Casmir blurted, halting.

Zee surged past him, grabbed the marines, knocked their rifles aside, and spun them into the wall. Casmir scurried back into the corridor and out of the way. The marines recovered from their surprise enough to fight back, but Zee was stronger than they were, even with the armor enhancing their human muscles, and they couldn't break his grip.

"Don't fire!" Ishii called from the command chair in the center of the bridge. "Dabrowski, tell your robot to knock it off." He sounded more exasperated than alarmed.

"I am a Z-6000 programmed to protect Kim Sato and Casmir Dabrowski," Zee said sternly over the thumps and bangs of ongoing struggles.

"Yeah, yeah," Ishii said. "I know. Dabrowski, get in here."

"It was a mistake, Zee." Casmir lifted his hands in placation as one of the marines thudded into the door frame. He *hoped* it had been a mistake. "Let them go, please."

Zee released the marines, but he stood in the doorway with his back to Casmir, so nobody from the bridge could get to him. Silence fell inside, punctuated only by a few pained grunts and soft curses from the marines.

"I said to *pretend* to apprehend him," Ishii said, "and loom at his side for this comm call with the prince."

"We *were* pretending, sir," one of the men muttered sullenly.

Casmir bent his head—he didn't have to bend it far—to peer under Zee's armpit. "Good morning, Sora. Maybe if you'd warned me that we were going to perpetrate a ruse, I could have informed Zee."

Ishii stood and faced him. "I didn't realize he'd be trailing you like an enraptured lover."

"Or perhaps a bodyguard?"

"Maybe an enraptured bodyguard." Ishii gave Zee a dyspeptic look and waved for Casmir to come inside.

Casmir patted Zee on the shoulder. "I think you can move aside now."

"Your supposed human allies do not treat you with appropriate respect, Casmir Dabrowski." Zee looked at Ishii, then at the marines. One of them was flexing his arm and glowering back.

"I've failed to earn   it then. Let me go in and practice my negotiating and people skills on Captain Ishii. He won't be nearly as hard to win over as Prince Jorg."

Judging from the way Ishii folded his arms over his chest and glared at him, he didn't agree.

Zee stepped aside but walked close behind as Casmir joined Ishii at the command chair.

"Can you have him stand over there?" Ishii pointed at a wall. "Prince Jorg is comming in three minutes, and he believes you've been in the brig since I captured your shuttle, not loitering at the new sickbay coffee shop like a feckless university student meandering through his major on his parents' crowns."

"I didn't know word of the coffee shop had spread." Casmir pointed for Zee to move to the indicated spot. The last thing he wanted was for Ishii to imprison him for real.

"I understand Doctors Sikou and Angelico were upset when Sato sneaked off the ship and failed to leave instructions on the espresso machine's operation."

"I didn't realize it was such an advanced piece of machinery."

"One minute, sir," the communications officer said.

Ishii glanced at the large forward display. Currently, it showed a field of stars. Casmir wished it could go on showing that. He didn't want to see a giant version of Jorg's face. Or any version at all.

"Is there any point in me suggesting that you cooperate wholeheartedly with him?" Ishii waved his marines to come closer and frame Casmir. "While bowing deeply, groveling, and perhaps throwing in some genuflections?"

"I don't think I can do all that at once without falling onto your deck."

"Just don't have a seizure. It won't win any sympathy from him."

Casmir doubted *anything* won sympathy from Jorg.

As the communications officer announced, "Incoming comm, sir," Casmir clasped his hands behind his back and tried to look like a forlorn prisoner, though it troubled him that Ishii felt the need to perpetrate the ruse. If not for Casmir and his friends, Dubashi wouldn't have lost his potential mercenary army—and his entire moon base. Shouldn't he be rewarded for his initiative? Or at least, shouldn't Bonita and Qin be let go because of that initiative?

Zee glared at the two marines as they stepped close to Casmir. One lifted a hand, as if to grip his shoulder and hold him in place, but Zee leaned forward, and the man dropped it.

Prince Jorg's face appeared on the display. Ishii and Casmir bowed deeply, as did everyone else on the bridge. The hawk-nosed Jorg wore a faint sneer, and this polite display of respect did not alleviate it.

"You are on course to Stardust Palace Station to retrieve the rest of the crushers, Captain?" Jorg asked without preamble.

"Yes, Your Highness," Ishii said, his tone much more reverent now than it had been with Casmir, "though we have not yet been given permission to dock there."

"Has the sultan explicitly denied you permission?" Jorg demanded.

"Yes, Your Highness. We did ask."

"Find a way to acquire permission, load the crushers onto the *Osprey*, and while you are there, I want you to get the slydar detector from Shayban."

Ishii blinked. "Your Highness?"

"Your Intelligence officers must be aware that such a thing exists now."

Casmir knew from firsthand experience that it did and that Shayban had one. He didn't know if it was a device or software that worked with existing scanners, but he had witnessed Stardust Palace Station effectively firing on Rache's slydar-camouflaged ship.

"We are, Your Highness, but we've also learned that the devices have to be purchased from Sayona Station in System Cerberus. As you know, we can't leave Stymphalia right now."

"The *Chivalrous* is going to go work on that problem now while acquiring more allies."

Go work on that problem? Where would Jorg go? It would be harder for Casmir to get his friends back if he had to fly halfway across the system to catch up to the *Chivalrous*.

HOME FRONT

"But you misunderstand me, Captain," Jorg continued. "I don't want you to buy a slydar detector from some unscrupulous huckster. I want you to get the one that's proven to work from Sultan Shayban. Either copy his software, if that's all it is, or get him to give you the device. You are authorized to pay him a fair price for it. If he is unwilling to give it up, you will force the issue. We will need it as soon as we're able to return home. Sooner. We must find Prince Dubashi's ship and destroy him before he can take those rockets to System Lion."

"I see," Ishii said carefully. "I'll attempt to get Shayban to sell it to us, or perhaps lend it to us."

"You will not *attempt* this. You will succeed at it."

Ishii only hesitated a second before saying, "Yes, Your Highness."

Casmir wondered why he'd been called up to the bridge for this. Jorg hadn't looked at him yet. Casmir would prefer to keep it that way, but he had to take a shot at getting Qin and Bonita back while they were still close.

As he opened his mouth, Jorg looked at him.

"Dabrowski."

"Ah, yes, Your Highness?"

"Your friends are being held safely. As long as you cooperate with the crown's wishes, they will be freed and permitted to return to their ship, which I magnanimously allowed Captain Ishii to collect and repair."

Magnanimously. Right. Given the way Ishii's lips twisted, Jorg had probably thrown a fit when he'd first learned the *Osprey* was towing it.

"And what are the crown's wishes?" Casmir asked.

"As I said, pick up the rest of the new crushers and retrieve the slydar detector by whatever means necessary. Since my intel officers have informed me that you've established a rapport with Sultan Shayban—" Jorg's eyebrows twitched, "—you will personally be responsible for getting the slydar detector. If you fail at either of these things, your friends' lives will be forfeit."

"But they haven't done anything," Casmir blurted before he could stop himself.

"Since they are bounty hunters, I highly doubt that is true. Regardless, their deaths would be completely your responsibility. It was your choice to defy my wishes and suborn two of my knights that prompted this action. Your actions have been treasonous from the day you first left Odin."

"Your Highness." Casmir calmly spread his arms and bowed, though his brain was gibbering and he wanted to collapse on the deck and thump his fists against it. "All I've done is seek to end the war and help our people. If what I thought was taking initiative you consider treason, I apologize. I will happily trade myself for them and serve you to the best of my abilities. From your brig if you wish."

"You'll serve me to the best of your abilities from Ishii's ship and from between those two marines. Only if you do so will I release your co-conspirators."

Casmir stared bleakly at him. These orders to steal from Shayban were criminal.

"If you do anything else, Dabrowski," Jorg said, his eyes slitted, "or if you try to rescue my prisoners, I will consider you an enemy of the Kingdom and order you shot on sight. And the prisoners will be executed."

"Will you let me speak to them?" The horrible thought occurred to Casmir that Bonita and Qin might already be dead. "Or at least see them?"

"No. That will be your reward for compliance. Take him to Stardust Palace, Ishii." Jorg closed the channel.

One man's compliance was another man's theft…

"Officers talk," Ishii said quietly, waving the marines back. "I've heard your friends are still alive."

"I hope so," Casmir said.

"I need you to get us invited to Stardust Palace. Even with the other warships with us, Shayban has enough firepower to give us trouble if we try to force our way in. There are weapons platforms all over that asteroid. Even if we get past them, he has all those crushers. Fully finished and operational, I assume. How many are left there? Eighty-eight? Hell, I don't want to send my people against that army."

"Comm him." With defeat making his heart heavy, Casmir didn't point out that the crushers wouldn't be a problem. He could order them to stand down. Everything *else* was the problem.

Ishii flicked a finger toward his communications officer. It didn't take long for Shayban's face to appear on the display, his white hair mostly covered by a turban, his bushy eyebrows drawn down in a V.

"I told you that you people don't have permission to dock here, but our scanners show you are still en route to our station with three of your warships." Shayban's scowl deepened. "We *will* open fire on you if you approach. The Kingdom is not welcome here." His gaze shifted to the side, and his tone lightened. "Professor Dabrowski?"

"Yes, Sultan."

The marines had stepped back but still stood behind Casmir, and Shayban asked, "Are you… a prisoner?"

Casmir considered the question. When he'd first met Shayban, he'd implied he was on the outs with the Kingdom. It hadn't exactly been a lie. Unfortunately.

"I'm being offered the chance to remedy past grievances so my friends will be safe."

Ishii's eyes narrowed, but he didn't refute anything. Shayban also squinted, if for a different reason, and Casmir suspected the intelligent and self-made Miners' Union leader had no trouble understanding far more than he'd said.

"May we be permitted to dock?" Casmir asked.

"The ship carrying *you*, Professor, may dock. The others may not. And when you arrive, only you and your most trusted allies may walk onto my station."

Ishii's eyes were now so narrow, Casmir wondered if he could still see.

"He's not going to kidnap you and your team, is he?" Ishii growled under his breath.

Casmir shook his head. "Thank you, Sultan. I look forward to seeing you again."

Casmir did *not* look forward to trying to swindle the man out of his slydar detector. But with Bonita's and Qin's lives at stake, what else could he do?

CHAPTER 2

KIM SATO PACED IN HER LAB, TRYING NOT to think about the data-based simulations she'd run for how rapidly the modified Orthobuliaviricetes virus could spread if those rockets were detonated over Odin's population centers. It was hard.

"Solutions," she muttered to herself. "Think of solutions, not how bad the problem is."

If she *had* the virus, she could have attempted to work on a vaccine, even though virology wasn't her area of expertise. But even if she'd carried samples away from Dubashi's base, Captain Ishii would have forbidden them on his ship. Understandably. The *Osprey* didn't have a lab capable of safely isolating such a deadly virus.

"Scholar Sato?" came a male voice from the doorway.

"I'm not making any more, but you can use my machine if you want espresso." Kim waved to the counter—she was tempted to move it out to a counter in sickbay so the crew wouldn't bother her in their quest for superior coffee, but she was reluctant to let it out of her sight. If something happened to it, she would be stuck drinking those dreadful coffee bulbs with all the suspicious ingredients.

"That's not why we're here."

Kim faced the newcomer, a sandy-blond-haired lieutenant it took her a minute to place. Meister, one of the ship's Intelligence officers. He'd had a long conversation with Casmir a couple of months earlier about his relationship to Rache. And now he was looking intently at her.

Behind him stood Lieutenant Grunburg, the chipper young programmer who'd helped Casmir come up with a solution to the astroshaman computer virus that had stripped the *Osprey* of power and nearly sent it crashing into a moon. All that seemed like long ago now.

"Are you looking for Professor Dabrowski?" Kim hoped whatever they wanted had nothing to do with her—or Rache.

"We'll be speaking with him too."

Why did that sound ominous?

"But I need to talk to you first, Scholar Sato. If you'll permit it?" The way Meister raised his eyebrows seemed like he was testing her.

What happened if she *didn't* permit it? She was a civilian, not in the military's chain of command. They couldn't order her to go along with an interrogation.

Which this might not be. She shouldn't make assumptions. Maybe all they wanted was her mocha recipe.

Nodding curtly, Kim waved them in. The lab had only one seat—a stool that was locked to the deck in front of the counter. She put her back to the wall, not feeling comfortable enough to sit.

"Ambassador Romano has requested that I ask you a few questions." Meister smiled briefly.

"Is there a malfunction at one of the nineteen speech-assisting points between his vocal folds and lips that precludes him from speaking for himself?"

Meister walked in with a tablet under his arm and didn't respond other than to furrow his brow slightly.

"From what I've heard, he yells a lot," Grunburg said. "Maybe his uvula is sore."

Meister shifted the frown to him. "You may wait outside. You're here to talk to Dabrowski when he's done on the bridge."

"I thought I'd get a drink first." Grunburg winked at Kim as he walked to the espresso machine. He eyed the various handles, knobs, and steamer nozzle. "If Dabrowski can work this thing, I'm sure I can."

"He can't." Kim wasn't sure if that wink suggested she had an ally or only that Grunburg thought Meister was a twit, but she doubted an interrogation would get intense with him in the room. He had a puppy-dog mien about him, and she remembered that he'd once taken classes from Casmir and liked him.

"He *can't?*" Grunburg pointed at the appliance in disbelief.

"Because of a lack of interest, not aptitude. He's more interested in hot cocoa than coffee. If he wanted, I'm sure he could give it intelligence

HOME FRONT

and have it anticipate the needs of nearby humans and dispense perfect beverages at a glance."

"Sounds right." Grunburg grabbed one of the small magnetic cups someone had brought in and stuck to a wall and set to work.

Meister tapped an impatient finger on his tablet, apparently not interested in asking his questions until Grunburg left. Kim hoped the programmer took a long time making his drink.

Casmir, she sent a message through her chip. *What are you doing?*

Debating my current problematic and uncomfortable position between a rock and a hard place. You?

Lieutenant Meister from Fleet Intelligence is here to ask me questions. Romano sent him. He wants to speak with you too.

Does that mean I should hurry down or do my best to avoid your lab until we reach Stardust Palace?

It's up to you. I believe I'm stuck here.

I'll come down soon in case you need moral support. Ishii is briefing me on how not to piss off Jorg further.

That would require an encyclopedia set of knowledge, not a briefing.

Likely so.

Grunburg slurped loudly from his cup, a straight espresso now in hand.

Meister jerked his chin toward the door. "Wait outside until Dabrowski shows up. Then *knock* before entering. Wait to be called in."

"You know we're the same rank, right, Meister? And you're not in my chain of command."

"I'm in Intelligence."

"So? I'm the ship's chief programmer. I can make that tablet self-destruct in your hands if I want."

"It must be fabulous to have super powers. Now, shoo." Meister waved him toward the door.

On his way out, Grunburg rolled his eyes for Kim's sake. She was starting to like him.

As soon as the door shut, Meister started speaking. "Tell me, Scholar Sato, how you came to be in Rache's hands and on his ship *again* this month."

Ugh.

Once, she'd had a good reputation with the Kingdom and the Fleet, but then she'd run away from Jorg instead of obediently coming to his ship to make a bioweapon. Now, it seemed, she would be held in suspicion.

She considered whether she could get in trouble for not answering. She was *horrible* at lying. With silence, however, she could also imply guilt. But would Meister have come down here if guilt wasn't already implied?

"I don't believe I shall answer your questions, Lieutenant. Or Ambassador Romano's questions, if that's what this is. I have watched as every time Casmir does something for the good of the Kingdom, he is deemed less trustworthy and more criminal in the eyes of the Fleet and the king. It's a poor precedent for enticing me to tell truths."

"So there *is* a truth to tell."

"Events happened, as they do. You can call them whatever you wish."

"Are you sure you don't want to describe those events to me? One of our Intelligence officers was able to acquire video footage from the ship bay on Stardust Palace. The ship bay where Rache came in and—it appears—kidnapped you. You were conveniently waiting in that ship bay. That being the natural place for biologists and roboticists to spend time."

Kim had always found extended eye contact uncomfortable, so she didn't stare mulishly at Meister as she withheld commentary. She went to the stool and sat down before the display, bringing up the virus data again. Previously, looking at it had alarmed her, but she now found it more soothing than the lieutenant's implications.

"Several days ago, that officer also noticed a signal sent from a hidden ship in space that we believe to have been the *Fedallah* to the *Osprey*. It took him a while to pinpoint whose chip it went to—he suspected Dabrowski, at first. Interesting that it went to yours."

Kim stared at the display without seeing anything. Had Intelligence broken the encryption and been able to read Rache's message? She had it saved on her chip, so she could look up exactly what it said. It hadn't been a proclamation of love, but the words made it clear that she and Rache were... not enemies.

She barely kept from reacting when she realized the contents also implied that Casmir was the one responsible, or at least had made the request, for having the gate shut down.

"Do you have anything to say now, Scholar Sato?"

"I do not. If you're prepared to arrest me and question me under eslevoamytal, you may find me chattier, but I will remind you that I am a civilian, not a soldier, and I've taken no oaths to the king or the service. I have committed no crimes, nor assisted anyone in committing any. It's within my right to speak with whom I wish."

"Not a man who's murdered thousands of soldiers," Meister snapped, losing his cool for the first time.

"Assisting him with a crime would be illegal. Speaking with him is not."

"It's always delightful to find a barracks lawyer on a ship."

"I have work to do, Lieutenant."

Meister came over to loom beside her, so she couldn't miss seeing him. "For your information, I *have* been given the authority to arrest you and question you under a truth drug."

Kim kept her face from showing any reactions, but a bio-scanner would have read her heart rate climbing. Sweat pricked at her armpits. What might she babble out under the influence of eslevoamytal? That she liked seeing Rache with his shirt off and liked *him*? Maybe that she thought she could one day fall in *love* with him? She hadn't even admitted that to herself, but who knew what her subconscious mind would spew out if no restraints were in place?

"Whose authority?" She was impressed how flat and indifferent her voice came out, as if she had nothing to worry about at all. As if every soldier on this ship wouldn't line up to shoot her if they knew her true feelings. Even Casmir thought she was crazy to care for Rache. "Ambassador Romano doesn't have any—"

"King Jager himself."

Kim couldn't keep from glancing in surprise at him. "The wormhole gate isn't working. Such a message couldn't have gotten through."

"It came through before the gate stopped operating. You've been a suspect since you disappeared from the *Osprey* weeks ago. Ambassador Romano, Prince Jorg, and I have been discussing your situation since we captured you."

Captured. Was that truly what had happened? She'd thought she and Casmir—and Asger and Bjarke—were being given a ride because the *Dragon* had been inoperable and the shuttle they'd borrowed from Rache hadn't had long-range capacity. Ishii had been friendly enough with her, and he hadn't even yelled at Casmir. Had she been foolish in believing he'd been helping them?

"What do you want, Lieutenant?"

"To question you. I might have settled for doing it without drugs, since I've been trained to read people, but after spending ten minutes with you, I can see that you're good at hiding your thoughts. I believe I'll use eslevoamytal after all."

Kim stood and faced him. He didn't back away. She didn't like how close they were, but with the stool behind her, she couldn't gracefully put more space between them.

"Lieutenant," she said, struggling not to give away how afraid she was that she would babble condemning evidence under that drug, "my family is on Odin. My father and brothers. My work is on Odin. Colleagues that I care about. You have in me someone willing to work very hard to ensure that Dubashi's virus isn't unleashed on Odin, and someone with the knowledge to deal with it when we find him. Very few people in this system who are qualified to work with such deadly viruses will do a damn thing to assist with what is, in their eyes, the Kingdom's problem."

She didn't know that was true, but it sounded plausible. It wasn't as if Jorg had made friends here.

"I will not stop you from working on a cure, if that's truly what you're doing." Meister glanced at the display.

"How generous of you. But what I meant to imply is that I will *not* do this work for you if you treat me like a criminal and ignore my rights."

"You just said your family is there. You'll do the work even if we question you."

"Will I?" Kim lifted her chin, hoping she was better at bluffing than she believed. She kept from wiping her damp palms on the legs of her galaxy suit—barely. The garment should have adjusted its temperature to keep her from sweating, but this was cold fear-sweat.

Meister squinted into her eyes. As uncomfortable as it was, she made herself stare back into his. Nothing in them was elucidating. He might think she was hard to read, but she was abysmal at reading other people too.

The door opened, and she jumped.

"He said to knock, Professor," Grunburg's voice floated in from the corridor.

"Did he?" Casmir stood in view. "You don't usually have to knock at a coffee shop. Kim promised me a hot chocolate."

"In that case, maybe he won't mind."

"Good." Casmir ambled in, smiling broadly at Kim and Meister while ignoring the tension hanging in the air. "Hi, guys. What's going on? Lieutenant, mind if I help myself?" He waved at the espresso machine.

"Your interview isn't until after Scholar Sato's," Meister said.

"No? Why don't you just do us both at the same time?" Casmir waved Kim to the side and sat on the stool, placing himself between the two of them. He wasn't even remotely an intimidating or inhibiting presence, but then Zee strode in, his bulk making the lab feel claustrophobic. "It'll save time," Casmir added. "Back home, we're roommates, you know. We tell each other everything. We don't have any secrets."

"Maybe you're the one I should drug." Meister grabbed his tablet off the counter and stepped back, glancing warily at Zee.

"With what? Most drugs give me seizures. Or put me into anaphylactic shock. Cashews and pomegranates also do that. You wouldn't want to be me, Lieutenant. Going through life in my shoes means constantly dodging bullets."

"Cashew bullets?" Kim asked, hoping Casmir's blatant attempt to diffuse the tension—and sidetrack Meister's train of thought—would work.

"Just so. Fortunately, I've got Zee now." Casmir waved at the crusher, giving him the warmest and most authentic smile a killing machine had ever gotten. "He steps in front of a lot of bullets meant for me."

"It is my duty to protect Kim Sato and Casmir Dabrowski from all threats," Zee said in his typical monotone. "Including bullets, energy bolts, and highly allergenic food projectiles."

"And he'd naturally step in if someone wanted to drug me. Or drug one of my friends." Casmir's voice didn't do cold and menacing, not the way Rache's did, but he did lose his usual affability as he gave Meister a pointed look.

He must have stopped to chat with Grunburg and get the gist of what was going on.

"I would do this," Zee agreed.

Meister glanced at him again, then squinted at Kim. "We'll continue this later. After I discuss with Dr. Sikou if you're as integral to solving this virus problem as you're telling me you are."

Meister stalked toward the door, the gesture less imperious than he surely intended, since Zee didn't step aside for him. Why he'd thought Zee would, Kim didn't know, but he stopped short just before crashing into him. Swearing under his breath, Meister went around and strode out.

"Dr. Sikou should vouch for me," Kim said quietly. "My expertise anyway. I'm not sure she'll agree that I'd withhold my help simply because they drugged me."

About Rache? Casmir asked, switching to chip-to-chip contact. The lab—the entire ship—was probably monitored.

Yes. They're suspicious of that supposed kidnapping. Kim sighed. *And I'm afraid I'll admit to how I feel about him and that'll be enough to condemn me to a firing squad.*

I'm sorry. That kidnapping was my idea. Casmir grimaced. *Come to think of it, I'm the one who suggested you flee the* Osprey *instead of going to work for Jorg.*

You are. Later, when Zee isn't around, I'm going to pelt you with pomegranate seeds.

Casmir didn't smile. His face was contorted with grief and regret.

It's not your fault, Casmir. I chose to go along with your ideas. And if I hadn't, I would have ended up in Jorg's brig weeks ago. And probably questioned weeks ago. I couldn't have made that man a bioweapon. She hoped Jorg didn't still have it in his head that she should.

How did we both end up as criminals in the eyes of our people, Kim?

I don't know, she replied, though she could have made a bullet list of all the things they'd done to irk the king and the Fleet. *We should be heroes after risking our asses to stop Dubashi. Or at least pardoned of any crimes.*

I wish we'd actually caught him. Then our heroness would be less up for debate. Is that a word?

It's not.

No wonder we're in trouble.

Grunburg knocked on his way in. "Professor?"

Ugh, what now? Casmir messaged Kim, but he forced a smile for his former student. "Whatcha need, Davy?"

"Remember that virus we worked on?" Grunburg glanced at Kim's display. "The computer one that knocked out the ship, not a human one."

"I remember it well. So do the pirates we used it on in System Hydra. Or they would if any had survived." Casmir's face was grim at the memory of how he'd inadvertently caused all those deaths.

"Ah." Grunburg hesitated, not appearing certain how to respond. "Better pirates than our people."

Casmir's hand wave connoted helplessness rather than agreement.

"While all this other stuff has been going on—" Grunburg gestured vaguely toward the ship, or maybe the entire star system, "—my department has been working on finding a way to nullify it in case it's ever used on us again. We believe we've now got a subroutine in our anti-virus software that accomplishes that."

HOME FRONT

Casmir nodded, though it wasn't apparent, at least to Kim, what Grunburg was getting at. She'd assumed Intelligence also wanted to question Casmir about Rache.

"We've also been trying to figure out how to deploy the virus ourselves, as a weapon to deal with enemies such as those blockading System Lion's gate, but we're missing something." Grunburg frowned. "We tried to use it against Dubashi's base, but they wouldn't accept a file from us. The mercenaries weren't as bright—we tricked some into taking it. But nothing happened. Unless everybody in the Twelve Systems now has a defense for it, we're missing something."

"I doubt the mercenaries have a defense," Casmir said. "Dubashi probably would have, even if one of his minions had been fooled into accepting it. He's an astroshaman himself."

"Yeah, Meister dug that up. But will you work with us on this, Professor? Right now, Intel hasn't been able to locate Dubashi's ship, but I heard Sultan Shayban might give us his slydar detector."

Casmir snorted. Kim didn't know the story there, but she doubted Shayban would *give* the Kingdom anything more helpful than a case of space shingles.

"Once we can locate Dubashi's ship," Grunburg went on, "we can go after it and unleash the virus. Maybe it won't work, but if it does, we could blow up his powerless ship—and destroy the virus-laden rockets he has—and maybe put an end to the war at home before we even arrive." He raised his eyebrows, looking hopeful. And naive.

"Didn't you just say Dubashi would have a counter to the computer virus?" Kim asked Casmir.

"I don't *know* that he has one. I just wouldn't be surprised if he had prior knowledge of it and is prepared." Casmir tilted his head. "But that doesn't mean all the ships he sent to System Lion would be prepared. It's worth getting it ready so you guys can try to send it when we get there." Casmir nodded to Grunburg.

"Oh, good. Come this way, Professor. I'll show you our computer lab and introduce you to the rest of my team." Grunburg smiled, as if they were on their way to camp and would have a delightful time making fires and toasting marshmallows. Or, more likely, programming robots and computers.

Why can't you make friends with our world leaders as easily as you make them with random enemies and the common man? Kim messaged as Casmir left the lab, Zee trailing dutifully behind him.

I don't think Grunburg is representative of the common man.
That's true. You make friends with geeks and nerds.
Precisely. The problem is that those aren't the people who rule the Kingdom.

Kim sighed, wondering if there was any way she could avoid Meister's drug needle for the rest of the trip. *Maybe that* is *the problem.*

Sweat bathed Asger's face as he and his father broke apart. They'd been sparring for over an hour. The low gravity on the *Osprey* made it less onerous than it would have been on Odin, but they were both breathless.

Asger had been ready to stop twenty minutes ago, but he hadn't wanted to be the one to suggest quitting first. He was relieved that sweat also bathed his father's face and dampened his short gray beard.

"Towel?" Asger stepped off the mat to grab two.

His father grunted. He hadn't spoken much during their match, and Asger had gotten in a few blows that suggested he was preoccupied.

Thinking about Bonita? Asger wasn't sure how close they were, but he'd seen them flirt—if throwing insults at each other could be called flirting.

Asger himself was worried about Qin and frustrated that the person who held her wasn't a person he could attack. How the hell were they supposed to get Qin and Bonita off Jorg's ship?

He tossed a towel to his father. They'd exercised together each of the three days since leaving Dubashi's moon base, where they'd formed an unspoken truce. Asger wasn't sure what had happened, but during that incursion, his father had opened up to him for the first time that he could remember.

It was good not to be arguing with him or stomping around in anger, but their new bond was hard to appreciate when Asger was worried about Qin. There had been a time—a long time—when he never would have believed a friend could be in danger from the Kingdom or any officer in the Fleet, but that time had come to an end. He'd seen the video Jorg had sent to Casmir—to ensure his compliance—of bruised and battered Qin in the brig of the *Chivalrous*. Jorg didn't deserve to command a ship with that name. Or any ship at all.

"I've heard the *Osprey* is going to Stardust Palace." His father wiped his face with the towel. "The sultan has agreed not to fire on us, but he doesn't yet know we have orders to take his slydar detector."

"We do?" Asger hadn't officially been kicked out of the knighthood yet—he'd been hoping vainly that helping to defeat Dubashi and thwart his plans might ultimately put him back in better standing—but he wasn't in the loop. This was a reminder of that.

"Dabrowski has those orders, specifically, but Captain Ishii already told me the *Osprey* is going in to back him. Jorg and the *Chivalrous* are heading elsewhere." He clenched his jaw. "To gather more allies. Or take more prisoners. Who knows?"

Asger switched to the privacy of messaging via his chip to ask, *Are you thinking about trying to do something about Jorg's prisoners?*

I'm thinking about it, yes. If I want to rescue them, it would have to be soon. His father closed his eyes, his face pained. *It would mean the end of my career, maybe the end of my citizenship in the Kingdom and the loss of our family land, but I don't trust that Jorg won't kill them.* His jaw tightened again. *They're not Kingdom citizens. What are they to him?*

I'll go with you if we can figure out a way to get invited to his ship.

His father shook his head. *I'll go alone. Better to lose one career than two.*

My career is already at its end. And it's not like I wouldn't be suspect even if you acted alone.

His father grimaced but didn't deny it.

Once, his father never would have questioned the crown. But times had changed. Asger was a little glad that his father understood now, but he never would have chosen these circumstances as a way to make that happen.

The gym door opened. Asger wouldn't have thought anything of it, since crewmen in exercise togs had been in and out, but Ishii strode toward them in uniform, a lieutenant with Intel tabs on his collars walking at his side.

"Are we in trouble?" Asger muttered, wondering if Intel was monitoring their chip communications somehow.

If so, they'd reacted to that conversation quickly.

Asger's father draped the towel over his shoulder, folded his muscular arms over his chest, and lifted his chin as the officers approached.

Asger, deciding to appear formidable and unconcerned, as befitting a knight, adopted a similar pose. It probably wasn't the time for it, but he noticed as they stood side by side that his arms were more muscular. His father was still as fit as any knight, but he'd either lost some of his mass as he approached sixty, or he wasn't as large as he'd always been in Asger's mind. Memories etched in boyhood were hard to alter, after all.

"Sir Asger, Sir Asger." Ishii nodded at both of them. "Lieutenant Meister has a few questions for Bjarke."

"Does that mean *I'm* not the one in trouble for once?" Asger smiled, though nerves pounced in his stomach.

"Neither of you is in trouble with *me*," Ishii said. "How Prince Jorg and your knightly superiors feel about you is up for debate."

"Our knightly superiors are all on the other side of two blocked wormholes," Asger's father said. "We're the only representatives of the Order in this system."

That was true, since Tristan—formerly Sir Tristan Tremayne—had been kicked out of the knighthood. Asger didn't bring him up. He had remained on the *Stellar Dragon* during repairs, and Asger didn't know if Ishii or Intelligence even knew about him.

"Since I'm a loyal officer of the crown," Ishii said, "I won't say that I wish the prince was."

Meister frowned at his captain, then led Asger's father away.

Asger caught the name *Druckers* as the lieutenant started to speak. That wasn't what he'd expected the questioning to involve.

"What's that about?" Asger asked Ishii.

"There's a big queue of ships waiting at the gate while scientists and engineers from a few of the system's governments attempt to figure out what's wrong," Ishii said. "Among the waiting craft are two of the five Drucker pirate warships. Since your father worked for them for a year, Meister is asking him about them."

"Do we care about the Druckers? They're pirates, not mercenaries. It's not like Jorg could hire them to help us, even if he would consider lowering himself to speak with them."

"We care only if they become a threat to the Kingdom because somebody *else* hires them."

"Is that likely to happen?" Asger asked.

"Probably not. We're just keeping an eye on them for now. Once we complete our mission at Stardust Palace, we're going to have to join that queue for the gate, along with those pirates and a lot of the mercenaries that Dubashi almost hired to attack us."

"Ah. It could get tense."

"Yes. I want to wish that the gate is repaired before we're ready to go through it, but if we can leave, Dubashi can leave."

Lieutenant Meister returned to Ishii's side. "I'm done, sir."

Ishii nodded to Asger and his father, and the officers left.

"Did you have anything useful for him?" Asger asked his father.

"Not really. I promised to send all the technical details I can for the two Drucker ships. I spent a few months on the *Jian*, so that one is easy, and I have some specs on the *Scimitar*." His father looked thoughtfully toward one of the view ports.

"Fondly reminiscing about your time there?"

"Hardly that. I was thinking of… what we discussed earlier." His father switched back to chip-to-chip messaging to admit, *I'm worried about Bonita. And her first mate.*

Qin. Asger was prepared to bristle if he called her a freak or said anything derogatory.

Yes, Qin. They never would have been captured if Jorg didn't have all those crushers. She's quite a fighter. His father smiled briefly. *They both are. Jorg has somewhere around a dozen crushers and numerous men on that ship. I need to think about a way to free Bonita and Qin.*

He tossed his towel in the recycler and headed for the door.

You mean we *need to. Don't forget I'm coming with you.*

His father looked back. *Very well. We. But do not blame me when we're both ostracized from System Lion and your second cousin is running the estate.*

Asger didn't point out that he was likely *already* ostracized. Only their travels in another system had kept that from being made official. Well, even if his own life was a shambles, maybe he could fix someone else's.

"We're coming for you, Qin," he murmured to himself after his father was gone. "One way or another."

CHAPTER 3

IN BASILISK CITADEL IN ZAMEK CITY, PRINCESS OKU was wedged between the rumpled, gray-haired Senator Boehm and the stout, authoritative Senator Andrin, one of her father's cousins. A dozen other senators sat at the table with them, though this wasn't an official meeting.

Her father, who was pacing to one side with his hands clasped behind his back, had invited these men for an "informal chat," as he'd called it. More likely, he wanted their opinions before the next vote. Her father hadn't invited Oku, but he also hadn't kicked her out when she'd slipped in.

She was listening, taking notes, and getting the gist of who was an unquestioning supporter of her father and who was more likely to speak out instead of nodding and going along with anything he said. This was her third time coming to one of these meetings, though she rarely said anything, only observed, trying to get more of a feel for the politics both in the room and in the Kingdom as a whole. And also trying to be, as Casmir's mother Irena had suggested, a confidante for any of the men who wanted someone largely apolitical to speak with. Her own mother, Queen Iku, had also suggested she be more involved, so she hoped nobody thought her presence at these meetings was suspicious. Her younger brother Finn was also there, not because he wanted to be but because their father ordered it.

"Forseti and Vidar Stations have been attacked this week," her father said without stopping his pacing. "You've seen the footage that made it out and onto the media. You know how many have died, how much damage has been done, and how many others are without homes. Even though the bombers haven't gotten through Odin's orbital defenses again, we remain on high alert as construction crews repair the damage already done here. The blockade remains in place, and we are now further cut off from Prince Jorg and the reinforcements he is gathering, because something has happened to the System Stymphalia gate. Nobody knows what. It's been almost a week since any messages have come out of that system. We must assume that the gate will be shut indefinitely, and that we have no reinforcements coming."

Grim-faced, he stopped pacing and faced the table, leaning between two senators and pressing his fingertips to the surface. "We are on our own. Earlier this year, I stood before all of you on the Senate floor, asking for your vote to allow me to send our forces to other systems, to strike preemptively because the tidings of war were already out there. I wanted to secure allies and bring new stations and planets into the Kingdom. The Senate voted no, saying my tactics were too aggressive, too antagonistic."

"You can't say that we were wrong, Sire," Senator Andrin said. "If we'd given the okay for the Fleet to go off to war, our forces would have been spread even thinner when this invasion came. Our system might have already fallen."

"We all thought we had a lot *more* forces," one of the other senators said. "I don't understand why we haven't made mincemeat of the blockade ships."

"Because we must defend Odin, along with every inhabited moon, habitat, and station in the system," Oku's father said. "Many of the enemy ships have slydar hulls, so we can't find and confront them face to face. Instead, they sneak in around our ships and attack. This could have been prevented if I'd been allowed to send our forces out into the Twelve Systems. We would have learned, with time enough to acquire one, that there is now such a thing as a slydar detector. This would have turned the tide in the war before it ever began."

Oku leaned back in her chair as others shared startled looks and whispers. But she, like a few others, had heard about the new technology the week before and wasn't taken by surprise.

"We've discussed this, Sire," Boehm said from Oku's side. "Why not send a team in a fast ship to run the blockade, fly to System Cerberus, and get a bunch of these slydar detectors to bring back?"

"I intend to try just that, but it's possible that System Cerberus won't want to deal with us. Royal Intelligence has given me reports from the other systems, and the belief out there is that the Kingdom is *losing* this war. Already, the crown has dropped precipitously on the systems-wide monetary exchange tables. Gentlemen." He didn't bother looking at Oku, the only woman in the room, but she didn't mind. She was invisible, and that was fine. "I've called a full meeting for the end of the week. I am going to press for the declaration of a state of emergency and King's Authority—the right to act and make decisions regarding this war without a majority vote from the Senate."

The men exchanged long looks. They were less surprised by this announcement, though it startled Oku more than the last.

"Whether you support this or not is your decision." Her father looked around, meeting everybody's eyes in turn, even hers. "But you know how I feel about this matter. If you intend to object, I hope you'll tell me now, or today at some point, and allow me to debate my case to you before the vote."

"*I* object," Boehm said. "You've wanted an excuse to expand all along. It's possible you've even been diddling with the Fleet to keep it from performing its best so that we would feel pressured into giving you what you want."

Oku expected her father to explode at the accusation. He merely narrowed his eyes and stared at the old senator.

"I do not know whether I'm more insulted that you question my willingness to protect my subjects or my integrity in general, but I *am* insulted, Boehm. That said, I will speak to your points when I address the Senate, and I shall hope to convince you that your fears are not truths."

"So be it."

"Anyone else?"

If any of the other men intended to vote against him, they didn't say it aloud.

"Then this meeting is adjourned." Her father stepped back from the table and waved for them to go. He drew Finn aside to discuss something with him.

Oku was surprised when Boehm rested a hand on her shoulder. "Am I foolish to speak out against your father?"

She thought he was brave but didn't know if that equated to wisdom. She didn't want to think her father would punish him for having a contradictory opinion, but she didn't know that for certain.

Oku smiled at him and tried not to let her concerns show. "I think you're supposed to have an opinion if you're on the Senate. Or if you're human."

"It's always easier and less dangerous to go along with the strongest one in the room. But you get tired of it as you get older and you've got less left to lose."

Oku had a feeling Casmir didn't go along with the strongest person in the room that often, age regardless. Maybe that was why he'd found himself at odds with her father. She wished she dared send a message to him, to let him know she'd been forced to stand beside her father and nod during that weird promise of an arranged marriage, but she dared not as long as Royal Intelligence was monitoring her chip. It was a moot point, anyway, if he was stuck in System Stymphalia with the mysteriously inoperable gate.

"We'll see who else stands up to him," Boehm said quietly. "He may get his way this time. The people are scared, especially Senators Hagiwara and Schmied who flew in from the half-destroyed Forseti Station."

"I know he's ambitious, but my father should truly want what's best for the people." Oku hoped she wasn't lying.

"Good." Boehm patted her shoulder, then lowered his hand, but instead of moving away, he leaned in and dropped his voice even further. "Whatever happens in the months and years ahead, watch your back, girl. Your brother has his eye on it."

The topic switch startled her, but she didn't pretend to misunderstand him. "Jorg or Finn?"

"You're in Finn's way, not Jorg's. But you may want to pass the same message on to your older brother when he returns home." Boehm looked over to where her father and Finn were still talking. "That one is hungry. You would be wise to gather allies outside of your family, if you can."

Boehm nodded to her and headed for the door, joining a couple of other senators on the way out.

Oku bit her lip as she watched them go, wondering at the timing of that warning. Yes, she'd been working on making herself approachable and spending more time around the senators and her father's aides and assistants, but what had compelled Boehm to speak now? Had he overheard Finn speaking to someone about her and Jorg? Why would

HOME FRONT

Finn be worried about his ambitions right now? Their father was fit and healthy enough to live for many more decades.

Boehm's suggestion of gathering allies worried her. Who would she gather? She had friends among academics both here and on stations and planets throughout the Twelve Systems, those she'd met at conferences and exchanged data and ideas with over the years. But what could any of them do if Finn decided to have her removed because she was in the way of some plot he'd hatched to get the crown? Write papers about how vile he was? She didn't even *want* to be between him and the crown.

Oku found herself wishing she could speak with Casmir. He wouldn't be any more familiar with the senators and the machinations of court than she—less, surely—but as he'd proven these last months, he had an out-of-the-box way of thinking, and she wagered he would have useful advice.

If only that gate were working and she felt free to send him notes. How had Royal Intelligence intercepted their messages anyway? She knew for a fact that Casmir had encrypted them well. He'd sent her a code for decrypting them before he'd started sending videos. A code stored in only one place.

Her finger strayed to her temple. Was it possible Royal Intelligence had access to her chip?

Bonita's head was already pounding when the lights in the brig cell flared to life. She winced and flung an arm over her eyes. She'd been lying on one of two rock-hard bunks, willing her body to heal in case some opportunity to escape presented itself. Unfortunately, her body didn't heal as quickly as it once had, and everything ached. She kept forgetting not to move her lips, and the split she'd taken to the bottom one when Jorg's cronies had roughed them up periodically broke open and bled.

On top of all that, Qin, her loyal companion of almost a year, was driving her nuts.

Qin had her own bunk on the other side of the small cell, but she was never in it. She was doing pushups, sit-ups, shoulder stands, and all manner of shadow boxing. The growls and grunts that apparently had to accompany the vigorous exercises were getting on Bonita's nerves. Normally, she would applaud this level of dedication to fitness, but sitting a foot away from it was making her *loca*. She was glad when a female lieutenant walked into view, trailed by two soldiers with rifles and in full combat armor, if only because it made Qin take a break.

A break from fitness, not from being ready to escape or attack. Qin sprang to her feet and focused on the trio through the force field that had thus far made the cell escape-proof. If she'd had a tail, it would have been twitching.

Qin would, Bonita had zero doubt, test herself against those armed guards if she got a chance. And she might win. Bonita didn't see any crushers.

"I'm Lieutenant Croix, a nurse." The woman lifted a medical kit. "I've been sent to check on you."

"More than four days after we were imprisoned and beaten up for no good reason?" Bonita asked.

"There have been arguments about whether or not you should be treated for injuries. The medical staff was *for* helping you." Croix eyed Qin. "In case that makes you less inclined to maul me when I come in."

"Nobody's going to maul you, ma'am," one of the soldiers said. Surprisingly, it was a female soldier behind the helmet's tinted faceplate. Bonita hadn't seen many women on the Kingdom ships, at least not among the grunts with guns and armor. "That's why *we're* here."

"I still vote for stunning them before we let her in," the other soldier, a man, said. "I've seen that one fight." He had a stunner on his utility belt, but he jerked the rifle toward Qin.

"Let me guess," Bonita said. "His stuffy and uptight Highness was against treating us."

"That's correct. The captain was for, but he wouldn't argue much with the prince."

"Arguing probably gets you thrown in the cell next door," Bonita said.

The lieutenant didn't smile.

"Step back." The male soldier twitched his rifle again. Focused on Qin, he didn't even glance at Bonita.

HOME FRONT

That made Bonita's hackles rise, but she knew she didn't look like much of a threat. The soldiers had taken their armor and weapons and even their shoes. She looked like the seventy-year-old woman she was as she stood in socks, trousers, and a shirt, the yellowing bruises on her face and forearms on full display. Qin wasn't wearing more, but she still looked ferocious, the light fur on the backs of her arms reminding onlookers that she wasn't fully human, even if they somehow missed the fangs. Qin was baring those fangs now.

She stepped back from the force field, but she raised her eyebrows and looked at Bonita. Asking if they should try to attack?

These soldiers didn't seem like the cream of the crop. She and Qin might not get a better chance, but she had little familiarity with the ship—she'd barely been conscious when those crushers had dragged them to the brig—and couldn't access her chip to check the network, message friends who might have helped, or even plot with Qin. The cell's walls were blocking all connectivity. In the days they'd been in here, nobody had visited them or told them anything. Meals had been delivered by robots with crusher guards to ensure Qin didn't mount an attack.

Bonita had no idea if Bjarke, Casmir, Asger, and the others had escaped Dubashi's base, nor did she know what had happened to her ship. What if the *Dragon* had been so damaged that Viggo hadn't been able to maneuver it away from those asteroids? What if it'd smashed against them and been wrecked beyond repair? All she owned was in her cabin there, and almost all of her net worth was in the ship itself, the part that was paid off. If she had to start over from scratch one more time…

She shook her head at Qin, then flopped back onto the bunk. Unless something major happened to distract the crew, she doubted they would be able to escape this ship, even if they managed to get out of their cell. She also didn't know if it—it was much smaller than the big Kingdom warships—had a shuttle they could potentially commandeer. They would have to steal the whole ship. Something that would have been daunting even without the cadre of crushers aboard. Congratulations to Casmir for inventing henchmen—henchbots—that drained all hope from the hearts of prisoners.

"I will not attack you if you are here to heal my captain's wounds," Qin said, speaking for the first time.

Whether that swayed the soldiers or they'd planned to come in anyway, Bonita didn't know. A faint buzz sounded as the force field vanished.

The armored soldiers remained in the corridor pointing their rifles at Qin. Lieutenant Croix came in and sat on the edge of Bonita's bed.

"How old are you, Captain?" she asked.

Bonita bristled at the question. Nobody would ask Qin that, she was sure. Or even Bjarke, if he'd been captured alongside her. Just the frail-looking woman with the braid of gray hair hanging limply over the edge of the bunk.

"Too old to get the snot beat out of me by crushers."

"Is there any age where that's fun?" one of the soldiers muttered.

The nurse glanced at Qin as she ran a diagnostic scanner over Bonita. "Are you injured, uhm, ma'am? I'm not sure how to treat genetically engineered… soldiers."

Had she been about to say *freaks*? Bonita would clobber her if she did.

"I'm fine," Qin said, though she'd been beaten up as badly as Bonita and still had bruises under her shirt. The kid had a high tolerance for pain. She must not have cracked any bones, though, or she would have struggled to do all those exercises.

"Good." The nurse sounded relieved, probably more because she wouldn't have to figure out how to treat Qin than because she cared. Or so Bonita thought. Then Croix added, "I'm from Zamek City on Odin. I was on leave when all the terrorist stuff was going on, the bombing of the Jewish temple. I saw on the news that you and your ship helped out with that, even though you didn't get much credit." Her lips wrinkled in a self-deprecating smirk. "The Kingdom is insular. We don't like to give praise to people from other systems."

"Yeah, we helped," Bonita said. "And we're being rewarded so generously."

Croix winced. "I'm sorry, Captain," she said quietly, putting away her scanner and pulling out a jet injector.

"Sorry enough to forget to put the force field back up when you leave?"

"I can't do that." Croix glanced toward the ceiling.

Whatever security camera was up there wasn't visible, but Bonita had no doubt the cell was monitored.

"How about having that meal-delivery robot send some painkillers and coffee?"

"I might be able to manage that." Croix held up the injector. "This will help with pain and inflammation in the short term. Your lip is fatter than the neck of a geoduck."

"A what?"

"You may not have them in your system. They're clams with long, thick siphons or necks that stick out. We dig them up on the beaches outside Zamek City."

"I grew up on a space station. I only know vaguely what a clam is."

"I've never seen one with a neck." Qin sounded curious.

Bonita didn't think she wanted to see a necked clam. Especially one that had been brought to mind by her split and puffy lower lip.

A shudder coursed through the ship.

The nurse leaped up, and Bonita rolled off the bed, not sure what was happening but immediately on the defensive. Another shudder rocked the brig. Bonita wobbled, and Qin lunged forward to steady her. The soldiers must have thought she was trying to escape. One grabbed Croix, pulling her out, and the other whipped up his stunner and shot Qin.

Bonita swore, but she wasn't strong enough to keep her tall and muscular friend from crashing to the deck.

An alarm wailed, and the soldiers and nurse backed out of the cell.

"Battle stations," a computerized voice came over the speakers. "All hands to battle stations. We are under attack."

"I'll come back later, Captain," Croix promised, as the soldiers ushered her out.

As Bonita knelt beside the unconscious Qin, the deck shuddered again.

"Just our luck," she muttered. "We got captured by the guy who's annoyed everyone in the system and probably all eleven others."

What if they died here on this Kingdom ship? Stuck in a cell for no good reason?

Bonita shook her head. She'd gotten the distraction she'd hoped for, but with Qin unconscious, she couldn't take advantage of it.

CHAPTER 4

"IT LOOKS LIKE YOU'RE MISSING A COUPLE OF files." Casmir pointed to the display. He was in the ship's programming section of engineering with Lieutenant Grunburg and a couple of crewmen who worked with him. The office wasn't posh, but it was better than that server closet Casmir had started out his stay on the *Osprey* in.

"Why would that be?" Grunburg wondered. "I copied everything we got from that android."

"Tork," Zee said from his self-appointed guard spot by the doorway. Grunburg blinked and looked over at him.

"Zee and Tork have a relationship," Casmir said.

"He is an inferior android," Zee said.

"That you still like to play network games and trade barbs with."

"Yes. With the gate down, I cannot do these things. It is unfortunate."

"I understand." And Casmir did. Even though he'd composed a few messages that he could send to Oku—he'd decided to stick with friendly and playful and pretended the one Jager had sent about marriage hadn't been serious—he couldn't send them. To distract himself from that, he was using tools and spare parts to make things. So far, only a toy, but he had a vague notion of crafting something for Oku, should he ever get to see her in person. He wished he had the materials to make those robot bees for her work project.

Grunburg looked back at him. "Do you have all the original files?"

"Yes, I should." Casmir touched his temple. "Let me check."

"You kept that awful virus on your *chip*? Right next to your *brain*?"

"I'm pretty sure software commands aren't going to convince my brain to shut down."

Grunburg shuddered.

"The files are still there," Casmir said, scanning his folders, "but... That's interesting. The date stamp suggests they tried to do something to themselves about two weeks ago. *I* didn't access them or do anything to them. Maybe there's code in there to cause the virus to delete key components after a certain time."

"Why would it—the programmer—have done that?"

"So a useable copy wouldn't get out? But none of mine seem to be missing."

"Why would yours have failed to delete when mine did?"

"I'm not sure other than that I have a lot of safeguards on my chip to keep other people from accessing it and deleting or uploading anything. Much more than industry standard. I'll transfer the files, and we can run a comparison."

The door opened, and Captain Ishii walked in.

Casmir looked warily into the corridor behind him, expecting Lieutenant Meister to follow. Kim had told him about what had happened before he walked in on their encounter. Since then, Casmir had been leaving a crusher in the lab with her with instructions not to let anyone stick a jet injector into her. He feared it was only a matter of time until Ishii heard about it and stuck them both in the brig—or tried to force the matter.

Meister wasn't with him, but Ishii pointed at Casmir and gestured for him to join him. He didn't look pleased.

"I think we can get the virus working." Casmir decided to open with good news in the hope that Ishii would forget about whatever unpleasantness he had on his mind.

"Good. What happened with you, Sato, and Rache? And why doesn't she want to answer questions about it?"

"Uh, basically, he picked us up from Stardust Palace and tried to turn us over to Dubashi. Dubashi wanted her to finish his bioweapon, and he wanted me, well, dead."

"But you somehow escaped from Rache in a shuttle, rescued Sir Tremayne—who I only recently learned is here stowing away on Lopez's ship—and picked up the two Asgers and went in to infiltrate Dubashi's base."

"Yes." Casmir smiled. "You're all caught up."

Ishii gave him a sour look. "I have a hard time believing you left your best friend behind on Rache's ship." His eyes narrowed. "*If* she was in danger."

HOME FRONT

"She *was* in danger. We barely got to her in time. Dubashi had ordered his minion to upload her brain to the computer and kill her if she didn't work on his bioweapon."

"I meant if she was in danger from Rache."

Casmir knew exactly what he'd meant. He was trying to give answers that didn't reveal anything important without being obvious about it, but he feared it wasn't working.

"Meister wants to use eslevoamytal on you too, you know. Dr. Sikou and the nurse who watched you have a seizure in sickbay pointed out that you're allergic to it."

"I appreciate them remembering that. Perhaps, whenever I'm in Kingdom hands, I should wear a medic-alert bracelet." He'd meant it as a joke, but Ishii scowled.

"Whenever you're in *Kingdom* hands? You are *from* the Kingdom. Being with us shouldn't be problematic for you."

"And yet..." Casmir turned his palm toward the ceiling.

"You're getting *yourself* in trouble. And taking Sato down with you."

Casmir resisted the urge to point out that the only thing Kim was worried about divulging had nothing to do with him. He'd tried to get her *not* to develop feelings for Rache.

"Are you going to put me in the brig?" he asked.

"I'd love to, but not until you get my virus working. And retrieve that slydar detector from Shayban. I can't even send a team onto the station unless you're with it." Ishii scowled again. "If you were in cuffs, I'm sure he and the eighty-eight crushers you left in his hands would rescue you."

Casmir almost pointed out that the crushers shouldn't be obeying Shayban, but it was possible they would rescue him. Zee would.

"Are you going to put Kim in the brig? Or question her?" Casmir worried what would happen if Meister tried to drug her and a crusher stepped in. One of the crew might get hurt if Meister tried to force the issue.

"I'm tempted." Ishii glanced at Grunburg, but he and his helpers were focused on their work. He still lowered his voice to whisper, "You know I'm ambivalent on Jorg's choices, and I understand why you're not complying, but what have you two been *doing* with Rache?"

"Trying to thwart his plans. You know he took an assignment from Dubashi, right? To assassinate Jager." Maybe if Casmir gave Ishii some free intelligence, it would get him to back off, to focus elsewhere. Besides, this wasn't information that the Kingdom couldn't already guess. "I think he may be after Jorg too."

Ishii didn't look surprised. He shook his head. "Which makes it all the more alarming that you keep showing up in his orbit."

"For most of our encounters, he's shown up in *my* orbit."

Ishii snorted. "Yes, I'm sure he's fascinated by you."

"Well, we are inextricably linked."

"What do you mean? Why?"

Ah, was Ishii not in the know on the clone matter? Casmir had assumed the Intelligence officers all knew by now, and that Meister would have shared that information with his captain, if Ishii hadn't known all along, but it was possible Ishii had a lesser security clearance. "Maybe you're the one who should have a frank chat with Meister."

Ishii opened his mouth but paused, touching a finger to his temple. "One moment. I have an urgent message coming in." He stepped out into the corridor and commed someone on the bridge.

Casmir was debating what to tell him, assuming he returned, when he received a message of his own. It was from Viggo.

Greetings, El Mago. You have not come over to visit during the period of repairs.

Sorry, Viggo. I'm not free to leave the ship. How are the repairs going?

They have been completed. Tristan and I have been discussing the possibility of rescuing Bonita and Qin.

I would dearly love to have them extricated from danger. I have reluctantly assumed I will have to go through diplomatic channels to get them back. Maybe I can offer to fix Jorg's robot vacuums to win him over.

That won me *over, but your prince is…*

Misguided? Rash? Impolitic?

A pendejo, *according to Bonita.*

Ishii stalked back in and grabbed Casmir by the front of the shirt. Zee surged forward, and Casmir barely had time to jerk a hand up to keep him from grabbing Ishii and hurling him across the room.

Ishii didn't seem to notice the exchange. "The *Chivalrous* is under attack."

"By whom?" Casmir asked, though dread and certainty sank into his gut like an anchor.

"Someone with a slydar hull. Someone we can't detect." Ishii pulled Casmir into the corridor. "We're changing course to go help. You're going to figure out if that's Rache and if it is, you better use your inexplicable link to him to get him to knock it off."

Inextricable was the word Casmir had used, but maybe Ishii was deliberately changing it.

Grunburg surged to his feet, hearing everything since Ishii wasn't speaking in a low voice anymore. "How far away from the attack are we, sir?"

"Too damn far to get there in time."

Casmir didn't fight Ishii as he dragged him to the bridge, but his mind was whirling. What could he do to stop Rache? And why was Rache attacking *now*? Kim had said *he'd* said he would wait until Bonita and Qin were off the *Chivalrous*. Why had he changed his mind?

Dr. Yas Peshlakai adjusted the setting on the lower-back exercise machine as mercenaries grunted and clanked heavy free weights in the background. This was the only ship he'd been on where he'd seen such things. What happened if the spin gravity went out while people were in here? It would only be a matter of time before a fifty-pound dumbbell floated over and clunked someone in the head. But perhaps the mercenaries couldn't feel manly using the machines that were safely bolted to the deck with all of their pieces attached.

Rache was over there with the grunts, in his usual black, wearing the usual hood and mask. One would think it would be difficult to exercise in. Yas imagined face sweat and having to breathe through mesh, but the man fought battles wearing it—and a huge pile of combat armor—so he must find it suitable.

"These are weenie exercises, Doc." Chief Jess Khonsari wrinkled her nose at him.

Yas didn't share that the gesture was cute or that he liked that their physical therapy sessions gave him an excuse to spend time with her. Jess should have had the services of someone who actually had a background in this, but he was the best the ship had.

"You can increase the resistance more next week, but remember what I said. Using your—"

"Yeah, yeah, the side with my cyborg bits is stronger than the side with my human bits, and my human spine is caught in the middle."

"That's the technical explanation I put in my notes, yes."

"Did you use the word bits?"

"Every chance I could."

"I don't believe you."

"Your mistrust wounds me."

The door opened, and Lieutenant Amergin ambled in. The Intelligence officer was a rare sight in the gym, despite the frequent fitness tests and exercise sessions Rache demanded of his crew. Maybe the cybernetic headset permanently integrated with his skull made him worry about gravity and dumbbells. That wide-brimmed cowboy hat wouldn't protect his head.

As Jess finished another set of her back exercises, Amergin approached Rache and the two stepped away from the other men.

"Maybe he's telling Rache that the gate is open again," Yas said, "and we can go to a nice peaceful system where a cybernetics surgeon can modify your spine to be stronger and a real physical therapist can work with you afterward."

"You dream big, Doc."

"I like my patients to get better."

When Rache and Amergin stopped to talk, they were close enough for Yas to hear. Rache glanced at him, but he must not have cared if his doctor and engineering chief overheard, because he didn't walk farther away.

"You're sure it's Dubashi?" Rache was asking.

"He may not be there personally, but ships working for him are chasing the Kingdom's *Chivalrous*. They're hidden from us by slydar hulls and distance, but I intercepted their encrypted transmissions to him and decrypted them. I figured you'd want to know if someone else completed the job and took out Prince Jorg first." Amergin lifted his chin. "I was surprised we didn't go right after him ourselves, Captain."

"I was asked not to," Rache said shortly. "How far away are we from the battle?"

The last Yas had heard, they'd been trailing the largest chunk of the Kingdom ships and keeping an eye on them. Most of their vessels were spread around the system, still trying to gather allies, but the

HOME FRONT

core warships were heading to Stardust Palace. The day before, the *Chivalrous* had broken away from those warships and headed off in a different direction. The *Fedallah* had opted to stick with it.

"If we boost to max speed, we could catch up in less than an hour," Amergin said. "Might be fast enough to make a difference. Uhm, are we trying to make a difference, sir?"

"We don't get paid if we're not the ones to kill Jorg."

"Right, but can we boot our own allies out of the way to do it first? Their presence is problematic, isn't it? Dubashi might not pay us then."

"Maybe we'll sidle up and see if they need some help," Rache said. "I assume the *Chivalrous* is fighting back."

"Yes, but it's only one ship. It's well armored and has a good amount of firepower, but it's outnumbered. I picked up desperate comm messages from it to the rest of the Kingdom fleet. Unless you're planning to switch sides and help Jorg, I don't see what we can do to change anything."

"We will not side with the Kingdom. Not now, not ever."

"I figured not, but—"

"Victory, Lieutenant, comes from finding the opportunities in problems."

"That one of your book quotes, sir?"

"Something like that."

As the two men walked out of the gym, Yas wondered what victory Rache sought. Not only Jorg's death but getting *credit* for Jorg's death? Or something else altogether?

"I don't think we're going to find that nice peaceful system of yours, Doc," Jess said.

"I have that fear myself."

CHAPTER 5

QIN WOKE UP WITH HER BODY THROBBING AND Bonita kneeling on the deck next to her.

"Wake up, wake up, wake up," Bonita was chanting while shaking Qin's shoulder and glancing toward the force field.

"I'm 'wake," Qin mumbled, her tongue thick. Memories of being stunned rocketed to her mind. She'd taken the blast full in the chest.

The ship jolted hard enough to knock out the spin gravity for a second, and Qin's body lifted from the deck before thunking back down.

"If that would go out permanently, I could haul you out of here over my shoulder," Bonita grumbled.

"Is the force field down?" Qin lifted her head but still saw the faint waver of an energy field blocking them in.

"It's been up and down. We're under attack, and the power has gone out a few times, but it's come back on quickly. I was afraid if I tried to drag you out, we'd get caught in the middle when it came back up and get fried."

"That would be unpleasant." Qin rolled to her hands and knees, strength and awareness gradually returning. "Are there guards out there?"

"I don't think so. Everyone was called to battle stations." Bonita lowered her voice. "If you're well enough to risk jumping through the next time the power goes out, this could be our chance to escape."

"I'm well enough." Qin shifted into a crouch, ready to spring out of the cell.

"And then we have to hope there's a shuttle we can take. And that whoever's out there firing on the ship doesn't fire on the shuttle."

Qin grimaced. "I suppose we can't just take over the ship and negotiate with whoever's attacking."

Not likely, she answered her own question. She wanted to avoid those crushers if possible, and half of them were probably on the bridge, guarding Prince Jorg.

"That seems ambitious for two women without shoes or weapons." Bonita also positioned herself in front of the force field to jump.

"I have my fangs."

"Do they sink nicely into a crusher's shoulder?"

"Not really."

Another shudder wracked the ship, and a fire started somewhere. Qin couldn't smell the smoke through the force field, but she could see it in the air.

"Do we know who's attacking the ship?" she asked.

"Take your pick. Everybody who's met Jorg hates him."

"Are we not flying alongside the rest of the Kingdom warships? You would think they'd protect him."

"I hate to break it to you, Qin, but aside from that twenty minutes you were knocked out, we've been experiencing the same things the whole time. I don't know more than you do."

"I thought it might have been an illuminating twenty minutes."

A jolt hammered the ship, pitching Bonita toward the wall. Qin caught her arm and sank low to keep her balance. The last thing they needed was to have their chance to escape ruined by being too injured to take it. The idea of dying helpless in this box made her growl.

The gravity went out, and they floated off the deck.

"Come on, power," Bonita urged, making a rude gesture at the force field.

As soon as Qin floated near a wall, she did her best to anchor herself so she would have something to push off from if the power failed. But without magnetic boots, it was difficult.

The smoke in the corridor increased, hazing the view of the empty cell across from them. Something out of view spat and hissed. The lights remained on, but the force field dropped.

"Now, now," Bonita urged.

She'd also maneuvered to a wall and pushed herself out of a corner and toward the corridor. Qin did the same, but Bonita made it out of the cell first, only to spot something and curse.

A stun bolt lit up the corridor, taking Bonita in the shoulder. Qin grabbed the corner of the cell and pulled herself out and toward their attacker. A woman in combat armor had just come into the brig and was striding toward them, her magnetic boots keeping her on the deck. She shifted her stunner toward Qin, but Qin reached her in time to knock it away. The bolt fired uselessly toward the ceiling.

Qin grabbed the woman's shoulders, knowing from experience that she had to keep in contact with her foe to do anything in zero-g, and yanked as she drove a knee into her groin. It didn't hurt the soldier through her armor, but it did knock her boots off the deck, leaving them both grappling in the air.

"The prisoners are out," the woman commed, her voice audible through her helmet. She reached for a rifle on her back.

Qin tore it away before she could bring it to bear and hurled it into a cell. She rammed her palm into the soldier's faceplate, worried that reinforcements—like those damn crushers—would show up any second. Her blow knocked the woman's head back, but didn't crack the Glasnax.

A gauntleted fist punched toward her stomach. Qin managed to shift aside, only catching a glancing blow, but without armor of her own, it stung like a dagger thrust and almost knocked her away.

She managed to keep her grip on the soldier and shoved her head against the wall. Her faceplate thwacked against it. Qin dug one of her claws into a seam in the armor, trying to rip it open. Her claws were like steel, but armor was tougher than steel. Growling, Qin slammed the woman's faceplate against the wall again.

An elbow came back, catching her in the stomach. Qin snarled through the pain and scooted closer, wrapping her arms around her foe's armored neck. The soldier tried to twist away. Her armor made her stronger than usual, but Qin was stronger still. She squeezed hard enough that the neck piece groaned and finally cracked.

The woman got her boots against the wall and shoved backward. They sailed across the corridor, and Qin's back struck the opposite wall. The soldier twisted and punched toward her face. Qin let go and ducked below the blow, then brought her legs up, jammed her feet against her foe's waist, and pushed off down the corridor. She floated past the unconscious Bonita and grasped the stunner where it dangled in the air.

The lights went out. A few indicators glowing on a panel near the door gave Qin's feline night vision enough to work with, and she turned and aimed at her target. The soldier was pulling herself along the wall, trying to get into the cell where her rifle floated. Qin fired at her cracked neck piece, though she worried the breach wouldn't be enough to matter. The woman's momentum carried her into the cell and out of sight.

Qin's socked foot clunked against a wall, and she used the leverage to push off. If the woman got that rifle, she could kill Qin *and* Bonita.

But the stun had done just enough. When Qin rounded the corner, she found the soldier floating unmoving in the air near the rifle.

Another jolt coursed through the ship. Qin grabbed the weapon and Bonita, and maneuvered up the corridor toward the exit, but she paused. Should she try to remove the soldier's armor? It looked like it might fit Bonita.

No, they would be better off finding their own. If they had any luck at all, it would be in a closet in the brig.

As Qin searched, she also looked for oxygen tanks. Who knew what would go out next on the ship?

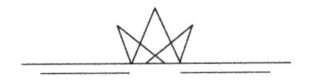

"Is there any chance of us coming up with a vaccine?" Dr. Sikou asked dubiously, eyeing the display full of virus details and Kim's notes on the modifications that the deceased Scholar Sunflyer had made. "Based on how difficult it was to immunize against the original version of the virus…"

"Odin would have to have the vaccine and plenty of time to implement it, yes," Kim said. "And what we can do here is unfortunately limited. I'm running hypothetical tests on computerized simulations, not a live virus. But I do have all of Scholar Sunflyer's notes. I was able to download his data both from Dubashi's base and also from his lab on Stardust Palace. My main goal is to send a thorough study to private and government infectious-disease laboratories back home as soon as the gate here is operable again. Transmissions fly faster than spaceships, so there's some hope they would have time to come up with something, especially if the Fleet can find Dubashi and detain him here. Or stop him altogether."

Kim glanced at the door as someone walked in, but it was a nurse. She kept expecting Lieutenant Meister to return and force the issue of drugging her for questioning, which could get ugly, since two of Casmir's new crushers were stationed nearby with orders to protect her.

With luck, the ship's officers were too worried about the prince right now to pester her. The deck vibrated as the engines worked hard to take the *Osprey* to help the *Chivalrous*.

"I can't say I'm sad that you don't have a Petri dish of the virus in your pocket," Sikou said.

"I wish Dubashi didn't either."

Kim had been so close to thwarting him. If only she'd had a little more time.

A message alert popped up on her chip, and she barely held back a groan. Rache.

Greetings, Scholar Sato. Do you have a minute?

I shouldn't be speaking with you. Intelligence here caught your last message. Kim wondered how far away the *Fedallah* was and how much lag there would be between responses.

Not much, it turned out.

Did they have an opinion on whether Prince Jorg would like a purse?

If they did, they didn't tell me. I'm trying to avoid a lieutenant who wants to question me under eslevoamytal.

Are you a prisoner there? Not a guest?

There was no way to tell through text if Rache's emotions had turned cold and hard, but she had a feeling anger accompanied the questions.

It's a little nebulous right now, but I'm positive I wouldn't be allowed to leave if I had a means. Such as the *Stellar Dragon*. She'd heard from Casmir that Bonita's ship was fully repaired, even though the *Osprey* was still towing it.

If you can't leave, that makes you a prisoner.

I'm in danger of becoming a more serious one because of my relationship with you. Realizing that made it sound like she blamed him, when she couldn't, not this time, she added, *It's possible I haven't made the wisest of choices. What do you need?*

You see what's happening to Jorg's ship?

I've heard he's under attack, yes. The captain thinks you're *doing it.*

Your captain is misinformed.

Is it Dubashi?

Ships he commands and that are reporting to him, yes. We've identified at least four.

We're going to help, but I don't know if we'll make it in time.

Likely not. The Fedallah *is closer. Are your friends still on Jorg's ship?*

As true prisoners, yes. They're in the brig. Kim grimaced, imagining Qin and Bonita dying simply because they were locked in a cell and couldn't escape. They should never have been taken prisoner. They had nothing to do with Jorg's enemies or the Kingdom war.

They are the reason we didn't attack originally, Rache messaged.

What are you going to do now? Kim imagined him swooping in and finishing off the *Chivalrous* so he could get credit for and be paid for killing Jorg.

How would you feel if I could get in, retrieve your friends, and get out while the Chivalrous *and those other Kingdom warships are distracted by Dubashi's ships?*

And assassinate Jorg along the way? She wanted to believe he was capable of altruism, but it was hard to imagine him risking his life and his ship for Bonita and Qin.

Really, Kim, I don't pry into your business plans.

If you could get them out, that would be noble and heroic. If you assassinated Jorg and killed all the Kingdom officers on board while you were doing it, that would be horrific and villainous.

I'm a mixed bag, aren't I? Tell Casmir I'm messaging him.

He's not in the lab with me.

I assume he is also nebulously held on the ship somewhere.

Kim worried about what the Intelligence officers would think if Casmir also started getting messages from the Kingdom's most notorious and loathed enemy, but if there was a possibility Rache could save Bonita and Qin…

Yes, she sent, *he's here.*

Good. If you find yourself in need of being broken out of that Kingdom ship, do let me know.

Kim shook her head, envisioning Rache and his armored men running through the corridors, blowing away Kingdom soldiers left and right. It was already doubtful that she would find a way of satisfactorily explaining his presence in her life and be allowed to go home, but that would seal her coffin—and the coffins of many others.

CHAPTER 6

THE CRUSHERS HURLED THEMSELVES AROUND THE SHUTTLE BAY, managing to avoid putting dents in the walls but denting each other regularly. Those dents filled themselves in, leaving the crushers as sleek as ever. Meanwhile, Casmir paced and worried about Bonita and Qin being stuck in the brig of a ship under attack.

"Perhaps we should instruct them about other important things, instead of just having them practice combat." Casmir said when he drew even with Zee, who was overseeing the sparring. The crushers were running ship-boarding drills in case the *Osprey* caught up with the *Chivalrous* in time to help, but they had been at it all morning, and all the banging and thumping was starting to grate on his frazzled nerves.

"What other important things should a crusher be versed in?" Zee asked.

"Puppies, kittens, love."

Zee looked at him.

"By learning about human interests, emotions, and motivations, it might make it easier for our two kinds to work seamlessly together." Casmir didn't truly intend to show them kitten pictures, but it would be nice to see the crushers do something besides practice fighting.

"We learn more about humans and other species naturally through our interactions with them," Zee stated.

"True. We could provide more environments for those interactions. You play games with Tork, right? They must be of some interest to you. Do crushers like to gamble?"

"When necessary, we calculate the odds and make informed and rational decisions based on them."

"Did you answer my question?" Casmir smiled. "I don't think you did. Humans sometimes gamble for prizes. What they value and what they're willing to risk to obtain it can show a lot about them."

"Tork and I challenge each other to games to see who is superior, not to win prizes."

"Isn't establishing your superiority a prize of a sort?"

"Not one that is won through gambling. It is won through *being* superior."

"It's not necessary to always be superior. It's relaxing to find a way that all can enjoy interacting with each other."

"Relaxing," Zee stated in a flat tone that suggested crushers did not *relax*.

Casmir patted him on the shoulder. "Let's try a game with everybody."

He fished the children's toy he'd made while working with Grunburg out of his pocket. After waiting for a lull in the combat, he walked into the group of crushers, where he felt like a child with them looming almost a foot taller than he. If he were ever to abandon his human body and upload his consciousness into a mechanical construct, he would choose a crusher over a droid. Kim's monkey-droid mother was sturdy enough for her size, but if Casmir had a second chance to live, he would enjoy trying out life, at least a semblance of life, as something difficult to kill. Difficult to push and bully around.

"You guys may represent creator wish fulfillment," he murmured.

"Do you have an assignment for us, Casmir Dabrowski?" the crusher he'd named Reuben said.

Casmir hadn't shared his names for them with any of his friends, but when he'd realized he had twelve, he'd named them after the twelve sons of Jacob. What he would do when he had the other eighty-eight, he didn't know. He hated the idea of calling them by numbers. Even Zee should have had a better name, had Casmir been thinking of that at the time.

"No. You've all been training hard. I thought you might like to play a game."

"To what end?" The crushers looked at each other.

Casmir took note of that response. He hadn't noticed that Zee ever looked to others before making decisions. These crushers had some social dynamics that he didn't remember putting into the programming. Was that a natural adaptation since a group of them had been created together?

"Fun is the end goal," Casmir replied. "And to take your mind off your problems."

HOME FRONT

All right, he was trying to take his mind off *his* problems. When he'd suggested comming the ships attacking the *Chivalrous* to try to strike a bargain with the captains, Ishii had forbidden it. Ishii hadn't wanted to tip their hand that they had something in the works—the virus. Casmir had already tried sending a chip-to-chip message to Dubashi—Kyla Moonrazor had given him his access code—but Dubashi either hadn't received the request to open lines of communication, or he'd ignored it. So Casmir was stuck twiddling his thumbs and hoping Jorg's ship could take care of itself. If the *Dragon* could have gotten there faster, he would have contemplated sneaking off in it.

"This is a dreidel." He held up the metal top he'd made, the letters *nun*, *gimmel*, *hey*, and *shin* written on the sides in black marker. The toy didn't look much like the wooden one he'd had as a boy, but he'd at least weighted it properly so the sides should come up randomly. "You take turns spinning it, and depending on which letter comes up, you either pass the dreidel to the next person—er, crusher—add a token to the pot, get the pot, or get half the pot. You play until one person has all the tokens."

Zee walked up behind him. "We have no tokens."

Casmir poked into another pocket and pulled out a package of dried currants he'd taken from the mess hall. "Now we do."

He distributed them evenly to the crushers and himself as he further explained the rules of the game.

"Nothing reveals humanity so well as the games it plays," Zee told the crushers, getting into the spirit of things—or plotting how he could, through this game, prove his superiority.

"That is a quote by David Hartley, a philosopher from 18th-century Old Earth," the crusher named Gad said.

"Maybe a game will reveal crushers as well." Casmir smiled.

Even though they didn't likely see any point to his gambling game, they crouched in a circle, taking turns spinning the dreidel and placing and removing currants from the pot. Casmir sat shoulder to shoulder with Zee and Reuben and made jokes depending on the results. He also tried to make it educational by asking them the odds of Zee or Gad winning more than five or ten times in a row, as he might have done with his students. The math was simple for them, and they ended up competing to see who could blurt out the answer first.

Ishii jogged into the shuttle bay, his Fleet galaxy suit managing to look rumpled even though the SmartWeave material was supposed to make that impossible. "There you are. I thought you were exercising your crushers in the gym."

"A grumpy sergeant kicked us out," Casmir said. "He said they were leaving dents in the walls when they threw each other around, but I think he found them disconcerting."

"Imagine that." Ishii frowned. "*Are* you exercising them? What is that thing they're spinning?"

"We're playing a game." Casmir patted Zee and Reuben on the shoulders and backed away to speak with Ishii.

"They play games? Aren't they just supposed to make people dead?"

"I'm broadening their horizons."

A message came in from Asger as Ishii stared at the crouching crushers.

Casmir, my father and I are planning to do something rash. Are you in?

Does it involve stealing the Dragon *and rescuing our friends before Jorg's ship is destroyed?*

I see you've been contemplating it too.

I want to help them, yes, Casmir messaged. *The problem is that we wouldn't be able to get there any faster on the* Dragon *than the* Osprey.

I know, but we would have autonomy. And be able to launch a boarding party without having to ask for permission. Qin is in danger, and doing nothing is driving me insane. Qin and Bonita.

Casmir smiled as he spotted Asger's preferences showing. *When are you leaving?*

As soon as we can get the ship. If you and Kim are coming, pack up and meet us at the airlock.

Ishii was turning back to him, so there wasn't time to ask if Asger planned to "get the ship" through cajoling... or force.

Let me see if I can extricate myself from my current company. Without Meister noticing, Casmir added silently. The lieutenant wasn't present now, but he'd wandered past the shuttle bay less than an hour ago and peered in. Casmir suspected he was being monitored.

I'll let you know when we've got the ship.

"Why does that one have a big stack of raisins?" Ishii pointed.

"They're currants, and he's lucky. Or cheating. But probably lucky. You should stand behind him during battle."

HOME FRONT

"How would I know in the heat of battle which one was the lucky one? Or how would I know five minutes from now? They're all the same."

"I call that one Zebulun, if it helps."

"That does *not* help." Ishii shook his head. "Look, Grunburg has that virus ready to go, and I've ordered him to transmit it to the ships harrying Jorg's, but he said they have to willingly accept a transmission from us."

"That's right."

Ishii's face twisted in exasperation. "They're never going to do that. We didn't do that when that android sent the virus to us. He found some back door, right? What did you do when you sent it to those pirates?"

"Tricked them into accepting a file transfer. The back door, as you call it, involved a transmission from our own shuttle—remember that we went out there to collect Tork, the medium for the virus at that time, and he was the one to slip it through our comm system."

"So unless we throw an android in the way of those ships and hope they pick it up, we can't send them the virus?"

As Casmir opened his mouth to reply, a message came in to his chip from someone he'd given access to but had rarely heard from.

Dabrowski, I need that virus, Rache texted without preamble.

Casmir struggled to send a calm response, though panic welled up in him at this contact. If Meister was monitoring who sent messages to Kim, the lieutenant was surely monitoring Casmir too. *I assume you don't refer to the Great Plague.*

The computer virus you used to wipe out those pirates.

I didn't wipe them out. The virus took the power from their ships.

And someone else wiped them out, yes, yes. If you want me to get your friends off the Chivalrous *before it's annihilated, send me the virus, preferably encapsulated so that it doesn't affect* my *ship, and details of how to unleash it on the ships chasing Jorg.*

I would love to have my friends safely removed from the Chivalrous, *but I believe the king—and every soldier who serves him—would shoot me if I sent you a virus that makes incapacitating enemy ships possible.*

Don't they have anti-virus measures for it yet? You've had it in your hands for weeks. Send it over with details on how to deploy it.

The Kingdom ships weren't the only targets Rache could use that virus on. Casmir would be giving him another weapon to use against… anyone he wished to attack. But if he was willing to help Qin and Bonita and was close enough to do so… was it worth it?

They need to be willing to accept a transmission from you, Casmir warned, *so you would need to be sneaky.*

I am very sneaky. I am also their putative ally. They should talk to me.

Casmir closed his eyes at the unintentional confirmation that Rache was working for Dubashi. It wasn't anything he hadn't known, but it was another reminder that he shouldn't be having this conversation with him, not when all messages were being relayed through the ship's routers.

Rache… are you truly going to help Bonita and Qin? For… Kim's sake? I can't give this to you if you're going to use it to kill Jorg.

You don't have a choice. Dubashi's ships are close to succeeding. Someone is going to kill Jorg one way or another. Send it to me, and maybe I can get your friends off.

Casmir bent forward, gripping his knees, and stared down at the deck. His vision blurred, and the light seemed to waver, though he was sure that was an artifact of his brain, not reality. Damn it, was there no way he could escape without more blood on his hands? If there was a way to help Qin and Bonita, he had to take it, but at what cost? And what would the cost be if he did nothing? He could lose them forever. Viggo would have no crew, nobody to banter with, nobody to fly him between the stars.

Ishii poked him in the shoulder. "Are you listening to me?"

"I…" Was he hyperventilating or was that his imagination? Casmir swallowed, trying to focus his vision and slow down his breathing. His mouth was dry, too dry. "I think I've found someone who can transmit the virus and is close enough to do something about it."

"Who?"

"You don't want to know."

Casmir shook his head and bundled up the files and instructions to send to Rache. His brain felt numb as he did it, as he imagined Rache not only using that virus against Dubashi's ships but against Kingdom ships. Grunburg had said they had come up with a defense against it, but had they tested it? Was it true?

"Am I making a mistake?" he whispered, but the words didn't come out right. His tongue was heavy.

"Dabrowski." Ishii gripped his shoulder, his voice sounding distant as he spoke. "What are you talking about?"

The light wavered and grew bright, too bright, and belatedly Casmir realized he was having his first seizure since taking Rache's immune booster. Ishii asked something else, but Casmir couldn't understand. His body and his brain stopped working, and he lost awareness.

You're not here, Father, Asger messaged.

I'm working on something, came the prompt reply.

I thought we were going to work on that together, assuming you mean sneaking away on the Dragon. Asger paced outside of the airlock bay. He'd told Casmir to meet him here with Kim in five minutes if they were coming along but hadn't heard back from him. And now his father, who'd said he would be here to help take the ship, was off "working on something."

Asger didn't want to delay further—the longer he waited, the more time there was for the crew to figure out he planned to take the ship. He would have to handle this on his own.

He strode into the quiet and almost empty bay. A single soldier stood at the airlock tube leading over to the *Dragon*, the freighter tucked in under the *Osprey's* belly for the tow. Asger, wearing his knight's silver liquid armor and carrying a rifle and his pertundo, approached as if he had every right to bypass the soldier and stride onto the ship.

But the soldier stepped in front of the airlock entrance. "The repairs are complete, Sir Knight. I have orders to keep anyone from going aboard the civilian ship."

Asger wondered if any of the people who'd been repairing the freighter had encountered Tristan. Neither Ishii nor anyone else on the *Osprey* had mentioned him. The ex-knight was proving to be good at hiding.

"I left something on board, and I need to get it. If there's going to be a battle, Captain Ishii might release the tow ship. I can't leave this item to be snatched by pirates or scavengers." While Asger spoke to the soldier, he sent a message via his chip. *Tristan, are you over there?*

"What item?" The soldier eyed his armament suspiciously.

"A pertundo like this one." Asger patted his weapon. "I was ordered to get it from an ex-knight on Stardust Palace Station. I did so, but it's still on the freighter. My superiors will bust me if I fail at that simple mission."

I'm here, eating Captain Lopez's food, practicing combat maneuvers with an antiquated robot Fit-1000, and listening to her ship complain that nobody is mounting a rescue mission.

I'm trying to come over there to help. I've met an impediment.

"Do you have permission from the captain to get it?" the soldier asked.

"I do not." Asger put a hand on the soldier's shoulder, not too worried since he was only armed with a stunner. "But I'm going over there. You can step aside and let me pass, or you can be thrown aside and let me pass."

"Sir Knight." The soldier wore a mulish expression, and Asger could guess what the rest of his response would be.

He was about to lunge in and hurl the man to the side when a clank came from the airlock hatch. The soldier jumped and glanced back as it opened. Asger took advantage of the distraction and snatched the stunner out of the man's grip.

The hatch opened, and Tristan stood there with his pertundo in hand. He was wearing a borrowed galaxy suit instead of armor, but he still managed to look strong and intimidating. All that work with the Fit-1000, no doubt.

The soldier swore and backed away from them. "I'll have to report this to my superiors."

"I expected nothing less," Asger said.

"You won't be able to uncouple that ship and fly away without someone on the bridge working the controls. You'll just be stranded over there."

"We'll see about that," a new voice said from the corridor. Asger's father had arrived.

The soldier looked bolstered as the senior Asger walked in. Believing he had backup? Not likely. Asger's father also wore his armor and carried his pertundo, in addition to toting a full pack on his back. Determination stamped his face.

"I've been ordered to keep anyone from going to the freighter," the soldier told him.

Asger's father flicked a finger toward the man. "Ishii knows we're taking it. Go check with him."

"I—" The soldier paused, his eyes going glassy as he accessed his chip. "Oh." He looked at Asger. "Why didn't you say you had permission, sir?"

"Recent development." Asger raised his eyebrows at his father.

"I decided to try negotiations rather than brute force," his father said.

"And that worked?" Asger stepped aside as his father approached the airlock chamber and looked toward the exit to the bay, expecting Casmir and Kim to show up at any second. "I thought you were also in questionable standing for having helped Casmir with his last scheme."

"With Jorg, yes. Ishii knows he was on course to get his fleet annihilated by a bunch of moon defenses and dozens of mercenary ships. And he knows we derailed that. Also, I promised him we'd ram an enemy ship with the freighter if things got desperate for the *Chivalrous*."

"Aren't things already desperate?"

"I'm afraid so."

Asger sent Casmir another note as his father passed into the airlock tube. It had sounded like he wanted to come along, but maybe he'd been detained. Or thrown in the brig. He tried Kim.

Give us a few minutes, was her terse reply. *Then go if we can't make it. Do you need help?*

Not as much as Qin and Bonita. I heard Ishii is bringing Casmir to sickbay. I'm guessing he had a seizure.

That answer didn't reassure Asger, and he almost headed back into the warship to help, but what could he do to assist with a seizure? And Kim was right. Unless someone was pointing a rifle to Casmir's head, he wasn't in as much danger as Qin and Bonita.

Though worried, he followed his father and Tristan through the tube and into the *Dragon*'s cargo hold.

"You brought back knights, Tristan," came Viggo's voice from a speaker.

"Yes. I believe we're going to try to rescue the captain and Ms. Qin now." Tristan smiled lopsidedly. "I hope the people I'm going to rescue need to be rescued this time."

"I'm positive they do." Asger hesitated, realizing they were assuming Tristan wanted to come. He seemed game, but this could be dangerous. Very dangerous. "Tristan, do you want to stay on the warship? We could use your help, but I realize you didn't sign on for any of this and probably just want to go back to the station."

"I would rather help than keep hiding. I wouldn't volunteer to risk myself for *Jorg*, but for you and your friends, yes, I'm in."

"Good." Asger clapped him on the shoulder. "Thanks."

"Will El Mago be joining us?" Viggo sounded hopeful. A couple of his robot vacuums vroomed across the cargo hold deck and paused at the airlock, their noses pointed toward the tube.

"Who?" Tristan asked.

"That's his name for Casmir," Asger said. "Or Bonita's name for him. I'm not sure."

"Hers," Viggo said, "but she's allowing me to use it. Is he coming?"

"He wants to, but I'm not sure yet if he can. I heard he's going to sickbay."

"*Sickbay?* Was he wounded? By the Kingdom troops?" Viggo sounded like an attack dog ready to spring to protect his master.

"I don't have all the details."

Faint clunks emanated from the hull.

Asger's father commed down from navigation. "Are your friends here yet? The *Osprey* is making preparations to release us, and we'll have to retract the tube."

"Not yet. Give them a few minutes." Asger bit his lip. How long could they wait?

"Ishii is letting the ship go?" Tristan asked. "Without a fight?"

"I believe my father promised we would use it to ram one of the prince's attackers," Asger said.

"*What?*" Viggo demanded.

Asger lifted a hand. "That's just a contingency plan, Viggo."

"It had better be. I just got everything in working order again."

"William," his father said. "We're less than an hour from the battle. If we're to detach and act anonymously, we need to do so now."

"Just wait a couple more minutes." Asger bit his lip and paced. "Casmir wouldn't want to miss this."

"*Casmir* would keep me from being used like a clunky tree trunk hurled against a castle door," Viggo said.

"That's true," Asger said, "and it's why I'd prefer he join us."

He sent another message. *Casmir, what's going on?*

Once again, he didn't get an answer.

CHAPTER 7

AFTER THE LIGHTS CAME BACK ON, QIN FOUND her and Bonita's armor and weapons in a cabinet near the exit of the detention center. It was locked, but her irritated fist found a creative way to unlock it. One that left her knuckles bruised, but she didn't care.

Fighting the zero-g, she pulled on her armor. It didn't help that the ship was engaged in evasive maneuvers and kept twisting and thrusting, making even Qin's usually ironclad stomach object.

Bonita was still out from the stun. Qin didn't think she could dress the captain and reluctantly locked her boots to the deck by the door to wait for her to wake up.

Now that she was out of the network-blocking walls of the cell and corridor, a stream of messages came to her chip. Many were from Asger, asking if she was all right—that touched her. One was from Bjarke, asking if Bonita was all right, and one was from Casmir, asking if they were *all* all right. He'd also let her know that the *Dragon* was being repaired and towed. He was the only one who'd given all the details on the freighter's repairs and Viggo's state of mind—such as Viggo had a mind—clearly believing they would be as concerned about their computerized friend as anyone would be about a human. Bonita *would* want to know about her ship.

The last message in the queue startled her. It was from one of her cohort sisters on the *Scimitar*, Qin Liangyu Seven, or Mouser, as they'd called her when the pirates hadn't been around to scowl at the nicknames. They were from the same batch of clones and similar to all their sisters, but everybody had their own personalities. Mouser had always been curious and a little mischievous. Even when she'd been punished for it, it hadn't dampened her spirits.

She and Qin had been close, but Mouser hadn't sent a message for the entire year that Qin had been free. Why now?

A new jolt coursed through the ship, and the lights flickered again. An alert on a nearby panel warned of an imminent failure to the main environmental system and that the computers were switching to auxiliary. Qin and Bonita would have to search for oxygen tanks before heading to the shuttle bay that Qin hoped existed.

"The hull has been breached by an invasion force," a computerized voice warned. "Defense Pattern Tango-Ten."

"Now would be a good time to wake up, Captain," Qin murmured.

If there was an invasion team, did that mean the attack would stop while the intruders tried to capture Jorg or whoever they'd come for? It had to be Jorg. Who else was here that they would care about? Qin wished someone was coming for her and Bonita, if only because it meant they would have a ship to leave in, but Casmir, Asger, and the others wouldn't—couldn't—attack a Kingdom ship. This had to be someone else.

While she waited for Bonita to wake, Qin read the message from Mouser.

Liangyu 3—Squirt—I am relieved you are alive and, I hope, well. We are in the system, trapped because the gate is inoperable, and I've learned that you are also here. I should say that Captain Framer *has learned that you are here, but since you seem to be wrapped up in this mess with the Kingdom, he said we're not going to try to get you back at this time.*

Good. Qin didn't need anything else to worry about right now.

I've thought of you often since you escaped and wondered what the universe is like for you now. Did you find a job? Are you getting to do all the things you dreamed of doing? What's it like out there? With freedom?

Qin could almost hear the longing in Mouser's voice, and a pang of homesickness—or maybe that was nostalgia—stuck in her throat. She'd hated being a slave to the Druckers, but she hadn't felt any animosity toward her sisters. They'd been through so much together. If anything, she felt bad that she'd been so busy of late that she hadn't thought of them much.

I'm afraid I'll be caught and get in trouble for asking this, Mouser went on, *but I heard you're a bounty hunter now and that you know mercenaries. Is there any chance we could hire you to get us off this* ship? And away from the Druckers permanently? You know how it is and that we've never been permitted to earn much money on our own, but a few of us have some. And we're not helpless waifs. We could help with the breakout. It would just be difficult. You know about the chips and the mind-messing they've done to us.*

Qin did know. Right after she'd escaped, she'd paid a doctor to remove that chip, afraid the Druckers could use it to track her and even more afraid that they could have delivered pain to her from across the star system.

It's hard to turn a hand on our owners, the message continued. *But if someone else were fighting them, and we could get out while they were busy, you know we'd be an asset. We've all talked about this. It might have been my idea, but everybody wants to leave. Even the older cohort. We want the chance to be free. You were so brave to do it, Squirt. Do you remember when that was your nickname? When we all made up secret nicknames because the pirates said we could only call each other by our numbers?*

Qin swallowed the lump in her throat. She did remember.

I may get caught sending this, the message went on, *but it was worth it to try. If you can get some mercenaries to help us… we'll help you with whatever you need. You know what good warriors we are! Just find a way to let me know. We're stuck here on the* Scimitar *until the gate is fixed. There might never be a better opportunity.*

Whatever happens, love you. Bye!

Qin blew out a slow breath. She'd dreamed of somehow buying out the contracts not only for herself but for all her sisters, but it had only been a dream. She'd known she would never make enough money to do that. But that wasn't what Mouser was asking. She wanted a *raid*. Qin was disappointed that she didn't have enough new allies for something like that. Bonita and Qin couldn't go up against the Druckers by themselves. She might be able to talk Casmir into helping with his crushers once he was done with his obligations to his own people, but there were hundreds of fighters on any given Drucker ship. Could even the crushers take on so many?

A boom sounded in the distance, rattling the ship and bringing Qin back to the present. Unless they could get out of here, she couldn't begin to think about rescuing someone else.

Bonita groaned. She had floated up to a corner of the ceiling, and Qin pulled her back down, feeling guilty that she hadn't kept hold of her.

"Captain?"

Another groan, and Bonita opened an eye. "Yeah."

"You were stunned."

"No kidding." Bonita turned her head. "I was rather hoping you would have carried me farther than ten feet while I was out. Completely off the ship would have been good."

"There were warnings that the ship might lose environmental controls. I wanted you to be in your armor." Qin pushed the bundle toward her. "And to be armed. There's an invasion team on the ship."

"*Whose* invasion team?" Emotions flashed across Bonita's face, hope, then wariness.

Like Qin, she'd probably first thought their friends had come for them before realizing that wasn't possible.

"I don't know," Qin said. "They haven't come to the brig yet. Nobody's come to the brig. I—" Her keen ears caught the buzz of DEW-Tek weapons firing. The closed door to the corridor muffled it, but the fighting couldn't be too far away.

"I'm dressing." Bonita must have heard the weapons fire too. She hurried to don her armor.

Qin held her weapons for her, then returned to the door. There was a small Glasnax window at eye level. She jerked away as two figures in black combat armor ran past carrying rifles and wearing belts and straps loaded with backup weapons. One figure had a grenade launcher.

"I may know who the invaders are," Qin whispered, her back to the wall beside the door. If they hadn't seen her, she wanted to keep it that way.

"Who?" Bonita, struggling to keep at least one boot magnetically locked to the deck as she dressed, hadn't seen the men.

"I suppose there could be lots of people who have black combat armor…" Qin had seen it often in her work for the Druckers. "But I only know of one outfit who wears it and would want a Kingdom prince dead."

Bonita paused to look at her. "Rache?"

"That's my guess."

"I'm not sure if their presence here is good for us or bad for us. Rache probably doesn't have any love or hatred or strong feelings at all about us, but they could shoot us without even identifying us. We better avoid them and find a shuttle. This boat has to have one."

"I hope so." Qin grimaced as more weapons fired in the corridor.

Another black figure strode past the window. Qin expected more troops in combat armor, but it was one of Jorg's crushers. She grimaced.

HOME FRONT

Hunters stalking the hunters? How many were on the bridge or wherever Jorg was, guarding him, and how many were roaming the ship?

A part of her almost wanted to warn Rache, but he was Kim's ally, not hers. Let the Kingdom and Rache's mercenaries brawl it out while Qin and Bonita escaped.

"I'm ready." Bonita lifted a gauntleted hand. "Throw me my rifle."

As Qin tossed it, something soft scraped at the door. An armored figure faced it, helmet bent toward the window so she couldn't see through the faceplate.

It was her instincts rather than any noise that alerted her to trouble.

"Get back," she barked and pushed away from the wall. She grabbed Bonita, pulling her back into the corridor toward the cells with her.

"What are you—"

An explosion roared as the door blew inward. The shockwave sent Qin and Bonita tumbling head over heels down the corridor. But that didn't keep Qin from glimpsing eight armored men striding in and fanning out, rifles pointed at them.

Kim was packing her medical equipment and expecting Casmir any moment when Lieutenant Meister walked into sickbay with two large stone-faced soldiers. She glanced at the spot where her crusher bodyguard had been all morning, but Zee had rounded them all up earlier for a training session elsewhere on the ship. She would have to defend herself if it came to that.

As she turned to face the three men, she reminded herself that she *had* defended herself before. Just because this was a Kingdom officer on a Kingdom ship didn't mean she couldn't kick him in the nuts. Maybe someday, she would find a pair of bokken again. The practice swords were laughable when compared to modern weapons, but they were handy for bopping someone in a sensitive spot.

When she met the eyes of the soldiers, they drew their stunners. Mind readers, no doubt.

"I don't suppose you're here for a cup of coffee?" Kim looked toward the door, expecting someone to bring in Casmir at any second. His seizures didn't usually knock him out for that long, though he would be groggy. Getting him to the *Dragon* might be a challenge... assuming she could escape this *current* challenge.

"No," Meister said. "Prince Jorg's ship has taken a lot of damage, and we don't know if we'll make it in time to help. They were fighting back, but the ship has taken a lot of hits, and their comm officer's distress call said their environmental systems are threatening to go offline." He gave her a long, hard look, as if she was responsible. A sinking feeling entered her stomach even before he said, "We believe Rache is responsible."

She almost blurted that he'd said it was Dubashi's people, but how could she without admitting she'd been communicating with Rache?

"You don't know?" Kim asked, buying time while she thought.

"The ship or ships attacking Jorg are hidden behind their slydar hulls." Meister sneered.

"Don't many mercenaries use such tactics?"

It was the wrong question she realized as soon as she asked it. He would think she was defending Rache.

Meister clenched his fist. "Only one who wants our prince dead."

Kim kept her mouth shut. The lieutenant was angrier than he had been before, and she didn't want to goad him into drugging her. She eyed the soldiers' stunners, wondering if she should try to get herself knocked out. They couldn't question her if she was unconscious. At this point, there was probably no hope of escaping to Bonita's freighter with the others.

"My cousin serves on the prince's ship. That aside, it's my duty to protect the crown, the king, and his children. I *will* question you to learn how I can find and stop Rache." Meister snapped his fingers, and a nurse with an apologetic expression walked over with a medical kit. The nurse had been coming into Kim's lab for coffee for several days and avoided making eye contact as she prepared an injector.

"He's not answering our hails. Can you communicate with him?" Meister asked Kim. "I know you have before." His lip curled. "Tell him to break off the attack. Ambassador Romano will speak with him about compensation." The lip remained curled, and indignation burned in his eyes. "Whatever it takes to save Jorg and the others aboard."

HOME FRONT

A part of her wanted to be mulish and not cooperate, but it might help the situation if they knew Rache wasn't the one attacking.

Knowing she was further incriminating herself, she took a deep breath and said, "I know his chip ident and can send a message to him, yes."

Triumph surged in Meister's eyes. The soldiers and the nurse gaped at Kim in shock.

"But he's not the one who orchestrated the attack on Jorg's ship. He believes those are Dubashi's people after the prince."

"He told you this?" Meister's tone oozed skepticism.

"You know Dubashi tried to hire Rache to assassinate Jorg, right?" Kim said as reasonably as she could. "*He's* the one who wants Jorg and Jager dead. And Odin for himself."

"*Prince* Jorg and *King* Jager," came a voice from the doorway.

Kim stifled a groan. The lean, gray-haired Ambassador Romano walked in wearing his gray civilian clothes and fur-trimmed robe instead of a galaxy suit. His dark eyes were cold as he stared at her.

The nurse held up the injector, her face no longer apologetic. By admitting to having Rache's contact information, Kim had declared herself a traitor to everyone here.

"You will use proper respect when speaking of the royalty and your world leaders." Romano stopped a few paces away, folded his arms over his chest, and nodded to Meister. "Proceed."

"Now? When we're about to fly into combat?" Kim silently messaged, *Casmir, if you see this, I could use a crusher bodyguard in sickbay.*

Maybe she shouldn't have sent the message, should have stoically accepted her fate, but fear of all that she might reveal about Rache under that drug made her desperate. It wasn't just that her feelings would get her in trouble—if not shot—but she might blab all his secrets to this roomful of people. And Casmir's secrets as well. Some people at Royal Intelligence knew who Rache was and knew he and Casmir had both been cloned from Admiral Mikita, but if this many new people heard about it, people without top-level security clearances, the news would be all over the ship—and all over the Fleet and the media—within days.

"Do we have to restrain you?" Meister asked.

"Do it," Romano said before Kim could answer.

As the two soldiers stepped toward her and Kim tensed, torn between trying to defend herself—getting herself stunned—and accepting her fate, the door to sickbay opened again. Casmir's voice floated in ahead of him, though it didn't sound like he was charging in to the rescue.

"I'm fine," he said as Ishii and a sturdy young soldier escorted him into sickbay. "Really, I'm fine. I don't need an escort. Or to inconvenience anyone. I'm sorry."

Despite his protestations of fineness, his words had a postictal slur to them, and Kim realized it had probably been a bad seizure. Maybe he hadn't seen her message yet, or grasped it, even if it had floated down his contact.

Ishii's eyebrows rose when he saw Romano, Meister, and the rest, and surprise flickered across his face. At first, Kim thought he might be unaware of this and would try to put a stop to it, but realization replaced the surprise, and he didn't comment other than to point Casmir toward a bed.

But Casmir stopped and looked at Kim. His eyes were bleary and tight with the pain of a headache, but they weren't confused.

"What's going on?" he asked.

Meister ignored him. "Grab her and inject the drug," he told his minions.

A crusher walked in, and the soldiers hesitated to obey. More crushers followed him—was that Zee in the lead?—and sickbay was abruptly much more crowded.

Ishii gripped Casmir's forearm. "Don't make trouble. You *know* who she's been talking to. And who you've been talking to, I'm sure. If not for your drug allergy, you'd be getting an injection too."

"I am a Z-6000," several crushers spoke at once, "programmed to protect Kim Sato and Casmir Dabrowski."

"Can't all this wait until after we rescue Bonita and Qin?" Casmir lifted a placating hand, though whether it was for the now-nervous soldiers or his crushers, it wasn't clear. "And Jorg? Sora, you know our friends are on that ship. If we knew how to stop whoever's attacking them, we would."

Have you talked to Asger recently? Casmir messaged Kim without looking at her. His pleading eyes were toward Ishii.

If he ordered the crushers to attack, they could overpower the soldiers in sickbay, but it wasn't as if they could fight off the entire crew of hundreds. And if they hurt anyone... Kim and Casmir would never be able to go home.

But maybe that point had already come and gone. And all they could do now was make it worse. A *lot* worse.

HOME FRONT

Yes, Kim replied silently. *We were supposed to meet him at the* Dragon *ten minutes ago, but it doesn't look like that's going to happen now.*

"It's all right, Casmir," she said aloud, lifting a hand toward the crushers, as if she could halt them. "I'll let them learn whatever they want to learn."

His eyes grew a little wild, and she realized he might act to protect her, even against her wishes.

Asger and Bjarke are already on the Dragon. Casmir must have sent a message to Asger and received an update. *They got permission to take it before this started. If we can get out of this mess and run down there… maybe we can leave before that permission gets revoked.*

You can barely walk right now.

I'll be fine.

Meister stepped forward—nobody else was moving—and reached for Kim's arm. She reacted on reflex rather than conscious thought and jumped back, avoiding his grasp.

Either Casmir messaged the crushers to attack, or they interpreted Meister as a threat and acted on their own. They surged forward to place themselves between her and the soldiers.

"Dabrowski, damn it." Ishii tightened his grip on Casmir's forearm and reached for his shoulder—or maybe his neck—with his other hand.

Kim jumped toward them, afraid Casmir would be used as a shield—or a hostage in negotiations with the crushers—but Zee reached him first.

"Don't hurt anyone!" Casmir blurted as Zee shoved Ishii, sending him spinning away. He struck a sickbay bed and went down.

A stunner fired. It was meant for Kim, but two crushers blocked it, and the weapon was useless on them. The rest of the crushers surged toward targets, disarming soldiers and capturing everyone else.

Kim reached Casmir's side, and he grabbed her arm. *Airlock Five!* he messaged and stumbled toward the door.

She gripped him, helping him stay upright when he wobbled. Despite his words, he was not *fine.*

An alarm wailed from the speaker, and dread thudded into Kim's stomach. They would have to deal with more than the soldiers in sickbay.

"If you run," Romano cried from where he was pinned to a wall by a crusher, "you two are dead. And that's not hyperbole!"

But the crushers not restraining people ran past Kim and Casmir and out the door first. They sped into the corridor, and when armed soldiers—these men carried rifles, not stunners—rushed out of a lift, the crushers created a shield to protect Kim and Casmir. Two of them ran forward to engage the armored team.

Two others followed Casmir as he veered into an access tube with a ladder leading to the lower decks. Kim had never been in it and didn't know where it went, but Casmir must have brought up a schematic.

He stopped at the bottom—Kim heard footsteps in the corridor they needed to enter—and pressed himself flat against the tube wall. There wasn't room for the crushers to pass and go out first. Or so she thought. Then they turned into amorphous blobs of black liquid and flowed past and out into the corridor. Crimson energy bolts slammed into them as they re-formed into their bipedal shapes, but the blasts did nothing to slow them down. They ran toward the soldiers firing at them.

Thuds and yelps of pain and anger sounded as Kim and Casmir waited in the access tube.

"We're screwed even if we escape this," Kim whispered. "I'm sorry, Casmir." She should have allowed Meister to question her back in her lab, before all this had escalated.

"We're going to get out and fix this." He patted her arm as two more crushers flowed down from above, oozing past, then re-forming in the corridor.

"Follow us, Casmir Dabrowski and Kim Sato," one said.

Zee? Kim had no idea at this point, but the weapons firing had stopped.

Casmir led the way out, following the crushers past doorways and the entrance to a shuttle bay. Kim glanced back to see that other crushers had broken the soldiers' rifles in half and were pinning the struggling men against the bulkhead. What were the odds that nobody would be seriously hurt—or worse?—in this flight of madness?

Casmir tugged her around a bend. "There's the door to the airlock bay."

"They're never going to release the clamps on the ship and let us escape now," Kim warned.

"I'm working on that."

They followed the crushers into the airlock bay.

"After what we just did, they may fire on us," Kim added.

"Working on that too."

"I'd feel more reassured about your abilities if you weren't stumbling and there wasn't a slur to your voice."

HOME FRONT

The hatches were still open for Airlock Five, the tube visible stretching toward the freighter, and they hurried toward it. One of the knights stood partway through, silver armor and helmet obscuring his face. He waved his pertundo.

A bang came from behind them, and Kim jumped, but it was more of the crushers rushing into the bay. Others remained in the corridor as shots fired.

Kim put her helmet up in case a stray shot made it around the crushers. She should have done that earlier. The galaxy suits weren't combat armor, but they provided some protection.

The airlock hatch slammed shut as they were about to enter the chamber.

"Did you do that?" Kim asked.

"No. They're trying to stop us."

"Imagine that."

"Give me a second." Casmir rested his hand on the nearby control panel, but his fingers didn't move. He would have to gain access through the ship's network.

Casmir shifted from foot to foot. DEW-Tek bolts zipped through the corridor beyond the door, but the crushers kept anyone from running in. Someone had found firearms with bullets, and the booms of propellant-fired projectiles filled the air. If they did anything to the crushers, Kim couldn't tell. So far, explosives were the only thing she'd seen damage them, and even then, they could usually reassemble themselves. Her benevolent, humanity-loving roommate had made very effective super soldiers.

"There it is," Casmir said, a click sounding.

The control panel flashed angry red indicators, denying entrance, but the hatch swung open. They stepped into the airlock chamber with several crushers squeezing in with them. The outer hatch was still closed. Casmir sighed.

As he worked on getting it open, Ishii's voice came over their helmet speakers. Kim expected orders for them to cease and desist or else.

"You've fucked up beyond all chance at redemption this time," was what Ishii said. "Romano has ordered me to shoot that freighter out of the stars if you succeed at getting away with it."

There was a pause before Casmir said, "Understood," and Kim wondered if Ishii had added some silent message straight to his chip.

The outer airlock hatch swung open, the tube stretched before them, the open hatch of the *Dragon* waiting for them. The armored figure lifted a beckoning hand. It had to be Asger. Bjarke wouldn't want to invite this trouble aboard.

"I have to do something so he doesn't get in trouble," Casmir muttered as they started across.

"He? Ishii?"

"Yeah." *I'm temporarily disabling the ship's weapons*, he added in a chip message. *Long enough for us to get away but not long enough to interfere with his ability to assist Jorg's ship.*

Kim wondered if it was too late for that. Would Jorg—and Bonita and Qin—still be alive when they got there?

Should you be able to do that?

No, but I set it up for myself to have access a while ago. I figured something like this might happen.

"You're making a mess," Asger said, looking back toward the crushers still in the bay, keeping the soldiers from following them.

"I know," Kim said sadly.

"The rest of the crushers are going to try to join us," Casmir said, patting Asger on the shoulder as they entered the *Dragon's* cargo hold. "Keep the hatch open."

Asger snorted but stood by it with his hand on the control panel.

"Casmir!" Viggo's voice was filled with delight, and several robot vacuums zipped toward Casmir.

He returned the greeting, but he sounded weary. He sank down to his knees on the deck, probably still working on the *Osprey* to make sure it let them go and didn't fire on them.

Kim wished they were safe now and that Casmir could rest, but they were leaving one danger and heading into another one.

CHAPTER 8

IN THE AFTERMATH OF THE DOOR BEING BLOWN open, Bonita ended up floating near the ceiling with her back to the far wall, her rifle pointed at the men in black armor who'd streamed inside. Qin had managed to get her magnetic boots locked to the deck and was a more serious threat as she faced the intruders, their tinted faceplates keeping anyone from identifying them.

"We're here for Qin Liangyu Three and Captain Bonita Lopez," a dry voice said.

Bonita recognized it even though she hadn't spoken often with Rache. How many other people could be dry in the middle of invading an enemy ship?

"To kill us or what?" Bonita asked.

"To rescue you."

"Uh." She couldn't fathom why he would. Was someone paying him? Bjarke? No. He had the money, but he would never hire this loathed enemy of the Kingdom. Casmir and Kim? Maybe they had talked Rache into it somehow. "Don't take this the wrong way, but we were in the middle of rescuing ourselves."

"I see that. We have a shuttle. Follow us, and we'll take you there."

Several of the mercenaries backed out through the open door, but Rache remained—he was shorter than all of his men—and lifted a hand, gesturing for them to come. Waiting to see if they would?

Qin looked at her, her eyes as uncertain as Bonita knew her own were. Heading off with criminals. What could go wrong?

"Don't you have Kingdom enemies to battle?" Bonita pushed away from the wall. She didn't know if they should go with Rache—avoiding everyone on this ship seemed wiser—but she didn't want to stay in the brig.

"We've taken the bridge. The one we're looking for isn't there. My teams are searching the rest of the ship." Rache waved his gauntleted fingers. "Come. We'll put you in a shuttle before we complete our mission."

The way he said *complete* sounded very final. Did he have plans to set charges and blow up the ship as his men were leaving?

"Coming," Bonita muttered. It might not be wise, but staying here could get her killed as easily as going with him. "Keep an eye out," she whispered to Qin.

"Always."

My dear Captain Laser, a message popped up on her chip as they followed Rache's men into the corridor. Bjarke. *My son and I and a few of your friends have departed from the Kingdom warship* Osprey *in your freighter and wish to pick you up, thus to return you to your rightful place. Are you in the brig there? Are you... all right?* A hint of genuine concern made it through Bjarke's usual flippancy. *We know Dubashi's ships have been attacking the* Chivalrous. *We're going to try to slip in and retrieve you while everyone is distracted. Let me know if you receive this message.*

We just got out of the brig, Bonita replied, delighted to have a second would-be rescuer. *Where would you like us to meet you?*

Going with Bjarke on the *Dragon* sounded a lot better than going with Rache anywhere.

Excellent work. There's a cargo bay on the bottom level with two airlocks. Meet us there.

We've got a few obstacles to get through— Bonita eyed the dark armored backs of the mercenaries ahead of her, *—but we'll do our best to be there.*

Qin is all right too? Bjarke asked. *William wishes to know.*

So far.

As they followed Rache's men down a ladder well and through a wide carpeted corridor, they passed statues and busts floating free from alcoves where they had sat on pedestals. Some were still there, secured even in zero-g, but others had been damaged, the pedestals blasted by rifles. A tapestry floating out in the corridor was scorched and smoking. Bonita was reminded that this was the prince's personal yacht, not a warship. She was amazed the defenses were good enough to have staved off their attackers for as long as they had.

HOME FRONT

The mercenaries stopped to exchange fire with crushers and men in blue Kingdom combat armor. Qin started forward to help, but Bonita pulled her into one of the alcoves, shoving a suit of ancient armor out of the way.

Let them fight, she messaged Qin. *We're not picking sides.*

I saw a crusher, Captain. It's not going to care which side we're on. They'll be focused on the bigger threat. Rache.

Rache's men also used the alcoves for cover, methodically trading fire with their enemies, blasting helmets and armored torsos with perfect accuracy. One of them spun a grenade down the corridor. It blew up, taking a crusher's head off, at least until it could regroup.

"Down that other ladder." Rache glanced back and pointed them toward what Bonita had thought was another alcove. "We'll hold them off."

Since Bjarke wanted to meet them on a lower deck, Bonita obeyed Rache's order without hesitation, pushing off toward the spot. A few energy bolts zipped past the men, and one almost careened off her helmet. She was glad Qin had found their armor.

The headless crusher re-formed itself and charged the lead mercenaries.

Bonita reached the ladder as Rache pulled out another grenade. Making sure Qin was behind her, she pulled herself down the rungs upside down, the lack of gravity making directions inconsequential. When she'd gone down as far as she could go, she poked her head out before committing to leaving the ladder well.

It was the cargo bay Bjarke had told her about, with a small shuttle in the center—it was closer to an escape pod than a true shuttle, and she doubted it could carry more than four people. Men in Kingdom armor were getting it ready for departure while eight crushers stood guard around it.

Naturally, the two airlock chambers Bjarke had mentioned were on the far side of the bay. Bonita and Qin would have to run past all those crushers and Kingdom men to get to them.

Casmir pulled himself past Tristan and into the *Dragon*'s compact navigation room. Asger was in the pilot's seat and Bjarke in the co-pilot's seat, so there wasn't much room. Kim was in the corridor with Zee and Reuben behind her.

"Are we out of range of the *Osprey's* weapons?" Casmir's head throbbed, and he still felt hungover in the aftermath of that inconveniently timed seizure, so he stared blearily at the forward display, not trying to focus on the instrumentation panels in front of the pods.

"We are. The *Osprey* didn't fire." Asger looked back at Casmir. "When I saw that mess of soldiers chasing you, I was sure they would."

"Ishii had orders to from Ambassador Romano. He made the mistake of—no, he made the *choice* to warn me."

"He warned you he would fire at us?" Bjarke asked.

"Yes. I temporarily deactivated their weapons system. It'll come back online in time for them to deal with—we believe it's Dubashi's men attacking the *Chivalrous,* right? Nothing changed while I was, uhm, fuzzy?" Casmir decided not to mention that Rache had been the one to tell him that.

"If it's not Rache, it's Dubashi," Asger said. "How can you, a civilian advisor with no military clearance whatsoever, deactivate a protected weapons system on a Kingdom warship?"

"I made myself an account and gave it clearance."

"You're not supposed to be able to do that."

"No," Casmir agreed, then smiled and shrugged. He'd spent numerous days on the *Osprey* by now. Foreseeing potential emergencies, he'd given himself access to everything important long ago.

"Rache said Dubashi's ships are the attackers," Kim said from behind Casmir.

"That doesn't make it the truth," Bjarke growled. "If anything, I'm more inclined to believe it's *his* ship now."

"I'm not." Asger pointed at something on a proximity display, then adjusted their course. "There's wreckage out there. A lot of wreckage.

We're coming up on it now. It's scattered all over the place, some of it still with heat signatures."

"A destroyed ship?" Bjarke asked.

"*Several* destroyed ships."

"We're not too late are we?" Bjarke shook his head. "I just sent a message to Bonita—Captain Laser—and she messaged me back."

"No." Asger pointed again. "There's the *Chivalrous* up there. I think this is wreckage from their pursuers. It has to be. How did anyone target them? They have—*had*—slydar hulls."

"Pursuers that the *Chivalrous* destroyed?" Bjarke sounded confused. "All the reports we were getting on the bridge of the *Osprey* said the *Chivalrous* was outmanned and outgunned and losing the battle. At one point, Jorg was screeching for us to hurry up and get there to help."

Casmir looked over his shoulder, meeting Kim's eyes. He was a lot less confused, despite his *fuzzy* period.

As Ishii had been helping him to sickbay, he'd wondered if he'd gotten his message off in time—the files with the virus and the information on how to deploy it—but he must have. This much destruction and of several ships... Rache must have successfully sent the virus and convinced them to open it. And then annihilated Dubashi's ships when they'd lost power and defenses.

Kim nodded back at him. She had to be thinking the same thing.

Should he confess to Bjarke and Asger what he'd done? Casmir was shocked that Bjarke had joined in on this fiasco. Of course, he'd planned to leave on the *Dragon*—with *permission*—before he'd known Casmir and Kim would get themselves in trouble.

"It's a minefield out here." Asger adjusted course again.

Casmir's boots left the deck, queasiness creeping into his stomach. They weren't accelerating or decelerating quickly enough for the ship to have a sense of gravity.

"I'm going to have to slow us down," Asger added, "or we'll end up with a piece of somebody's hull plowing through this ship."

"You can't slow down." Bjarke gripped the console as if he might take over the navigation controls. "Bonita said she's in trouble. Technically, she said there were a *few obstacles* in her way, but she's big on understatement and sarcasm. That probably means a platoon of soldiers. Or of crushers."

"We have crushers too." Casmir pointed over his shoulder. "I can send them in to fight Jorg's crushers."

"Are yours bigger and better?"

"Yes," came Zee's deadpan response behind Kim. "Human friends, this should be apparent simply by comparing the new line—of which I am a prototype—with the old line. We are substantially bigger."

Casmir smiled and decided not to point out that size was the only difference he'd made. That desperate night on Forseti Station, he'd been afraid to tinker too much with the original schematics. He'd only hoped that by giving Zee the weight advantage, Zee would fare well against the crushers that had been chasing them.

"We are also considerate and work well with our human allies," Zee said, then held something out to Casmir. "I did not get an opportunity to return your toy to you earlier, but I kept it safe for you."

Casmir plucked his makeshift dreidel out of Zee's hand. It was undamaged, even though Zee had gone into battle recently.

"Thank you," he said.

"Where did he keep it?" Bjarke asked. "He doesn't have pockets."

"He can *make* pockets," Casmir said.

"Easily." An indentation opened up in Zee's side, and he poked a finger into it before filling it in again.

"Now there's a super power." Bjarke turned back to watch the forward display.

"A super power?" Zee asked, then ran a search. "Yes, I see. Like superheroes in Casmir Dabrowski's comic books. Crushers have super powers. That is correct."

"Now you've got him thinking he's a superhero?" Kim asked.

"Zee is developing his own sense of self," Casmir said.

"Uh huh. If his ego gets any bigger, he's going to tip over."

"Not as long as the gravity is nonexistent." He winked at her.

"At least the *Osprey* is having trouble with this junk field too," Asger said, focused on piloting. "We may be able to get there first. They're bigger and having to pick a more careful route. They just fired a couple of blasts to clear debris."

"Is anybody firing at the *Chivalrous* right now?" Casmir asked. "Or did Rache take care of the threat?"

"Rache *is* the threat," Bjarke growled. "One of them at least."

HOME FRONT

Casmir wished he could object, but if Rache came face to face with Jorg... he would take out the prince as surely as Dubashi's men would.

"True," Casmir said, "but he's a threat we could more easily negotiate with. We've dealt with him in the past."

Bjarke waved to the comm panel. "Negotiate away."

Casmir started to lean past his pod toward it but paused and looked back at Kim. "He's not one to hide on his bridge while he sends people over, is he?"

She shook her head. "He said—he asked what I would think if he rescued Bonita and Qin, so I'm guessing he's leading a team over there."

"I'll try his chip."

"*I'll* try not to find it alarming that he's given you permission to contact him that way," Bjarke growled. "And vice versa, presumably."

"I've learned a few tricks for getting through to people who haven't given me permission to contact them." Casmir didn't mention that his tricks hadn't been needed in Rache's case. He leaned back and composed his message.

"I've got visual on the *Chivalrous*." Asger tapped a few controls for the display, and a distant ship hanging listless in space came into view as the *Dragon* soared around a piece of wreckage.

Scorch marks and spots where the armored hull had been blown away riddled the yacht. One of its two weapons turrets had been destroyed, and the other was inactive. Everything about the ship appeared inactive. Did they have life support over there?

"There's a shuttle out here too." Asger frowned at the scanner display. "It doesn't have any markings. I'm not sure if it's one of Rache's or if it's an escape shuttle that came out of one of these destroyed ships."

"Don't hail it," Bjarke said. "We're not taking on any of Dubashi's minions as refugees. They can wait for the *Osprey* to save them."

"The shuttle is snugged up to what's left of one of the wrecks, a spot near the bridge." Asger sounded puzzled. "I see what I thought were a couple of bodies outside in spacesuits but what may be workers. Maybe some passengers were trapped on the bridge, and they're cutting through the hull to get them out?"

"Not our problem," Bjarke said.

"I thought knights were supposed to be noble and chivalrous and help everyone in need," Kim said.

"Not Dubashi's people. I've had enough of them."

Asger nodded and rubbed his shoulder, the one that had been injured in Dubashi's base. "We're flying past without hailing them. Let's just get our friends."

"Agreed," Bjarke said.

Kim didn't object. Even if she would have normally wanted to help stranded refugees, she had to want to get Bonita and Qin out of danger first. As did Casmir.

Hello, Rache! Casmir strove for cheer in his message, even if it was false cheer. They flew past a body, Asger swearing as he tried and failed to keep it from bumping against the *Dragon's* hull.

It was a grisly reminder that Casmir had shared the computer virus that had allowed these ships to be blown up. They were enemy ships that had been trying to kill Jorg, but it was hard for him to justify this, especially since Rache was as much of a threat to Jorg as these people had been.

Casmir made himself continue with the message. *Have you managed to find Captain Lopez and Qin over there yet? We're coming to pick them up. We would also appreciate it if you could bring Prince Jorg to us for transport to one of the Kingdom warships. Alive, if you please. We don't mind if you put a gag in his mouth. If you're willing to trade him to us, I'll be most pleased to hand over that crusher I believe I once promised you. I'll even throw in a second, since I already owe you for giving us that ride to Dubashi's base. I'm also beginning to suspect that they are social constructs and are happiest with another crusher around. I will be happy to share with you the details of Zee's quest to find a mate, if you would find that interesting.*

He stopped, rolling his eyes at himself. He wasn't even face to face with Rache, and he was falling prey to his usual nervous babbling.

As they flew closer to the yacht, Asger still cursing at all the wreckage they had to maneuver around, a combat shuttle came into view. It was docked to one of two airlocks on the *Chivalrous*.

"That has to be Rache's shuttle," Asger said, though it was unmarked. "They're already aboard."

"Take us in." Bjarke leaned forward in his pod.

Kim? Casmir messaged. *Are you in contact with Rache? He's ignoring me.*

HOME FRONT

Casmir supposed it was possible that Rache had been knocked out or killed in the fighting—or was too busy to respond—but he had a feeling Rache didn't want to talk to him about saving Jorg.

I haven't spoken to him since before we left the Osprey.

Will you try asking him to save Jorg instead of killing him? I offered him two crushers. There's not much else I have that I can negotiate with, but we can try something else. Casmir didn't technically own the crushers or have the right to trade them, but surely the rational minds in the Kingdom would see it as a fair trade for Jorg's life. Even if Jorg later didn't.

You know that's not going to work. He wanted this assignment.

He wanted to kill Jager. Does he really care about Jorg?

Kim's lips thinned. *Jorg is even more of a dick than his father.*

But he's not old enough and hasn't been in command of anything long enough to have screwed over Rache. I assume Jager did that at some point. You've never told me his story.

It's never been mine to tell. Kim lifted a hand. *I'll send him a message and see if there's anything he will trade.*

Offer him two crushers. And a kiss.

I'm not offering him sexual experiences as a negotiation tactic.

I'll kiss him if he refrains from murdering our monarch's son. Kim, we blasted our way off the Osprey. *We're in trouble no matter what, but if we could get Jorg out of there alive, maybe it would mitigate things somewhat.*

A long minute passed before Kim shook her head. *I sent a message, but he also isn't responding to me.*

Casmir sighed, and Bjarke looked back.

"Rache doesn't seem to be open to negotiations." Casmir waved at his temple.

"Shocking," Asger muttered.

"Just take us in." Bjarke touched his pertundo. "Maybe there's still time to help."

"Help? Or kill Rache?" Asger asked.

"Help *by* killing Rache." Bjarke glanced back at Casmir again. "Will you send your crushers in with us?"

"Yes." Casmir nodded.

If he didn't send them in, Asger, Tristan, and Bjarke, as talented as they were, wouldn't stand a chance against Rache's entire strike team.

Kim opened her mouth, as if she wanted to ask him not to order them to kill Rache, but she didn't voice the request. Maybe she already knew that he wouldn't. He would order them to save Jorg and Qin and Bonita and nothing more. He hoped it would be enough.

CHAPTER 9

BONITA LOOKED UP THE LADDER WELL, HOPING RACHE and his men were on the way down—and hoping the crushers hadn't spotted her peeking out into the cargo hold.

"What is it?" Qin whispered.

She'd stopped in the ladder well above, her head downward, her feet floating back up behind her. If Rache's mercenaries were up there, Bonita couldn't see them.

Crushers, Bonita sent via her chip. *Ssh. I'm hoping they didn't—*

A black form stepped in front of the ladder well, not two feet away. Bonita couldn't keep from squawking in alarm.

Before she could swing her rifle out to shoot at the crusher, it grabbed her and yanked her away from the ladder. It hurled her with gut-wrenching force across the cargo hold.

She tumbled through the air, unable to halt herself in zero-g until she crashed against a wall. If she hadn't been in armor, the impact would have broken bones. As it was, the force battered her body and made her bite her tongue. The metallic taste of blood tainted her mouth.

Qin pushed out of the ladder well of her own accord and grappled with the crusher. She shoved it back, but it was as strong as she was, even with her genetic modifications and her armor enhancing her power. As they wrestled, the crusher's magnetized feet were knocked from the deck, and Qin soon grappled in the air with it.

Bonita brought her rifle to bear only to see that the barrel had been bent, either by the crusher when it had grabbed her or by her impact. She couldn't do anything unless pushing herself back over there to club it would help.

Another crusher broke away from the formation and strode toward her. Bonita cursed, looking for somewhere to run, but the doorway leading out of the cargo hold was on the far side of the ship from her. She was closer to the airlocks. From her spot, she couldn't tell which one led to empty space and which one to Rache's shuttle, but she would take either option over being mauled by a crusher.

As she was scooting down the wall, trying to stay in contact with it so she wouldn't float free and hang helplessly in the air, someone strode through the doorway, someone in purple combat armor with a matching cape. Two soldiers in more typical blue Kingdom armor flanked him, carrying luggage and crates of food.

The crusher either didn't notice the newcomers or didn't care. It kept coming toward Bonita.

Before it caught up with her, a warning shout came from the ladder well. Qin. She'd managed to kick the crusher she was battling away from her, but she gripped her shoulder, injured despite her armor.

The first of Rache's men pushed out of the ladder well, with several others right behind. They fired into the bay. One shot at the crusher advancing again on Qin, but most of them spotted the Kingdom men and shot at them. The man in purple had almost reached the ramp leading up to an open hatch, but he flinched as weapons fire bounced off the crushers and skipped off the deck all around him.

One of the soldiers released the luggage he was carrying and shouted, "Guard him!" as he pulled a rifle off his back.

All of the crushers, including the one that had been coming for Bonita, rushed back toward the ship. They arranged themselves around the ramp and the man in purple, his ridiculous cape floating around him even though his magnetic boots kept him on the deck.

Rache's men fanned out, facing the crushers and trading rifles for grenade launchers. Bonita waved for Qin to come join her. Nobody was paying attention to them now. It was their chance to escape to one of the airlock hatches.

But which one? Earlier, she would have chosen either, but if there was a chance the *Dragon* could get here in time, she didn't want to board the mercenary shuttle.

The combat paused, neither side firing for a strangely silent moment.

Rache faced the man in purple combat armor, who now stood at the base of the ramp up to the little shuttle, the hatch open behind him. He

HOME FRONT

could have fled into the interior, but he must have been confident that the crushers would keep him from being captured and that his armor would deflect a few shots.

It had to be Jorg. Bonita hadn't seen him in his armor before, but only some royal twit would wear purple armor.

Surprisingly, he carried a pertundo in his hand, with the more practical rifle slung across his back. He was probably correct that he was safe. Rache's men were equal in number to the crushers and Kingdom men, but the crushers seemed to be worth more than any one man, even a cybernetically enhanced mercenary.

"I knew it was you," Jorg said, and Bonita did indeed recognize the snotty voice. "Running up on us like a coward and firing from behind your camouflage. Like you've been doing for ten years. A guerrilla sniper assassinating good Kingdom men and then slinking away into hiding."

Thus far, Rache hadn't said anything. He stared at Jorg, his mask on behind his faceplate.

Bonita couldn't tell if he was debating if he could kill the prince, debating how to get rid of the crushers, or sending silent messages to his men elsewhere in the ship. How many troops had he brought over? She didn't care. She just wanted to get out of there.

Bjarke? she messaged. *We're in the cargo bay, but there's a showdown going on here. Which airlock are you coming to, and will you get here soon, by chance?*

We're almost there. We're navigating through a lot of debris. Rache destroyed Dubashi's ships before boarding that one, and we're not sure where the Fedallah *is, but it must be nearby. We have to use caution.*

"Have you ever fought a crusher, Rache?" Jorg asked.

"Yes," Rache spoke for the first time. "Several times. Explosions discombobulate them long enough to get past them or throw them out an airlock."

Jorg had shifted slightly, and Bonita could see his expression through his faceplate. A flash of uncertainty stole his haughtiness for the first time, but he replied as pompously as usual. "I hope you brought a *lot* of explosives. These guys are nearly indestructible."

"Will you hide behind them like the coward you accuse me of being?" Rache asked.

"A prince must have an army."

"You trained as a knight once." Rache pointed at the pertundo. "Do you remember how to use that thing, or is it merely decorative? The same way you are in your father's court?"

"What do *you* know about my father's court?"

"Do you not recognize my voice, Jorg? Has it truly been that long?"

Jorg stared at him, his lips parted. Rache's men exchanged quick glances with each other, though they remained focused on the crushers.

The crushers did not react to anything the men said.

"I don't care who you are," Jorg said. "You are a criminal. That's all that matters. And I am *not* decorative. I am my father's heir. One day, I will be king."

"Not if you don't get off this ship alive," Rache said, his tone turning to ice. "Even if you do, someone else will assassinate you. You accuse me of being a coward, but you are standing there behind the robots someone else made to protect the Kingdom. They weren't meant to protect a spoiled brat who had to cheat to pass the knight's exams. Did your father ever find out about that, Jorg?"

Bonita expected a righteous denial from Jorg, but the prince's face grew a few shades paler.

"Did Baron Farley ever find out?" Rache went on. "That you blackmailed one of the administrators for a copy of the math portion because you knew you wouldn't pass? And that the administrator, a former knight himself, took his life afterward, because he believed he'd broken the Code? Did anyone else ever find out what a bastard you are, Jorg?"

"None of that is true," Jorg finally managed to snarl after a long stunned silence. "You don't know what you're talking about. Whoever told you those things was trying to besmirch my honor. As if you would know anything about honor. You're a wart on the face of humanity."

"Then come out here and test yourself against me and show everyone your honor. Fight me one on one as a knight would. If you're not afraid."

What is he trying to do? Qin messaged to Bonita. *Why don't Rache's men just fight them all?*

Goad Jorg into attacking. Or challenging him to a duel. Hell if I know. Bonita shook her head. *His men probably don't know if they can win against that many crushers. Just hold still. They're not paying attention to us, and Bjarke should be here any minute.*

"I'd be foolish to fight you, coward," Jorg said. "You'll play some trick and run and hide."

HOME FRONT

"The only trick I ever played on you was to make you believe I was dead." Rache lifted his hand and beckoned to Jorg, inviting him to come fight. "I took my exams at the same time you did. And I was there when you blackmailed old Oskar."

Jorg shook his head. "Impossible. You are not…" He licked his lips and glanced at his men, the few humans in armor.

"I am." Rache beckoned again. "The ward your father had created to lead his armies because he knew he couldn't count on his own children to be smart enough or strong enough for the job."

Anger boiled in Jorg's eyes. "David Lichtenberg is dead! My father would have told me if he weren't. I don't know how you got this information but—"

"Your father wouldn't have told you anything. You're weak and not fit to rule after him. Not now. Maybe he sent you out here to prove yourself. Did it really have anything to do with proposing to a woman—a woman who rejected you and chose a lowly commoner—" Rache laughed shortly, "—or did he have this all planned and know you'd end up in charge? Tell me, Jorg. Did he say this was your chance to prove yourself? I know he's big into that."

"You don't know anything, you murdering asshole." Jorg hefted his pertundo and ran across the deck, almost sending himself floating off it because he ran too quickly for his magnetic soles to catch. "Get the mercenaries, crushers. But leave Rache to me. I *will* prove myself. I will kill you, and my father will know I'm his deserving heir."

Bonita looked at Qin. *I feel like we came in at Act Three.*

Yeah, I have no idea what's happening, Captain.

Metal rang out as Rache caught Jorg's pertundo with the shaft of his rifle. His mercenaries surged toward the crushers, who sprang to attack them. The Kingdom soldiers took cover behind the ship's ramp and fired. They might have ignored the prince's orders and fired at Rache, but Jorg was in their way. The two men grappled instead of trying to shoot each other, and soon, they tumbled away from the deck, wrestling in zero-g.

Bonita, Bjarke's words came across her contact. *We're coming into the airlock on the right.*

You better hurry. I think your prince is about to get his ass kicked.

Shit. Can you help him?

She barely kept herself from spitting a caustic response about how the asshole had imprisoned her and Qin and she was rooting for Rache. And only because she worried Bjarke would be in big trouble if Jorg died—all those Kingdom people would be.

I don't think so. My rifle was damaged. There are a bunch of crushers in here fighting Rache's men, and Jorg and Rache are in the middle of it. They wanted to duel with each other, and everyone seems content to let them.

Jorg wanted to duel with Rache? What is that fool thinking?

Bonita might have explained the goading, but a stray DEW-Tek bolt blasted into the wall inches from her helmet. She scooted toward the airlock. She and Qin could wait in the chamber behind the hatch for the *Dragon* to attach.

Is Jorg still alive? Bjarke added.

For the moment. He and Rache are grappling instead of blowing each other's brains out like normal, sane people. We're waiting for you at the airlock.

We're coming in with the crushers first. We have to rescue Jorg. Stand to the side until we pass.

When Bonita and Qin reached the airlock, Bonita grabbed a handhold to the side of the hatch. A porthole allowed her to see the *Dragon* outside, extending its airlock tube. For the first time since they'd been captured, her heart soared. Her ship was all right and she would be back on it soon.

"You bastard," came Jorg's voice, rough with pain, just audible over the weapons firing as Rache's men continued to battle the crushers. The two Kingdom men who'd accompanied their prince were now floating near the ceiling, neither moving. "Cheating again. You're *enhanced*."

"I don't need enhancements to kill you. Your knight's training was a joke. *Oku* could have beaten you in a fight." Rache's voice was ice cold and utterly calm.

"Fuck you," Jorg panted.

Rache gripped Jorg from behind, an arm around his neck, Jorg's back to Rache's chest. If they hadn't been armored, it would have been an easy position for Rache to break Jorg's neck. With his strength, maybe it still would be.

Qin lifted her rifle—she and Bonita were the only ones not engaged in battle, the only ones who might have done something. She aimed at Rache's helmet.

HOME FRONT

Bonita pressed Qin's arm down. "This isn't any of our business."

If she'd believed Jorg was a good man and that this was a true crime, Bonita might have felt differently, but he wasn't, and she didn't believe it was. Rache had set it up to be a fair fight, inasmuch as that was possible.

Qin must have felt conflicted, because she let Bonita derail her aim. A wrenching sound came from the pair as Rache twisted off Jorg's helmet. Then a ringing snap echoed through the hold.

As Rache released the now-limp Jorg and pushed him away, the airlock hatch beside Bonita flew open. Two armored knights—that had to be Bjarke and Asger—shoved themselves out into the cargo bay, arrowing straight toward Rache's men. A dozen crushers streamed out of the airlock after them.

Bonita was glad she wasn't expected to stay and fight because she had no idea how to tell the new crushers from the old unless they were standing right next to each other—Casmir's were a little larger. Would they all engage in battle against Rache's team? Or would the old crushers, with no leader to command them, default to defending the ship from all intruders?

"Captain Lopez." Tristan, protected only by a galaxy suit he'd scrounged and not armor, stood in the airlock chamber, a rifle in one hand as he waved for her to come with the other. "And Ms. Qin. It's time to go."

Bonita didn't have to be invited out of this hellhole twice. She pulled herself past him and into the airlock tube. Good riddance to the Kingdom and Rache.

"Jorg's crushers are fighting ours!" Bjarke yelled. "Tell Casmir to do something!"

Bonita paused, her hand on the hatch to her own airlock, her own ship. The alarm in Bjarke's voice made her pause. If she'd had a working rifle, she would have turned around to help him, but he was right. Casmir was the only one with a shot of turning the Kingdom crushers from foe to friend. If that was possible.

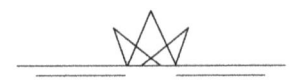

The sounds of weapons firing and explosives detonating boomed on the other ship, the din echoing down the airlock tube. Kim raised her rifle as someone rushed through it toward the *Dragon*'s cargo hold, but it was Bonita. She spotted Kim right away.

"Tell Casmir—"

"He knows." Kim nodded toward the battle, toward the old crushers fighting the new crushers. "He thought that would be a problem, and he's working on it."

She'd left Casmir in navigation to work on it remotely—and safely—via his chip, but he came out of the ladder well and pushed off across the hold toward them.

Kim held up a hand to stop him, assuming he didn't intend to pass into the airlock and had miscalculated his trajectory.

But he shook his head. "I have to go over there and talk to them."

"*Talk* to them?" Kim shifted to block him. Like her, he wore only a galaxy suit. It would be madness to run into a battle zone full of crushers and armored men. "Talk to who?"

"The crushers. And Rache and his men. And Jorg and his men. We shouldn't be fighting each other. Dubashi's attackers were the only real enemy here, and they're dead."

Kim thought Bjarke and Asger would object to Rache being classified as anything other than a *real enemy*, but that wasn't what Bonita objected to when she lifted her hand. "Jorg is dead."

Casmir's shoulders slumped. "We were too late?"

Kim digested the news without emotion. She knew Casmir never wanted anyone to be killed, but she couldn't stir up any remorse for the man who'd ordered her to build him a horrific bioweapon.

"Only by seconds," Bonita said. "Though Rache may have been, uh, not playing with him exactly, since there was a small war going on all around them during their fight, but he turned it into some wrestling match instead of just blowing up Jorg's shuttle—or *Jorg*."

"Was just blowing him up an option?" Kim asked.

HOME FRONT

"I don't know. Maybe not with all the crushers guarding him. Rache goaded him into running out and making it a one-on-one battle."

Casmir recovered, shook his head, and moved Kim's hand out of the way. "If Jorg is dead, then there's *really* no reason for the remaining people and crushers to be fighting. I'm going to try to get them to surrender, or at least cease hostilities."

"Can't you talk to the crushers over the network?" Kim's fingers twitched—she wanted to stop him from going over there and getting himself caught in the crossfire.

"Not the original ones. I intentionally set them up so people couldn't hack into them easily and change their orders."

"Even *you*?"

"It was what the military wanted." Casmir shot past her and into the tube. He didn't even have a weapon.

Bonita headed in the other direction. "I'm going to get the *Dragon* ready to fly in case we have to leave in a hurry."

"I am already prepared," Viggo announced, "but I welcome your return to navigation, Bonita. Two Kingdom warships approach. The *Osprey*'s weapons appear to be working again."

Kim pulled herself after Casmir, more worried about him than the warships, though when the *Osprey* arrived, they would have another problem. Ishii might try to recapture the *Dragon,* especially after he learned Jorg was dead. Would Rache's *Fedallah* fire on the Kingdom ships? Kim and the others hadn't seen Rache's warship on their way in, but it had to be nearby, waiting for the return of its combat team.

A sick feeling wrenched her stomach. What if Rache ordered his people to destroy the *Osprey*? She wouldn't mourn Jorg's loss, but Dr. Sikou and Captain Ishii were another matter. Ishii had only ever been trying to obey his orders and do the right thing. He'd looked the other way when Kim had fled to avoid the bioweapon duty.

Rache, she sent another message to his chip, though he hadn't responded to the last one. *The* Osprey *and another ship are coming.*

This time, his response was prompt. *I know.*

Maybe he'd been engaged in his battle with Jorg before, and that was why he'd ignored her.

Please don't have your ship attack them. Bonita and Qin—Kim saw Qin up ahead in the airlock chamber with Tristan, both trying to keep

Casmir from going out into danger—*are safe. Just get out of here, please. The* Osprey *is*... Kim groped for an argument that would sway Rache. He wouldn't care that Captain Ishii was a decent man. He wouldn't care that every ship the Kingdom lost would make it that much harder for them to stop the war. He wouldn't care that Ambassador Romano, who would probably be in charge of gathering troops now, was on there. *I left my espresso machine in sickbay.*

It was a stupid thing to say, but maybe it would convey that the ship meant something to her in a way that long detailed explanations wouldn't. If he was in the middle of battle, he wouldn't have time to read those anyway.

The one I gave you?

Yes.

Really, Kim.

That was all he said. Did that mean he agreed not to attack the ship? Or was disappointed in her?

There's also all the work I've put into studying Dubashi's virus. Almost everything is on the sickbay lab computers. We had to leave in a hurry, and I didn't get to copy everything.

You were in danger?

Of being injected by eslevoamytal and blabbing everything I know about you.

He didn't respond. Maybe it was self-serving to imply that she'd fled out of a desire to keep his secrets for him. She'd been as worried for herself back in sickbay.

A thunderous boom came from the *Chivalrous*. If it hadn't been completely out of commission when the battle had started, it had to be by now.

"Crusher friends," Casmir called out into the melee.

Kim would have dropped her face into her hand if she hadn't had her helmet up. Instead, she scooted up and tried to see past Qin and Tristan—they'd taken positions in front of the tube, firing from the cover of the airlock chamber, but they had let Casmir squirm out.

"The mercenaries have fled," Casmir called, though the bangs and thumps emanating from the cargo hold didn't suggest the melee had ended. "These knights are from the Kingdom. You should have been programmed to recognize their armor. And these other crushers are also from the Kingdom. They were made to serve the prince and the king."

HOME FRONT

"The prince is dead," someone—a crusher?—said in a flat monotone.

"But the war at home continues. Our people need us—*all* of us. It is our duty to protect the Kingdom and all the humans and robots that live there."

"Robots?" Tristan whispered. "Is protecting robots in the original programming?"

"I wouldn't be surprised," Kim said.

He hadn't noticed her behind him and now shifted to the side so she could see. Smoke clouded the air, but DEW-Tek bolts were no longer ricocheting off walls. Half of the crushers were on the deck, locked in grappling matches, with their soles magnetized and keeping them near a small shuttle. The other half were tangled up and floating in the air—there were armored bodies floating up there too. But Casmir was right—she didn't see any of Rache's men. Had they thrown the grenade and taken the opportunity to get out of there?

A purple armored figure with an equally purple cape dangled above the ramp of the shuttle. Kim stared, knowing that had to be Jorg, even though she'd never seen him in his armor and couldn't see his face. His helmet was missing, and from across the hold, she could tell his neck was broken.

"Listen to Casmir Dabrowski," one of the crushers called out. They all had identical voices to Kim's ear, and she didn't realize that was Zee until he spoke further. "He is our creator. You must have his face in your databanks. He made you, as he made us. He programmed us to protect Kingdom subjects and to obey orders, and he also battles to protect the interests of crushers and lesser robots."

The fighting stopped, and as one, the crushers—all of them—rotated toward Casmir. He was standing in front of Tristan and Qin, his hands spread, an unarmored man without a weapon. Kim wanted to grab him by the scruff of the neck and yank him back to safety.

"We do recognize Professor Casmir Dabrowski," another crusher said. "He is not an enemy."

If only Jager and the rest of the Kingdom believed that.

"Who is your commander now that Prince Jorg is dead?" Casmir asked.

"Captain Nieman commanded the *Chivalrous* and was second-in-command of our forces, but he is also dead."

Another crusher chimed in: "Some of us wished to defend him and remain on the bridge to protect key personnel, but Prince Jorg ordered us all to accompany him during his retreat."

"I'll bet," Tristan muttered.

Even though it chilled Kim that Rache had killed Jorg—ripped off his helmet and broken his neck—she felt more relief than sorrow in knowing the man could never end up ruling the Kingdom.

"In that case," Casmir said, "you should report to Captain Ishii on the *Osprey*. His ship should be here, uh, any second now probably. He's the senior-ranking Kingdom officer in the area."

Kim noticed he didn't mention Ambassador Romano.

"Who commands these crushers?" One of them pointed to Zee.

Zee lifted his chin. "We are programmed to protect Kim Sato and Casmir Dabrowski. We obey Casmir Dabrowski. Only he cares about the fate of crushers."

Kim had no idea if Casmir had programmed that notion into the crushers or if that was an indication of the opinions that Zee was forming as he developed. Quite possibly the latter. Kim couldn't imagine Casmir inputting commands to flatter people, even him.

The crushers looked at each other. Were they communicating over a network?

We are leaving, a message came in over Kim's chip. Rache. *Unless you need us to stay and protect you from the warships.*

Did she? How would Ishii react when he learned Jorg was dead? No, how would *Ambassador Romano* react?

But she couldn't ask Rache to open fire on the warships on her behalf. That would only further cement Kim and her friends as enemies in the Kingdom's eyes. Especially after Rache had just killed Jorg. What if there was video footage of everything that had happened out here? Queasiness twisted her stomach as she realized there almost had to be. Unless power failures had knocked out the ship's security, all the key public areas would be monitored.

We'll handle it one way or another, Kim replied, hoping she was right and that they could. Romano had to realize he needed Casmir to convince the rest of the crushers to work for him and he needed Kim to work on an antiviral. He *had* to grasp that.

I hope you're able to recover your espresso maker.

So do I.

Kim wanted to say something more meaningful in parting, but what? Rache had killed the heir to the throne and his next target, as soon as he could get out of this system, would be the king himself. It was ludicrous that she kept having conversations with him. But...

HOME FRONT

Thank you for rescuing Bonita and Qin. She couldn't ignore that he'd done that.

He had risked himself to go over there in person. He could have joined Dubashi's ships in firing from space and just as certainly killed Jorg that way. It might not have been as satisfying as breaking his neck—she didn't want to contemplate if he'd found that satisfying—but it would have been less risk for his men.

You are welcome. But I must admit they were already out of their cell when we arrived and in the process of rescuing themselves.

They are capable women.

Indeed.

That was the last thing Rache sent, which was good because she found an army of crushers heading toward the airlock tube. She had to scoot back, as did Tristan and Qin. Casmir, like the Pied Piper of Old Earth lore, was leading the crushers in a queue behind him.

Kim backed all the way to the *Dragon's* cargo hold and, as she watched the two sets of crushers enter, hoped the new ones wouldn't be trouble. She trusted the ones Casmir had made personally starting with Zee. As far as she knew, he'd only overseen the creation of the others, and they'd been off murdering people on Jager's behalf since then.

What would Romano say when he found out Casmir had taken all the crushers aboard the ship they'd only an hour before stolen from the *Osprey*?

"I hope this doesn't backfire," Kim muttered.

CHAPTER 10

OKU WOKE TO A KNOCK BEFORE DAWN, AND Chasca, who had been sleeping on the end of the bed, woofed a protest at the noise. The sound of soft voices came through the door. Oku shuffled out of her bed to open it.

Back in the castle, she'd had a suite of rooms, but like almost everyone else, she had only one small bedroom and attached bathroom here in the Citadel. A bodyguard was usually stationed in the hall outside, someone who would have objected to an unauthorized person visiting her. Because of that, she wasn't surprised to open the door and find her mother outside, already dressed for the day.

"May I come in for a moment?"

"Yes." Oku sat on the edge of the bed.

Chasca thwapped her tail against the comforter, and Mother patted her on the head.

"I see your second bodyguard is always on duty," she said.

"On duty from under the covers usually. What's up? I assume you didn't come to invite me to brunch at Sigler's."

"I'm afraid not." Mother folded her hands in her lap. "I came to let you know that Senator Boehm passed away in his sleep last night."

An anchor of icy steel sank into Oku's stomach.

"I know you've been spending time with him since we've all been stuck in the Citadel and thought you would want to know."

"Yes." Oku's mouth had gone dry. "Thank you. He died of, uhm, natural causes?" *Were* there natural causes anymore in this medically advanced age? Even when someone died in their sleep, the reason could be determined, but maybe a doctor hadn't examined the body yet.

Oku shook her head slowly. Boehm had been the one man to object to her father's plans at that meeting. And now he was dead.

"We believe so. This is the most secure installation on the planet right now, and everybody who's here has had a background check. Even your collection of commoners from the city." Her perfectly shaped eyebrows rose.

"They were all collected from one building." Oku frowned. She didn't want to be distracted. She searched her mother's eyes, wondering how much she and her father actually shared. Her mother had always seemed amiable but not adoring with him, but it was hard to know how she truly felt. She didn't speak negatively about any of her family. Or anyone at all, for the most part. A gossip, she was not. That little dig about commoners was as snarky as she got. "Does Father know?"

"Yes. He said he'll make funeral arrangements as soon as it's feasible and that the meeting of the Senate will go on today."

Of course. His obstacle was gone. Why wouldn't he want it to go on?

Mother patted her leg and rose. "I'll see you at breakfast."

"Thank you."

As soon as she was gone, Oku got dressed. Chasca hopped out of bed and picked up one of Oku's shoes and plunked it down in front of the door.

"Yes, I know." Oku took the dog out, found that the morning fog outside the protective dome of the Citadel hid evidence of the sunrise, and debated if she should do anything. And if so, what?

On the way back in, she took a circuitous route and walked toward her father's office.

Before she reached it, someone else entered the hall from the other end. Senator Andrin. He lifted a hand in greeting to Oku, then stepped into her father's office without knocking. The door closed firmly behind him.

It was early for a meeting. Oku stopped at the door and pointed for Chasca to sit, so her claws couldn't be overheard clacking on the old flagstone floor. Oku could hear the murmur of voices inside the office, but she couldn't make out distinct words.

Aside from Chasca, the hallway was empty. Oku bit her lip, then leaned her ear against the door. If Casmir were here, she was certain he would have suggested a more sophisticated way of eavesdropping. In the castle, where all the royal suites and offices had been retrofitted with modern technology, this wouldn't work, but Andrin and her father were standing close enough to the door that she could hear them.

"…could have gotten what you wanted without this?" Andrin was asking.

"Do not question me," her father said.

"I wouldn't dare to now."

"Just make sure to argue my side to anyone who objects. It's what you wanted as much as what I wanted. You were the one to argue for the crusher program."

"This will be *your* legacy. History won't remember me."

"Unless you make yourself significant. Stand at my side, and you won't be forgotten."

The words grew softer and impossible to make out. They must have moved away from the door. Oku beckoned Chasca to follow and hurried off, not wanting to be caught. Besides, she had to think about this. Did the conversation suggest what she already suspected? That Senator Boehm had been killed because he'd been an open dissenter? Or because his vote might have kept her father's request for King's Authority—essentially the right to act as an unquestioned dictator—from passing? What would her father do once he *had* that? Pursue the war and expansion he'd longed for? Something else?

No matter what he planned, was it her place to step in and try to do something? What could she even do? Warn her academic friends in the other governments around the systems? Right now, she dared not even send a message to Casmir.

Oku wished she could. She would have valued his opinion. She felt so alone here in the Citadel, even with hundreds of other people staying in the secure facility.

Maybe if she could make sure Royal Intelligence didn't have a way to download data from her chip, she would be freer to act and speak with others.

"What do you think, Chasca?" she murmured. "Should I take a trip?"

Chasca wagged her tail in approval.

Asger returned to the *Stellar Dragon,* his armor dented and his ears still ringing from the grenades that Rache's men had detonated in the other ship's cargo hold. He'd fired at Rache as the mercenary had been leading his troops back to his ship, and he'd contemplated going after him, but to what end? Jorg's dead body had been floating in the air for all to see, and Asger couldn't manage any rage or indignation. The prince's death had seemed inevitable ever since they'd learned that Dubashi's ships were after him.

He was glad his father had been too busy battling a crusher to see Rache leaving. *He*, Asger was certain, would have felt differently and might have gotten himself killed trying to chase Rache back onto his own ship.

"Is everybody aboard?" came Bonita's voice over a speaker. "The *Osprey* is about to be breathing down Viggo's neck, and I want to get us out of here."

Qin shut the airlock hatches and retracted the tube. "We're ready, Captain."

"It's only a matter of time before Ishii or Romano comms." Asger's father grimaced and headed up to navigation.

Asger stood near a wall, staying out of the way of what seemed like an army of crushers—there were more than twenty now. He had no desire to speak with Ishii or Romano. Let his father handle that.

After the *Dragon* pulled away from the *Chivalrous*, Qin leaned back, her helmet thunking against the hatch.

"Are you all right?" Asger shifted over to stand next to her.

She removed her helmet, her dark hair damp with sweat, her pointed ears peeking through it. He had the urge to stroke the side of her head but felt self-conscious with so many witnesses in the cargo hold. Even if most of them were crushers and not paying attention to him. They had formed a circle around Casmir, who was chatting amiably about their mission and their goals, as if the menacing crushers didn't faze him at all. Asger supposed they didn't. He'd made them, after all.

"I'm okay," Qin said. "That was a weird experience."

"Being captured or seeing crushers fighting crushers?"

"Watching Jorg with Rache."

Kim and Tristan were nearby—they didn't seem to want to get close to Casmir's legions—and Kim looked over at the comment.

"What happened?" she asked.

"I'm not sure," Qin said. "He was basically making sure Jorg knew who he was. I'd always assumed he was from the Kingdom, since he has that accent, but his true identity has always been part of the mystery of his persona, so it was strange that he was openly talking about it in front of us and all his men—unless they've always known."

Kim shook her head. "They know—knew—very little about him. Not many of them have seen him without his mask."

"Have you?" Qin asked.

Kim hesitated and glanced at Asger. "Casmir and I have, yes. He showed Casmir the day they met."

"Why?" Qin asked.

"Hm. Whatever he revealed in that cargo bay, I guess it wasn't everything."

Qin looked at Asger, but he could only shake his head. He didn't know who Rache had been before he'd become Rache, and he didn't care.

"The *Osprey* is attaching to the *Chivalrous*," Bonita said over the comm. "I hope none of you left anything condemning over there."

Asger shook his head. His time on board had been brief, ineffective, and too late to matter. He was surprised Bonita hadn't said the *Osprey* was comming them and demanding they surrender the freighter and wait to be boarded.

"He's always been secretive about his identity though," Kim went on, studying the deck, not reacting to Bonita's comment. "It sounds out-of-character for him to have blurted out clues in front of everyone."

"Maybe it was important to him that Jorg know who was killing him before he did it," Qin said.

Kim flinched at the word *kill*. But all she said was, "Maybe he doesn't care anymore because…"

"Because he's been hired to kill Jager?" Asger guessed. "And he thinks that once that's done—Kim, I know you don't think he's your enemy, but we can't let him kill our king—it won't matter because nobody will be left who cares about hunting him down? That's not true, you know. Every soldier and every knight out there loathes him with good reason."

"I know. Maybe he doesn't care anymore," Kim repeated, her expression grim, "because he doesn't expect to survive that mission."

Asger *hoped* he didn't. If the *Osprey* let the *Dragon* get away, if they could make it to Stardust Palace, and if Casmir could get that slydar detector, maybe they could find a way home in time to keep the *Fedallah* from getting anywhere near Odin or the king. And what was Rache without his ship full of mercenaries? Just one lone assassin. Imperial security had been dealing with would-be assassins their whole careers.

"Why would he take the mission if he doesn't think he can make it out alive?" Qin asked.

Kim spread her arms. "It's the one mission he's always wanted. Nothing else seems to matter to him."

"Why does he hate Jager so much?" Qin was much more curious about all this than Asger.

All he could feel was bitter hatred for the criminal.

"It's a long story," Kim said. "And his to tell."

William, Asger's father messaged him. *You better come up here for this. And get Dabrowski.*

I take it the Osprey *has commed us?*

Correct.

"Casmir." Asger patted Qin on the shoulder and headed to the knot of crushers. "It's time for you to have a chat with someone who isn't likely to worship you."

"That's most people from what I've experienced." The crushers parted to allow him out of the circle.

"Is that why you prefer to spend time with robots?"

"Well, I don't know if *prefer* is the correct term, but they are logical and nonjudgmental. And rarely shove you in a locker."

"Be glad if that's all Ishii does to you the next time he sees you in person."

Casmir smiled sadly. "I will."

CHAPTER 11

CASMIR SHIFTED FROM FOOT TO FOOT BEHIND BONITA'S pod in navigation. The *Dragon* was accelerating toward Stardust Palace Station, so they had a semblance of gravity again.

It had been almost a half hour since the *Osprey* had commed, a communications officer putting them on hold, pending the outcome of "an investigation," as she'd called it. The *Osprey* was still attached to the *Chivalrous,* boarding parties probably collecting the bodies of the deceased Kingdom men—and all the video footage the ship's security system had collected. Surprising to all of them, the ship hadn't fired or done anything when the *Dragon* departed.

Judging by the way Bonita kept checking the scanners and nibbling on her fingernails, she didn't trust that they would continue to do nothing.

Asger stood behind Bjarke, who sat in the co-pilot's pod, not nibbling anything but staring at the forward display while wearing a pensive expression. Had they done the right thing? He seemed to wear that question on his face. But they had retrieved Qin and Bonita, and it wasn't as if they'd made matters worse. Unfortunately, they hadn't made anything better, either, not for Jorg and not for the Kingdom.

Casmir hoped he and Kim wouldn't somehow be blamed for Jorg's death because Intelligence now believed they had a relationship with Rache. If that happened, Casmir didn't know what he would do. He already doubted he could go home again. The thought of leaving Odin forever saddened him, especially if he couldn't see his family and friends again. Could he smuggle his parents off-world? Would they even leave? They had such long-standing ties to the community. He hoped he hadn't put that in danger. He hoped he hadn't put *them* in danger.

Kim came up to navigation, joining him in the back of the small space, and he thought about asking her opinion on relocation. Before he could, the hold-screen dissolved, and Ishii's face came into view.

Judging by the dim background and furnishings behind him, he was in his quarters, not on the bridge or in a briefing room. Casmir didn't know what to think of that, but he was relieved Romano wasn't there. He could have been standing out of view of the screen, but Casmir doubted Ishii would invite the man to his quarters for a drink.

"Dabrowski, this is for you."

Casmir, not trusting his tongue, only nodded in acknowledgment. The fact that Ishii hadn't opened by snapping some sarcastic comment at him attested to how tired he was. And probably how worried and distraught he was.

"After that fiasco in sickbay, Ambassador Romano wants you hunted down and shot. Sato too. Chasing you down isn't our priority, so I don't have to decide if I agree with him or not, but I suggest you take advantage of our distraction to do something useful for the Kingdom. Maybe it'll matter when we catch up to you and it's time to determine your fate."

"You still want me to go to Stardust Palace?" Casmir guessed.

"Assuming Captain Lopez will cooperate, yes. Get the rest of the crushers. Get the slydar detector. Have the Asgers help."

"Are we... still authorized to offer Sultan Shayban what he paid for it?" Casmir asked.

Bjarke frowned at him.

Casmir spread his hand. What? It remained an act of theft if they didn't.

"*You're* not authorized for anything. Sir Bjarke..." Ishii rubbed his forehead with the heel of his palm. "I don't know. Prince Jorg was the one who had access to the king's coffers. The warships have already been out here longer than planned, and without access to the systems-wide banking database, we can't withdraw or even prove that we have funds to pay for things. We're barely finding ways to get supplies for our ships. Just try to smooth-talk him into giving it to you. It's what you do, Dabrowski."

People had developed some odd notions about what his secret powers were. Smooth-talking *robots* was what he did.

"I'll see what I can do," Casmir said.

"Good. Keep him from doing anything too stupid, Bjarke."

Bjarke frowned. "I'll try."

Why did he sound so skeptical that such would be possible?

"Ambassador Romano and I will be spearheading the collection of troops and ships in the system, taking up where Jorg left off," Ishii continued. "Captain Timmons of the *Raptor* is the senior-ranking Kingdom Fleet officer in the system, but he's working on the gate. I've got Romano with me, so we're the new flagship for the Fleet apparently. We're going to do our best to put together an impressive number of ships to take home in one swoop."

Casmir almost mentioned all the mercenaries that had been stuck in the system and that it would be easier to hire them than form new alliances, but if Ishii didn't have money for supplies, he didn't have money for mercenaries.

"Which brings me to my next question." Ishii had been focused on Bjarke instead of Casmir, but his gaze shifted, and his eyes closed to slits. "Do you know anything about the gate and why it's inoperable?"

"Er."

"You're a horrible liar."

"All I said was er."

"That was enough."

Casmir pushed his bangs out of his eyes—he needed a haircut. Maybe Zee would do it.

"Speak," Ishii added.

"I know the astroshamans were responsible for taking it down. I don't know how they're doing it or how long it will last. Or even where they are." Casmir didn't point out that Moonrazor had done it at his request.

"Do you have a contact for any of them? We need it fixed."

"Might I point out that as long as the gate is closed, Odin is safe from Dubashi and his bioweapon?"

"But we can't get back home to help with the blockade. You saw the news showing Odin being bombed, I'm sure. Zamek City included. That's your home. You must care."

"Of course I care. My parents and all my friends back home are there. I'm just pointing out that it would behoove us to find and capture Dubashi and destroy his virus-laden rockets before opening the gate."

"If you have a plan for doing that, I'm listening."

Casmir kept himself from saying *er* again. Barely. "If we can borrow Shayban's slydar detector…"

Ishii nodded. "That's why we want it. Dubashi and Rache. The sooner we can get it, the sooner we can hunt them down."

Casmir doubted the slydar detector would be such a simple fix. It probably helped with detection close up but didn't make it possible to spot a ship on the other side of a star system. But if Dubashi was near the gate, waiting to get out, then it might be possible to use it to find him. And wouldn't Rache soon be in the same spot if he meant to go after the king?

"I'll do my best," Casmir said.

"Don't forget to chat up the astroshamans too. Whoever you have to schmooze so we can go home." Ishii closed his eyes. "And so news can get home. King Jager needs to be told… what he needs to be told."

After Ishii cut the comm, Casmir leaned forward and gripped the back of Bonita's pod for support.

"That comm wasn't as bad as I feared it would be," Bjarke said.

He only felt that way because Ishii hadn't singled him out as someone Romano wanted shot.

"I suppose it would have been worse and more demanding if Romano had been with him." Bjarke looked at Bonita. "Do you mind taking us to the palace?"

"It's not like I can leave this system," Bonita said, not with rousing enthusiasm.

"At least you're back on your own ship."

"There is that. On my own ship with twenty hulking crushers."

"At least crushers," Viggo spoke up, "do not slam the lavatory stall doors."

"I hope our knights are past that now too." Bonita shot Bjarke a warning look.

Bjarke looked over his pod at Asger.

"We're fine," Asger said.

Kim touched Casmir's shoulder. "Are you all right? You're not going to have another seizure, are you?"

"I hope not." Casmir made himself straighten and blink away what had probably been a glassy-eyed stare at the deck. "I just feel daunted and… responsible."

"For what? Jorg's death?"

Casmir didn't have words for all the regrets he had and all the failures he'd inadvertently instigated, so he only shook his head. "Let's hope Sultan Shayban is a reasonable—no, *generous*—man and isn't disappointed that I can't drop Dubashi in his lap, as I was supposed to do in exchange for all the materials for building those crushers."

"Ah." A troubled furrow creased Kim's brow. "I'd forgotten about that."

"I haven't." To ask for more favors when he hadn't even fulfilled his part of the bargain...

Casmir shook his head and went to find a place to lie down. He still had a headache from his *last* seizure.

Numerous mercenaries came to sickbay after the battle on the Kingdom yacht, and Yas called in the ship's single nurse and also a recruit with a steady hand to help. The men's armor had protected them from energy weapons and bruises, but many had broken bones and other internal injuries. The crushers had thrown them around so hard that even the insulation of their equipment hadn't been enough to cushion them. Yas had heard variations of the same story from several of the men.

He was almost surprised when Rache walked in, his helmet off but his mask on, as usual. Since he had numerous enhancements to speed his healing, he usually bypassed sickbay and suffered in silence in his quarters until his body mended itself.

Rache nodded to the men as he passed. "Report, Doctor? Are Chaplain and Drang doing all right?"

Those two had been carried into sickbay unconscious.

"They both have skull fractures and swelling in their brains. Chaplain also looks like someone drove a jackhammer through his ribs and into his liver."

"Crushers hit hard. They'll make it?"

"They should, but they'll be out of commission for a while."

Rache nodded. "Until that gate is open, we don't have anywhere to go."

His voice sounded determined rather than accepting, and Yas wondered if he had some plan to figure out how to open the gate.

"I am contemplating searching for Kyla Moonrazor," Rache added in a quiet tone. "I've heard she's in this system. There aren't many people Dabrowski could have contacted with the power to wave a hand and render an advanced piece of ancient technology inoperable."

"We could just wait. If he was responsible for the gate, well, he's going to want to go home eventually."

"As soon as the Kingdom has the ships it needs to stop its war. But it would be easier for me if we could get through now, while there's a blockade and all of the Kingdom is distracted."

"Do you still have… that mission in System Lion?" Yas stepped into his small private office in sickbay, and Rache followed him to collect his report. "Won't Dubashi find out you blew up his ships? Those *were* his ships that were attacking the Kingdom yacht, right?"

"They belonged to people working for him, yes. It depends if they got a report out before they were destroyed." Rache sounded indifferent to the notion. Maybe he didn't believe Dubashi would care, as long as Jorg was dead. That was hard to believe.

"I heard the Kingdom warships were swooping in as we left the scene. Are you sure… Is Jorg truly dead?"

If he'd been left near death or even dead with the possibility of resuscitation, it was possible the Kingdom men had found him and brought him back on board.

"He's dead," Rache said with certainty.

"Did you do it?"

"Yes."

"A DEW-Tek bolt to the back? Or face?"

"I broke his neck." Rache said it simply, stating a fact, and without remorse. "He attacked me first. I did goad him into it, but that was out of a notion that some people would find it less inappropriate if it were a fair fight. He was willing to be goaded. He called me a wart on the face of humanity and slavered and foamed at the mouth when I brought up his delinquent past."

"*Some* people?" Yas tapped his tablet to send a report on the men's status to Rache's chip. "Like Kim?"

"Kim and perhaps my doctor." The mask hid any facial expression Rache might have shared, but Yas imagined an eyebrow raising. "I also went to the brig to collect her friends, Lopez and Qin, when we were there. I intended to rescue them, but they mostly rescued themselves."

HOME FRONT

"Frustrating when you try to rescue someone who doesn't need rescuing."

"Yes. Do you think Kim will kiss me if I subtly let her know that my distraction was integral to their escape?"

The question almost made Yas drop his tablet. Maybe it had been better when Rache had ignored him most of the time and never shared anything personal.

"Maybe if you don't mention the slavering and foaming and neck-breaking of her monarch's firstborn."

"Hm." Rache, having received his report, wandered off.

Sometimes, Yas wondered what went on in that man's mind. Other times, he didn't want to know.

CHAPTER 12

Q IN RAN ON THE TREADMILL IN THE LOUNGE, needing the exercise after so many days cooped up in that cell, and needing something for her body to do while her mind raced. She kept thinking about the strange showdown between Rache and Jorg and what the ramifications might mean for her friends. The Kingdom wasn't her world, and had nothing to do with her, but she'd come to care for Casmir and Kim and—of course—Asger. Would they ever be able to return home after failing to save their king's son?

Was there something Qin could do to help them? Or would Bonita, once they dropped everyone off at the station, head for the wormhole gate, eager to put as much distance between the *Dragon* and the Kingdom war as possible? The idea of leaving them to their own fate when she might be able to help bothered her.

And then there was Qin Liangyu Seven—Mouser—asking for help. Qin hadn't mentioned that to the others yet, but she would say something to Bonita when there was a quiet moment. Maybe she would have some ideas. Earlier, Bonita had been chatting in navigation with Bjarke—if trading sarcastic comments about which of them had the shiniest, lushest gray hair counted as chatting—and Qin hadn't wanted to disturb her.

The door opened, and the warm, familiar scents of her friends preceded their entrance. Casmir and Asger.

Asger pointed at Qin and thumped Casmir on the chest. "One of the treadmills is taken. We'll have to arm wrestle for the other one."

"Let's save my joints some pain and just say you won," Casmir said. "Unless you want to let one of the crushers stand in for me."

"I do not. I'm still sore from the one I arm wrestled with earlier." Asger rotated his shoulder gingerly. "Couldn't you have convinced them they were on our side *before* it hurled me against a wall?"

"Sorry."

"Qin?" Bonita's voice came over the speaker, a strange note to it. "Are you still up?"

"I'm exercising in the lounge."

"Did you know the Druckers are in this system?"

"I heard that two of their warships are here, yes."

"And did you hear that they're coming this way?" Bonita asked.

"The last I heard, they were at the gate, waiting to leave." Concern spilled into Qin, and she slowed down the treadmill. Could this have something to do with Mouser's message? "By *coming this way*, do you mean flying in this general direction or… chasing us?"

Viggo was the one to answer. "They could be heading to Stardust Palace, but they are following our route directly. They're about to fly through the wreckage of Dubashi's ships."

"Is the *Osprey* still there?" Casmir asked.

"They left the area towing the *Chivalrous*," Viggo said.

Qin turned off the treadmill and dropped her chin to her chest. Was it possible the Druckers had decided to come find her, after all? Maybe they figured as long as they were stuck in the system, why not collect their wayward slave?

"They're not going to get you, Qin." Asger came over and put an arm around her shoulders.

"There's no way," Casmir added. "We have twenty-*five* crushers now. And some knights who aren't bad fighters either."

"Thank you so much for your high accolades," Asger said.

"You're welcome."

"Thank you. Both of you." Qin leaned into Asger, appreciating his support, and that he no longer shied away from her after they touched. If life weren't so crazy, maybe they could have gone on a date and shared another kiss. But it didn't seem that the universe wanted her life to be simple. "There's something more you should know. Bonita, too."

"We're listening," Bonita said.

Qin hadn't planned to tell Bonita about the message over the comm system with the whole ship listening, but she supposed everyone on board was a friend, so it didn't matter.

HOME FRONT

She pulled up Mouser's message and read it aloud. At the end, she added, "I'm worried someone intercepted it and maybe that's why they're coming for me. Which could also mean Mouser is being punished right now."

"It's a shame we can't free your sisters," Asger said.

"Are we sure we can't?" Casmir asked.

"Have you seen how large those pirate warships are?" Asger asked dryly. "And how many weapons and crew are aboard?"

"No. I don't spend a lot of time studying pirates. They're too biological."

"That's the least of their flaws," Qin murmured.

"Maybe your father could come down and give us a slide presentation on them," Casmir said.

Asger grunted. "I'm sure he could. But you've got another mission, Casmir. And we've been assigned to help you with it."

"Hm." Casmir walked to the comm panel and tapped it. "Bonita and Bjarke, would you mind coming to the lounge for a confab? And Kim, if you're awake, and Tristan too. Oh, and all crushers who would like to confab are welcome. And intelligent ship's computers."

"Why don't you invite his vacuums too?" Asger muttered.

"Should I?"

Bonita cleared her throat. "The ship-wide comm is for the captain to make announcements to everyone, not for the passengers to use."

"Is it?" Casmir asked. "Huh."

"You're not even supposed to be able to do that from down there."

"Sorry." Casmir ambled to the table and sat down.

"What are you thinking?" Asger asked him suspiciously.

"Just that we should do some brainstorming. Maybe there's some way to accomplish our mission and help Qin's sisters. They should be free, if that's what they wish. And if a person asks for your help, you should give it."

"You can't help everyone, Casmir," Asger said. "The Kingdom has to be our priority, saving Odin and our families—*your* family. That must be what you want more than anything, to make sure they're safe. After the war is over and our people aren't at risk any longer, we can come back and get them. I'd be willing to help." Asger nodded to Qin.

Casmir gazed at the deck as Bonita, Bjarke, and Kim filed in, trailed by a few of the crushers.

"Ensuring my family and friends back home are safe *is* what I want, yes," Casmir said. "But as my father is fond of saying, the way to get what you want in life is to help others get what they want."

Qin didn't want her friends to land themselves in trouble by taking on the Druckers, but she couldn't help but get her hopes up. Even though the *Dragon* wouldn't be able to get close enough to one of the Drucker warships to send over a boarding party, she imagined Casmir's crushers—*all* of them—storming the corridors and throwing pirates around left and right.

"Qin," Bonita said, "you know I want to help you—and I guess the dozen mirror-yous out there—but going up against the Druckers last time didn't go well for us. And the only one we were trying to fool was some tattooed knight in disguise."

"A superior opponent, surely," Bjarke said.

"We don't have the resources to take on the Druckers, even if only two of their warships are in the system. I don't care how many crushers El Mago here has. We wouldn't be able to get close enough to send them over. It's not like they can turn themselves into an attack ship and take out the warships' weapons."

"I have turned myself into a couch," one said—that had to be Zee.

"Gee, that's almost the same thing," Bonita said.

Zee turned to Casmir. "I have observed that many of your human colleagues employ sarcasm when they are daunted or uncomfortable with the situation."

"Yes." Casmir smiled briefly.

"The Drucker ships have stopped," Viggo announced.

"Stopped?" Bonita wrinkled her nose. "What do you mean stopped? Nobody stops in the middle of nowhere in space."

"They are in the middle of the wreckage from the battle site."

"Running salvage?" Tristan suggested.

Bjarke scratched his jaw. "When I was with them, they weren't above salvaging ships, but they preferred richer and more obvious treasures. They preyed on live ships—and their crews—to get them."

"What if they're suffering the same problem the Kingdom warships are?" Casmir asked. "What if they're cut off from the systems-wide banking infrastructure and find themselves in need of cash until that gate opens?"

"Wouldn't they run some raids then?" Asger asked.

HOME FRONT

"With the gate inoperable?" Bjarke asked. "How would they escape afterward? Several governments in this system have sizable militias."

Qin was relieved that the Druckers weren't truly after her, at least not at this moment, but also a touch disappointed. If they had been coming, she and her friends might have been forced to figure out a way to deal with them—and maybe free her sisters in the process.

"Captain Laser," Casmir said. "I'm not suggesting a frontal assault, but perhaps if we gather some intelligence on the Druckers, an opening will present itself. Why were two Drucker warships in this system to start with? Had they planned to attend Dubashi's meeting but then were detained? Where are their other three ships? Were their forces split when the gate closed, or does this represent some schism in the organization? Qin has an inside source. Perhaps she should communicate further with her. If that's not dangerous for her sister." Casmir stroked his jaw thoughtfully. "Rache has intelligence people. Maybe he has information on the Druckers and we could convince him to share it." Casmir extended a hand toward Kim, who hadn't spoken yet and frowned at being singled out.

"Why do you say *we* when you mean *me*?" she asked.

"I'm happy to try," Casmir said, "but Rache was unmoved by my offer of a kiss."

Bjarke stared at him. "I hope that's a joke."

"Desperate times require flexible lips," Casmir said.

"You better focus on using your lips on Shayban for now," Kim said.

That earned several nods from around the room.

"Once everything with the Kingdom is resolved," Bjarke said, "perhaps we can help Qin and her sisters."

Casmir wore a determined expression and was probably still mulling over ideas, but he allowed the others to lead him out. Soon only Qin and Asger remained in the lounge.

"I guess Casmir forgot he wanted to use a treadmill," she said.

"I think he forgets that often unless Kim is there to prod him." Asger squeezed her shoulders, then released her. "If he figures out a way to get your sisters off that ship without it being suicidal, you know I'll help. I wonder if he's envisioning recruiting your sisters as allies against Dubashi."

"If they were suddenly free for the first time in their lives, they would have to find employment. That could be for the Kingdom. If they're like me, they would find working for almost anyone preferable to the Druckers."

"Casmir must have something like that in mind. He's an altruistic guy, but he's also a man on a mission. As we all are."

Qin wasn't, but somehow, she'd gotten wrapped up in their mission. She reached up and touched Asger's face. He lifted his eyebrows and laid his hand on hers, and she decided she didn't mind.

It was a foggy morning when Oku left Basilisk Citadel for the first time in weeks, slipping out with only her bodyguard Maddie. She hadn't checked in with her father or security before taking one of the government vehicles parked near the exit, and she'd had to order the gate guard twice to open the secured entrance before he'd relented and done so. At least he'd seemed overly protective rather than overly suspicious. It hadn't been long since automated ships on a kamikaze run had slipped past orbital defenses and damaged one of the main cities on the southern continent.

As Maddie drove them through the foggy streets, detouring around work crews, Oku stared bleakly at their own city. Before leaving, she'd commed the clinic where she went for her beta cell treatments to make sure the building hadn't been damaged and that it was open. The receptionist had assumed she had a health concern and made an immediate appointment.

Not a health concern. A security concern.

Oku's fingers strayed to her temple, to the chip that had been implanted when she was five years old and had been there ever since. To the chip she now suspected was monitored by Royal Intelligence.

She wished Casmir were here so she could ask him if getting a new one would truly solve her problem. What if Intelligence had workarounds? She would ratchet down the security settings before it was implanted and hope for the best.

Oku also would have asked Casmir if Intelligence would be alerted when she removed the old chip. People *did* have them replaced—after decades, they grew obsolete and sometimes before then, they malfunctioned and couldn't be repaired *in situ*—but they typically had all their software and data transferred over first. She couldn't risk reinstalling Intelligence's monitoring program. She planned to have her old chip saved so she could do that later, but not now.

"Are you all right, Your Highness?" Maddie asked.

Oku realized they had arrived, and she was staring at the glass windows. "Yes. Thanks for driving."

Unlike with the busy hospital they had passed on the way, the parking lot was empty. Nobody was worried about knee surgeries or stem-cell infusions this week. There were too many larger things to worry about.

As Oku stepped out, she couldn't help but eye the sky warily. The fog would have made it impossible to see enemy ships even if they were up there.

Maddie came around to her side of the vehicle but paused to frown at someone on the street instead of heading in. Oku glimpsed a man in a suit before he disappeared into the fog.

"Intelligence is keeping an eye on you," Maddie warned.

"That was someone from the Citadel?"

"Yes. I recognize the agent."

"I don't suppose you'd like to go beat him up, tie and gag him, and leave him in an alley?"

Maddie blinked a few times at this unusual request.

"I'm joking." Sort of.

Oku hurried for the door, telling herself there was no way Intelligence could know why she had come. It was disturbing that they were trailing her, but it was probably because she'd left and headed into an unsafe area, not because they knew her plans.

The receptionist escorted her back to her usual room where her usual doctor waited. That was a relief. Maybe this would be easy.

A curly-haired woman in her forties, Dr. Pulinski appeared to have aged ten years since the last time Oku had seen her, only a couple of months earlier. She'd always been lean, but she bordered on gaunt, the tendons on the backs of her hands standing out when she gripped her tablet.

"Are you all right, Doctor?" Oku asked as Maddie came in to stand guard by the door.

"I lost my husband in the first bombing."

"I'm sorry." Oku gripped Pulinski's hands, wishing she could say something more useful.

"It's been a difficult couple of weeks. We can't even arrange a funeral now because it's not safe to be out in the city." Pulinski looked toward the ceiling, not saying but doubtless thinking that it wasn't safe anywhere.

"Thank you for seeing me. You could have—I wouldn't have blamed you if you shut the clinic for a while."

"I would rather work than not. I wish it were busier." Pulinski tapped her tablet. "What brings you in? I wasn't expecting to see you again so soon. Are you having trouble maintaining your blood sugar levels?"

"No, they're fine. Better than most people's given all the stressors, I'm sure. I came because I'd like you to remove my chip." Oku touched her temple.

"What? Why? Is it malfunctioning? You should see a cyberware programmer before doing anything drastic."

Oku hesitated. "Would they be able to remove something I suspect has been there since it was installed?"

"Maybe. What?"

"A back door that lets Royal Intelligence past my passcodes."

Oku expected surprise from Pulinski, but she opened her mouth in an understanding, "Ah."

"You know about it?" Oku had been making assumptions on little data.

"It's typical for the king and queen to have such measures employed on the chips of their children and closest staff that work with the family. It's not a program for monitoring activity around the clock, but information can be gathered at intervals. The senators must all agree to them, too, when they're sworn in to their positions. Many of the senior knights who are likely to be involved in top-secret missions too."

"I feel naive. All this time, I hadn't realized."

"Royal Intelligence doesn't announce it. There was a point in our history, when the chips were becoming commonplace, that they argued that every subject should be monitored thus, but the university students came together and started protests. The government backed down, and everybody assumed that was the end of it. But some people and positions are deemed too important not to be monitored."

"Important. That's me."

"I think with the royal children, it's more that they want to be able to find you if you go missing rather than a concern that you're a threat to security." Pulinski smiled, as if to reassure her.

HOME FRONT

Oku was not reassured. "If that were true, the locator beacon would be sufficient. And considering how many monarchs have mysteriously died in the past, with their heirs coming to power rather young, I'm sure kings and queens like to monitor their children for other reasons."

She wondered if Royal Intelligence had ever caught Jorg scheming in such a way. Or Finn? Senator Boehm's warning came to mind.

"You may be right. They'll know soon if you remove it—as soon as they go in for a data dump or to check your most recent files."

Yes, and that worried her, but she lifted her chin and said, "I don't care if they find out. They'll have to come to me and ask me for permission if they want to install something on the new chip. I just want this one out. Aren't the newer models faster anyway? We'll chalk it up to whimsy and wanting the latest tech."

Pulinski hesitated before nodding. "As you wish, Your Highness. Let me go get the right equipment, and you'll need to do a backup first, in case the chip is damaged during the removal and you can't get data off it later."

"I understand. Thank you."

When the doctor left, Maddie stepped forward, her eyebrows drawn down. "Is there anything you want to tell me, Oku? Such as that you're planning a coup?"

"Nothing that dramatic. I just want to be able to talk to a friend without being monitored."

Maddie made a face. "Is *he* planning a coup?"

"No. What makes you think it's a he?"

"Girls usually only care about secrecy if a boy is involved."

"If he's out there obeying my father's orders to the letter, he may become my fiancé."

"Oh?" Maddie hadn't been privy to the message Oku's father had forced her to send. "Do you think he will?"

"Obey my father's orders to the letter? No."

"Is that a relief or a disappointment?"

"I'm not sure. We've only met twice." Oku smiled wistfully. Strange that their fates had become entwined after so few encounters.

"Well, do let me know if I need to prepare for a coup of any kind."

"I will, but you ought to know me well enough to know I'd rather work in a lab at a university for the rest of my life than have anything to do with politics."

Maddie considered that. "You have made many friends with political influence on other worlds through your academic work."

"Only friends with political influence who *also* prefer labs." Friends that Oku missed. She longed for the day when the Kingdom was once again safe and it was possible to fly to other systems.

Pulinski returned. "I'm ready to begin, Your Highness."

Nerves jangled in Oku's belly, but she made herself nod and say a confident, "Good. I'm ready too."

She hoped she was right.

CHAPTER 13

THE NIGHT HAD PASSED UNEVENTFULLY, WITH NO PURSUIT from the Drucker warships, and the *Dragon* was an hour out from the asteroid that held Stardust Palace Station. Bonita sat in the pilot's pod, looking forward to docking there for a few days and hopefully being safe.

She didn't appreciate that she'd been brought in as a pawn in the Kingdom's war and wouldn't have minded hunkering down at the station until all their soldiers and warships disappeared from the system. But she supposed she should look for a cargo while she was there. The Kingdom engineers had done a decent job repairing the *Dragon*, and Casmir had also been wandering around with his tool satchel, but the freighter needed new parts.

Beyond finding work, there was the question of Qin's sisters. Bonita wanted to help them—to help *Qin*—but was there truly a way it could be feasible? What she didn't want was to end up with a Drucker bounty on her head.

A soft clang came from the ladder leading up to the navigation deck, and Bjarke's voice preceded his arrival. "You've left an empty seat for your distinguished company? I'm so pleased."

"Yeah, I thought Zee might like it."

Bjarke swung into navigation, brushed the side of her head with his fingers, and slid into the co-pilot's pod. "A robot couldn't possibly be as engaging and appealing as I am."

"I am sure Casmir would disagree."

"If he'd seen the extent of my charms, he wouldn't, but he is admittedly not my type."

"No? He has those flexible lips."

"That he'll be able to use to schmooze the sultan, I hope." Bjarke settled back into the pod. "I would prefer not to mount a raid and steal from this man, especially when we don't have a fast, heavily armored escape vessel to get away in afterward."

"Or anywhere to escape *to*." Bonita waved vaguely in the direction of the gate. Whatever Casmir and the knights planned, they had better not get her and her ship in trouble. Again.

"I think Dabrowski knows something about that malfunction. Or, given its impeccable timing, that sabotage."

"He said that?"

"It's what he doesn't say."

"There's not much that he doesn't say, from what I've seen."

"He's not a man without secrets," Bjarke said.

"Casmir is a delightful conversationalist," Viggo chimed in. "Just this morning, we were discussing advancements in energy efficiency among newer models of Kingdom manufacturing robots. He believes that we could employ those techniques and, with minimal retrofitting, drastically increase the battery life of my cadre of vacuums."

"Delightful," Bonita said.

"Extremely so."

Bjarke gripped his chin in contemplative silence.

"What do you think of his idea about rescuing the Qins?" Bonita asked. "This business is full of deadbeats and backstabbers. Qin has been such a loyal friend. If I could help her, I would."

"I would be happy to see those girls—women—rescued, or given the opportunity to rescue themselves. It's not as if they aren't capable. I don't know how practical it is right now. I'm afraid that if you annoyed the Druckers to that degree—took all of their special warriors—you had better have plans to destroy them outright, or you'd be forever looking over your shoulder, waiting for a dagger to find your back. And the women would also be forever looking over *their* shoulders." Bjarke lowered his hand. "I wondered if he was thinking of ways to use that computer virus on their ships. Even this freighter with its single railgun could take out a warship that was completely powerless."

"I can't imagine Casmir making plans that included killing hundreds of people. He was upset when the pirates in System Hydra were blown up."

"If the pirate warships were powerless, one could bring over a combat team. A combat team of a couple of knights and crushers could be particularly effective. But there would still be the problem of the Druckers retaliating later. Unless you could somehow put the blame on someone else. Or kill the key pirates. You wouldn't necessarily have to get rid of hundreds of people, just the heads of the snakes. Others would take their place but probably not with a vendetta against those who stole the Qins. If anything, they ought to be grateful for the shift that placed them in power."

Bonita glanced at him. "You've spent some time contemplating this."

"You didn't invite me to your bedroom last night, so I had little else to do."

"Some people use the night cycle to sleep."

"What a waste of time. That's what power naps are for."

"You could have knocked on my door if you had randy thoughts in mind," she said.

"I didn't want to presume. We hadn't engaged in foreplay in a corridor or lift."

"The ship has been pretty crowded lately. I keep stumbling over knights and crushers. It tends to inhibit a woman."

"Maybe Dabrowski could lock them in a closet."

"The knights or the crushers? Because I agree that knights should be locked up whenever the opportunity presents itself." She grinned at him.

Bjarke grinned back. "In closets or in handcuffs attached to a bedpost?"

"A bedpost? Where does one find a bedpost? The bunks on the *Dragon* and every space station I've been on are built into the walls and decks."

"There are these fabulous things called planets where gravity is a constant and you don't need to worry about fluctuations sending the wooden furniture crashing into the ceiling."

"Planets are strange, not fabulous."

Bjarke tilted his head. "Do you not enjoy visiting them on leave?"

"Not really. I get uncomfortable when there aren't defined spaces around me. I've always lived on habitats or ships. You must not mind it yourself. It sounds like you're rarely home."

"It's true. William might as well have the estate. If I had more appealing work to do when I'm down-side, maybe it wouldn't be so bad, but I equate it with getting bogged down in the administrative duties of owning property and having inherited numerous family businesses."

"It must be tedious to own things."

"There's a lot of paperwork involved. And managing people. I'd rather be in combat and testing my mettle against enemies."

Bonita could understand that completely. She wouldn't mind being financially independent—who would?—but she'd never equated that with settling down in a house in some dirt-licking town with rain and snow and wind. She much preferred the climate-controlled and always immaculately clean corridors of the *Dragon*. She just wished she owned the freighter outright and had money enough to afford to pass up jobs that didn't sound pleasant.

The comm panel beeped.

"That should be Stardust Palace responding to my earlier request for a landing pad in one of their ship bays." Bonita tapped the button. "This is Captain Lopez."

"Many pardons for the delay in responding to you, Captain," a polite female voice said. "I've been checking for openings here. Our ship bays are completely booked up. Will you send over the size specs for your freighter? I will see if we have an airlock available for you."

"Completely booked up? Is it some kind of Miners' Union holiday?" Or—Bonita made a face—had the sultan heard about Jorg's death and decided to host a celebration?

"Sultan Shayban's talks are starting soon, and we have dozens of ships visiting from the other systems. Thank the stars most of them flew in before our gate was rendered inoperable. Unfortunately, a few did not make it and will not be able to participate."

"What kind of talks?" Bjarke asked as Bonita transmitted the requested information on the *Dragon's* size.

"I'm afraid that information is for invited guests only, but if we're able to find you a place to dock, you will of course be permitted to enjoy all the amenities and shops on the station. We've added extra robots and human staff this week so the spa can be open around the clock. If you and your significant other are interested, I can submit a booking request for a Delyaran intelli-gel wrap, a dimsyn algae soak, the heated humming salt caves, or an old-fashioned couples massage."

"All we need is a bedpost," Bjarke said. "Thanks."

Bonita snorted.

"We are happy to service all preferences and kink levels here on Stardust Palace Station. Simply forward your preferences for booking. I have received your dimensions. Please hold."

"This is a more sales-pitchy conversation than I remember from our last visit," Bonita observed.

HOME FRONT

"If the place is packed for whatever these talks are, the sultan must have told his people to take advantage. At least someone around here has money." Bjarke shook his head. "Too bad he's not a Kingdom ally."

"Thank you for holding," the woman said. "We can accommodate your freighter on Auxiliary Lock Lane J, unit 17. I will forward a map to help you find it. It's around on the back side of the station."

"I didn't know a cylinder in a rock could have a back side." Bonita imagined having to dock her ship between a garbage scow and a fuel-delivery tanker, while being bathed by toxins from the station's exhaust vents. Viggo would complain.

The woman ignored the comment. "I will forward you an invoice for a deposit. Once you've paid, I'll place your reservation. How long will you be staying?"

Good question. The last time Bonita had been here, station security had told her she had to beat it, since she'd delivered the sneaky Kingdom stowaways. That had only been a couple of weeks earlier. Had grievances been forgotten so quickly? Maybe the sultan *had* heard about Jorg's death and held no ill will toward the rest of the Kingdom.

"Uh, put us down for a week. We'll see, but with the gate not working, there's no hurry for us to go anywhere."

"Indeed. That's been excellent for business."

The transmission came in, and Bonita gawked at the display. "This deposit is more than we paid for our whole stay last time."

"Due to high demand, prices have increased."

Bonita wondered how much she would have to pay to perch on the outside of the asteroid and spacewalk in. "Were you aware that we have the sultan's personal friend Professor Casmir Dabrowski with us?"

"One moment, please." The hold signal came back on.

Bjarke raised his eyebrows. "I talked to Casmir last night, and he's not positive we'll be well-received. He was supposed to deliver Dubashi to the sultan's brig, not let him escape into the system."

"I doubt the rates can get any *worse*."

"Greetings, Captain Lopez," the woman said with new enthusiasm. "I've managed to free up a space in Ship Bay A, Slot 2 for the sultan's esteemed guest Professor Dabrowski. We will waive all docking fees, and I will arrange to have a free spa day for two, with a complimentary couples' massage and intelli-gel wraps for the professor and a guest. Thank you for choosing Stardust Palace for your travel needs."

"Well," Bjarke said after the comm ended, "I don't think the sultan is irked at Casmir."

"When I met that kid, I never would have guessed that he would turn into someone who could get me invited to swanky places."

"Swanky places like Ship Bay A? Where we stayed before when the station wasn't busy?"

"Like the spa. He's going to need someone to go with him to take advantage of that other ticket." Bonita, as his pilot, was the logical choice.

"True, but maybe he wouldn't mind if we both went in his place. He doesn't have anyone to take for a couple's massage, does he?" Bjarke lifted his eyebrows. "I understand he and Scholar Sato are just friends."

"Yeah, but he and Zee are close. Nothing shows how grateful you are to your bodyguard like inviting him for a massage."

"I'd think a wash and lube would be more to a crusher's tastes."

"I'm sure they do that there," Bonita said.

Even though Casmir had parted ways with Sultan Shayban on good terms, and Bonita said the *Dragon* was receiving preferential docking treatment on his behalf, he was nervous when he walked down the *Dragon*'s cargo ramp and into the large ship bay. They'd been there only a few weeks earlier, departing when Casmir had arranged to have Kim and himself kidnapped by Rache, but it was much busier this time. Every landing pad had a ship on it, ships of every make and model, including a nearby yacht that appeared to be crusted with diamonds. At the least, it sparkled brightly under the artificial lights.

People of all skin colors, genetic modifications, and clothing types imaginable streamed to and fro, carrying shopping bags and luggage. There weren't any other freighters, nor did Casmir see the robot loaders that had whisked about loading and unloading cargo before. Maybe, due to the busyness of the station, freighters had been relegated to a less central location. Bonita had said something about talks.

HOME FRONT

Casmir hoped the sultan would have time to see him. His current plan was—assuming Shayban was pleased with his crusher and that nothing untoward had happened with the automated manufacturing of the rest—to ask if he could see the slydar detector and try to reverse engineer it so he could make one for the Kingdom. Or many. Even that seemed a lot to ask—Shayban had mentioned it being a prototype, and it was possible he'd signed documents agreeing not to let others copy it—but it was a better solution than theft.

Princess Nalini and Prince Samar walked into view, accompanied by a couple of security androids. Tristan, who'd been discussing a few last-minute things with Bjarke and Asger in the cargo hold, sprinted past Casmir on his way to greet them. No, to greet *Nalini*. Samar only got the briefest of waves.

Even though he knew trouble was unlikely, Casmir braced himself as the security androids walked up. What if, in the intervening weeks, Shayban had realized the kidnapping by Rache had been a ruse? Or what if he'd decided he wanted to keep *all* the crushers, not only one?

No, no, it would be fine. Shayban had sent spa tickets to the ship. People didn't give free spa appointments to enemies.

Zee stepped up beside Casmir as the androids approached, always the consummate bodyguard. Reuben was also coming along to act as Kim's bodyguard, even though she seemed more dubious than grateful of the assignment. She was going to break the news about Scholar Sunflyer's death to his daughter Natasha in person.

"That is an enthusiastic kiss," Kim observed, looking toward Tristan and Nalini. "What do you think the appropriate time length is for a reunion kiss?"

"Uh, maybe there are studies out there on the network." Casmir didn't want to think about why she was curious about that. He planned to go through life assuming that she never had been and never would be intimate with Rache. Casmir smiled wistfully at Tristan and Nalini, though not for long. He didn't like to intrude on other people's privacy. "I wonder if anyone will ever be that excited to see me."

"Viggo choreographs dances for his robot vacuums and plays opera music when you arrive," Kim said. "If that's not excitement, I don't know what is."

"True, but I was envisioning female excitement. *Human* female excitement."

"Of all people, you should have a mind open enough to accept other possibilities for companionship."

"They're fine for others, but I'd like to be able to give my parents the grandchildren they want." And he admittedly had a specific human female in mind for kisses, though the odds of even getting to ask her out for coffee were getting poorer by the day.

"This way, Professor Dabrowski," the android leading the security team said, "and Scholar Sato." He glanced at Zee and Reuben but didn't acknowledge them. "We will take you to see the sultan, and then you will be free to enjoy the amenities of the station."

Asger, Bjarke, and Qin watched them depart from the top of the cargo ramp. Asger had offered to go with them, in case Casmir needed to force the issue of acquiring the slydar detector, but if he needed a knight, he feared their cause would be long lost.

The androids led them down a corridor of potted date-palm trees decorated in colorful silks. Casmir's nostrils itched, and his eyes watered. More evidence that the immune system boost he'd received from Rache's potion was wearing off. Unfortunate. Until a couple of days ago, it had been a pleasant month devoid of motion sickness, seizures, and allergies.

"You can probably veer off at any point to look for Scholar Sunflyer," Casmir told Kim. "Reuben will go with you."

"You named him?" Kim glanced over her shoulder.

"I named all of the twelve. I haven't yet gotten to know the earlier-model crushers. They don't have as much personality as I would have expected, given that they've existed for two years."

"If they've been hanging out with Jorg, that's to be expected."

Casmir grimaced in a semblance of agreement, but he didn't comment. Even if Jorg had been difficult to work with—difficult to obey—he didn't want to speak ill of the dead.

The androids took them not to an unfamiliar corridor of offices but to the very familiar manufacturing and smelting facility where Casmir had set up the crusher-creation factory. Those crushers had all been completed and were out on the floor, not testing their combat prowess, but standing and answering questions for the dozens—hundreds?—of guests milling around the area. As with the people he'd seen in the hangar, they seemed to represent fashion and genetic modification preferences from all the

HOME FRONT

systems. The crushers were the only thing familiar. A few of them were demonstrating their versatility by shape-changing into liquid puddles or geometric shapes and then back into their bipedal human forms.

"It looks like we're going to a party," Kim said. "The only thing that's missing is crushers carrying trays of sherry and brandy."

"Is that what goes on at your lab parties back home?"

"Yes, but with less sophisticated robots that wear tuxes. Usually, there are also fruits cut into flowers and chocolate truffles."

"That sounds a lot classier than the bring-your-own-beer faculty parties I've been to. How come you never invited me?"

"I tried once. You were going to gaming night with your friends, I believe to slay a dragon threatening the castle, which was very important."

"Did you mention the truffles and the flower fruits? I might have abandoned my friends for such luxurious fare."

"You know you wouldn't."

"Ah, Professor Dabrowski," came Sultan Shayban's booming voice from the middle of the gathering.

He strode toward them wearing light and dark blue silks, a vibrant blue feather sticking up from the front of his turban. One of the crushers followed behind his shoulder, clearly on bodyguard duty. Shayban spread his arms wide and gave Casmir a hug while Zee sized up his mirror-image counterpart.

"Welcome back, good professor," Shayban said. "You're just in time for the talks. I know the people from System Hydra hoped to see you."

"People?" Casmir looked at Kim. "I only know one person in System Hydra, and I doubt President Nguyen is here."

"Her vice president is, actually. Vice President Phan. There's also an android named Tork and a scholar in a monkey-droid body that I believe is related to Scholar Sato." Shayban extended a hand toward Kim, who blinked in surprise.

"My mother is here?"

"Several representatives from System Hydra are, along with a number of scholars with expertise on—" Shayban lowered his voice and leaned close to him, "—the ancient wormhole gate that was discovered under the ice on a moon in System Lion. I've been learning all about it. Everyone you see here was invited because of their expertise on gates or because they're government or Miners' Union leaders willing to work together on this project. I was fortunate I learned of the gate so I could get involved—more than that, I offered to host the first talks. Did I tell you about that last time you were here? Perhaps not. You are from the Kingdom, and nobody wants to get the Kingdom involved. Also, you were building me crushers." Shayban patted his crusher on the shoulder.

"I am a Z-6000 programmed to protect Sultan Shayban," he stated.

"I am a Z-6000," Reuben said, "programmed to protect Kim Sato and Casmir Dabrowski."

"I am Zee," Zee said. "Did you say my acquaintance Tork is in this system? And he did not contact me previously? He is an inferior android, but it is his turn in our game of *Stars and Battleships*."

Shayban looked at him. "Your crusher is chattier than mine."

Several of the other crushers were also looking at Zee with as much curiosity as their vague faces were designed to display.

"They tend to develop more personality over time," Casmir said.

Kim was peering around the gathering. Looking for her mother?

"I look forward to that," Shayban said.

"Sultan, uhm." Casmir took a deep breath. "I must inform you that I haven't yet managed to capture Prince Dubashi. We infiltrated his base, but he slipped away."

"Oh, I know. The word is all over the system that he's still out there, and he messaged me personally to accuse me of financing that little expedition. Can you imagine?" Shayban looked toward the sea of crushers that he had indeed financed. "He told me I'd rue the day I first met him, as if I don't already. What a disgrace to the Miners' Union he's always been. But you struck him a mighty blow, Professor." Shayban clapped him on the shoulder. "You destroyed his base in this system, thwarted his attempt to hire that army, and have got everyone blaming him for the gate malfunction. Best of all, you've thoroughly embarrassed him by revealing that his war spending has turned him into a pauper." Shayban threw back his head and laughed. "What a fool. This is why you leave war to the planetary governments and profit by supplying equipment to them. Much safer that way too."

Casmir remembered the clip of a message on Dubashi's computer with Jager goading him, or at least it had seemed that way. He still felt there was more to that and wished he could have found the complete correspondence.

"I am delighted by your work, Professor. All of it. Yesterday, a representative from a trade partner trying to jilt us got lippy with me, and my crusher grabbed him by the scruff of the neck and hoisted him into the air. When I told the much-quelled man to have a seat, the crusher turned into a seat with cuffs. The representative wet himself, apologized for raising the rates, gave me a discount, and left posthaste."

"I see."

"My offer of employment still stands, but I am still hoping you'll capture Dubashi first. We can't have him zipping around the system, causing trouble. He still has plenty of resources with which to do that. I've been keeping an eye out—" Shayban tapped the side of one eye, "—for his ships. With the slydar detector. Unfortunately, I believe it only works at close range. We know it works because we caught Rache's ship sneaking up on us, but I'm not able to scan the entire system."

"Maybe Casmir could take a look at it," Kim said, pulling her searching gaze back to them. "There could be ways to improve its range."

"Oh?" Shayban's brows rose.

Casmir struggled not to squirm at this hint of dishonesty. "I am a passable mechanical engineer, but I don't even know if this detector is hardware or software. And I..." He looked at Kim, but she'd spotted her mother.

She waved, said she would be back in a minute, and strode through the crowd.

"Sultan, perhaps we could discuss it in your office when your party is over," Casmir said.

"Ah, yes, I will try to make time. But I may have to send you in alone to look at it. Or maybe my son Samar could go with you. This party is the prelude to several days of talks we have planned. I think you'll find them interesting and could add to them—you're invited to come." Shayban tilted his head to the side. "I've heard some interesting rumors about you from some of the new guests."

"Oh?" Casmir asked warily.

"I'll ask you about them later in a more private setting. But as for the talks, I intend to facilitate the study of this old gate, the production of many new ones, and if I can manage it, strong alliances between the Miners' Union rulers and several of the systems' larger governments. I'll never need to fear a rival again if I am tantamount in uniting much of the Twelve Systems."

It occurred to Casmir that this sounded like how he had hoped those gate pieces would be used, bringing humanity together rather than creating secrecy and mistrust. He hadn't envisioned Shayban at the center of the wheel, but better him than Jager.

He was also, he realized, being offered a chance to look at the slydar detector without a chaperone, or at least not much of one. He'd met Samar briefly and knew he would be easier to work around than a sharp-eyed security chief.

Shayban's gaze shifted past Casmir's shoulder, and his affable smile turned to a frown. "Queen Dya. I did not expect to see you here. I am certain you do not have an invitation."

Casmir turned as a woman of indeterminate age flowed up, the loose folds of a voluminous gown swaying with her steps. A party of six extremely handsome bodyguards with sleeveless uniforms revealing muscular arms accompanied her. The woman was bedecked in rings, bracelets, necklaces, and piercings, all featuring what appeared to be diamonds. Casmir wondered if she was the owner of the ship with the diamond-covered hull.

"Prince Galen was kind enough to let me know of this shindig and extended an invitation to me, Sultan." She—Dya—spread her hand toward him. "I knew you wouldn't mind if I came. Our grievances are such old grievances. I don't even remember what they were."

Shayban accepted and kissed her hand briefly, then dropped it. "You slept with my sister's husband and drove her to suicide when she found out about the affair. If it was indeed suicide. The doctors were never sure."

"Ah yes, but that was so long ago. And it was certainly not my fault that your brother-in-law wasn't honest with his wife about the open nature of their relationship."

"It wasn't supposed to be open," Shayban snapped, then took a breath and recovered his equanimity. "As long as you're here, enjoy the buffet and do have your staff make use of my services."

"At a discount?" She smiled.

Casmir wondered if she was one to enjoy humming salt caves and intelli-gel wraps.

"No." Shayban made a shooing motion.

Dya lingered to look Casmir over. She was almost a half a foot taller than he and was still beautiful, thanks to however many anti-aging treatments she'd received over the years. He expected a dismissive sniff from her—the reaction he usually got from striking women.

"Is this the professor who's making all your formidable robots, Shayban?" she asked instead.

"Yes, and he's not available to work for my competitors."

"Is that so?" She flashed a smile—it was only in Casmir's imagination that she had fangs—then slid an arm around his shoulders. "What if I were to extend him the same deal? That I'd provide all the materials and the manufacturing facility and pay him for his time and expertise?"

"Word gets around quickly, I see," Casmir murmured as Shayban's face flushed.

He didn't know what to make of the one-armed hug or that she had sidled closer. No doubt to irritate Shayban. Should he step away? *Spring* away? He wasn't used to having to rebuff women, though this was more akin to someone claiming a favorite chair than a sexual advance.

"There are no secrets in space," Dya said.

"*You* are not able to reach your manufacturing facilities currently," Shayban said.

"I'm sure the gate will be back in working order shortly. If the techs of this system are not talented enough to repair it, perhaps the professor could have a look." She squeezed his shoulder and gazed down at him.

"Perhaps he can, but he's here for the talks first. Now, run along until it's fixed, Dya." Shayban made another shooing motion.

"Certainly. I'm invited to the talks, I trust?"

"*No.*" Shayban must have decided he sounded petulant, for he smoothed his silks and added, "Only those who control pieces of the gate have been invited."

"Ah. Unfortunate. I have so much to offer." She released Casmir and ran a painted fingernail along his jaw before stepping forward and patting Shayban on the chest. She sashayed away, her bodyguards frowning back as they trailed her, their faces oozing disapproval, as if Casmir and Shayban had been the ones flirting with *her*.

"My apologies for the interruption, Professor. The leaders of the Miners' Union are a contentious and arrogant lot. I suppose one must be to rise to such a position. Wrangling them into a solid alliance will be a challenge, but I trust they all see the opportunities for growing our little empires—and our wealth—by building gates to new systems and opening up more mining areas. You'll come to the talks?"

"Me?" Casmir had been distracted watching Kim's reunion with her mother—a stiff, hands-clasped-behind-their-backs reunion—and almost missed the question.

"As a voice of reason and a neutral third party. Technically, more like a sixtieth party, but Vice President Phan from Tiamat Station requested you be there, and I agree."

"I… could come for part of them if they start soon, but I'm still trying to help the Kingdom. I need to catch Dubashi and make sure he can't deploy his virus-filled rockets on my home world. I also need to help the Fleet evict that blockade of ships from our gate. And a friend needs assistance retrieving her family from the clutches of pirates."

His to-do list kept growing and sounding more impossible.

"Those things would be difficult for one man to do," Shayban said.

"Well, I will have help." Casmir smiled and extended a hand toward the crushers, hoping Shayban still planned to let him take them. He could force the issue, since they were programmed to obey his commands, but he would rather not state that.

"Ah, indeed, but I do plan to attempt to buy some of these crushers from you. Also, others here—not only the odious and self-aggrandizing Queen Dya—have expressed interest in them."

"Oh?" Casmir couldn't sell the crushers, though he felt guilty about that since Shayban had provided the materials. Even though Jorg was gone, Casmir assumed Jager knew about them—or had been the one to command them to be built—and would miss them if they didn't show up back at home.

"Yes. But what I meant to imply is that for all you plan to do, you will need allies and ships. And what better place to recruit than here?"

Casmir couldn't imagine how many crushers he would have to promise to secure the assistance of ship-owning Miners' Union leaders, and he suspected his smile was more bleak than enthusiastic.

A dark-skinned woman with elaborate braids of black hair wound about her head rode toward them in a float chair. It took Casmir a second to recall where he'd seen her before, but by the time she was near, he managed a semblance of a knight's bow.

"Good evening, Princess Tambora," he said. "I did not know you would be here or were coming to this system at all."

HOME FRONT

Where was she from? Shango Habitat in System Boar. Kim had introduced them on Tiamat Station, but he'd only spoken with her for a few minutes.

"Had I known we would be trapped here, I wouldn't have volunteered to come, but since I was on Tiamat Station when the first gate pieces were brought in, and happened to mention it to my mother, she thought I might like to tag along with Vice President Phan and learn more. And perhaps offer the assistance of our scientists in creating a new gate when the time comes. As you can imagine, we too would like access to more star systems."

"I'm sure all of humanity will want that access and be curious to explore the rest of the galaxy."

"Yes." She tilted her head and studied him, appearing far more mature than the eighteen or nineteen years he guessed she was. "I understand you share that opinion and acted to ensure all of humanity *could* potentially participate."

He spread a hand. "I don't know how successful I was in that, but science and technology should benefit everyone, not a select few, if we're to evolve as a people."

"It's also easier to get away from sisters you don't like if there are more gates going to more places." Her nose crinkled, and she looked her age again.

"I imagine so."

Tambora peered around and spotted Kim with her mother standing away from the main herd of people. "I want to talk to Scholar Sato, but I shall first express my condolences that your people have lost your eldest prince." She raised her eyebrows, as if uncertain if these condolences were in order. She was, Casmir recalled, an acquaintance of Oku's. What had Oku said to her over the years about her older brother?

Shayban had stepped aside for this conversation, but he remained close enough to hear, and he curled a lip. "Losing that toad can't be a sad event for anyone in the Kingdom. One wonders if his own parents could have loved him."

Tambora's eyebrows drifted higher. "I spoke briefly with Princess Nalini when I arrived about the, ah, attempted courtship."

"As if you could call it that."

Casmir, not wanting this to devolve into lambasting-the-Kingdom hour, said, "Thank you for your consideration, Your Highness. It is regretful that solutions could not be reached without death. It is a difficult time for the Kingdom."

"The Kingdom has made it so," Shayban grumbled.

"There is a rumor, Professor," Tambora said, "that you were responsible for the derailing of Dubashi's mercenary army."

After deciding she appeared more intrigued than concerned or annoyed—Dubashi didn't seem to have many fans—Casmir said, "I think that was Tristan, actually. He pulled up Dubashi's finances and put together spreadsheets. I just facilitated the delivery of the information to the mercenary leaders at an opportune time."

"Your Kingdom ought to appreciate that you kept him from forming an even larger army," she said.

If only.

Casmir smiled faintly. "If they don't, do you have room for a robotics refugee on your station?"

"I've offered you a job *here*, Professor," Shayban said. "You've no need to fly to another system for asylum."

"Of course, Sultan. I'm merely keeping my options open."

"We on Shango Habitat are interested in seeing Princess Oku's bee project be completed," Tambora said. "The last I'd heard, robot bees were going to assist natural bees with bacterial enhancements."

"Yes." Casmir's smile was more genuine as he realized she'd been talking to Oku about her—their—project at some point. "I hope all will be resolved with our war soon and that work may resume on that project."

From wherever in the Twelve Systems he ended up doing it.

"Good. We are one of many habitats attempting to grow all of our food that would benefit from natural pollinators." She nodded to him and to the sultan. "Have a good evening."

"Enjoy the party tonight, Professor," Shayban said when she'd gone, "and tomorrow, you will come look at my slydar detector and see if you can boost its range, yes? I will rest much easier once Dubashi is no more. I cared little when his sights were set on your Kingdom, but if he, like the rest of us, cannot escape this system, he may settle for a closer target."

"I'll be happy to take a look," Casmir said.

"Excellent." As Shayban clapped him on the shoulder and headed off to chat with other guests, a familiar android appeared out of the crowd, bland face, dark hair, and silver eyes.

HOME FRONT

Zee turned toward Tork as he approached. "Greetings, inferior android Tork."

"Greetings, single-track killing machine Zee."

"My tracks are many, as is proven by the fact that I am winning in our most recent strategy game."

"You only think you are winning. I am using cunning subterfuge to lull you into this false belief."

"Androids are as cunning as socks with holes in them. They were not designed to hunt down intelligent prey, but merely to do mindless tasks."

"You will see my cunning when I best you at this game, as I have bested you in previous games, and you will be forced to accept that hunting requires only fast reflexes and enhanced olfactory sensors. There is no innate intelligence in crushers."

Casmir would have left them to their bickering as he went to check on the contents of the buffet table, but since Zee was still on bodyguard duty, he followed. And Tork also followed so they could continue their discussion, if that was what it was. Casmir wondered what Zee would think if he posited that Tork might be the mechanical being he should select as a mate. Their interactions were much more spirited than any Zee engaged in with the other crushers.

CHAPTER 14

ASGER, HAVING ALREADY SEEN THE SIGHTS OF STARDUST Palace Station, remained on board the *Dragon* with his father, Qin, and Bonita. Bonita and his father were playing a holo game in the lounge. Asger and Qin sat cross-legged on the deck above the cargo ramp, looking out into the ship-filled bay. People watching, ostensibly, but Qin looked pensive, and Asger kept thinking about her sisters.

It bothered him that *Casmir* had been the one to suggest they might be able to find a way to facilitate their jailbreak. Asger was Qin's friend—maybe *more* than friend—so he should have been eager to help her with this quest, and he wasn't unwilling, but he'd encountered one of her sisters, such as they were, before he'd ever met Qin. She'd been from the older cohort, as he'd later learned, but had looked so similar that when he saw Qin the first time, he'd thought they were the same person. And that sister had killed one of his friends in battle. He was wrestling with the idea of risking his life to save the rest of them. Did he truly want to? They were the Druckers' creatures, brainwashed from birth to be loyal to them. Qin was different, *his* Qin. The others were an unknown.

"Are you thinking about your sisters?" he asked, since her pensive expression hadn't changed, not even when a boy had led an elephant off a ship and toward cargo doors in the back of the bay. A gift for the sultan, perhaps.

"Yes. Casmir said if we brainstormed a plan that could work, he would either go along, if it's after he's finished helping his people, or he would send some of his crushers."

"He had better make sure he can get them back from Shayban before promising that."

"I think he can get any robots he wants from anybody, whether he's programmed them or not."

One of Viggo's robot vacuums whirred past behind them—the whirring almost sounded like a cheerful hum.

"That is possibly true," Asger said.

"And he's got twenty-some already." Qin waved into the ship. "Fearsome warriors."

"Hm, yes." The last Asger had seen, the bigger crushers were teaching the batch acquired from Jorg's ship how to play a game that involved spinning a top and gambling with dried fruit and nuts raided from Bonita's provisions cabinets.

Qin's pensive expression turned to one of joyous contemplation that seemed more natural for her, and she leaned over and gripped his thigh with both hands. "Wouldn't it be wonderful if I could get my sisters away from those vile men? That vile life? Being killers with no choice in the matter? No choice in their destiny? They could be free to work as bodyguards or law enforcement officers or bounty hunters—whatever they wished. Or maybe they could even work with us, some of them at least. Sometimes, the captain talks about going back into bounty hunting, not just running freight. With a few of us… no criminal would stand a chance." Her eyes grew bright with this vision.

Asger heard her words, but his mind was distracted by her touch on his leg. He supposed it wouldn't be the appropriate time to suggest they retire to one of their cabins to explore some well-deserved time off. What would it be like to sleep with someone who thought he was a better knight than his father, and who always fought at his side when they went into battle? With someone tall and strong yet also sweet and funny, whose eyes always gazed at him without artifice?

They'd only kissed a couple of times, but those times had been memorable, and he well remembered Qin wrapping her arms around him, powerful, intriguing arms that were nothing like those of women he'd been with back home. And he remembered wrapping his arms around her, feeling the blend of feminine curves and raw strength under her galaxy suit. What would it be like to explore her body without any armor or clothing between them?

"You agree, don't you?" Qin asked, and he realized he'd been silent and staring at her with his lurid thoughts for a long moment.

"Yes. What was the question?"

Her expression grew confused, but when he dropped a hand to one of hers and rubbed his thumb across her warm skin covered with a hint of fur, she seemed to guess what had distracted him.

She smiled gently. "If you agreed that my sisters would be good warriors who could best criminals."

"I'm sure that's true. We just have to figure out how to get them away from the Druckers, right?"

"You're willing to help?"

"Of course." Even if he had reservations, how could he say no? She'd helped him so many times. To clear his mind from sexual thoughts and help focus, he stood up, patting Qin's shoulder to let her know he wasn't rejecting her touch, and started pacing. "We do need a plan. Casmir's crushers would only help if we got close enough to board."

"The Druckers tend to shoot down anyone who gets that close. They might not try to take on a Kingdom warship, but the *Dragon* would be an easy target."

"The *Dragon*," came Viggo's voice from the speakers, "would not be so foolish as to wander within firing range of a massive pirate warship."

"What if, instead of us trying to board them, we lured them into boarding us?" Asger mused. "It is a freighter. Could we somehow start a rumor that we're carrying something of great value? They must need money if they're salvaging those wrecks."

"But instead of carrying goods of great value we're carrying a dozen crushers?" Qin asked.

"Casmir would argue that they have great value."

"I'm sure." She tapped her chin with a claw. "I like the premise, using a bait ship to set a trap, but the *Dragon* is known to them. We used it to meet some of them when Bonita was pretending to hand me off for a reward. Granted, Bjarke was the one leading the Drucker operation to pick me up, but he had other legitimate pirates with him who got away and would have reported back. Also, I'm sure anyone could do a little research and find out I'm working on the *Dragon*. They would recognize it for a ruse, especially since we tried to trick them before."

"Another ship then. Maybe Sultan Shayban would lend us one."

Qin arched her eyebrows. "Lend us a ship to use as bait for trigger-happy pirates? I don't think he loves Casmir *that* much. A ship is a lot more valuable than tickets for a spa he owns. Besides, Shayban doesn't even know who we are."

"His favorite daughter does."

"Just because we had finger sandwiches in her suite after knocking out all the security guards along the way doesn't make us her new best friends."

"Hm, what about Tristan? We fought with him. Though I don't know how much influence he has here. Just because he's Princess Nalini's business partner doesn't mean he has a fleet of ships of his own." Asger didn't even know if Tristan would come back down to visit. He'd run over to meet his girlfriend and had only given the most fleeting backward wave as he left with her.

"There's the ship we need." Qin chuckled and pointed at the gaudy diamond-covered yacht parked near them. "You wouldn't even have to put a cargo in it. The pirates would want it based on the hull, and it's a new state-of-the-art ship on the inside too." Qin touched her temple. "I pulled up the specs. The equipment inside is worth a fortune."

Asger leaned against the frame of the hatch and considered the yacht. It was gaudy, yes, but he could appreciate the sleek lines under the ostentatious hull decorations. "It would attract a pirate's eye, but I doubt it's one of Shayban's ships, or that whoever owns it would lend it to us."

"I suppose not. I wonder how much engineering brilliance it would take to make a replica and borrow its ident chip."

One of the doors that led into the ship bay opened, and a woman wearing expensive clothing and jewelry entered, trailed by six burly bodyguards who were showing off their arm muscles to potential enemies—or perhaps for their employer's benefit. Asger couldn't tell how old she was—not young—but she had a faintly predatory mien and seemed like someone who would have a healthy sex drive.

As she headed toward one of the ships—was she going to the diamond yacht they'd been discussing?—she looked over at them. Her gaze skimmed indifferently past Qin but stopped on him. A half-smile pulled up one side of her mouth as she looked him up and down.

Asger was in his galaxy suit rather than his armor, and it showed off that he'd kept himself fit during his adventures. He puffed out his chest a bit—if she was interested in him, it might be easier to cut a deal with her.

Her gaze made it up to his eyes after lingering in other spots. When she reached the ramp to her ship—it *was* the diamond yacht—the hatch automatically opening at her approach, she crooked a finger to him in invitation.

HOME FRONT

Qin growled deep in her throat, not loud enough for the woman to hear. Maybe not even loud enough that she was aware of having done it herself.

The bodyguards noticed their boss's attention. One of them stepped closer to her, putting a hand on her shoulder and murmuring something in her ear. A warning that he was from the Kingdom? A knight? A troublemaker?

All true this week, but those seemed like things that might enhance his allure to some wealthy business mogul. He had no intention of sleeping with her, but if he found an opportunity to send that ship off in the right direction with a hold full of crushers…

The woman leaned against the bodyguard, smiled over her shoulder at him, and reached back and patted his stomach. Actually, that was *lower* than his stomach. The man glared over at Asger, his hand still on her shoulder, and nuzzled the back of her head. She smiled at Asger while receiving this attention, then made an inviting head tilt and walked into the ship. One of the other bodyguards had closed the distance and rested a hand on the woman's butt.

"What the hell was that?" Qin asked after their hatch shut.

"I think I just got invited to an orgy."

She looked tartly at him. "I assume you're not interested."

"Not with six other guys and only one woman, no. If the ratio were reversed…" Since Qin's expression was shifting from tart to full-out disapproving, Asger ended with, "I still wouldn't be interested. Knights are wholesome. Paragons of social and sexual mores. And monogamous when in a relationship."

"Good." Qin rose lithely to her feet, all power and agility, like the cat whose DNA had been spliced into her genes. She was a *lot* more interesting than that woman and her bodyguard orgy. "Because I'd hate to think that all the stories I'd read about knights were lies."

"They aren't."

"Good," she repeated, then rested her hands on his shoulders and leaned her chest against his. "We'll find another bait ship, one that doesn't come with a soul-sucking siren for an owner."

"I'm amenable."

Asger slid a hand down Qin's side and around to her back, or maybe a little lower, then bent his head to kiss her and show her how *much* more interesting she was to him. She returned the kiss hungrily and molded herself to him.

He decided it wouldn't be appropriate to let other women ogle him in the future as a way to spur on her libidinous and possessive side, no matter how arousing it was. And it was that. If they didn't stop soon, they would end up putting on quite the show for any passersby in the ship bay. Of course, they could close the hatch... or go somewhere private.

"Why don't we discuss further plans..." he murmured in between kisses, "in your cabin?"

"Yes," she said promptly, her hands tightening their grip on him.

He'd expected her to pause to think about it, since he was suggesting more than the kiss and date they'd talked about, but if she didn't want to pause, he didn't mind.

"I've wanted to... discuss things with you..." she said, a little breathless, "ever since the park."

"The park on Odin?" He pushed his hand through her thick mane of hair, gently brushing one of her pointed ears. "Where you were springing through the trees?"

"Yes."

"Because the trees got you in an amorous mood, or I did?"

She grinned. "Yes."

Kim did not like parties or large gatherings of any kind. She didn't think her mother did, either, but maybe the white-haired vice president of Tiamat Station had asked her to mingle with the other scientist guests. He'd come over and said a few words to her right after Kim had joined her.

Now, Kim was tagging along as her mother chatted with a blur of archaeologists, engineers, and historians that she didn't recognize. The conversations revolved around the gate and how long it might take to build a new one, given that the various governments, even after agreeing to work together, were missing a lot of pieces. Thankfully, her mother eventually stepped away from the scientists, and she and Kim found a relatively quiet spot under the potted trees along one wall.

HOME FRONT

"There are two other loaded droids here." Her mother pointed at a nearby female android and a male model across the room. "The male is a Miners' Union leader who lost his human body to old age last year, and the woman is a technology archaeologist, Scholar Mara Neem. She's been a droid for over a century and was one of the first to upload her consciousness, also to avoid death. I spoke with her earlier. She's seen so much and studied so many fascinating places and objects all over the Twelve Systems."

"Do you enjoy finding others who've made the choice you have?" Kim didn't know why her mother was pointing out the loaded droids, but it seemed polite to ask.

"I do. I was an oddity even when I was human—I imagine you can understand—but I'm more of one now. I don't regret my choice, as I'm alive in a fascinating period in human history, but the stares can get tedious."

"Would they stare less if you'd chosen a more typical android body?"

"Likely so, but then I'd be mistaken for a butler, nanny, or maid all the time. That happens to Scholar Neem, if you can imagine. We have odd preconceived notions about androids and what they're created for."

"I'm sure Casmir would agree."

"Yes, the crusher whisperer. His reputation is growing."

"His reputation for creating crushers?" Kim doubted Casmir would *want* to be known for that.

"No. This is all recent, isn't it?" She pointed at one of the tarry constructs showing off his ability to jump a great distance to a group of teenagers that had to be sons or grandchildren of one of the guests.

"The batch here is recent, yes."

"They're only a part of his reputation. President Nguyen has been spreading a rumor that he's Admiral Mikita's clone, raised by King Jager to serve him as an engineer and military strategist. But he's rebelled and fled his oppressive liege, and is now available as a free agent."

Kim was so busy gaping and rocking back on her heels—her calves bumped one of the potted trees—that she almost didn't hear anything after *Admiral Mikita's clone.*

"I tried to dissuade her of that notion—this is the boy who left fizzop stains on my coffee table, after all—but she found some old pictures and dredged up three-hundred-year-old rumors that King Ansel had preserved genetic samples of the admiral." Her mother peered up at her. "I admit there is a very strong resemblance in the pictures, but I am positive Jager didn't raise Casmir to be a military strategist."

"No," Kim said numbly. "That was… somebody else."

"There *is* a clone, then?"

"This is top-secret stuff in the Kingdom, Mother. Let's at least go somewhere else if you want to talk about this, all right?"

Her mother gazed up at her, and Kim wondered if she'd already given away too much. Should she have squelched any notion of Casmir being linked to Mikita? Would it matter? Her mother wasn't the one spreading rumors; President Nguyen was in another system.

Maybe Kim should ask Casmir how he felt about this before denying or confirming anything else. He might be able to—and even want to— use these rumors to his advantage.

"We can go somewhere else," her mother said after a long, contemplative pause. "It's good to see you again. I didn't expect to run into you here, but I'm glad you're safe. I'd thought those warships had gone back to the Kingdom and that you would be stuck on Odin for those bombings." She shook her head. "I do hope Haruto and the boys are safe. It's distressing that this closing of the local wormhole gate means we can't even get the infrequent news updates that were making it through the blockade before."

"If we get the chance, Casmir thinks we should convince our families to leave Odin and take up your offer to move to Tiamat Station." Kim shook her head, remembering the forlorn cast to his expression when he'd admitted he'd been pondering that.

"An excellent idea. Tiamat Station is rebuilding and will soon be the vibrant and welcoming community that it was before."

Kim had a few dozen other things to worry about before contemplating a move. Such as that virus. Kim had volunteered to break the news of the death of Scholar Sunflyer's father to her in person because it seemed like the right thing to do, but she also hoped to get permission to study her father's lab, assuming it was still there. Maybe she could get some insight into his work or more data on the virus.

"I need to speak with Scholar Sunflyer on this station," Kim said. "Do you want to come with me?"

There was no reason to take her mother along, but Kim didn't know how long she would be on the station, and she was reluctant to part ways after only a half hour.

HOME FRONT

"Is that the woman responsible for the mushroom gift shop?" Mother wrinkled her nose.

"I think she makes the materials and some enterprising entrepreneur here crafts the purses and gift baskets."

"I see you've been there."

"Yes." Kim started to smile, but a wave of bleakness washed over her as she remembered Rache's joke, that he wanted a recording of Casmir giving Jorg a mushroom purse. Well, that wouldn't happen now.

A part of her was glad that Rache hadn't sent her any messages since their ships had gone different directions—what would she say when there was no question that he'd killed Jorg? A part of her wondered what he was up to now and wished he *would* send a message, if only so she would know. And because, she admitted ruefully to herself, she still wanted to hear from him.

If she *did* move to Tiamat Station one day, it might be easier for a mercenary with a ship to come visit her, far easier than it would be if she remained on Odin—especially if Casmir got ahold of a slydar detector for the Kingdom.

"I'll go with you," her mother said. "You'll have to lead the way. I haven't downloaded a map of the station yet."

"Of course." Remembering that she'd promised to rejoin Casmir, Kim sent him a message as she scanned the manufacturing facility for him. She half-expected to find him in a cluster of crushers while completely ignoring the human guests. He did have a couple of the crushers and an android around him, but he was in a group of several older men and women, gesturing animatedly. And they appeared to be listening in rapt attention.

Casmir was not, she reminded herself, against parties and gatherings, and he did far better in social settings than she did. Not social settings full of jocks and gym rats, perhaps, but anywhere that discussions of technology could be appreciated, he fit right in.

But was this more than that? Maybe it was her imagination, but it seemed like quite a few people were glancing in Casmir's direction. What if Nguyen's rumors had spread wide and many of the sultan's guests were wondering if he was indeed Mikita's clone? She would have to warn him about that later. If she did it now, he might hyperventilate and have a seizure. That might happen anyway, but she knew he would prefer it didn't occur in a large public setting.

You seem to be doing fine, she messaged him. *I'm going to visit Scholar Sunflyer and try to secure permission to check her father's lab.*

Good idea, Casmir replied promptly, even though he was in the middle of talking. *You caught me by surprise earlier, but I think Shayban is going to let me in to look at the slydar detector. That was a good idea, too, though, uhm, a little disingenuous.*

Everything the Kingdom does these days is disingenuous. Kim would be happy to be disingenuous for Casmir, so he didn't have to be.

That's a sad truth I'm learning.

Let me know if you need help with the slydar detector. Or if you come across any fresh intelligence on Dubashi's location or the rockets while you're snooping in Shayban's control room.

Snooping? What makes you think there would be snooping?

You're probably snooping all over the station's networks right now, while sending me messages and speaking to all those people.

Really, Kim. That's not snooping. That sounds so nefarious. I'm merely gathering data, like the bots that roam the systems-wide networks to make searches more effective for users.

Just let me know what you find on the rockets.

Will do. I'm going to send Reuben with you.

One of the crushers left his gathering and jogged toward Kim and her mother.

I don't think that's necessary. I can take care of myself, you know.

Now you can take care of yourself twice as well. Casmir beamed a smile over at her. *Also, with this many people on the station, I don't think we should assume that everybody will have friendly feelings toward us. I assume that Dubashi still has a bounty on my head—though I hope people now believe he can't pay it—and he may also be irked at you for nullifying several of his rockets.*

Good point.

"Kim." Her mother tugged at her sleeve. "Should we be alarmed that one of those hulking crushers is running at us?"

"No. That's Reuben. Our bodyguard."

The crusher fell in behind them as they headed out of the facility.

"Does he make Rueben sandwiches?" her mother asked.

"I haven't noticed any of the crushers carrying out domestic duties."

"That's disappointing."

"You don't eat sandwiches anymore."

HOME FRONT

"True, but I'm disappointed on behalf of all crusher-owning sandwich eaters."

Kim looked down at her. "Do you think you're weirder since you transferred into the droid body?"

"Why do you ask?"

"No reason."

CHAPTER 15

Q IN WOKE TO A STARTLED CURSE IN THE corridor outside of her cabin—it almost sounded like a male scream. Surprisingly, her door was open. She sprang out of bed and almost rushed out to check on the noise—she could smell people out there… Asger and Bjarke. Then she realized she was naked and blushed when she remembered why.

"What are you doing?" Asger blurted. Why had he gone out there?

Qin grabbed her clothes—they were heaped on the deck beside the bunk with Asger's. Her strong, athletic, and talented Asger. She grinned wickedly in remembrance.

"Just loitering in the corridor," came Bjarke's response. "Wearing clothes."

"Those aren't clothes. Clothing. Whatever it is, it doesn't count." Asger sounded more flustered than she'd ever heard him.

It wasn't until Qin donned her shirt and pulled on some exercise pants that she leaned into the corridor and discovered why. Asger, his back and naked butt cheeks toward her, faced Bjarke, who was wearing a skimpy lavender robe that Qin recognized as Bonita's. That was *all* he was wearing, leaving his hairy legs on full display. The two men looked like they'd both been heading to the lav when they'd stumbled into each other.

Further down the corridor, the hatch to Bonita's cabin was open, and she leaned her head out. Judging by her bare shoulder, she wasn't fully clothed either. She caught Qin's eyes and grinned at her past the men.

"You two take turns if you need to," Bonita told them. "And don't violate Viggo's stall doors."

"*Thank* you, Bonita," Viggo's voice sounded.

Asger flung his arms up. "Is there anybody who isn't awake?"

Two robot vacuums vroomed down the corridor, weaving between the men's legs, looking more like cats playing chase than cleaning appliances seriously tending their duties.

"I'm going to the lav." Bjarke strode forward, lifting a hand in case he needed to nudge Asger out of the way.

Seeing a man's wrist and a forearm sticking out of that lavender sleeve was decidedly odd. Asger must have thought so too, because he sprang back. Then he turned and fled into Qin's cabin, but not before she caught Bonita checking out his ass and giving her a thumbs-up.

As soon as Qin leaned back inside, Asger thumped the door shut. Hard. He put his back to it.

"Are you all right?" Qin hadn't thought that Bjarke and Bonita had been that clandestine about their relationship, but maybe this had taken Asger by surprise.

"No. I have to pee."

"There's more than one toilet in there."

"I'm not going in there when *he's* in there. In that, that *robe*. What kind of man wears a woman's robe?"

"One who didn't bring one of his own? And doesn't want to catch a chill on the way to the lav." Qin patted him on the stomach.

Asger appeared more horrified than comforted. "I'm never going to be able to forget that. It's scorched in my mind."

"If it helps, the captain may have scorched your butt cheeks in her mind." From what Qin had observed, Bonita was perfectly capable of admiring one man's form while she was in a relationship with another.

"That does *not* help." Asger cupped a protective hand over one of those cheeks.

"Sorry." But Qin couldn't keep from snickering, even if this wasn't how she'd imagined the end of her first night with Asger going. It was fun. *He* was fun. That was something she'd never experienced back when she'd been a slave to those pirates.

He managed a lopsided smile and pulled her into a hug. He kissed her on the forehead, but when a clang came from the corridor, he lowered his arms.

"Will you check to see if it's safe?" he asked.

"Safe? You mean if Bjarke is done?"

"And locked back in his cabin where he belongs."

"Uh, I think it's the captain's cabin that he'll be locked in."

"Whatever. Just so I don't have to run into him again while he's…" Asger groped in the air with a flustered hand. "Not properly attired."

"You're really going to send me, an innocent doe-eyed damsel, out to check on the danger while you hide in here?"

"An innocent what?"

"Doe-eyed damsel. It's a line in one of my fairy tales. Never mind." Qin pushed him aside and went to check the lavatory. "It's safe for you to come out, brave and fearless knight."

He squinted at her as he passed. "Is that from a fairy tale too?"

"No, that was me teasing you."

"Meanie." He swatted her on the way past and didn't fully commit to entering the lavatory until he'd poked his head in and checked.

A message came in to her chip as she returned to her cabin. It was from Mouser.

She read it with trepidation, worried her sister would ask again for help that Qin hadn't yet figured out how to deliver. Earlier, when she'd sent a response, she'd said she would talk to her captain and see if anything seemed possible, but she'd tried not to commit herself or sound too optimistic. She hadn't wanted to get Mouser's hopes up.

But it was a warning, not a request.

Squirt, I saw that we were close to your freighter the other day— I'm relieved you were gone before our warships arrived to salvage the wrecks. But it looked like you might be on course for Stardust Palace. Is that correct? You know we're given only limited access to the network and ship's scanners down here, so I couldn't be sure, but if so, I am sending a warning. The Druckers, as well as all other mercenaries and pirates in the system, have been informed that there is a meeting going on at the station, and that the majority of the Miners' Union rulers, as well as other wealthy businessmen and influential government leaders, are there. It was pointed out that if those people were taken as hostages, each one could be worth a fortune. It was also pointed out that they likely had a lot of wealth on their own persons and in their expensive luxury ships. As far as I've heard, the Druckers are planning to stay here and finish this salvage and then amble over, perhaps to arrive after the others, hoping the fighting is over and those early arrivers have taken the brunt of the damage from the station's defenses. But in case you're there, I wanted to warn you. Perhaps you and your captain should leave before you're trapped there.

Qin sank down on her bunk. When Asger came in, she sent him a copy of the message. She also forwarded one to Bonita, Kim, and Casmir.

"Squirt?" Asger asked before he'd had time to read more than a line or two. His eyebrows twitched.

"It was my nickname when we were little girls. We all ended up about the same height, but I was the shortest of my sisters for a while."

"Like the runt of the litter?" The corners of his mouth joined his eyebrows in twitching.

"Like the squirt of the litter." She shoved him in the arm. "Read the rest."

"Yes, ma'am."

His amusement faded as he continued on, and he ended up swearing. "Who do you think tipped off a bunch of money-hungry pirates and mercenaries?"

"Those talks can't be that secret if people from all over the systems were invited," Qin said.

"Yes, but it sounds like someone deliberately sent the word out to all the disreputable sorts. All the disreputable sorts stuck in the system, twiddling their thumbs with nothing to do. And many of whom, it sounds like, are short on funds since they can't access the banking system."

"I'll send Mouser a message and ask if she knows who the source was, but she probably doesn't. We were never kept in the loop, just told who to fight and where, usually right before the mission. What little information we got came secondhand from gossipy pirates. The captains had the network wireless signals dampened in our pen to keep us from accessing much information or even communicating with each other unless it was out loud. They wanted their cameras to be able to record all of our exchanges. I'm not sure how Mouser is getting these messages out."

"These pirates are such lovely people. You make me want to get your sisters out more than ever."

"Thank you for that." Qin patted his knee and didn't make any more teasing comments about his bravery in the corridor, though she might bring it up again if he ever teased her about her old nickname. "But I guess we'll have to stay here and help defend the station against

HOME FRONT

attackers. Let's hope the weapons on the surface of the asteroid are powerful enough that the mercenaries and pirates will be too daunted to force their way in."

"Actually—" Asger rubbed his jaw, "—this may be a good time to try that plan with the bait. It doesn't sound like the Druckers want to risk themselves on this attack of the station, but if they need money, they might feel forced to. Unless a more appealing and easier target comes along."

"But we'd be fleeing from a battle."

"And into another battle. It's not an act of cowardice. Besides, if we won, we would take out two ships that might have joined in with the others. Even if those pirates are risk averse, if they came to believe that the attacking side was going to win…"

"They would be quick to jump in then."

"Let's chat with Casmir in the morning and Bonita and my father—" an involuntary grimace crossed Asger's face, and Qin envisioned him begging Bonita to implement a no-robes-in-public-areas policy, "—and see if any of them has the connections to get a bait ship. If not, the *Dragon* may still work. If we float a rumor that we're leaving Stardust Palace with a valuable cargo, it may be more believable now that everybody knows all these rich influencers are here."

Qin was skeptical that using the *Dragon* would work, but if they couldn't come up with anything better, she would try it. The chance to free all of her sisters… It was a fantasy she'd dared not dwell on that often, but now, it was impossible to stop thinking about.

Casmir was the first to respond to the messages she'd sent out.

Do you have any idea how long we have until this supposed attack will take place? he asked.

No, Qin replied. *I don't know any more than what's in the message.*

Hm. I'd been contemplating sleeping tonight. I guess I will put that on hold. Indefinitely.

Sorry. Qin felt bad that she and Asger—and Bonita and Bjarke— had been enjoying the night while Casmir was up there schmoozing the sultan and trying to gain access to his slydar detector. Not that Qin would have had any luck schmoozing people. She was lucky if they didn't run away in terror when they saw her fangs.

I wonder if Dubashi is behind that tidbit of information being leaked out, Casmir messaged. *The last time we were here, he sent a team to try to steal some of Shayban's ships. As far as I know, he is still in need of ships, now more so than ever.*

He could hope to send another team in while the station is busy defending against mercenaries.

Or another team could already be here.

You better keep your crushers close. Dubashi still wants you dead, I assume?

Now and forever, I suspect. Thanks for the heads up, Qin.

Let me know if you need any help. Or to be rescued when you're caught snooping around.

Funny, Kim used that same word.

It's the right one, isn't it?

As I told her, I'm gathering data.

Is that what snooping is called when a professor does it?

If it's a mathematics or engineering professor, yes. Liberal arts professors are shiftier.

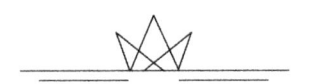

Prince Samar led Casmir to his father's office, which seemed an unlikely place for a slydar detector to be hooked up, but what did he know? But all they did was pass through the office to a secret door that led down a winding private corridor and eventually up a ladder to a trapdoor.

"Are you sure you're supposed to be showing me your father's secret routes?" Casmir asked.

Prince Samar was a man in his twenties who reminded Casmir of a lot of the art students from the university back home. A quick network search revealed that he painted and sculpted, occasionally putting on shows at galleries around the system, but he didn't sell much of his work. Thanks to being able to live off his father's funds, he might not care. Thus far, he seemed more accomplice than guard dog, so Casmir was inclined to like him.

"Of course I am. He loves you. He's five minutes away from putting you in his will."

"I assume that's a joke."

"Yes. It's probably more like five months, but if you give him another crusher, he might slip you in sooner." When Samar reached the top of the ladder, he pressed a thumb to a biometric padlock, and the trapdoor hissed and swung open. "Do watch out for his other children, who might feel jilted if their inheritance is smaller than expected."

"You're somewhat fixated on your father's death. He doesn't have any medical conditions to worry about, does he?"

"I don't believe so, but this is what life is like when you're the son of a sultan. Or when you're one of many sons and daughters of a sultan. You start speculating from a young age on your position in the family and what you might inherit." Samar climbed out into a large, blue and gray control room that was the first place in the palace Casmir had seen that wasn't draped in silks and decorated with potted trees or plants. It looked like the bridge of a ship.

"It sounds morbid."

"That's what it's like to be born into money. You're lucky you avoided it. I assume you did. You seem normal."

"Nobody's ever called me normal before." As Casmir climbed out, he realized the control room wasn't empty and he'd announced that to three puzzled workers. An open door also led to a busy utilitarian corridor that reminded him more of a military ship than the opulent palace.

"I'm an odd fellow, and my family is odd, so I assume everyone else is normal. Hullo, Chief Faramarz," Samar said to a dark-haired woman in a crisp uniform who rose and bowed to him. The two men working at computer stations did the same. "This is Professor Casmir Dabrowski," Samar added.

"The crusher maker?"

It appeared Casmir had a new job title he could put on his résumé back home.

"Yup. Father said to let him look at the slydar detector. He's going to see if he can boost its range to locate hidden ships."

"We would appreciate that," Faramarz said.

"Hell yes, we would," one of the men said. "We didn't detect that damn mercenary's warship until it was almost humping our asteroid."

"Language, Caveh." Faramarz pointed at Samar.

"Prince Samar doesn't care. He's not uptight like his sisters."

"It's true," Samar said, "though I am an enlightened soul on a spiritual journey and prefer language that brings us closer to embracing and understanding the cosmos and our place within it."

"See?" Faramarz swatted her colleague on the chest. "No humping."

Caveh looked more confused than enlightened.

"Is the slydar detector in here?" Casmir had to fight down a yawn. He'd left the party before it ended, though it had been far harder to slip away than he'd expected—he'd found himself unexpectedly well known and uncharacteristically popular. It was late, both by station time and ship time on the *Dragon,* but since he'd gotten that message from Qin about a possible mercenary raid on Stardust Palace, he didn't feel he could wait for morning to get started.

"It's that big ugly box with all the wires sticking out of it, Professor." Faramarz waved to a station behind the trapdoor.

"Oh." Casmir didn't like to apply subjective adjectives about aesthetics to machinery, but the box *was* ungainly. And hot-wired into an existing scanner console. That answered his question about whether it was hardware or software. It would have been nice to find a program he could easily copy, but he hadn't expected that.

The blocky housing hid its interior. Would these people allow him to open it up, take a few thousand pictures, and do his best to create a schematic?

"It's a prototype," Samar said. "I gather that's why it was acceptable that it arrived looking like a ten-year-old's science-fair project."

"It does work," Faramarz said, "so there's that."

"Mind if I take a look?" Casmir patted the tool satchel that he'd stopped by the *Dragon* to pick up.

"Just don't break anything. That's now the most expensive piece of equipment we've got."

Casmir nibbled on his lip. What would she consider *breaking*? He would have to open up the housing and start removing parts in order to find and record everything.

"If I give you a security tip about a possible threat, would you let me unplug it for an hour?" Casmir asked.

"Uh." Faramarz frowned at Samar.

"Would you give us the tip even if we said no?" Samar asked curiously.

"Yeah. It just came in—" Casmir waved to his chip, "—or I would have shared it earlier."

"You're not a very good negotiator."

"I know. But I'm on your station currently, so I'd like for it to be as prepared as possible in the event of hostilities."

"*What* hostilities?" Faramarz asked.

Casmir explained the information he'd gotten from Qin. "The source of this information is… unknown to me. This is one of those I-heard-it-from-a-friend-who-heard-it-from-a-friend instances, but perhaps if you have some intelligence analysts on the station, you could have them investigate."

"Intelligence analysts?" Faramarz looked at Samar again. "We have spies who specialize in corporate fact-finding and espionage among our Miners' Union competitors. I don't think we have agents placed among any mercenary organizations."

"A failing we shall have to remedy," Samar said.

"Before or after you find enlightenment among the cosmos?" Faramarz asked.

"When I said *we*, I meant some of my father's staff."

"Of course." Faramarz waved at Casmir. "Go ahead and poke around. I'm going to assume that the man who built those crushers won't break a box." Her mouth twisted, and Casmir wasn't sure she was that confident in her assessment.

"I'll be careful." He gave her a cheerful wave, pulled out a light and some tools, and set everything on the floor next to the device.

CHAPTER 16

OKU STAYED IN HER ROOM THE NEXT MORNING and didn't go to the Senate meeting. She had a slight headache from having her chip replaced, but that wasn't the reason. She didn't want to see Senator Boehm's empty seat, nor did she want to watch as the majority vote came down in favor of her father being given King's Authority.

She was composing a long message to Casmir, hoping the gate to System Stymphalia would be open soon and that it could get through. The last she'd heard, fast courier ships were still running the blockade periodically and delivering communications. They'd received news from the other systems, and Oku had learned that many delegates and Miners' Union leaders had been trapped in Stymphalia along with Casmir and the four Fleet warships. But like everyone else, she had no idea what was going on there. Nor had she been able to suss out where those delegates had been going and why. Kingdom news outlets were speculating that the rest of the systems were considering attacking System Lion while it was distracted and announcing it was a good thing that all those miscreants had been trapped.

Oku was decanting everything she knew in her message. What Casmir could do about it, she didn't know, but she needed someone she could talk to about everything that had been going on.

Her mother was too likely to share what she said with her father. And Finn was impossible, certainly not a confidant. She'd exchanged a few messages with her colleagues at the university, enough to learn that the majority of the populace had been living in fear for the last few weeks and were more relieved than upset that her father might soon be able to act without input—or interference—from the Senate.

More and more, she wondered if he'd set this all up, somehow causing the poor response of the Fleet to the invaders to ensure everything was scarier to the general populace than it should have been. Not just scary. *Deadly*. Many people had died in the bombings.

Oku didn't want to believe that her father would have set up such a scenario—maybe he'd only taken advantage of it after the fact—but with Boehm's mysterious death from "natural causes," she didn't know what to think.

Chasca, who'd been napping after her morning romp in the Citadel's garden, sat up and woofed. A few seconds later, a knock sounded at her door. Maddie was standing guard from inside Oku's room, and she opened it. A murmured discussion occurred in the doorway, and Oku couldn't see past her to tell who was out there. Maddie pointed at something in a covered tray and requested to see under the lid. Whatever it was must not have ruffled Maddie's honed bodyguard senses.

"Irena and Aleksy Dabrowski here to see you, Your Highness," she said.

Chasca hopped off the bed, wagging her tail, and slipped around Maddie to perform her own investigation of the tray.

"Come in, please." Oku got up from the desk, pulled Chasca back by the collar, and waved them in. "Stay," she told Chasca after waving her into a sit.

Her dog obeyed, but her tail swished back and forth on the old flagstone floor, and her gaze was focused on the tray.

"Princess Oku." Aleksy bowed as his wife came in after him. "We've been instructed to leave and go back to our home—we're relieved to do so—now that it's been a few days since any bombing ships have made it through to the surface and since…" He looked uncertainly at his wife.

"King Jager is all but assured to be issued King's Authority," she said, her face more irked than uncertain, but she glanced at the ceiling—suspecting monitoring cameras?—and didn't share her opinion on the matter.

"It's believed that he'll step forward now with the authority and power to finally defeat the blockaders and clean up the system." Aleksy spread his hands. "That's what they're telling the populace."

"I'm sure," Oku murmured, wishing she dared confess to them, but she was already taking a risk by sharing everything with Casmir. She hoped nobody could monitor the messages she sent and received on her new chip.

"But we wanted to thank you very much for coming to get us," Aleksy went on, "and our friends and family."

HOME FRONT

"I made rugelach for you." Irena came forward with the tray and set it on the desk. "Ingredients are understandably hard to come by right now, and the kitchen staff was skeptical about sharing their space with me, but they had the makings for these."

"Oh, thank you. Uhm, what are they?" Oku had never heard the term.

"Cookies." Irena pulled off the lid to reveal small rolled pastries. "Casmir likes them."

"Casmir likes *all* cookies," Aleksy said. "More apposite would be to find and share his favorite vegetable."

"He doesn't have a favorite vegetable."

"Exactly."

Irena elbowed him, and he grinned.

"There's also something here for Chasca." Irena picked up a blue paper bag with a curly paper ribbon tied around it. "It's a similar recipe to what I use in treats for our cat, all animal-friendly ingredients. I replaced the catnip with anise. I've read that dogs enjoy it."

"Thank you. That's very considerate." Oku was even more touched that she'd made something for Chasca than for her, though she wasn't sure whether it was the dog treats or cookies that had Chasca's attention.

"You're welcome," Irena said. "We thank you again for coming and offering us safety. I've heard from the neighbors that our building suffered a near miss and took some damage, but it could have been much worse, so we'll tidy up the best we can and move on with our lives and hope… our son comes home soon." Her smile turned sad and she offered her arms. "Is it permissible to hug princesses?"

"Of course."

Aleksy also came forward to give her a fatherly embrace.

"Be careful in the city," Oku told them. "Just in case…" She didn't finish the thought, that her father being given absolute power wouldn't necessarily mean all would be well and there wouldn't be more attacks on the city. She hoped it meant the end would come soon, but she had many concerns. Instead of sharing them, she made herself smile and repeated, "Just in case."

"Of course," Irena said.

"And we hope you'll also stay safe." Aleksy opened his mouth, as if to say more, but he closed it and shook his head.

For some reason, Boehm's warning—the last words he'd spoken to Oku—came to her mind.

They waved, and Maddie saw them out. Her broad shoulders slumped uncharacteristically when she stepped into the hall.

"Someone else is coming," Maddie warned Oku. "Maybe he's passing through and isn't here to see you." Maddie waited with the door open, frankly eyeing someone approaching, then looked in again. "No such luck."

Finn frowned at her as he walked in. "You've seen the news, Oku?"

"Which news?" She leaned her hip against the desk.

Finn came over to peer at the tray, then took one of the cookies.

Chasca put her paws up on the end of the desk. Before Oku could shoo her away and chastise her for climbing the furniture, she plucked up the blue bag of dog treats and hurried into the corner behind the bed. The bag didn't look to hold many treats or have any toxic parts, so Oku let her go. What did it say, she wondered, that Chasca had been worried that Finn would steal her treats?

"Help yourself," Oku said.

"Thanks." Finn chomped down the cookie and took a second before getting to the point. "You saw that Father's been given King's Authority, right?"

"I assumed his request for it would pass."

"It did, and he's summoning all of the remaining Fleet ships to Odin. He's going to take the launch loop up to orbit and join the *Space Hawk* to assume his role as supreme fleet commander. He's planning to bravely lead the ships to the gate and repel all the blockaders once and for all."

"That's good." Oku didn't know why he couldn't have done it a month ago—would the Senate truly have objected to that?—but if their father could finally end the blockade and drive all the invaders out of the system, she would be glad. She was long overdue to meet with Scholar Dubuque and Princess Tambora on Shango Habitat, not to mention getting back to work on her bee project. If the war ended, Casmir and Kim Sato could—she hoped—come home and they could all go back to finding a solution for natural—or robotic—pollination in the food-growing stations and habitats across the Twelve Systems.

"He's going to leave *me* in charge." Finn smirked smugly.

"Of the Citadel?"

"Of the planet." The smirk got smugger.

"I guess you'll get that chance to field all the paperwork that you wanted."

Finn's smirk faltered. Did he think she would be envious? Or angry because she wasn't being left in charge of *the planet*? It sounded like a nightmare, but she trusted her father's various aides would keep Finn from doing anything too stupid.

"In the past, Jorg was always in charge when Father was gone. Now's my chance to prove I'll be good at ruling. Will it bother you if he names me the second heir instead of you? Because I asked him to." Finn's eyes closed to slits as he watched for her reaction.

And if she objected, would she meet the same end that Boehm had?

"You know my interests and talents are in the sciences," she said. "I hope you study history and politics and learn how to do a good job."

"The sciences." He scoffed. "Planting weird things in dirt doesn't make you a scientist."

"My two advanced degrees in botany and biology do," she said, not able to hide her irritation at his dismissal. She truly didn't want political power, so she didn't care when he bugged her about that, but that he would belittle something she was good at… *That* was vexing.

"Yes, I'm sure you're quite the genius." Finn started toward the door but paused. "Once the Fleet is gone, I'm going to move us all back to the castle. There's no reason to stay hunkered down in here. Then you can get back to your planting in the greenhouse." He squinted over his shoulder at her.

What? Did he plan to arrange for an asteroid to fall on her greenhouse and *ensure* she wouldn't push to be the heir after Jorg? And what about Jorg? Did Finn have some plan to get rid of their older brother? He was only a few years older than Oku, so it wasn't likely that she *or* Finn would ever end up in charge of anything. By the time Jorg passed away, he'd have adult children of his own who would be next in line for the throne.

Maddie didn't move out of Finn's way, and his shoulder bumped hers. She was an inch taller than he and probably had more muscle, despite being thirty years older.

He glowered at her. "When I am in charge, you will learn your place, *bodyguard*."

He stalked out, slamming the door behind him.

"When he's temporarily in charge of the planet?" Maddie wondered. "Or is he hinting that he has more nefarious plans?"

"I think all of his plans are nefarious, but don't worry. He's not going to do anything to you. If the world goes mad, and he somehow ends up in charge of the Kingdom, we'll take a ship to another system and start a new life out there."

"*Out there* is full of weird people." Maddie looked more glum than excited by the prospect of leaving Odin.

"There are plenty of weird people here in Zamek City. But good people too." There was a heavy knot in Oku's stomach, and she didn't feel like eating, but she took one of the treats to be convivial and offered the tray to Maddie. "Cookie?"

"I was hoping Finn would accidentally eat the dog treats," Maddie admitted, taking a cookie.

"Chasca wasn't going to allow that to happen." Remembering that her dog had stolen the bag of treats, Oku went over to check on her.

Chasca was sitting daintily in a Sphinx pose, the neatly unwrapped bag and untied ribbon between her legs as she snuffled up the crumbs that were all that remained of the treats.

Oku recorded a few seconds of the scene to include with the rambling message of politics and war updates that she'd composed for Casmir. Mentioning that Chasca liked his mother's baking and was a fan of anise would be a cheerier way to end her note. She hoped System Stymphalia would fix its gate and it would reach him soon.

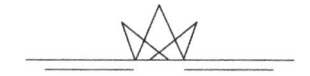

Yas was eating breakfast when Jess commed and asked him to come to the bridge with burn ointment. When he arrived, he found her on the deck on her back with her head and shoulders inside an open panel under a console. A big, ugly dented blue box rested beside her, wires snaking out of it. Nearby, Rache leaned his hip against the console, his arms folded over his chest.

"Someone called for a doctor?" Yas asked.

"Down here." Jess stuck her hand in the air in a semblance of a rude gesture, but that was probably accidental. Her fingers were splotchy and red and already starting to swell.

"Ouch." Yas sat on the deck next to her and opened his medical kit. "Do you want to come out of there?"

"I'm not sure it's allowed. I was told this is a priority."

HOME FRONT

Yas looked up at Rache, prepared to making biting comments about him working his people to the bone, but Rache flicked his fingers in what looked like permission for Jess to take a break. With her head under the console, she didn't see it, so Yas translated.

"He said you can come out, the better to receive and respond well to my excellent care."

"I'm positive he didn't say that."

"He flicked two fingers. I translated."

"With flair."

"Doctors are known for flair."

Jess scooted out, grimacing and refraining from putting her hand on the deck. "This is a piece of crap, sir."

"I understand it's an expensive prototype that costs more than a combat shuttle."

"That was before we blew it up."

"Blew it up?" Yas examined her hand with his diagnostic scanner, hoping it was a simple burn and the electricity hadn't done damage beyond the skin.

"After we sent the virus to the ships attacking the *Chivalrous*," Rache said, "three out of four lost power immediately. The fourth didn't take the bait, and we had to battle it straight out."

Yas nodded. He'd been in sickbay during the fight, but he'd caught the gist of it from others and from ship-wide announcements.

"*Somewhat* straight out," Rache corrected. "Because it had a slydar hull, there was a lot of guessing about where to shoot based on Amergin pinpointing their frantic comm signals. Interestingly, it not only had no trouble accurately shooting *us*, despite our lack of frantic comm calls, but it fired *first*. Well before we were close enough that their scanners should have detected us. Thus I guessed that they had one of these new slydar detectors. I sent a team out to scour the wreckage and find it." Rache extended his hand toward the box.

"We're so lucky," Jess told Yas.

"Is this the only spot you were burned?"

"Uh, here too, I think." She touched her shoulder. "It felt like the electricity shot through me. I grounded myself before opening the case, but it clearly wasn't sufficient."

"Let me scan the rest of your body. Electricity traveling through you can cause heart arrhythmia, seizures, and nerve injuries, among lesser maladies."

"Wonderful." Jess looked at Rache. "When do you need this online, sir? Do you have a specific target in mind that you need to detect?"

"I'd like to know where Prince Dubashi is, but more urgently, I want to find Kyla Moonrazor and convince her to open the gate for us. I believe she's the one responsible for closing it."

"Convince her with force?"

"Most likely. I doubt bribes and sweet-talking would work on her."

Yas almost pointed out that something along those lines had apparently worked for Casmir, but he doubted Rache wanted to be reminded of that, and Yas didn't truly know the details of Casmir's chats with the astroshaman leader. "If you open the gate, won't Dubashi also be able to get through and threaten your—the Kingdom home world with that bioweapon?"

Rache turned his masked gaze toward Yas. Maybe he hadn't appreciated that slip. But from what Yas had heard, Rache had dropped about twenty clues to his identity when he'd been facing off with Prince Jorg—rumors were flying around the ship like holiday fruitcakes in the Tiamat Station mail.

"That's why I want to know where he is," Rache said. "I only want to finish my mission, not see a population annihilated by a deadly virus."

His mission of annihilating one man with a dagger? Yas sighed and kept the thought to himself. He wouldn't convince Rache to abandon that mission any more than he'd been able to convince Rache to leave Jorg alone. He had a vendetta and wouldn't be stopped. What would happen when he completed his life's goal and King Jager was no more? Would Rache continue being a mercenary or would he retire? He was young for that, but if everything had been building to Jager's demise, what else would be left for him?

If he *did* retire, would he free Yas from his oath of serving him for five years? Maybe Yas could return home. Or, if they weren't all marked as criminals in the Kingdom, take a trip down to Odin with Jess to help her see the surgeon and physical therapist that Kim Sato had mentioned.

"What will the *Fedallah* do when these slydar detectors become widespread?" Jess asked.

She was back to fiddling with the device while Yas smeared BurnBetter over her hand. Fortunately, his diagnostic scanner did not pick up notable internal injuries.

HOME FRONT

"It'll depend on what we learn from studying this one," Rache said. "If it allows scanners to pick us up across the system as soon as we enter a gate, then our days of hiding and striking with the element of surprise will be over. If it only helps with short-range scans, our slydar hull would still be useful."

"Do you think the Kingdom has these scanners yet?" Yas wondered if Rache would be deterred from his mission if he believed the planet Odin was protected and he couldn't get close to Jager without being detected.

"No," Rache said. "If they did, they would have picked out the kamikaze bombers before they broke atmosphere on their planet. No matter how inept Jager is making his forces be right now."

Yas squinted at him, not understanding that sentence. "You think he's sabotaging the defense of his own system?"

"Likely so his people have losses and close calls and are scared. Scared enough to give him King's Authority."

"Which is what?"

"Similar to martial law on your Tiamat Station, but it extends beyond absolute control over homeland security. It extends his authority to include making policies and decisions for the entire Kingdom without needing the majority vote from the Senate."

Yas would have guessed that their king could already do whatever he wanted, but he supposed he'd heard of their Senate and that it acted as a counterbalance against the supreme power of the throne.

"I wouldn't be surprised if the announcement has already been made," Rache said, "and we just don't know about it because we're cut off."

"Not for long, sir." Jess plugged in a cable, and a display on a console above her head flared to life. "I think I've got this thing working."

"Good," Rache said. "Let's fly over to the gate and see if any astroshamans are lurking nearby. If we succeed in forcing Moonrazor to repair the gate, perhaps we shall be lauded as heroes."

Yas doubted that. Especially when the news made it to the Kingdom that Rache had killed the king's heir.

"Sir?" Amergin ambled over. "I've gathered the intel you wanted. The Kingdom *is* trying to get ahold of a slydar detector so they can take it home, replicate the technology, and install it all over their system. You won't guess who they've put in charge of getting one of the prototypes."

"The prototype Sultan Shayban has?" Rache asked. "I can guess."

"Your little nemesis Professor Dabrowski."

Nemesis? Or clone brother? Apparently, Amergin's intelligence gathering hadn't stumbled across that information yet.

"Someone's also been putting the word out," Amergin continued, "to all the mercenaries in the system that there are a lot of powerful people with money meeting at Stardust Palace right now. And that if enough of the mercenaries—and pirates, I'm assuming—work together, they might be able to collect some valuable hostages and loot."

"Interesting. What are those powerful people gathered to discuss and who is included?"

"A lot of the Miners' Union rulers and government delegates from several of the systems. They're discussing the gate—the one that was hauled off Xolas Moon—and the bits that have been bartered and traded around the Twelve Systems for lots of money these past weeks."

"Maybe we should go to Stardust Palace instead of the gate," Yas suggested, more because he wanted to steer Rache from his assassination path than because he wanted to force a fight between him and Casmir. "It sounds like a hotbed of activity."

"No. We will go to the gate, find Moonrazor, get her to fix it, and fly through. Better for us if events here have people distracted. There shouldn't be any slydar detectors in System Lion yet. We'll bypass the blockade and complete our mission."

Rache strode off the bridge.

CHAPTER 17

HER SECOND DAY ON THE STATION, KIM APPROACHED the mycology laboratory where she'd first met Scholar Natasha Sunflyer. She hadn't been at work the night before when Kim had come by with her mother. Perhaps not surprising, given the late hour. Since Kim hadn't known where her residence was, she'd ended up having a cup of tea with her mother at one of the cafes around the station and getting updates on the gate research and archaeological opportunities in System Hydra. Her mother had suggested again that Kim should come live there and give up on staying anywhere in the backward Kingdom.

The thought of getting to spend more time with and getting to know her mother better wasn't unappealing, but being driven away from her home was. The longer she'd been away, the more she was having nostalgic thoughts about her little house back in Zamek City, enjoying coffee on the patio in the morning with squirrels running through the branches overhead, then going in to the laboratory where she liked her work and her colleagues appreciated her. The time away had made her realize that she had been content with her life back home. She'd found a place to fit in—something that had never been easy for her—and realized she should have taken the time to appreciate it more. It was far better than being dragged around the galaxy against her wishes, crossing paths with a man she could never truly have a relationship with.

"Then why do I keep thinking about him?" she murmured to herself.

"Did you utter a command, Kim Sato?" the crusher that had been trailing her around the station asked. Reuben, she reminded herself, though she couldn't tell any of them apart.

"No. Just talking to myself. It's a human thing."

"I am learning about human things, such as gambling and playing. It is desirable to win dried currants in games of chance."

"So I've heard." Kim waved at the door sensor. "Did you win any?"

"I did not. I am not lucky."

"Casmir told you that?" She had a hard time imagining him being anything but encouraging to his robotic children.

"The others heard him discussing luck with another and informed me that I am not lucky because I did not win any currants and lost all the ones I started with. It is a game of chance, as I told them, but several suggested the human superstition of luck is worth considering. I disagree."

"Good. You should."

The door opened, and Natasha stood inside. She started when she saw the hulking crusher behind Kim's shoulder.

"My new bodyguard," Kim explained.

"He's… ah, not as photogenic as the knight was. Sir Asger."

"I don't think Casmir was worried about aesthetics when he designed them. If anything, they're supposed to be intimidating and scary."

"I look in the mirror at my own face every morning, so I suppose I should be used to that." Natasha waved to her bulbous forehead and larger than typical skull with fingers too long to appear natural. Her long hair swept artfully around her head but didn't hide the size. She'd said her father had genetically engineered her and her sisters for superior intelligence.

"Your face is perfectly fine and presumably functional." Kim wasn't good at giving compliments. Maybe she should have said Natasha was beautiful? Such observations struck her as pointless, but she'd seen people glow in appreciation at receiving them. But Kim's attempted compliments rarely had that effect. Maybe it was best to get to the point of her visit. "Do you have a moment?"

"Yes. Is this about my father? I heard that Captain Lopez's ship had returned, but she hasn't contacted me."

Kim took a deep breath. "No. I was the one to go into Prince Dubashi's moon base, and I know most about the incident, so I volunteered to come speak with you. I regret to inform you that your father is dead."

Even though she was not good at reading people's thoughts and emotions, even she could interpret the meaning of the deep slump to

HOME FRONT

Natasha's shoulders as she turned away. Kim made herself detail what she knew of how Dubashi had kidnapped Serg Sunflyer, forced him to build a bioweapon, and how her father had taken his own life in the end.

"He didn't want to have created something that would be used to kill millions. Potentially billions." Kim didn't point out that the suicide hadn't done anything to keep the virus from being completed and loaded into rockets for deployment. She wished the senior Sunflyer had suffered his bout of morality *before* finishing the project.

"Thank you for bringing me this news in person. Will you excuse me for a minute? I need to tell Sultan Shayban and Princess Nalini and Prince Samar. They've been kind to us, and I know they'll want to know." Natasha didn't leave the room, but she sat down at a nearby console and composed a chip-to-chip message.

Kim didn't know if she should stay or go. What was the protocol for this? She hoped to be granted permission to look over any work her father had possibly done here that might give her insight into his mind and help her with creating an antiviral, but it seemed inconsiderate to make the request after delivering news of his death. What was the appropriate period of time to wait? And why did every other human seem so much better at intuitively knowing these things?

A message came in on her own chip.

Her insides tightened. It was from Rache.

Her first instinct was to deny it—or even remove his permission to contact her—but that was because it had gotten her in trouble on the *Osprey*. The Kingdom warships weren't nearby and nobody should be monitoring her messages now. The tightness unfurled a bit as she opened the message, realizing that, for the time being, she could talk to anyone she pleased. Including Rache.

Maybe she *shouldn't* talk to him, but she read the message nonetheless.

Greetings, Kim.

I understand you are on Stardust Palace Station currently, so I hope my contact will not get you in trouble. I wish to deliver a warning. I've learned that numerous mercenaries are being ushered to possibly attack the station. It might behoove you and Casmir to extricate yourselves from that asteroid before they arrive. I do not know who is behind rounding them up—I have my Intelligence officer looking into it—but

I suspect Dubashi again. He wasn't able to win those mercenaries over with money, but perhaps by implying they could gain wealth by acquiring the spoils of others, he hopes to manipulate them. Judging by the ships on a heading for that station, it's working. The question is what does Dubashi hope to gain? To repair the gate and slip out of the system while others are engaged there? To strike a blow against his nemesis, Shayban? He did not invite me to participate—I suspect he learned that I was behind destroying the ships he sent after the Chivalrous. *I do not know. I merely send warning.*

The note didn't say anything specifically about Jorg. Not that she had expected him to gloat or rub it in. Rache had known she didn't approve of his mission.

Thank you for the warning. We heard something similar from a contact of Qin's, but I will let Casmir and the others know that it is a certainty. She wondered if Shayban's people knew. With so many ships coming and going at the busy station, they might not have thought much of mercenaries heading this way, especially if they were several days out. Or they might know about the possibly hostile ships but hadn't wanted to announce anything. After all, a mass exodus would be chaotic and bad for business. *Are you in the area? I don't expect you want to get involved in a battle between mercenaries and a space station, but…*

But what? She wasn't sure why she'd even asked if he was close. There was no reason for them to work together again. Rache wished to serve Dubashi, and Kim and Casmir and the others wanted to *stop* Dubashi.

Casmir has his crushers, and I believe he promised you one. Or was it two? You'll have to let us know where to have them delivered. Kim rolled her eyes at herself. Why hadn't she said she was worried about him, and the choices he was making, and was wondering what he was up to?

Minutes passed as she waited for a reply—the *Fedallah* probably wasn't anywhere near the station now—and Natasha stirred.

"The sultan and Nalini are on their way to see me," she said.

"Do you want me to leave?"

"No. I'm sure they won't mind if you're here." Natasha glanced at Reuben and managed a wan smile. "I hear Sultan Shayban likes crushers, so he won't even mind your bodyguard."

"A bodyguard should be expected in the company of such an important scientific researcher as Scholar Sato," Reuben said.

HOME FRONT

"Please tell me Casmir didn't program you to say things like that," Kim murmured.

The crusher's head tilted in a human-like gesture. "He did not, but since I have been assigned to protect you, and I am a powerful and sophisticated being, I must assume your importance. A lesser individual would not receive a crusher bodyguard."

Kim looked at Natasha, feeling vaguely that she should apologize for this arrogance—and that Reuben was joining Zee in developing a personality. Maybe it started happening after someone named them.

"Seems logical to me," was all Natasha said.

I hope you'll forgive me, Rache's reply came in, *for not telling you exactly where I am. I do not believe that you or Casmir would approve of my current goal. I do have a post office box in System Cerberus that I can give you if he wants to ship a crusher to me, but it's possible the postmaster would be alarmed at the arrival of such a large and deadly package. Though he does receive all manner of packages for pirates, mercenaries, bounty hunters, and the like, so it's possible a crusher wouldn't even be the most disturbing thing to arrive that week.*

The fact that he didn't want to tell her where he was bothered her. He couldn't go after Jager until the gate was fixed, so that couldn't be what he was up to. What if he was trying to find a way to *open* the gate? Did he know where Kyla Moonrazor was?

Sultan Shayban and Princess Nalini came in with Tristan tagging along. He'd depilated his beard scruff and was finally in new clothing, and he looked much better than he had since he'd stowed away on Rache's ship.

Nalini came up and gave Natasha a hug while Shayban patted her on the shoulder. Tristan, who hadn't lived here long enough to know her that well, stopped beside Kim.

"I hear trouble may be coming to Stardust Palace," he murmured. "Not Rache, I trust."

"You mean the mercenaries? Word gets out. No, I think he's…" She only had a hypothesis on what he was doing, so maybe she shouldn't share it with others yet. "Elsewhere."

"Harrying the Kingdom ships?"

"That's a possibility." As plausible as her possibility, she supposed.

"This is heinous news," Shayban announced, lowering his hand and turning from Natasha. "I want Dubashi dead. I'm tired of him interfering with my business, my family, and my people." He squinted at Kim and also included Tristan in the look. "Let us go speak with Professor Dabrowski. I want to know what resources I can lend him to help him capture Dubashi once and for all."

"Has he made progress on, ah, extending the range of your slydar detector?" Kim hadn't heard from Casmir since the previous night. She assumed he was working on copying the detector rather than extending its range. It was also possible he had fallen asleep under a console and not made much progress either way.

"We'll go find out. My son has been helping him."

"Samar has been helping with engineering and electronics?" Nalini asked, an arm still around Natasha's shoulders.

"He has been ordering the staff to bring Dabrowski supplies and holding his tools."

"Well, that's more useful than he usually is." Nalini smiled. It sounded like a friendly dig between siblings rather than a genuine insult.

As the group headed for the exit—it looked like they would *all* go see Casmir—Kim lifted a finger, realizing she might lose her opportunity to study the senior Sunflyer's work.

"I'm sorry to bother you about this now," Kim said, "but Scholar Sunflyer, I was wondering if I could see your father's work and what he was researching here. It's possible he relied upon research he did in the past when he worked in System Cerberus, and I thought he might have saved copies here. In case we don't catch up with Dubashi in time, I'm gathering everything I can to send back to my people so they can work on a vaccine and antiviral agents."

"You will have everything you need," Shayban said in his booming voice before Natasha could open her mouth. "That virus could be a threat to us all, not only the Kingdom. Scholar, please assist her. Nalini, Tristan, come. Let us confer with the professor."

Kim wondered how Casmir felt about being someone that people wanted to confer with on martial matters. Puzzled, she suspected.

"I'll show you where he worked and open his files," Natasha said when the others were gone. "I may be able to help too, as I'm familiar with some of his work, even if viruses aren't my specialty."

"Thank you. But I'll understand if you'd rather take some time off."

"I'd rather work than think about things." Natasha grimaced. "Or compose the messages to my sisters that I'll have to send off. I've been hesitant to tell them anything prematurely, but two of them have sent videos this week, wondering why they can't reach Father." She shook her head. "Let's work."

Kim nodded and followed her into the bowels of the laboratory.

Realizing she hadn't responded to Rache's last message, she sent:

How much do we have to come up with to keep you from finding a way to open that gate? I have savings in my account back home, and Casmir keeps collectors' coins and his other valuables in a box under his bed.

He hadn't said he was trying to open the gate, and she was only guessing, but maybe he would give her the information.

I find it troubling that you can guess my intentions so easily, came the reply a couple of minutes later. *What kinds of valuables are* in the box? *I don't work for comic books.*

I believe his gold-plated membership pen to the Justice Dealers Starflyer League is among the valuables. And some of the comic books are signed.

She could almost hear Rache sigh from across the system.

If I succeed in opening the gate, I'll do my best to make sure Dubashi can't come through after me. And if he does... I'll keep him from deploying the rockets.

Kim's shoulders sank. He was doing exactly what she feared, trying to get the gate open. Probably trying to find and strong-arm Kyla Moonrazor.

I hope you can, was all she sent back.

After a day docked in Stardust Palace Station's bay, Bonita was growing restless. She was leaning against the jamb of the cargo hold door, trading barbs with Viggo and gazing out at the other ships on landing pads.

Rumors abounded that a mercenary fleet was flying toward the station, perhaps to interrupt the talks now going on in some atrium near the core, perhaps to prey on all the wealthy people and ships here. Bonita was rethinking her decision to linger in the area.

Clanks, grunts, and taunts emanated from the cargo hold behind her. Bjarke, Asger, and Qin were training together. Bonita was pleased that Bjarke seemed to accept Qin and her genetically modified differences. He might not be delighted that his son was sleeping with her—she'd caught him frowning a few times when they'd held hands or touched in his presence—but that was a less extreme reaction than she would have expected, given his roots. Maybe his years undercover in other systems had rubbed the edges off his Kingdom xenophobia.

"There are six mercenary ships less than a day away," Viggo told Bonita. "If we do not depart soon, we will be trapped here."

"I know. What about the Druckers? Are they still salvaging those destroyed ships?"

"They've finished and are sauntering this way, but they're moving extremely slowly."

"Still planning to let others go in first, eh?"

If they were going to try their bait-and-trap scheme to free Qin's sisters, this might be a good time. More than that, it might be their *only* opportunity.

A handful of delegates or whatever they called themselves ambled into the ship bay and headed toward the *Dragon*. Bonita didn't recognize any of them except for a blonde woman weighed down by diamond jewelry. Bonita hadn't spoken to her but knew she was docked at the landing pad adjacent to theirs.

The group of three men and three women headed straight to the *Dragon's* cargo ramp.

"Bjarke," Bonita called back. "We've got company. I doubt they're here for me."

She wasn't sure they were here for Bjarke either, but Bonita couldn't guess who else they would want.

"Hello, Captain Lopez, is it?" a stout, dark-skinned man in a flamboyant red and blue wrap asked. A mechanical parrot rode on his shoulder.

"Yup," Bonita said.

"I am Jemadari from Yemaya's Asteroid Belt. Have you by chance seen Professor Dabrowski?" He looked at Bjarke as he walked up to Bonita's side. "He flew in with you, did he not? After seeing him at the sultan's party the other night, we expected he would be at the talks."

Bonita was fairly certain Casmir was busy talking to a computer console somewhere.

HOME FRONT

"Are roboticists common at government talks?" she asked.

"He is more than that, you must surely agree. He has inside information on the new gate and may know better than we precisely who has gathered which pieces." Jemadari looked around at his comrades.

"Specifically, he might be able to verify our suspicions about which pieces the Kingdom got," the blonde woman said, looking Bjarke up and down while smiling at him.

"Why do you care which pieces the Kingdom got?" Bjarke asked, his face hard.

The members of the group exchanged looks with each other. "We're interested in negotiating for them."

Bjarke snorted. "King Jager won't give them up. He only got a handful of the five-hundred-odd pieces. He wanted them all."

"Well, he's not here. And others from the Kingdom who have proven more interested in furthering the goals and good of mankind as a whole are."

"Is that Dabrowski?" Bjarke asked flatly. "He's nobody in the Kingdom. And the gate pieces aren't here either, so I don't know what you think you stand to gain."

"They're not?" Jemadari shifted, and the faux parrot ruffled its feathers. "We had thought—were the pieces not originally recovered by your warships? The very warships that then traveled to this system to meet with your prince? And my condolences on his death. I just heard."

He sounded vaguely sincere. Surprising.

"They're not here," Bjarke repeated without expounding.

"So one would have to go to the Kingdom to retrieve them." Jemadari looked at the others again. None of them appeared pleased. "They may already be locked away in some obscure and heavily secured warehouse."

The blonde twitched a shoulder. "We assumed we would have to negotiate for them regardless. You and your tiny militia weren't planning to take them by force, I assume."

"Our militia is substantial, thank you very much."

"Why do the Kingdom's gate pieces matter?" Bjarke asked.

Jemadari opened his mouth, but another man gripped his shoulder. "They don't. We simply had hoped to get as many together as possible for study. Our chances of replicating the gate go up if we have more pieces."

"So they're not homogeneous?" Bjarke asked.

The man who'd interrupted hesitated.

The blonde rolled her eyes. "No, they're not. Perhaps we'll speak with Professor Dabrowski about it all. Do you know where he is?"

Bonita opened her mouth to tell them to find him themselves if they wanted him, but Bjarke lifted a hand.

"Queen Dya," he said, "it sounds like you need a favor. As it so happens, you may be in a position to help us in turn."

Her eyes closed to slits. "With what?"

Bjarke looked to Asger and Qin, who'd broken off and also come over to see what was going on.

"We'd like to borrow your ship." Bjarke pointed to the luxury yacht, its encrusted hull glittering under the bay's lights.

"My yacht!" The blonde—Dya—rocked back, touching a hand to her chest—or maybe the several gold-and-diamond necklaces draped over it. "You have a ship, however ancient and bug-infested. What could you possibly need with mine?"

"*Bug-infested?*" came Viggo's voice from the nearest speaker. "There is not a bug, insect, or arachnid anywhere within the confines of my hull. I employ a fleet of robotic vacuums and various sanitary measures to ensure my ship is clean. You could polish the entire cargo hold deck with your tongue and not pick up a single germ."

"Ew, Viggo," Bonita said.

"I am offended and affronted."

"We have some unfinished business with some pirates in this system," Bjarke said, ignoring Viggo's outburst. "We want to lure them into attempting to board a ship that will, unbeknownst to them, be full of knights—" he touched his chest and waved at Asger, "—genetically modified warrior women—" a wave toward Qin, "—and crushers."

Bonita wondered if two knights and one warrior woman qualified as *full of*, but she merely watched the exchange. This was what they had wanted. A chance to help Qin, and if it could be done without risking the *Dragon*, she would be pleased. But she couldn't imagine this supposed queen handing over a ship worth tens of millions of Union dollars.

"You want to use my ship as a Trojan Horse?" Dya demanded.

"Exactly." Bjarke smiled and bowed. "Your command of Old Earth history is excellent."

Dya might have been checking him out earlier—she'd also given Asger a long examination when he'd come over—but she looked too smart, and was likely far too old, to be taken in by a handsome smile.

HOME FRONT

"Maybe we could just borrow some of her shiny hull bits," Bonita said, "and stick them on my ship to make it look modern and expensive."

Dya gave her a scathing look. "Those are laboratory-grown adamantem potentia crystals. They have a purpose. They deflect radiation away from the hull of the ship. They're cutting edge."

"And shiny."

"I'm not sure you're helping," Bjarke murmured.

"She wasn't going to give you her ship anyway."

"That is correct. I'd possibly give him a ride in it if he was willing to put that tongue to use." Dya's gaze flicked toward Asger. "If either of them were. Or both."

"Bjarke's tongue is typically only used to deliver biting sarcasm." Bonita had recently learned it had a few other uses, but she didn't want to encourage this self-proclaimed queen.

"Perhaps she wants him to use it to polish her deck," Qin said.

"I do not recommend it," Viggo said. "I am positive the deck on that ship would not be as germ-free as mine."

"You're an odd lot of people, aren't you?" Dya asked.

"If we agreed to visit you on your yacht, would you also allow our crushers to visit and be willing to set a course past the Druckers' noses?" Bjarke asked.

Bonita elbowed him. The rest of the delegates had started muttering at this deviation from the gate topic, and they drifted away, speaking and gesturing among themselves.

Dya tapped her chin thoughtfully. "The Druckers have committed crimes in my territory in System Hind, including robbing from my automated mining ships. I hadn't realized they were trapped in this system."

"Two of their ships are," Qin said, a hint of hope brightening her eyes.

Bonita wanted to tell her to quash that hope, that they couldn't trust this Dya even if she changed her mind about working with them, but maybe she would be proven wrong. If Dya hated the Druckers, might she consider this?

"If you attacked two of them," Dya said, "and somehow managed to take them over or destroy them, you'd have to deal with the other three as soon as the gate is fixed. The brothers are vengeful."

"So we've heard," Bonita said.

"They would have to come to the Kingdom to challenge us," Asger said. "When the gate is operating again, we'll return home, stop the war, and once again have our full fleet and resources in System Lion."

"Pirates haven't dared encroach in System Lion for centuries," Bjarke added. "And it would be our problem to deal with, not yours. We could let it be known that we forced or tricked you into lending us your ship. No fault would fall on you."

"Sure it wouldn't." Dya snorted. "But I do not fear reprisal from scruffy pirates. I am merely debating the odds of you being successful. The *Congo* has some weaponry, but it is not designed to take on warships. Will your Kingdom Fleet help? I've noticed they have ships lurking by the gate."

"We can handle the pirates without help," Bjarke said.

"We'll have allies on the inside," Qin added.

Bonita wondered if even Qin's sisters and Casmir's crushers would be enough against two warships full of hundreds of pirates—hundreds of fighters—each.

After some consideration, Dya shook her head. "No. It's too risky. As much as I'd like to see the Druckers snubbed, or outright destroyed, my yacht could be damaged if not completely destroyed. I've not risen to this position by throwing away resources. But you knights and your tongues are still welcome to come over and visit for a couple of hours." She blew Bjarke and Asger kisses, ignoring Qin and Bonita, and sashayed back to her ship.

"I don't like that woman," Qin said.

"This being a civilized station," Bonita said, "I don't suppose we can kidnap her, lock her in a cabinet, and *take* her ship."

"That may be frowned upon," Asger said.

All except one of the delegates wandered off, Jemadari and his robo-parrot. He walked up the ramp to face them, and Bonita expected more questions about gate pieces or Casmir's whereabouts.

"My ship isn't as swanky as Dya's, but it's less than a year old and has the latest engines and equipment. I would consider letting you use it if you really could get rid of those pirates. They've also robbed from me before." Jemadari pointed across the bay at an elegant black yacht with aesthetically appealing curves. "I'd been thinking of leaving before the talks are over anyway. Rumors abound about mercenaries on the way to attack the station. Many of the others are convinced they'll be safe here under the asteroid's surface-mounted weapons. I'm not so sure. Mercenaries don't start fights unless they believe they can win."

"Do you have room for knights and crushers aboard that ship?" Asger asked.

"Even a fake cargo if you think they'll run scans before attacking."

"What would you want in return?" Bonita found the man's altruism suspicious.

"Besides the destruction of pirates that have vexed my people in the not-so-distant past?" Jemadari shrugged. "Protection as I fly from the station and to the gate. It's not safe to travel alone out there with all those mercenaries in the area. Your allies are the Kingdom warships, yes?"

Bonita started to say they weren't *her* allies, but Asger and Bjarke both said, "Yes."

"They will come to help if we get in over our heads." Jemadari smiled. His bird squawked semi-realistically, and he patted it on the wing. "Shall we make plans?"

"Come on in." Bjarke waved him into the cargo hold and led the way toward the ladder up to the lounge.

"Should we trust this guy?" Qin asked.

Bonita shook her head. Trusting any stranger, especially some wealthy Miners' Union stranger, was never a good idea.

"We'll look him up," Asger said. "I'm also going to let Casmir know we're going to need some crushers."

"Maybe you should let him know that half of the station is looking for him too," Bonita said.

"He may not *want* to know that." Asger spread his hand. "What's he supposed to do to help people get the gate pieces from the Kingdom anyway?"

"Maybe they think that since he facilitated the original free-for-all, he's going to be on their side."

"I don't know, but I better let Ishii know about this development. And that the Kingdom may have a bargaining chip. There must be something special about one of the pieces they snagged." Asger scratched his jaw. "I'll let Casmir know about it too. He's more likely than Ishii or Romano to use the information to his advantage in a negotiation."

Asger headed after Bjarke and Jemadari.

"When did Casmir become such a linchpin to everything going on in the systems?" Qin asked when she and Bonita were alone.

"I don't know, but it's probably going to get him killed."

Qin shook her head sadly. "I hope not."

CHAPTER 18

WE NEED SOME OF THE CRUSHERS, CASMIR, ASGER messaged from wherever he was on the station. *A couple dozen if you can swing it.* Casmir, his mind and his eyes bleary after being up all night and morning, couldn't remember why Asger might need crushers. He was lying on his back under a console in the station's control room, using his contact camera to take photos of all the circuitry in the slydar detector. He'd already spent hours examining and copying the software program. Soon, he should have enough data to recreate the slydar detector, but to do so, he would need access to a manufacturing facility again. And he hadn't admitted to Shayban what he was really doing here.

Are Viggo's robot vacuums not sufficient for keeping the Dragon in good shape?

They're fine. I understand you can lick the decks with your tongue if you want.

Why would you want to?

Maybe they're cherry flavored. I don't know. Casmir, I'm serious. We've got a nice ship that we can use for bait against the Druckers. We have to act soon if we want a shot to get Qin's sisters out.

Ah! Excellent. Who's going? I'm still working on the slydar detector, and I think Kim is working on an antiviral.

I think we'll be all right without you two great warriors.

I'm insulted that you don't recognize our value in combat, but yes, good. You and Bjarke are going?

That's the plan. With as many crushers as we can get. By the way, has the sultan actually said you can take them? I heard they were entertaining the guests at his party last night.

They'll come. I better not take them all though. I've heard from numerous people now about mercenaries heading this way.

Everybody has heard, Asger messaged. *A couple of ships in this bay are taking off, fleeing before the storm arrives, and I suspect more will follow.*

At this point, they might be better off staying. The mercenaries are coming in from a number of directions and could potentially pick off lone targets.

I think that's why this Jemadari guy is willing to give us a ride for our ruse. If someone gets aggressive and boards his ship, he'll have crushers to throw at them.

I'll send three dozen crushers. Is that Jemadari Sayyid? The Miners' Union leader from System Boar? He's been here representing not only his own people's interests but those of two governments and a university in his system. I met him at the party.

Does that mean I should kiss his ass?

I guess if you'd lick the deck of a cargo hold, a butt cheek isn't much different.

Trust me, it's a lot different. Jemadari didn't give his surname or a title. Does that mean he's less pompous than the others?

Maybe. Casmir sent an order to the crushers still in the *Dragon* and another dozen in the sultan's manufacturing facility. He would have to warn Shayban that he was deploying some of them. And make sure the sultan truly intended to let him have the rest of the crushers without a fuss.

"Is he sleeping?" a familiar voice asked from the middle of the control room.

"I don't think so, Father." That was Samar. "I've been giving him what he needs to stay awake and work all night."

"Caffeine tablets? Heart Jolt pills?"

"Candy and fizzop, which I believe is liquid, carbonated candy. See the cans and wrappers?"

"I assumed someone had mistaken that corner for a dumpster."

"No, that's his work area. You can see some tools amid the refuse."

Casmir scooted out from under the console, managing to not clunk his head on the edge. He staggered to his feet and bowed. Princess Nalini and Tristan were there as well as Samar, Shayban, and the staff working in the room—the shift had changed again and new people had come in. Was this the third group of faces he'd seen since the night before? Yes.

HOME FRONT

More people filed in after Shayban and his family, and they peered curiously at Casmir. He recognized some of the faces from the party.

"Hello?" He smoothed his rumpled shirt the best he could and grimaced when he noticed a grape fizzop stain on his chest. Maybe he should have kept wearing the self-cleaning and wrinkle-proof SmartWeave galaxy suit. Feeling self-conscious at all the gazes turned toward him, he was compelled to blurt an honest, "I haven't figured out how to extend the range of the slydar detector yet. I've mostly been studying it to see how it works, and I was thinking that it would be helpful to be able to replicate it." For the good of the Kingdom. But he caught himself before saying that. What came out instead was, "If every ship here could be outfitted with one, it would be a wonderful start toward making piracy in the Twelve Systems far more difficult for the nefarious types hiding behind camouflaged hulls. And if we could make our own, there wouldn't be any need for anyone else to pay what I assume was an exorbitant price for this unit, Sultan."

Was he babbling? Did they believe his intentions were altruistic? He *did* think slydar detectors for all was a good idea, even if it hadn't come to mind more than twenty seconds ago.

Shayban had grown hard to read. Nalini's beautiful brow had a faint crease to it.

"I would *love* a slydar detector," one of the delegates said. "Sultan, did you plan this from the beginning? I'd pay you a fair price, of course, for such a device, but what a relief it would be to know there were no pirates lurking between here and the gate. And on all future travels."

"It wasn't my plan," Shayban said, "but… I believe it is a good one." He nodded at Casmir, though something about his expression—his forehead was crinkled similar to his daughter's—suggested this wasn't what he'd wanted.

"I admit that the Kingdom has interest in such technology too," Casmir heard himself confessing. He was a horrible secret agent.

"Ah. I am not surprised." Shayban's brow smoothed, but his eyes grew shrewd as he tapped his chin. "But they will pay four times as much for theirs, I believe."

His guests chuckled. Casmir didn't point out that he'd downloaded the software and enough information to replicate the machines for his own people.

"Perhaps I could once again use your manufacturing facilities," Casmir said, "to start building some for your guests."

"There's something I want you to do first," Shayban said. "I want Dubashi dead. Or I want him here in front of me so I can strangle him." He lifted his hands, demonstrating how the strangling would work. "He's been a comet threatening to crash into us for decades, and he was responsible for Scholar Sunflyer's death, as well as that attempt to steal ships from me, the one you thwarted."

Casmir nodded, though Zee had thwarted it, and only because Casmir had asked him to break him and Kim out of the detention area. "You want me to go after him again? Unfortunately, I don't have the use of the Kingdom's ships, and I'm not sure how—"

"You have the use of *my* ships. I can't give you my entire fleet, since there's a mercenary threat on the horizon, and we'll need some ships to defend this station, but I'll give you ten."

"I'll send my second ship with him if it'll get rid of Dubashi," one of the delegates offered. "Especially if those who help will be first on the list to receive a slydar detector."

Three other delegates chimed in with offers to help. One man had brought four vessels to the talks and promised to lend two to the effort.

"Who will command this fleet that we're forming?" one delegate asked.

"Professor Dabrowski," Shayban said firmly.

Casmir lifted a finger, intending to suggest that perhaps the ships should be attached to the Kingdom fleet under Ishii's command, but was Ishii in command? He'd mentioned before that one of the other captains was his senior, and then there was Ambassador Romano to deal with.

"Are professors allowed to command fleets?" One of the delegates looked Casmir up and down, his gaze lingering on the fizzop stain.

Casmir dropped his hand over it.

"You can call him an admiral if you want," Shayban said. "Acting admiral. But I'm not putting any government bureaucrat in charge, and I'm certainly not relying on those meandering Kingdom warships to handle it. Professor Dabrowski was responsible for the destruction of Dubashi's base, and I'm positive he's the man to finish off this plague on the Twelve Systems." Shayban looked at his family and the delegates. "I'd bet a ship of the best iridium ore that Dubashi is behind the mercenary fleets flying to my station. I bet he promised them they could loot your ships while he slips in and steals mine. Well, that's not going to happen. Professor Dabrowski is going to hunt him down first."

"I…" Casmir wanted to object to everything from being called an acting admiral—how could a civilian even receive a military title?—to being put in command of a fleet, but having this many ships might allow him to find Dubashi more easily. It wasn't as if the *Dragon* was going to be able to hunt down the prince. And was it possible that if he completed this task for the sultan—a task the Kingdom also wanted completed—that the ship owners might be grateful enough that he could borrow the fleet long enough to fly to System Lion? These ships, combined with what Ishii and Romano were scraping together, might be enough to convince the blockaders to flee without a fight. "We won't have much luck finding him unless I can get slydar detectors on every ship."

"There won't be time for that," Shayban said, "unless you can get it done before the mercenaries arrive."

Which was in less than a day. "Ah, I can maybe have one done by then."

"If the fleet had even one, that would be an advantage," Shayban said.

"We *all* get them eventually, right?" a delegate asked.

"You all get to be on the top of the list of people who will be able to *buy* them once the professor makes more." Shayban patted Casmir on the shoulder. This might not have been his plan, but he was willing to capitalize on it.

"Whatever it takes to get one," the delegate said.

"You better get started promptly, Professor. Days pass quickly." Shayban turned the pat into a shoulder squeeze.

"I've… heard that."

Casmir had a grasp of how the slydar detector worked, but could he truly build one from scratch that quickly? He had better. He couldn't imagine how they would find Dubashi without a working slydar detector.

"Let's let the man work." Shayban lifted his hands. "And start prepping the ships you'll send after Dubashi. I'll do the same. Samar, see to it that the professor doesn't run out of snacks."

Samar's expression was wry as he looked at Casmir's pile of cans and wrappers, but all he said was, "Of course, Father."

Tristan and Nalini lingered after Shayban and the delegates filtered out.

"Do you need help, Casmir?" Tristan asked. "You look daunted."

"Do I? Huh."

Nalini poked Tristan in the shoulder. "I think you're supposed to call him Acting Admiral Casmir now."

Tristan eyed Casmir. "I think he'd prefer it if I didn't."

Casmir nodded in ardent agreement. "What kind of help? I could definitely use some engineering assistants. And I'll take your math expertise if you want to lend it."

"I'm not sure it would be helpful with software development or whatever you need for that thing, but if you want it, it's yours. I also thought I could go along with you and your new fleet as a representative of the sultan, assuming he'll approve. If I'm with you, his ship commanders might give you less lip. Asger didn't take my pertundo, so I could wave it menacingly if need be."

"You're planning on leaving again?" Nalini frowned at him. "Without me?"

"I appreciate the offer, but you don't have to come, Tristan," Casmir said. "I'll have Zee and the crushers I don't send with Asger. They can loom menacingly if needed."

"Hm, I thought it might be helpful to have someone who's almost in the sultan's family along in case you run into any red tape." Tristan held Nalini's hand. Did that mean he'd proposed? Or she had?

"*Or*," Nalini said before Casmir could figure out if he should offer congratulations, "you could take a current and blood family member along." Nalini patted Tristan's hand and squinted at Casmir. "If you end up chasing Dubashi through the gate and into a different system—or into your home system—it might be useful for you to have someone who can speak as his representative." She nodded, as if she'd decided without anyone else's input. "I'll make sure my father is all right with it."

Tristan scratched his jaw as she walked out.

"Did you expect her to throw herself into danger?" Casmir asked.

"It's not surprising. I was just debating if she has an ulterior motive. She's not a student of war tactics and strategy, as far as I know."

"Maybe she wants to come along this time to try to keep you safe."

"I don't think that's it," Tristan said. "She once mentioned being interested in real-estate development deals in the Kingdom. Maybe she thinks you'll end up back in System Lion and that there'll be opportunities there in the aftermath of the war. I once offered to show her the neighborhood where I grew up."

HOME FRONT

"Nice place?"

"Oh, no. It's a hellhole. But Nalini likes to take neighborhoods like that and develop them into something nicer. It's also possible that her father will want her to spy on the Kingdom and try to figure out where those gate pieces went." He shrugged. "I guess you'll have a chaperone, acting admiral."

"I'm hoping *someone* comes along who has actual military experience."

"Asger and Bjarke?"

"They're preparing for another mission. That reminds me. I need to send them three dozen crushers."

Tristan blinked.

Casmir yawned, his mouth opening so wide his jaw hinge cracked. "And then figure out how to mass produce slydar detectors."

"You're winning over the systems by making things for people. I wonder if that's ever been done before."

Casmir had no idea, so he only spread his arms. "Who doesn't like gifts?"

A new message came in on his chip, not from Asger but from his father.

Will you send along a copy of your virus? Bjarke asked. *And instructions on how to use it on the Druckers?*

I can send it. I doubt you'll be able to trick them into accepting a file download from you.

Figure out an alternative way for us to use it. We'll need an advantage against two warships with crews of hundreds. It sounded more like an order than a suggestion. Maybe he didn't know about Casmir's recent appointment as acting admiral.

Three dozen crushers aren't advantage enough?

I want something they won't see coming.

I can ask the crushers to turn into couches for the surveillance cameras.

You can do better, Professor. I've seen your work. William, Qin, and all her sisters are going to need your best.

I'll... try to think of something.

On no sleep. While replicating sophisticated electronics from pictures he'd taken. No problem. No problem at all.

Asger and Qin shouldered their armor, weapons, and other gear and headed across the *Dragon's* cargo hold toward the open hatch where Bonita and Bjarke were talking.

"I'll follow along at a distance," Bonita was telling him as they looked across the ship bay at Jemadari's ship the *Star Mirage*. "A *long* distance. They shouldn't think anything of me flying in the general direction of the gate. I'll plan to pick you up after your victory, unless you're planning to take over the Drucker warships and claim them for your own."

Bjarke gave Asger a long look. *Was* that his plan? A couple of new warships for the Kingdom Fleet?

Asger frowned. Achieving that would be a lot more difficult—and dangerous—than breaking out Qin's sisters.

"We'll plan for contingencies," Bjarke told Bonita. "I'll feel much better knowing you're back there and willing to pick us up. But I *am* hoping that Professor Dabrowski can send me his virus to use on the pirates."

"You know how to deploy computer viruses?" Asger asked.

"Rache did it. Dabrowski did it. An android did it. How hard can it be?"

"Rache is a criminal mastermind. And Dabrowski is… a do-gooder mastermind. Androids are smart computers."

"I'm a smart knight."

Asger grunted.

"Are parents supposed to be egotistical and delusional?" Asger looked at Bonita and Qin.

"I don't remember," Bonita said. "Mine have been gone a long time."

"I never had parents," Qin said.

Asger almost made a joke about how she wasn't missing out on anything, but her eyes were wistful.

"Just a bunch of sisters that you're about to reunite with?" He hoped that would raise her spirits.

"Yes." Qin nodded firmly.

Three dozen crushers strode across the bay toward Jemadari's ship.

HOME FRONT

"I suppose we should go introduce ourselves to them," Asger said.

Some of them he'd already met. Most of the crushers were six and a half feet tall, but a dozen of them were six feet tall, the originals that had come off Jorg's ship. As Asger headed out to join them, he hoped Casmir had sufficiently reprogrammed them to be loyal to him—and the knights in charge of this mission.

Bjarke and Qin trailed him off the ramp. After a farewell wave, Bonita drew it in and closed the hatch, ready to depart after they did.

Asger hoped she wouldn't be in any danger and had almost suggested she stay here, but she was right. They might need someone to pick them up, especially if his father's plan hinged on him deploying that computer virus successfully—multiple times. Besides, it wasn't as if the station was guaranteed to be safe this week.

The crushers queued up in front of the *Mirage* like a platoon of soldiers, all facing front, all at a semblance of attention. Asger felt strange addressing them, since they lacked the detailed human faces of androids—their eye, nose, and mouth orifices were only vague indentations in the right places. But he stopped and faced them.

"I'm Sir William Asger, and that's Qin and Sir Bjarke Asger." He pointed them out. "We're in charge of this mission to rescue a group of genetically modified warrior women who look like Qin. You're to assist us. Is that what you were told? Do you agree?" He was reluctant to bark orders at them. Casmir never did, and Asger didn't know how obedient they would prove.

"Yes," the crushers said together in a monotone. Then one up front added, "We have been instructed on the goals of the mission, and we were told to obey Sir William Asger first and foremost. He is in charge of the mission. Should he not be present to give orders, the second in command is Qin Liangyu Three, followed by Sir Bjarke Asger."

"Wait a minute." Asger's father scowled and hefted his pertundo. "I'm the senior-ranking knight. I should be in charge of the mission."

A few of the crushers gazed blandly at him. Most of them ignored him.

"Our creator, Professor Casmir Dabrowski, has instructed us that *William* Asger is in command."

Asger bit his lip and didn't look over at his father—he was afraid he would have a gloating expression on his face if he did.

"That's ridiculous," his father snapped. "I have ten times as much experience."

The crushers gazed at him without arguing, without wavering.

"Ten times, Father?" Asger murmured. "Are you even older than I realized?"

His father glared icy comets at him.

"Perhaps we can consider it a joint command," Asger offered. "If there's something you want them to do, run it by me, and if I agree, I'll tell them to do it."

"That's not a joint command. That's a chain of command with *you* above me. How about this. I'll tell you what I want done, and then you tell them verbatim without arguing."

Qin cleared her throat and stepped forward with raised arms. Even though she was diffident, she was too tall and strong to ignore. "They are Casmir's crushers, so it's fair that he choose who they'll obey. Can we please be glad they're helping us and load up and go? I've told my sister that we're on the way and not to do anything to tip our hand to the pirates, but if we don't leave soon, we may have trouble getting out."

The last Asger had heard, the first mercenary ships would arrive within twelve hours. And it was possible there were additional ships out there with slydar hulls, not yet close enough to show up on the slydar detector.

"We can load up and go—" Asger's father glared at the crushers, "—but we're not done discussing this."

"I'm sure you'll find further discussions with them scintillating," Asger murmured.

The glare transferred to him, but his father stalked up the passenger ramp through Jemadari's open hatch without further comment. Asger gestured for the crushers to file in after him while he hung back with Qin.

"Do you think this'll be a problem?" she asked quietly.

"I think he'll try to order them around through me. I'm sure we can make it work for one mission." Asger couldn't keep his tone from growing wistful as he added, "Maybe I'll perform adequately and he'll think more highly of my experience and abilities."

"You always perform adequately." Qin smiled shyly and looked like she felt she was being daring when she patted him on the butt. "*More* than adequately."

"I'm glad to know you feel that way." He put an arm around her shoulders as they headed up after the crushers but almost dropped it. His father had returned to the hatch and was glowering out at them.

HOME FRONT

Asger didn't know if it was a glower for the chain-of-command debacle or for his closeness with Qin. He kept his arm around her shoulders, refusing to hide his feelings for her. Besides, it wasn't as if there were any secrets about who was sleeping with whom after that appalling midnight meeting in the *Dragon's* corridor.

"Is he all right with us?" Qin murmured as Asger's father disappeared into the interior, barking orders about where the crushers should situate themselves.

"I'm not sure. I haven't talked to him about it. I don't care if he is or not."

"Truly?" She paused in front of the hatch and looked at him.

Asger hesitated. He wanted it to be true, but he hadn't yet convinced himself to stop caring completely what his father thought. "I'd prefer he not have a problem with it, but it won't change anything if he does."

"He always seemed… to not mind me. That I'm a genetically engineered warrior woman. Not when he was playing the role of Johnny Twelve Toes and not after he revealed himself as a knight. I didn't like *him*, but he never reacted like he hated me or thought I was a freak. But he's been giving me some weird looks lately. Since, uhm."

"The robe incident?" Asger noticed they had an audience—Queen Dya watching from the hatch of her yacht—and waved for Qin to step inside with him.

"When you two ran into each other naked in the corridor? Yeah, since then, I guess."

"*He* wasn't naked." Asger shuddered.

Qin must have also been aware of Dya watching them, for she glanced at her before stepping into the ship, where a soft blue-green illumination emanated from bulkheads, reminding Asger of bioluminescent algae in the tidal waters back home.

"Do you think she'll be trouble?" Qin asked.

"I don't see how. We're leaving." Asger closed the hatch behind them.

Similar to the outside, the yacht was all curves inside, with no hard edges. Cabins and common areas blended together, a cushy carpet that looked more like lush moss than anything synthetic flowing between the spaces. The crushers had all entered a large lounge and gaming room full of pods interspersed with fountains and trees that appeared to grow up out of the carpet. This wasn't the combat transport vessel Asger had envisioned for his troops.

"She could send a message to the Druckers," Qin pointed out. "We revealed our plan to her when we asked for her help."

"Let's hope she doesn't have a reason to wish us or Jemadari ill will." Asger led the way to a pair of empty pods—they seemed to be made from the stumps of ancient logs, but when he sat in one, it cupped his body reassuringly, the same way a normal one did. "She said she has reason to hate the Druckers."

"I hope so."

"Do you know something I don't know?"

"Lots of things, I'm sure." Qin smiled at him. "You hardly know anything about fairy tales. Which is silly, considering you're a knight."

"It's a wonder you can stand to be around someone so ignorant."

"I'm willing to educate you on important matters."

"Like unicorns?"

"Goblins and griffins and mermaids too. Bonita tells me you're never too old to learn new things."

Somehow, Asger doubted the things Bonita liked to learn involved fairy tales.

The thrum of the engines coming online reverberated through the deck. The interior doors were all open, and Asger could hear his father, Jemadari, and a pilot speaking quietly in the navigation cabin up front. The pilot asked the station for permission to enter the depressurization area and take off.

Qin leaned out of her pod and reached over to clasp Asger's hand. She'd painted her claws with purple and pink rainbows for the mission. "Thank you for agreeing to help me with this. I know your Kingdom wouldn't care and probably would forbid you to have anything to do with this if they knew."

"You're welcome." Asger laid his other hand atop hers. "I don't think the Kingdom—the part of it that knows what's going on in this system—cares that much about me and my father right now." Especially about him. Asger had hoped he might redeem himself with his attack on Dubashi's base, but they had only partially accomplished their goal, and Ishii might be the only one who knew and acknowledged that he had helped.

The *Star Mirage* lifted off, and they leaned back in their pods as it flew out of the bay and into the hollowed-out interior of the well-lit asteroid that housed the station. A nearby display showed them zipping toward the main tunnel leading out into space.

"The offer still stands," Qin said. "If your people don't let you come home, you can come work with me and the captain."

"Are you allowed to make that offer?" Asger raised his eyebrows. "It's Bonita's ship, right?"

"Yes, but you're traveling with Bjarke, and I'm positive she would let him stay. She said she likes the dimples in his butt cheeks."

Asger curled his lip. "I didn't want to know about that."

"I thought you might be wondering." Her eyes twinkled. "Since the robe hid that part of his anatomy."

"That robe hid next to nothing." A horrified thought came to him. "*I don't have dimples back there, do I?*"

It had been a while since he'd looked at his butt in the mirror, but he'd always assumed it was fine. After all, he'd gotten modeling gigs in the past.

Qin shook her head. "I think you get them when you're older."

"Well, he *is* old. And apparently has ten times my combat experience." Asger rolled his eyes. "His math has got to be fuzzy. Or he thinks I'm younger than I am. Or he's way *older* than I am."

"That's probably it," Qin said, going along with him.

Asger's father came out of navigation and sat in an empty pod facing him. "That woman—Queen Dya—is following us. Do you know anything about it?"

"Just that she was eyeing us as we departed." Asger looked at Qin.

"She never spoke to me," Qin said. "She was far more interested in you."

"And in my father too." Asger waved at him. "And anything male and ambulatory."

"I didn't see her ogling the crushers."

"They're not anatomically all there."

"No butt dimples?"

Asger's father blinked a few times, then recovered. "I've spoken to Bonita. She's taking off shortly and will follow Dya for as long as she follows us. She promises to blow her crystal yacht out of the sky if it does anything threatening."

Asger rubbed his head. "What happens if the Druckers see our odd trio of ships flying past and are suspicious and ignore us all? Or what happens if they attack us all?"

"The *Mirage* is the only one we've put rumors out about. The whole system should think it's full of vast riches." His father flicked a finger toward the crushers.

"That doesn't mean they won't see through our ruse. Especially if Dya tells them about it."

"I'll stay in navigation and keep an eye on her ship."

After his father left, Asger slumped down in his pod. "Why do I already have a feeling this mission isn't going to go according to plan?"

"Maybe we should abort." Qin's anguished expression promised that wasn't what she wanted to do. "I want to get them, but…" She gazed bleakly at him.

"We'll make it work." Asger had his doubts, but he forced a smile and hoped he was telling the truth.

CHAPTER 19

YAS GAZED OUT THE PORTHOLE IN THE MESS hall at the orderly queue of ships lined up at the wormhole gate, waiting for it to be repaired so they could leave the system. There weren't as many as he expected, even counting the rogues that had arranged themselves haphazardly and looked prepared to cut the line if the opportunity arose. Nobody was bothering the three university science vessels anchored right next to the gate, their crews going in and out of their airlock hatches in spacesuits.

The *Fedallah* didn't anchor itself anywhere. The ship was circling the area, like a hunting dog trying to find a trail.

"Hey, Doc." Jess ambled up to join him, a sandwich in one hand and a water bottle in the other. Grease and less identifiable stains smeared her coveralls, and a smudge had found its way onto her cheek.

"Chief Khonsari." Yas doubted she would appreciate it if he pulled out a saniwipe and washed her cheek for her. And her hands. Who ate a sandwich with engine grease and lube on their fingers?

"I think we've established that you can call me Jess."

"I wasn't sure if you would revoke that after I ran that scan on you and healed your vertebrae without permission."

"If you have to be knocked out and manhandled by a guy, there are worse things that could happen." Jess grinned and took a chomp out of the sandwich. Her face was as elegant as ever, even while chewing, even while grease-besmirched, and even while discussing molestation.

"I hope the danger of anything untoward happening to a woman on this ship is low."

"You're more likely to get punched in the face here than molested."

"Some people would consider *that* molestation."

"Not if it happens in the boxing ring. And not if you punch them back even harder."

"The mercenary life is an interesting one," he observed.

"Not that different from sports, really. More killing and fewer scoring of goals, but the people are kind of the same."

Yas didn't know what to say to that, so he opted for, "How's the burn?"

"About gone. Thanks. And we got the slydar detector online." Jess pointed her sandwich at the porthole. "The captain has already located three ships hiding out there. We're making scouting passes now, trying to figure out exactly what the range is. And trying to find an astroshaman ship. Nobody ever sees them flying about, so we're thinking they've all got slydar. They could have some *other* kind of camouflaging tech— who knows with them?—but we hope to find them."

"Yeah." Yas had already voiced his objections on the matter, so he didn't say more. Besides, Jess wasn't the one in charge of the ship.

She finished chewing and gazed at him as she drank from her water bottle. The light by the porthole was soft and played across the planes of her face, creating mysterious shadows here and there. There were a few other mercenaries in the mess hall, but it was late, and he doubted anyone would notice if they kissed. Not that they would. He'd given up on her ever falling for him. She was more likely to thump him on the shoulder and call him "Doc" rather than some term of endearment. Or even use his name.

"I really do mean thanks," Jess said. "And not just for the burn. My headaches have been a *lot* better since you tinkered." She waved over her shoulder toward her back. "I'm trying to be careful not to re-injure my spine by lifting too much, but I got so used to being able to pick up heavy things with my cybernetic side that I'm fuzzy on what a normal and appropriate weight is. I've tried lifting things with my other side, but it's so puny." Her nose wrinkled.

She probably didn't mean for it to be cute, but it was, and he laughed.

"That's how it is for us mere unmodified mortals. We're all puny."

"Maybe you can get some nice enhancements after we finish our mission," Jess said. "With bigger arm muscles, you could lift large unconscious mercenaries without the assistance of tools."

"I don't mind tools. Tool use was how we developed large brains and separated ourselves from the apes. I'd rather see *you* get an upgrade to your spine. That would be far more useful than me getting cybernetic biceps so I could win arm-wrestling contests against mercenaries."

"I'm a little scared of having more surgeries," Jess admitted. "The last one was major and left me alive but messed up. And spines are somewhat important."

"Somewhat. You could always retire from this job and do office work. It's hard to fracture your vertebrae while sitting in a chair and composing messages on your chip."

She grimaced. "Unless you're so bored you fall out of the chair and break your back."

An alert blared over the speakers, and First Officer Mendoza on the bridge called key personnel to battle stations. Yas didn't see anything threatening outside the porthole, but he trusted the slydar detector had picked up a ship. Dubashi? The astroshamans?

"Guess I was wise to just get a sandwich." Jess started to back away but paused, looking at Yas again.

He had been enjoying their banter and wished the night had gone on being quiet and uneventful.

"Thanks again for helping. For *caring*." She stuffed her half-eaten sandwich into her coveralls pocket.

Yas was on the verge of pointing out that the robotic mess-hall attendant wouldn't punish her for taking a plate to engineering, but she stepped in close, and he forgot to speak. She lifted her hands to the sides of his face. He froze, forgetting to breathe as he wondered if—

Jess leaned in and kissed him. It wasn't the kiss of a friend or a colleague, but a mouth-open, tongue-teasing actual kiss that prompted thoughts of bedroom activities to stampede into his mind.

The deck shifted, gravity fluctuating as the *Fedallah* switched direction too quickly for the spin gravity to compensate. Yas might have gripped Jess harder—at some point, his arms had wrapped around her waist—and ignored it all, but she smiled against his mouth and stepped out of his embrace.

"They usually notice if I'm not at my duty station in a battle," she said.

"Uh, yeah. Me too. I think."

"They usually notice if you're not at your station *after* a battle." She squeezed his hand as she stepped away. "Coffee later?"

"Oh yes."

Yas gathered his scattered thoughts, realizing he needed to get to sickbay and into a pod if he didn't want to be thrown all over the place, but glanced at the porthole before leaving. A ship had come into view, a sleek, dark blue cylinder with what looked like circuitry all over the hull. An astroshaman ship?

The *Fedallah* was right behind it, so close that whatever camouflage the foreign craft had was no longer effective. The warship opened fire at its back end.

Aiming to destroy it? Without warning? The other ship wasn't even trying to maneuver yet. The crew must not have guessed the *Fedallah* had obtained a slydar detector.

The astroshaman ship was tiny compared to Rache's big warship. How could the captain not feel like a bully for picking on it? The other ship had shielding, and the attack didn't blow it away, but it was hard to imagine them winning in a battle.

When Rache had spoken of convincing Moonrazor to repair the gate, Yas had assumed he meant to negotiate. Maybe blackmail or bribe but not blatantly attack.

With Yas's thoughts of romance shattering into a thousand pieces, he rushed to sickbay. Before he reached it, the other ship fired back.

A surprising jolt flung Yas against a bulkhead. Whatever weapon that was, it had sliced right through the *Fedallah's* shields. Gravity disappeared briefly, his feet flying free of the deck, and he caught himself before his head crashed against the ceiling. He lacked armor and magnetic boots, but he put up the helmet of his galaxy suit for some protection.

As he passed the last porthole before turning toward sickbay and the protected interior of the *Fedallah*, he saw the enemy ship firing back, strange pulsing blue bolts that widened and wrapped around the warship's hull. Maybe Yas had made the wrong assumption about who would win the battle.

Alarms went off, and a computer voice warned of the hull being breached on the port side of the ship. As soon as Yas reached sickbay, he locked himself into a pod and pulled up a display of the battle. He was in time to see one of the *Fedallah's* blasts slam into the side of the astroshaman ship. This time, its shields weren't enough to fully repel the attack. The ship's running lights went dark.

Rache's calm voice came over the speaker. "Doctor Peshlakai, we've taken out the shields and possibly main power on the astroshaman ship. I'm sending over a boarding party to collect prisoners. Be prepared for casualties, possibly among our side and most likely among the astroshamans."

Yas should have issued an obedient, "Yes, sir," but he couldn't help but ask, "Is Moonrazor among them? Did you fire because they wouldn't agree to fix the gate?"

"I don't know if she's among them. We'll find out. Rache, out."

He didn't know if she was among them, and he'd fired anyway? That meant there had been no negotiation. If Kyla Moonrazor *was* over there, she would be dagger-hurling mad.

Grimacing, Yas braced himself for angry patients... and pulled up what medical records he could find pertinent to treating astroshamans.

Casmir moved from the control room to the now-familiar manufacturing facility, completely and unfortunately bypassing the room Shayban had given him to sleep in. There wasn't time for sleep.

He had Tristan, a handful of engineers from the station, and Zee and several other crushers helping him to retool the equipment once again. Right now, he was crossing his fingers that he'd figured out enough about the slydar detector to replicate it. Even loading the software onto another system was proving problematic—he'd encountered numerous security precautions installed by the original builders, designed to prevent anyone from doing exactly what he was doing. He'd ended up sending some of it over to Lieutenant Grunburg on the *Osprey* to work on while he tinkered with the hardware. He'd also sent all the specifications and the schematic he'd put together, figuring the engineers and programmers on the Kingdom ships could work on building their own slydar detectors if they could kludge together the necessary parts with what they had. At the least, they would have a head start on preparing the interface for their scanners.

Nalini came in a few hours into the evening and went straight to where Casmir and Tristan were working and deposited takeout boxes of hot food on a conveyor belt. That prompted Tristan to kiss her and proclaim his love for her. Casmir, had he thought she would appreciate it, might have done the same. Not only had she brought food, but she'd also taken over supplying and organizing the fleet he'd never expected to end up in charge of.

The only problem was that said fleet might end up being sent out of the asteroid only to help protect it. They could hardly fly off to hunt for Dubashi and leave the station with half its defenses.

I have a problem, popped up an unexpected message from Kyla Moonrazor.

Casmir held up a finger and stepped away from the others so he could concentrate. *Is it me?*

It's your mercenary clone.

Maybe it should have alarmed or surprised Casmir that Kyla Moonrazor, a woman he'd met exactly once and very briefly, knew about his relationship to Rache. And likely who their progenitor was. But it did not. He assumed she could gather information as well as the best Royal Intelligence analyst, if not better. With all the cybernetic upgrades she had, she could probably surf the network like a data packet zipping around at light speed.

What's he doing, and how can I help?

He's captured the ship I left monitoring the gate. It has several of my people aboard. They and the ship are only there because you requested we deactivate the gate—I'm still waiting for the crusher you promised, FYI.

Where would you like him delivered?

To Rache's ship to kill him. She sounded frustrated enough to strangle Casmir as well as Rache.

He grimaced. She'd only diddled with the gate as a favor to him. *I'm not sure the postal service would be up to that.*

He's willing to return my people and my ship to me if I open the gate. Which I am considering. I'm not like that idiot Dubashi, who's so obsessed with getting retribution that he abandoned his followers. Oh, he's supposedly promised to take them to a new land, but he's scarcely communicated with them in a year.

I'm surprised he has followers. Casmir noted how quickly her responses were coming back to him. Moonrazor couldn't be far from the station. He hoped that didn't mean she would join in with the mercenary attack. *His base was practically empty of human life.*

HOME FRONT

His main residence is in System Hydra, but yes, he has followers there and here. Or he did. While he's been busy with his plots against the Kingdom, I've slid in and reminded them of the true ways of the astroshamans and that we care nothing of planets or pleasures of the body. Once we transcend to fully machine entities, we do not need the sun on our faces or anything except electricity to survive.

That's what you're doing now? Making the rounds and collecting his wayward acolytes?

The opportunity to do so, and the belief that Dubashi will soon be extricated from this existence, is what brought me to System Stymphalia.

You foresaw that? Through, uhm, divination? When he'd been in her base, he hadn't seen evidence of livestock sacrifices or portents drawn in chicken entrails. But he had been sick at the time. Maybe he'd failed to notice the signs.

When your mind is like a computer, you find it easy to calculate odds and permutations. Thousands of possible outcomes and their likelihoods. Dubashi made two mistakes: going to war with the Kingdom and drawing you into his world. At that point, many of the outcomes veered out of his favor. There was a pause before she added, *Though I admit, I hadn't factored this damn mercenary into my calculations. Foolish of me. I should have realized the other clone could not help but play a role. Is it strange that I believe he'll keep his word when he attacked my ship without warning? I hope he has some of your honor. I do not sacrifice my own, so I must open the gate. You have been warned.*

Wait! Can't you delay him? Or do you at least know where Dubashi is? Casmir imagined the prince with his ship full of rockets poised to fly to System Lion as soon as the gate came online.

I know where he is not. Like your mercenary clone, I also have an equivalent of your new slydar detector. I regret not installing it on my assistant's ship. Then she would not have been caught by surprise. I did not realize that technology had become so widespread.

Casmir wondered how many mercenaries were coming to the station in addition to the ones the scanners could pick up. Soon, they might be close enough for the slydar detector to pick up. Maybe foolishly, Casmir was more worried about Dubashi.

If he's not by the gate— Casmir intended to check with Rache to see if he could and would confirm that, *—then where do you think he* *is? There's nothing left of his base. The mercenaries know he can't pay them, so they should be ignoring him now.*

He'll need ships to complete his invasion of your system. And I'm sure he still wants to kill you.

You think he's coming here? Is that why you're here? Or near here?

Am I? I'm certain you don't see me, and I must go attend to the man using the lives of my kin to extort me.

Any chance you can let him out and then close the gate again?

It is not a light switch you can instantly flip on and off, nor do I intend to stick around indefinitely in this system to do your bidding. You have your warning, Professor. The gate will open soon. I'll send instructions on where to deliver my crusher.

"Shit." Casmir rubbed his head. He didn't know if he was more alarmed that they were out of time when it came to the gate or that Dubashi might be coming here with the mercenaries or in the *wake* of the mercenaries—using them as a distraction?—to get Shayban's ships. And maybe to get Casmir. "Better corroborate her story first."

Thus far, Moonrazor had been fairly honest with him and even helped him, but he couldn't guarantee that was still the case. She'd been irked by Rache's meddling.

"So he's the natural person to message for corroboration, right?" No, but he didn't know who else he could try.

Rache, Casmir composed his message. *You never let me know where to send your crusher. I hear you're by the gate harassing astroshamans. Will you be there long enough for a postal ship to find you?*

It took a while for the response, lending credence to the notion that Rache wasn't near the station. *Subtle, Dabrowski.*

Aren't you calling me Casmir these days?

I don't know. You're still calling me Rache.

Well, I know Tenebris isn't your first name. I suppose I could call you David, but you haven't invited me to.

This is true. What do you want? I already gave my post office box in System Cerberus to Kim.

Was he being sarcastic, or was that true? *I can't ship a crusher to Cerberus. The reputable mail services don't deliver there. The crusher might be stolen along the way.*

Are you telling me that one of your crushers couldn't keep itself from being stolen if it wishes?

It might not wish. Zee has been relaying stories about you. Are you torturing astroshamans and forcing Moonrazor to open the gate?

Nobody has been tortured.

Just threatened with death if she doesn't comply?

My doctor is treating the injured astroshamans. Nobody has even been killed. It's time for the gate to be fixed, Casmir. Dubashi isn't in the area—I checked. You'll have to deal with him before he can get to the gate. I'm going through to finish my mission.

Casmir closed his eyes. *No chance I can talk you out of it?*

None.

No chance you'd like to be a hero instead of a villain? Fly to Stardust Palace Station and help drive off the mercenaries attacking us because Dubashi has manipulated them to do so.

Perhaps the Twelve Systems will one day consider me a hero for getting rid of Jager, Rache messaged.

Only if you can do it without assassinating him. Why don't you kidnap him, handcuff him, and throw him in an anonymous extinct volcano with food and water to last him the rest of his life? Old Earth was full of conquered rulers being sent into exile.

Yes, and volcano exile is so much nicer than death. Please, should you ever be assigned to hunt me down, just shoot me.

You know I don't like guns, Casmir replied.

But volcanoes are okay?

They're less permanent.

I'm busy, Casmir. Go find that deluded Miners' Union prince. I don't want to feel guilty about him getting through and detonating that rocket where it can harm our people.

By all means, let's ensure you can sleep at night.

Rache didn't respond. Casmir sighed. Maybe he shouldn't have resorted to sarcasm. And maybe he should stop believing that deep down, Rache wanted to change his stripes and become… if not a good guy then a dependable ally. And someone who wanted to make the universe better instead of contributing to entropy and chaos.

Tristan touched his shoulder. "You all right, Casmir?"

"I'm tired, and I keep expecting too much from other people and from myself. I'm not sure either is realistic." His left eye blinked twice.

"And *I'm* not sure you answered my question."

"Nor am I." Casmir yawned and rubbed his eye. It was a wonder his entire body wasn't twitching and spasming.

"You should get some rest. Nalini says our new fleet will be ready to deploy in a couple of hours—and that we can't delay. We need to fly out of the asteroid so we can help deal with the mercenaries if necessary—we're hoping a display of strength will send them skittering away—before we can search for Dubashi."

Casmir grimaced. "A mission that's more important now than ever."

He wished he could skip the posturing with the mercenaries and go straight after Dubashi. But if Rache was right, he might already be lurking nearby.

"Why?" Tristan asked warily.

"Rache has captured some astroshamans and is forcing their leader, Kyla Moonrazor, to repair the gate. She's the one who originally deactivated it."

Tristan took a minute to digest that. "Who was your source? Any chance it's an unsubstantiated rumor?"

"Moonrazor told me, and then I checked with Rache."

Tristan's mouth drooped open. "You have… high-level sources."

"I believe in going direct."

"When did you speak with them?"

"Just now. When I was over here moaning and rubbing my temple."

"You weren't doing that. You were staring blankly at a wrench. I think Zee would have poked you soon if I hadn't."

"Correct," Zee said from behind Casmir's shoulder. "I was trying to determine if Casmir Dabrowski was about to have a seizure. I have been unable to learn reliable methods for ascertaining this from human studies on seizure-sensing dogs."

Tristan's forehead furrowed. "What?" He chopped a wave. "No, never mind. This is big news. I have to tell… Hell, I don't even know. It's not Sultan Shayban's problem, but if the gate opens and Dubashi escapes…"

"I know," Casmir said glumly. "I'm going to send a message to Ishii to warn him. I don't know where the Fleet warships are now, but they need to get to the gate and barricade it if Dubashi shows up." Something they could only do if Grunburg and his engineering buddies succeeded in making a slydar detector of their own in time. "We can't let him get into System Lion."

"Damn that Rache."

"He has his own agenda. We have to focus on ours."

"Right. I'm going to find some combat armor that fits me, just in case we get boarded." His eyes narrowed. "Or get the chance to board someone else. Do you want me to see about finding you some?"

"I have a galaxy suit on the *Dragon*… which I just realized I should have retrieved before the *Dragon* left the station."

"Likely so."

"I've been distracted. It's Bonita's anyway. I've been borrowing it from her. Yes, if you can find me a galaxy suit or, I guess, armor, I'll take it."

"You're supposed to sound more enthused about armor. It keeps you alive when people fire at you."

"I know, but if people are firing at me, it means I've failed to achieve my goals through diplomacy, charm, or appearing too inept for them to bother shooting. In that case, the mission is doomed."

"I'll find you some. Nobody can be charming all the time." Tristan patted him on the shoulder. "You should get some rest. Even if it's only in a supply closet for a couple of hours."

Casmir smiled bleakly. "I need to make sure a slydar detector is on one of those ships when we launch, and I don't think the sultan is going to give me the one in his control room."

CHAPTER 20

"ARE YOU FINDING ANYTHING ENLIGHTENING?" NATASHA SUNFLYER ASKED. Kim leaned back from the three displays scrolling data and showing images from slides under microscopes. "Actually, yes. I'm debating what to do with it."

Natasha approached, her hands clasped behind her back. She had been working in her lab while Kim scoured through her deceased father's files at another work station.

"What did you find? I don't think he was working on viruses here, nothing deadly certainly. We don't have a facility with the proper biosafety level for that, and Sultan Shayban specifically said he didn't want anything virulent and lethal being experimented on here. This last year, my father was helping me study positive-sense, single-stranded RNA mycophages."

"I'm sure he was, but he brought his data with him from System Cerberus. See?" Kim pointed to one of the displays. It was full of the Orthobuliaviricetes virus, not mycophages.

"He didn't bring any live samples with him, did he?" Natasha peered around the lab with fresh concern.

"I don't know. Probably not. This is old research, and I think he refined it further when he was captured by Dubashi. But it was based on something he'd started years earlier."

"Would it be useful in creating a vaccine?"

"Yes. If I were back home—in Zamek City—at my lab there, *we* have frozen samples of the Orthobuliaviricetes virus that I could modify. I could create a live culture and experiment on it. Or better yet, hand it off to four virologists far more qualified than I to work on it. They could come up with an antiviral." Kim thumped her fist on the table. "I know we want the gate to stay closed so Dubashi can't get out, but I wish I could bundle all this data off to them. Then they'd have a shot at coming up with something before Dubashi's ship could get there. Maybe." Kim considered how long it took to create and test vaccines and how long it took a ship to fly from the gate to Odin. Her maybe was a big one. She would at least bundle everything up to send as soon as possible, but she had better hope that Casmir succeeded at replicating the slydar detectors and finding Dubashi.

A letter came in from Rache.

Greetings, Scholar Sato, it started formally, as usual, *I hope you are well and will not be hurt in what's shaping up to be a scuffle at Stardust Palace Station. I was tempted to fly over there and retrieve you, but I am no longer in the area, and coming close would be difficult for me, now that Shayban has that slydar detector. I have arranged for something to be delivered to you, should you need help in battle. But please remember that there's no shame in hiding in a cabinet in a laboratory, not when you're a scientist and it would be a crime for your mind to be lost at the hands of some hoodlum with a gun. Be careful.*

Kim arched her eyebrows. He was having something sent to her? On this station? All she could think of was the psychedelic mushroom trail mix in the gift shop.

If I am successful with my current endeavor, I will be leaving the system soon. I would offer to deliver messages to your family and friends in System Lion, but they would be suspicious of any missives routed through me.

Yes, her father and brothers had heard of the notorious criminal Tenebris Rache. Everyone on the planet had. If the chance to bring him to a family dinner ever presented itself, that would be a very awkward meal.

I have searched the area near the gate with a slydar detector of my own that I've acquired, Rache went on in his letter, *and Dubashi's ship is not currently here. He could be anywhere in the system. But as I already warned Casmir, I think it's likely he's trailing behind those mercenaries. Remember, cabinets.*

Take care of yourself and... should you ever feel the urge to compose another story and send it in my direction, I would be delighted. By ever, I mean in the next week. I fear my time may be limited. I know it's a lot to ask, but I was pleased that you shared the last one. I hope you live a long life and have time for both writing and research and development in it.

For my closing, I thought to insert a poem, perhaps from Shakespeare or Elizabeth Barrett Browning, to say without saying the thing that has been on my mind but that I've feared to confess, knowing that our time is likely limited, knowing that we should never have met, and knowing you'd likely have preferred that fate hadn't inserted me into your life. We can't blame fate for all *those kidnappings though. At some point, people should acknowledge that they wish to be together, whether it makes sense or not.*

Kim felt her eyebrows drift upward again at the uncharacteristic ramble.

I should have said this in person before we parted last, but I was too focused on my plans, and perhaps that is still true. My fatal flaw, if you will. But I will say it now, on the chance that I never get the opportunity to do so in person. I love you.

~David

Kim leaned her hand against the counter, aware of Natasha in the room and wishing she'd thought to read the letter in private. So she could sit and consider it in private. And maybe cry a little for someone who knew his obsession was doomed but couldn't stop from pursuing it anyway.

Did she love him back? She cared for him and was depressed that he'd chosen this path for himself, but feeling fondness and wanting to spend time with someone... Was that love? How would she even know? She'd never fallen in love before, never truly believed she was capable of it.

Maybe if there was time, she would write the story he'd requested and let the words of a character say the things she'd never been capable of saying in person.

A chime sounded, followed by a familiar voice. "Hullo? Is this lab open for visitors?"

Kim attempted to swallow the lump that had formed in her throat and said, "That's Casmir," in case Natasha was tempted to shoo him away. She'd lost all track of time, but she thought night had come around again. If not another night and morning. "Back here, Casmir," she called.

A moment later, Casmir stuck his head through the doorway. Bags darkened the skin under his eyes, his shirt was rumpled and stained, and his shaggy hair was more unkempt than usual.

"Have you slept?" Kim asked.

"Last week, I think. I have to go get changed into the armor that Tristan found me. I'm taking my fleet out to fight mercenaries and look for Dubashi." He pointed ceiling-ward, then, likely after reconsidering the way the cylindrical station spun on its axis inside the asteroid, pointed floor ward.

"You have a fleet?" Kim looked from him to Natasha and back. "Did I miss something while I was looking at viruses?"

"Probably so. In other news, Rache captured some astroshamans and is forcing Moonrazor to fix the gate. For good or ill, we'll be able to get messages through soon." He grimaced. "That means, among other things, that Jager is going to learn about his son's death and that we haven't been the most loyal Kingdom minions."

"Oh, but I can send all the information on the virus back to my lab then. They're more qualified to work on an antiviral than I am. And they have the necessary facilities. They just need time. Probably more time than we have, unfortunately."

"For what it's worth, Rache said Dubashi isn't near the gate."

"I know," Kim said. "He sent me a letter too."

"Good to know he hasn't been too busy plotting villainy to send you poetry."

Natasha had been standing quietly, not commenting on the conversation, but she gaped and rocked back on her heels at this.

"Sorry," Casmir said to Kim, then held a finger to his lips and met Natasha's gaze. "The poetry is a secret. Don't tell anyone."

"Knock it off," Kim said. "There isn't any poetry."

Just short stories? Casmir switched to text, sending that to her chip.

He doesn't send those. I do. And it was just one. She hesitated and added, *He asked for another one.*

Maybe you should send it before he goes and gets himself killed.

Kim wanted to object to the notion that Rache would get himself killed, but she couldn't. He himself believed that was his fate, and for whatever crazy reason, he was willing to give his life if he could take Jager down with him. It frustrated her for reasons that went beyond the morality debate.

Why, when he'd been trying to make her care for him all these months, would he throw away the possibility of them having a future together? Because he didn't see a way they could? Kim admitted she'd never hinted to him that it was possible. She hadn't told him she'd occasionally speculated about joining her mother on Tiamat Station. He wouldn't be popular there, either, but it would be easier for him to visit her there than on Odin.

"I need to go," Casmir said. "I just wanted to offer to take you along—both of you, if you're game for an adventure."

"An adventure?" Natasha asked dubiously.

"Maybe I should say a way off the station if things go terribly and horribly wrong." Casmir smiled, but worry lurked in his eyes. Did he think that was possible? "Sultan Shayban was adamant that his asteroid's weapons platforms will have no trouble handling invaders, but I heard he's sent some of his children and grandchildren off in an armored transport ship."

"Is the *Dragon* still here?" Kim had gathered the information she could and didn't have a reason to stay, though the idea of heading off into a battle wasn't that appealing. Her mother was still here somewhere, presumably.

Casmir shook his head. "They're off to help Qin get the other Qins."

She knew what he meant, but her brow wrinkled at the phrasing.

"Don't worry," he said. "If they don't have individual names, I'll be happy to help. You know I like naming things."

Kim looked toward where her crusher was standing in the corridor with Casmir's crusher—Reuben and Zee. "Yes. Is there room on your ship—how did you say you got a ship?—for my mother? In case she doesn't want to stay?"

"Since your mother could fit in a lavatory cabinet, I don't think room is a problem. I have twenty ships, I believe. Temporarily, for the purpose of finding Dubashi. Ten are Sultan Shayban's, and the others are on loan from the various delegates and Miners' Union leaders."

"Who's in charge of them?"

Casmir smiled lopsidedly and raised his hand.

"How did *that* happen?"

"I'm not sure. I was under a console most of the day, spilling fizzop on my shirt. Princess Nalini and Tristan will be there. We can pretend they're in charge if that makes you feel safer."

"A real-estate agent and a guy who got kicked out of the knighthood. The perfect people to lead a fleet."

"She's a developer, not an agent."

"That makes her *much* more qualified to lead people into battle."

"It might." Casmir's eyes grew abstracted for a moment. "We're leaving from Ship Bay C in twenty minutes if you want to come. If not—" He started to raise his arms for a hug, then shifted to offering a handshake.

A sense of foreboding went through her as she realized they might be separated and she might not see him again if she didn't go along. She didn't know what help she could be, but if she stayed here—allowed herself to be trapped here—she might regret it later.

She hugged him, in case she didn't make it to that ship bay in time, and because normal people were supposed to be capable of such things. Of hugs and admitting to caring for friends and falling in love with strange men in black masks. What was wrong with her that she struggled with these things?

"I'll contact my mother and see if she wants to go. She should still be here with the Tiamat Station vice president." Kim assumed her mother would have told her if she was leaving.

"And Tork. Yes, I know. He and Zee have been reacquainting themselves." Casmir thumped her on the back, then bowed to Natasha and headed out. "Don't forget to bring creative knockout grenades if you come," he called back as he disappeared into the corridor.

Kim stared at the doorway. Did he anticipate the battle turning into boarding parties and close-combat encounters?

"Was that reminder for you or for me?" Natasha asked.

"For me, I believe, but if you can do interesting things with fungi, he'd probably take them."

"Hm."

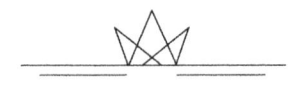

Oku was visiting her mother in her parents' suite in the Citadel and showing her some of her plans for engineering higher-yield grains when news came that the System Stymphalia gate had been repaired. Ships still had to run the blockade to escape System Lion, but a few were daring it, allowing communications in and out.

HOME FRONT

The message she'd had queued up to go out to Casmir finally showed as being sent. She hoped that before the end of the day, a message or two from him would come through for her, though the last thing he'd seen was that awkward promise-of-a-proposal that her father had strong-armed her into recording.

"Have you tested the strains in the lower-gravity environments of space yet?" her mother asked.

"I've done computer models, but I've been stuck here in the Citadel with everyone else, so no. Maybe when all this is over, I can take a trip up to one of the orbital stations and get some growing. You're right that I can't send anything out until I've seen the crops succeed myself."

A curse and a startled roar of, "What!" came from her father's office.

He'd been in there all morning, working while his servants packed for his trip, or so Oku had thought. He stepped out and looked at Mother, his face ashen.

Fear drilled into Oku's heart. She had never seen a stricken expression on her father's always-in-control face. Her first thought was that news had come of Casmir's death, but her father wouldn't react so strongly to that. Unless the entire Kingdom Fleet presence in System Stymphalia had been destroyed?

A new message appeared in her inbox, and her heart leaped. Casmir.

She would check it as soon as she was alone.

"What's wrong?" Mother asked.

"Several reports came in all at once from numerous sources including Ambassador Romano and Captain Ishii of the *Osprey*," Father whispered, the words barely audible. "One might have been a mistake, but so many... I'm afraid it's not a mistake."

"What?" Now Mother's face was turning ashen.

"Jorg is dead."

They stared at each other.

Neither looked at Oku. She didn't know what to say. How had Jorg gotten himself killed? Hadn't Kingdom ships protected him on all sides? Or had the entire fleet been annihilated? Her previous concern returned to mind, and she promptly felt guilty that she was more distressed over the idea that Casmir might be dead than the fact that Jorg apparently *was* dead.

But Jorg had no more been close to her than Finn. Her brothers had always existed in their own world of war and politics and practicing to be future kings, and they'd never included her. The castle was so large that it had grown easy not to see them, especially since they'd all become adults. She wasn't *glad* Jorg was gone, but she was more surprised than sad or horrified.

Her mother recovered first and masked her face—she'd always been so much better at that than Oku. She didn't say anything, didn't make any accusations, but maybe her father guessed that they existed behind her mask.

He clenched his fists. "I sent him out there to *prove* himself, to gain real-universe experience of what it's like to deal with other governments and lead a fleet. I knew he needed this, but I thought he could handle it. I thought he would grow up and prove himself worthy to one day take my position as ruler of the Kingdom."

Mother's first real reaction came as a weary sigh. "Must everyone always *prove* themselves to you?"

"Everyone who wishes to rule the Kingdom or have great privilege and power gifted to them, *yes*." His face twisted with anguish Oku had never seen in him before, and he lowered his voice and his gaze. "I thought he could handle it," he repeated. "That it would be a good exercise, a chance for him to learn to act independently from me. Maybe it was a mistake, but he was almost thirty. We can't *coddle* them."

"Can't we protect them?" Mother asked quietly, glancing at Oku.

"He *had* the Fleet with him." Father lifted his gaze, his eyes growing hard and determined. "He was betrayed. I'm sure of it. I'll find out who was responsible, and they will pay."

Without another word, he spun and stalked into his office and locked the door behind him.

Mother blew out a slow, sad breath and shook her head.

"I'm sorry." Oku came and wrapped her arms around her mother's shoulders.

She was sorry for Jorg's death, sorry it would hurt her mother, and sorry she didn't feel any sadness at the loss of her older brother. Maybe that would come later, when they had a funeral and she'd had more time to process it, but she wasn't sure.

"Thank you," her mother murmured, resting her forehead against Oku's shoulder.

Oku couldn't remember her mother ever needing her support and accepting it. She stroked her hair, wishing they'd been closer these last years. But her mother was as busy as she, traveling the world for her diplomatic and educational missions, and Oku had been gone so often to scientific centers and universities in other systems, working on her botany projects. They'd never been as close as some mothers and daughters, but Oku had always felt more kinship to her than to her brothers or her father. She and her mother were more alike than different.

"Whatever your father's plans were exactly," her mother murmured, leaning back and dabbing at her eyes, "this was not a part of them. I don't know if he will change anything, but be prepared for it." Her mother's dark eyes were troubled as well as moist as she gazed at Oku, and it seemed like there was more that she wasn't saying.

Oku thought of Boehm's warning about Finn. Would he start planning to get rid of her now that Jorg was gone? Did he need to? It sounded like their father meant to make him heir above her regardless of their ages.

"Do you think I should volunteer to officially abjure any interest in being part of the succession?" she asked.

"No," came her father's voice from behind them.

He'd stepped out of his office, his face once again masked, and he pointed for porters to take out his luggage.

"I plan to live for another hundred years," her father said tightly, "but if that's less feasible than I think, Finn is too young to take over. And he wants the throne too badly. He hasn't even attempted to hide his ambition." His eyes narrowed as he studied Oku, as if wondering if she had ambition that she *was* hiding? No, not even remotely. Her ambitions were to have peer-reviewed articles published in prestigious journals and to create new fertile plants that could thrive in space-station environments. Her most grandiose dream was to have what might become a popular cultivar named after her and used for centuries to come.

As the seconds stretched, Oku fought not to shift uncomfortably under her father's scrutiny. How long had that door been open? She didn't think she had said anything condemning.

"And you want it not at all, I believe," he finally said.

"That's right." Oku couldn't hide the relief in her voice. It wasn't as if she'd been joking when she'd told Finn the job would involve paperwork. Paperwork and the responsibility over billions of people spread across the planets, moons, habitats, and stations of the entire system. Even if she had wished for that power, she wasn't qualified to do a good job.

"I will consider this matter on my way to end this blockade," Father said. "I suppose our people would not accept a ruler who had his consciousness uploaded into an android in the event of his unexpected death."

"Just do your best to stay alive, if you would," Mother said.

"I shall endeavor to do so." He bowed to her and started for the exit but paused and looked back at Oku. "Have you heard back from Professor Dabrowski?"

"Not yet." She didn't let herself focus on the new message in her inbox, the one she hadn't read yet. "Have you?" she asked, more to deter him than because she thought Casmir would be sending her father notes about his progress.

"No." There was that steady gaze, that scrutiny again.

"System Stymphalia's gate just came back online, didn't it? Maybe something will come through. Uh, do you want me to respond if something comes in while you're gone?"

"No. Do not communicate with him until I've *fully* learned what he's been doing in Stymphalia."

Did that mean he had a partial idea already?

"Yes, Father," Oku said, though she intended to disobey that order. Hopefully, with her chip replaced, she could do so without worrying about Royal Intelligence finding out.

"And if he had anything to do with Jorg's death," Father added darkly.

Oku rocked back. "I can't believe that he would."

Why would her father even think that?

"We'll see," was all he said before walking out.

CHAPTER 21

ASMIR DIVVIED HIS CRUSHERS UP SO THAT EACH of the ships in his mishmash of a fleet got at least a couple to help out in the event they were boarded. He was sending most of the crushers on two of Shayban's vessels that were designed for combat. They weren't warships or anywhere near the size of the Kingdom spacecraft, but they were heavily armored and bore numerous weapons—the vessels usually accompanied Shayban's mining ships to protect their rich loads as they ventured far from civilized space.

Shayban didn't have a militia, but he'd scrounged up security officers with armor and spaceship combat experience. They had boarded earlier with the crushers. Only Casmir, Tristan, and Nalini remained out in the bay, directing people where to go as Shayban paced and watched these final preparations. He didn't interfere, but a couple of times, he paused and lifted a finger, as if he wanted to. But he inevitably lowered it again and returned to pacing. Casmir hadn't seen Shayban nervous before, and it rattled him a bit. Did he know more than he'd let on?

Casmir was nervous himself. A deluge of messages from back home had flooded his chip earlier, meaning the gate was open and a courier ship had come through from the Kingdom. That meant Dubashi could leave any time he wanted, and it meant everything that had happened here would have made it back to Jager by now. Casmir felt time pressing on him from all sides.

"Time to board, Professor," Tristan said. "Half of our fleet has already flown out, and if we mean to get out before any shots are fired, we need to leave too."

"I know. I'm ready."

Casmir checked the exits one more time before heading to the ramp of the armored ship that he, Nalini, and Tristan would ride in. Even though he'd hugged Kim and said goodbye, he hoped she would show up at the last minute and join him. Maybe it was silly—he didn't know if she would be safer out there or safer in here—but they'd been through so much together since leaving Odin. It seemed strange to go somewhere without her now.

Shayban hugged Nalini, shook Tristan's hand, and then the two of them headed up the ramp. He offered Casmir his hand too.

"I think you know what I want done, Professor."

"The mercenaries driven away and your enemy vanquished, or at least kidnapped and brought back to you."

"Indeed. Do you realize that the rest of the ships—those that aren't mine—were lent to your fleet for more reasons than a desire for a slydar detector?" Shayban arched his eyebrows.

"Oh?" he asked carefully.

Casmir still wasn't sure if Shayban was pleased that his expensive prototype was in the middle of being mass produced. The first detector off the line had been installed in the combat ship he was about to enter. It was all he'd been able to get ready in time, and they had yet to test it.

But Shayban didn't bring up the slydar detector. "I know you were working and missed the start of the talks—the talks that we've unfortunately had to pause until we're sure everybody will be safe—but I trust you gathered that the various scholars—and the government leaders backing those scholars—are interested in the gate pieces that your Kingdom ships made off with."

"I did wonder about that, sir. The Kingdom did get a number of pieces, but I believe the mercenary Rache got more, and of course Kyla Moonrazor herself took away half of them."

"Through luck or design—I am assuming luck—the Kingdom ships got what the scholars believe is one of two control pieces. They believe the astroshamans got one of them and that Jager now has control of the other. It'll be difficult for them to replicate the gate without studying one of those integral pieces. They've already asked the astroshamans if they'll share theirs—the answer, I'm told, was a resounding no—so the Kingdom is their only other possibility."

"How do they know our ships got that particular piece?"

HOME FRONT

"Apparently, there are unique markings on the exterior, and someone got camera footage of the gate piece being slurped up into one of your warship's holds."

"Huh. I wonder if Jager knows yet what he has."

"It's possible. The scientists know about the control pieces from their studies of the twelve original gates *in situ*. The Kingdom will figure it out quickly too. At which point, they'll get smug about what they lucked into or they may consider bargaining with it. I can't predict Jager. He doesn't act like a rational and logical businessman."

Casmir almost pointed out that he was better than Jorg had been, but he caught himself before he could speak ill of the dead.

"My point in telling you all this—I know you need to leave now—is that everyone's eagerness to help you may be born of ulterior motives. Be careful what you agree to out there. They know you're from the Kingdom, and they also believe you're not Jager's pawn and might be willing to act against him."

Casmir's stomach sank as he imagined being asked to sneak into some highly secured government warehouse on Odin to steal a gate piece. He was already going to find himself in exile, if not outright hunted, after all the news filtered back home. But he still had a vain hope of capturing Dubashi, destroying the bioweapon, and halting the blockade—all with witnesses who would testify on his behalf in the king's court—and returning home with all forgiven.

"Acting against him would be unwise for my health."

"For most people's health, I should think. I just wanted to make sure you were aware that any favors that are granted to you may have strings attached."

"Right. Thanks." Casmir made himself smile. "And thank you for all the help. Can I leave you an extra crusher?"

"Yes," Shayban said promptly and grinned like a boy being offered a second dessert. "Will your Kingdom Fleet commander be annoyed with you if you show up missing one?"

Probably. The person who'd ordered them made might be dead, but Romano and Ishii knew about them. The order might have originally come from Jager.

"I'm hoping nobody counts that closely." Casmir didn't point out that he'd already offered crushers to Rache and Moonrazor. It might make the offer seem less special.

"They do all look alike. When they're all assembled for inventory, maybe you could have a few that have already been counted rush to the back of the line to be counted again."

"I'll keep that idea in mind."

Kim walked into the ship bay in a galaxy suit, with Reuben walking behind her and carrying a trunk of her belongings—or more likely her research equipment. Her mother and Tork were with them. Kim waved to Casmir, her expression somewhat bemused. Maybe she hadn't invited her mother or Tiamat Station's android delegate along. The vice president was the only one from that station who wasn't with her.

"Is the inferior android Tork-57 coming on this mission?" Zee asked.

"He may be," Casmir said as the group approached. "Is that acceptable to you?"

"I have begun instructing the other crushers on network games that are satisfying to our kind, but Tork is a spirited opponent."

"I am ahead in our current round of *Pirates and Ore Ships*," Tork said as they arrived.

"Because I am luring you into a trap," Zee said.

"One does not sacrifice one's premier mining ship for bait."

"That you believe that is precisely what makes it a good tactic."

"Are you incapable of acknowledging when you've made a mistake, crusher?"

Casmir left them arguing and led Kim and Reuben up the ramp and into the ship. Her mother had already bypassed the squabbling duo to go inside.

"Vice President Phan thought it would be a good idea to send along Mother and Tork with all the project data in their android brains in case things don't go well down here," Kim explained.

"Is that the sentiment on the station now?" Casmir asked. "That things won't go well?"

"As more and more ships head over to join the action, yes. When it looked like only a handful of mercenaries were coming, most of the delegates believed the sultan's promise that they would be safe in his well-defended asteroid. Now, they're less certain. People have also realized that there could be a lot more ships out there with slydar hulls that aren't yet in range of the sultan's new detector."

"Very true." Casmir led her to a lift that would take them to a bank of cabins on the second level. "It makes me wonder how many more ships were at the gathering on Dubashi's base than we realized."

HOME FRONT

None of them had possessed a slydar detector then.

"Would you have gone in if you'd known it was twice as many?" Kim asked.

"I was committed. Would you have?"

"I was committed."

"I am also committed," Reuben stated, stepping out carefully to avoid clunking her big trunk against the lift doors.

"I'd intended him to be more of a bodyguard than a porter, you know," Casmir said dryly.

"He volunteered to carry it," Kim said. "I was in the middle of hunting for a hover cart."

"I am not lucky," Reuben said, "but I am versatile and a hard worker."

"You're not lucky?" Casmir raised his brows as they walked down the corridor.

"I have been unable to win dried currants in the game of chance."

"I told him that luck isn't supported by scientific data," Kim said. "You had to give me the superstitious crusher."

"They're developing their own unique personalities." Casmir clapped Reuben on the back. "It's wonderful."

"If he starts avoiding black cats and throwing salt over his shoulder, I'm going to complain to the manufacturer."

"Perhaps my lack of luck will benefit you, Scholar Sato," Reuben said. "An enemy's fire intended to strike you will be more likely to hit me."

Kim sighed, but she did say, "Thank you for carrying my stuff for me, Reuben," when they reached the door to her cabin and he set the trunk down inside. "You are a hard worker."

Casmir beamed, pleased that she could acknowledge the usefulness of crushers. "I'm surprised you've managed to keep so many of your belongings with you for all this moving around. Is that the same trunk you took from the *Osprey* when you snuck off to avoid Jorg?"

"Yes. Luckily, I'd retrieved it from the *Dragon* before Bonita left. It's been there most of the time since I *stealthily* departed the *Osprey* for the good of humanity. Scholar Sunflyer also lent me some of her equipment in case of an emergency situation."

Casmir frowned. "What kind of emergency situation?"

"In case we manage to capture Dubashi's ship and need to deal with the rockets and their contents."

Casmir's frown deepened. "I was hoping that spacing the rockets and blowing them into a few billion pieces from a distance would be an acceptable way to deal with their contents."

"It will be if you find the opportunity to do so." Kim looked down at the trunk, her lips quirking in wryness. Or was that puzzlement? "I also received a gift. I have not opened it yet."

"A gift from whom?"

"An acquaintance."

"I didn't think that acquaintance was anywhere near the station." Casmir wished Rache and his big powerful warship *were* near the station. And willing to help.

"He's not. He ordered something local and had it delivered."

"Maybe it's a puzzle, and you'll have something to do during the flight." Casmir wondered what Rache's idea of an appropriate gift for a girl was—and if it had involved shopping at the all-fungi gift shop.

"The ship will take off in five minutes," Princess Nalini said over the speakers. "Prepare for maneuvers out of the asteroid and possible battle maneuvers shortly after. Acting Admiral Dabrowski, please report to navigation."

Kim's eyebrows flew up. "They've seriously given you that title? I thought it was a joke."

"I think it's for the sake of our hodgepodge fleet. Shayban's people will follow Nalini, but the commanders of the various Miners' Union and other government ships might not appreciate it if they thought Shayban was in charge of the entire fleet. I guess I'm considered a neutral third party. Which seems odd since the Kingdom isn't neutral by anyone's standards, but Dubashi is an enemy to everyone, so maybe this works for them." Casmir shrugged, since he didn't truly know why he'd been given the lofty title, however tongue-in-cheek it might be.

Kim's eyes narrowed. "That might not be it. Did you hear that there are rumors going around about you?"

"Rumors? Did they find out about my Robot Remstar pajamas?"

"It's becoming widely believed that you are Admiral Mikita's clone."

"Oh." Casmir remembered that President Nguyen had caught that early on.

"It seems that other systems have a better memory when it comes to what Kingdom heroes from three centuries ago looked like."

HOME FRONT

"Then they'll be surprised if they learn I'm only wearing an Admiral Mikita mask for a forthcoming costume party at the university."

"I don't think anyone will believe *you're* the masked one at this point."

Casmir looked up sharply. The door was open and it was possible there were cameras in the cabin, so he switched to chip-to-chip messaging to ask, *You don't think any of them have caught on about Rache's origins, do you?*

Probably not. Based on the speculations I heard at breakfast about your origins, none of them know the real story. A few are guessing that King Jager had you made, but there are a variety of origin stories out there. A popular one is that one of the Miners' Union leaders is responsible, that Dubashi himself may have made you. Then you turned on him, and that's why he's put a bounty on your head. You snubbed him on the way out and took some of his money, and that's why he's in financial straits now.

And why I'm so clearly wealthy. Kim, I spent the last of my money on Rache's mushroom gift box. Casmir rubbed his head. He'd had no idea such elaborate speculation was going on about him while he'd had his head under that console.

Some people would interpret such a frivolous purchase as the act of a monied man.

Some people don't know me very well. I only make frivolous purchases when I buy gifts for friends, relatives, and mercenary captains I hope won't come after me.

Perhaps if you wear the Robot Remstar pajamas openly around the ship, these people will get to know you better.

I'll consider that.

You probably will.

"Admiral Dabrowski, please join us in navigation," Nalini repeated.

"I better go before all the good seats are gone."

Casmir told Kim there was a cabin next door for her mother, then left her to get situated as he hurried to the lift. He hoped that someone with actual spaceship fleet combat experience would be in navigation, because if these people expected him to be able to outmaneuver dozens of mercenary ships, their fleet and the entire station would be in trouble.

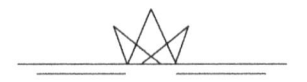

"Status, Viggo?" Bonita had woken from something more like a nap than a full night's sleep and slid into her pod in navigation.

"Queen Dya's crystal yacht is still trailing the *Mirage*. The *Mirage* is still heading toward the gate on a path that will accidentally take it past the two Drucker warships flying toward Stardust Palace at a geriatric turtle's pace."

Bonita grimaced, having flashbacks to her school days more than fifty years earlier and math problems that had started out, *If Sally's spaceship leaves the planet's orbit at 3 p.m. at one-tenth light speed, and Martina's spaceship leaves the moon's orbit at 4 p.m. at one-twelfth light speed, and they both head toward the gate, when will they draw even with each other?*

"Back at the station," Viggo continued his update, "four mercenary ships have flown within weapons range of the asteroid. A dozen more are on the way. Nobody is firing yet."

"Why is this system more of a mess than the one at war?" Bonita asked.

"It's full of mercenaries and pirates who didn't get the work they expected and can't get out of the system to seek other work."

"I wasn't expecting a logical answer."

"But I am a rational ship's computer. I shall always give logical answers. Do you think Casmir will be all right on the station? I got so little time to speak with him when they were aboard this time."

"I'm sure the sultan will put him in a special padded room to protect him. They're best friends now, you know."

"Best friends?" Viggo considered that for a few seconds. "I should like to think that Casmir, having known me for longer, would consider me at an equal or greater friendship level to a new acquaintance. Should friendship be quantifiable. I am not certain that it is."

"He'd probably let you put him in a special padded room too. Someone needs to." Bonita toggled the display and zoomed in to put Dya's yacht on the forward display. There wasn't enough light in space for its hull to glitter. Maybe the Druckers wouldn't have been drawn in by it.

"I'm thinking of comming her," she said. "Do you think she'll tell me what she's up to? Or is she busy having an orgy with her bodyguards?"

"I know too few factors to compute the odds of that."

"I hope she's not having a long chat with the Druckers about the ruse we're trying to pull." Bonita nibbled on her fingernail, then tapped the comm. "Let's see if she answers."

While she waited, she nibbled on another fingernail.

"Her ship has increased speed and is accelerating more quickly away from us," Viggo said.

"Really." Bonita tried comming two more times, but the system didn't even invite her to leave a message. "I feel snubbed."

"Do you want to accelerate to close the gap between our ships?"

If she did that, it would be hard to pretend, for the sake of onlookers, that the *Dragon* was ambling toward the gate with no interest in the other ships.

"How far is she from the Druckers?" She looked at the scanner display.

"Not too far. The *Mirage* is closer. They're on course to fly past the pirate warships—seemingly giving them a wide berth—on their way to the gate. So far, neither of the Drucker warships has moved off its course to intercept."

"Meaning they're not buying it?"

"Possibly," Viggo said. "I am detecting transmissions from Queen Dya's ship."

Bonita glanced at her comm panel, but it remained dark. "Transmissions to whom? Is she contacting the Druckers?"

She clenched a fist, frustrated and worried for her friends. If the Druckers recognized it as a ruse, they might do more than ignore the *Mirage*. They might attack it. That yacht couldn't withstand the might of the warships. Their whole plan was predicated on the Druckers wanting to board the ship and steal its fictional cargo.

"She is communicating with the *Mirage*." Viggo sounded surprised. "I shall try to intercept the transmission. It does not appear to be encrypted."

Bonita leaned back in her pod and made herself stop chewing on her nails. One of Viggo's vacuums trundled into navigation to suck up nonexistent dirt on the deck. It was important that the ship not go into battle dusty.

"The transmission ended, and the *Mirage* has not responded yet," Viggo said. "I am playing what I managed to capture."

"Dear Jemadari," Queen Dya purred. "I know you were enamored with my prototype slydar detector when I gave you a tour of my ship, but I didn't think that you and your minions would sneak aboard and steal it. Did you think I don't have cameras and wouldn't notice? It was thoughtful of you to leave my jewelry alone, but we both know the slydar detector is worth a lot more. Just because the gate has been repaired doesn't mean you can get away from me. Don't think I won't gun you down because I'm a woman. I'll give you fifteen minutes to decelerate so I can catch you and you can return it. If you don't, I *will* open fire."

Bonita gazed at the comm panel, as if the blank display might provide enlightenment. "I'm confused, Viggo."

"As am I."

"Did that actually happen? Did Qin, Asger, and Bjarke get involved in some Miners' Union-leader squabble?"

"Perhaps it is a ruse. The Druckers should also be close enough to intercept that communication. If they cared to do so. Maybe they're indifferent to anything other than what's going on at the station. That is still their heading."

"I'm going to check in with Qin. If there *was* another slydar detector that we didn't know about, and if Jemadari's people *did* take it, she should know by now, right?"

"If the passengers are not being kept in the dark."

Qin, Bonita messaged. *Did you know that Queen Dya is chasing the ship you're on?*

The last I heard, it's following us at a distance.

Check again. You guys just got an ultimatum from her. You may be in a battle soon if Jemadari doesn't reply.

A battle with Dya?

Bonita summed up the message, ending with, *You've been ordered to slow down.*

Uh, none of our people are in navigation, but I'm pretty sure we aren't.

"Is the *Mirage* decelerating, Viggo?" Bonita asked.

"Not that I can detect."

Figure out what's going on over there, and let me know if you need help.

Thanks, Captain. I'll get back to you soon.

Bonita grimaced. She'd hoped that Qin would have known exactly what was going on and already have a plan in action. Should she try

HOME FRONT

Bjarke? Or were he and Asger sitting in some passenger compartment right next to Qin, equally clueless?

"One of the Drucker warships is changing course," Viggo said.

"Toward the *Mirage*?" Bonita asked with sinking certainty.

"Toward the *Mirage*."

"The other Drucker ship hasn't deviated from its path toward Stardust Palace."

"Why would it? They only need one warship to annihilate either of those yachts. And us too, for that matter."

Bonita tapped the navigation console but didn't do anything to alter the *Dragon's* course yet. For now, they were probably an uninteresting blip on the Druckers' scanner display. As soon as she got involved, the pirates would have a reason to notice her. Better not to be a part of whatever calculations they were computing. Then maybe she could come in later as a surprise and be more useful.

"Has the *Mirage* replied to Dya?" Bonita asked.

"No."

"Have the Druckers tried to comm either of those ships?"

"Not that I've detected."

"So nobody really knows what—"

"She's firing," Viggo interrupted.

"Dya?"

"Yes. The *Mirage* is firing back."

Qin, Bonita sent. *You better take over in navigation, or your whole plan is going to go supernova.*

She didn't get a response.

CHAPTER 22

THE FIRST SHOTS WERE FIRED AS SOON AS Casmir's new ship, the *Moon Dart*, cleared the asteroid and flew out to join the growing fleet of defenders. Unfortunately, the fleet of mercenaries was growing too. Few of them had ventured close enough to be at risk from the weapons platforms mounted around the asteroid yet, but a couple of well-armored ships were zipping in, flinging fire, and zipping back out—taunting the defenders to fly away from the asteroid's defenses where they would be more vulnerable.

Casmir was seated in a pod he'd been given at a scanner station in navigation so he saw the asteroid's return fire light up the darkness of space. A missile slammed into one of the mercenary ships, but it was heavily armored and didn't appear to take much damage. It did zoom back out of range. Casmir hoped the hit had stung a little.

He made himself tear his gaze from the scanner display and familiarize himself with the computers and displays at the station. He'd found the slydar detector sitting on the deck next to it. Nobody had attempted to hook it up for him, so he had work to do now.

Tristan was at the nearby weapons station, Nalini in the central command pod, and three other crew members in colorful blue and purple uniforms from the station manned the communications and helm stations. Casmir had been relieved when nobody had pointed their new "acting admiral" to the command pod.

While the others murmured quietly, watching the displays and movement of the various ships, he opened his tool satchel and focused on getting the slydar detector plugged in.

Zee stood behind his pod in his usual bodyguard spot. The rest of the crushers were down near the airlocks, prepared to defend the ship if enemies boarded it. If they managed to find Dubashi, Casmir looked forward to sending all the crushers over to deal with him and destroy the rockets.

"Your father is warning the mercenaries to leave the area, Princess Nalini," the comm officer said. "He's telling them the station is fully prepared and that they won't find it an easy target. Do you want it on the speakers?"

"Yes," Nalini said.

After a few crackles of static, they heard the response from one of the mercenary commanders. "…have heard that you have a number of important people on your station right now, Sultan. Not to mention the wealth of equipment and riches you're known to have there in your home. Do you still have that collection of petrified drayka eggs in your suite? I understand those are selling for close to a million Union dollars each on the collectors' market."

"I'll pretend it's not aberrant that you've researched what's in my bedroom, *Captain* Delgado," came Shayban's familiar voice in reply, "but we both know better. I also know that you stole that ship and have no proper claim to that rank."

"Unlike the rank of sultan that you gave yourself after hollowing out that asteroid and building a tin can of a palace inside?"

"The station is firing again," Tristan said quietly.

"I can't imagine why," Nalini murmured.

"Targeting that ship—Delgado's. It's right at the edge of the station's range."

"Casmir," Nalini said, "let us know when you have that slydar detector online. Father is sending over some updates about hidden ships out there, but the interface between his computer down there and ours up here is clunky so far."

"I'll work on both those problems." Casmir was happy to comply—and to take orders rather than giving them, as long as they were reasonable orders. So far, he had more faith in Nalini to give them than he'd ever had in Jorg.

The ship deck tilted, the sense of gravity shifting as the *Moon Dart* changed course. Casmir's tool satchel tried to take a journey across navigation. Zee, his magnetic soles keeping him affixed to the deck, caught it.

"Do you need assistance, Casmir Dabrowski?"

HOME FRONT

"Usually," Casmir said. "Soldering gun, please."

Zee handed him the tool.

"You're a good crusher," Casmir said.

"Yes, I am. And also a good protector. Did you take your seizure medication today? I have noticed that when your sleep schedule is interrupted, you occasionally forget to take the necessary doses."

"Oh yes, I took it. As an acting admiral, I'd find it even more mortifying than usual to collapse in front of the crew. Thank you for checking."

"You are welcome. A canine would not be able to check." Zee was apparently still trying to figure out how to be superior to a seizure-detecting dog.

"This is true."

"One of the asteroid's weapons platforms is firing again," Tristan said. "At something short range that we can't see."

Casmir glanced at the scanner display. "Camouflaged ship. The telemetry the station is sharing with us is delayed by at least sixty seconds."

Seemingly from a point in empty space, a railgun opened fire, a powerful blast striking one of the asteroid's weapons platforms. As far as the scanners showed, the beams didn't do damage.

"The asteroid is shielded all around," Nalini said. "They should be able to take a lot of damage before there's any threat to the asteroid itself, and then the asteroid is nearly a mile thick around the station."

"So the mercenary ships can fire all day, and everyone in there will be fine?" Tristan asked.

"Let's hope so."

More hidden ships fired at the asteroid, determined to test those shields themselves. Dozens of weapons platforms were built into the rocky surface below, and thanks to Shayban's original slydar detector, they fired back accurately. Thus far, nobody was targeting the defending ships, giving Casmir the time he needed for his installation. Now and then, the mercenary captains, sounding confident in their ability to vanquish the station, taunted Shayban. He stopped answering, and Samar came on to field any comments worth responding to. There weren't many.

"That's a problem." Tristan came over to the scanner station and peered at one of the displays Casmir was ignoring in favor of getting the slydar detector up and running.

"What is it?" Nalini asked.

"It looked like that shot got through."

Casmir frowned and tapped a few controls. "The energy shield that was registering around the asteroid is gone."

"What?" Nalini pushed away from her pod and came to grip the console beside them. "It should have taken a *lot* more damage before failing."

"The weapons platforms are still firing," Tristan said, "but we should send our ships in to help."

"We can't until we can see real time what we're targeting. Right now, we'd risk getting in the crossfire." Nalini chewed on her lip. "We could go out and challenge the visible mercenary ships that are sitting back and watching. What do you two think?"

"Yes," Tristan said. "Let's send half of our fleet out."

Casmir pointed at the comm station. "Find out if the station's shields are down permanently or temporarily."

"Right." Nalini opened a channel. "Samar? Father? What's going on?"

A prompt curse came in reply. Shouts in the background were audible.

Shayban was the one to answer. "We have a saboteur on the station. Someone dropped the shield generator from within. I'm getting a team suited up. The generator is out in the asteroid itself, not here in the station."

"Your crusher and the other one I left behind can handle that," Casmir said.

"Yes. Good idea. We'll try to get it back online."

"I've sent half the fleet to attack the watchers," Tristan reported. "We better stay here, since we'll be the only ones outside the asteroid with a detector. Once it's up. How long for that, Casmir?"

"Good question." Casmir had everything hooked up, but he was struggling to get the software to come online and integrate with the ship's scanners. He grimaced, wishing there had been time to test his first slydar detector somewhere nice and quiet. A coffee shop or library, perhaps. "Soon." He tried to sound certain rather than hopeful.

Now that the asteroid's shields were down, the visible mercenary ships that had been lurking on the outskirts started inward.

Already, Casmir regretted asking Kim to come along for this. He'd envisioned quickly convincing the mercenaries to leave, easily finding Dubashi with the slydar detector, and then taking this fleet back to System Lion to help the Kingdom.

"Will this ship go into combat?" Zee asked. "The other crushers and I are ready to go into battle."

"I'm sure you'll get your chance," Tristan said grimly.

The long look he exchanged with Nalini was disconcerting.

Casmir was sure Tristan wished he were down on the station so he could personally go check on the generator.

After another adjustment, Casmir released himself from his pod so he could reboot the scanner system from underneath the console. Nalini swore as *all* the displays went offline.

"It'll be back," Casmir promised, but he held his breath, panicked thoughts spinning in his mind.

What if the original builders had put a failsafe in the software to keep someone from doing exactly this? Casmir hadn't seen anything like that, but it was possible someone skilled could have hidden it from him.

The scanner displays came back up, and he exhaled in relief. All the mercenary ships that had been there before reappeared. And then new ships started popping up, pale gray blips on the visual instead of white. There were a lot of them. Forty? Fifty? The appearance of the hidden ships tripled the size of the mercenary fleet.

"You better get those shields back up quickly, Father," Nalini murmured.

"I'm aware." Shayban had been looking at the total number of ships all along.

Tristan pointed at one of the pale-gray blips, one firing at the station. "Singh, take us after that one. We're going to have to start whittling away at our opponents."

"Yes, sir," the helmsman said.

The engines thrummed as the *Moon Dart* took off after its first real target.

Captain Ishii, Casmir composed a message, *I don't know if you're watching what's going on at Stardust Palace Station, but we could use some help here. I'm sure the sultan would be grateful if you flew in to blow away some mercenaries. It's also possible that Dubashi is lurking in the background, masterminding this trouble. It could be a chance for the Fleet to take him out preemptively.*

Casmir sent the note, knowing Ishii wasn't near the station, but hoping the battle would go on long enough that he could help. *If* he came.

Would he? Shayban had been snubbing the Kingdom for weeks.

"Casmir," Tristan said, "see if you can share this with all the other ships in our fleet. We're all going to need this data." He lowered his voice. "And to not worry about the fact that we're outnumbered."

"The weapons platforms on the asteroid even the odds," Nalini said.

"The weapons platforms that, with the shields down, those ships are now targeting?" Tristan pointed at a new batch zeroing in on the far side of the asteroid.

Nalini swore. "Let's get them."

Casmir's stomach plummeted as the ship accelerated, and he scrambled back into his pod. As the insulated sides cupped him protectively, he hoped his stomach would refrain from sending his last meal all over navigation. He was positive acting admirals weren't supposed to puke all over their crew members.

We're waiting for you and prepared to help, or at least not get in the way, a message came in from Mouser, making Qin forget to respond to Bonita's last text.

Earlier, Qin had sent a message to Mouser, asking her to tell the cohort not to attack if she, Asger, Bjarke, and the crushers managed to get aboard the ship. Qin didn't want to have to battle a bunch of warriors as capable as she was.

If it's at all possible, Mouser's message went on, *we'll get down to the airlock level to meet you.*

Faint shudders coursed through the *Star Mirage*. Qin gripped the armrests of her pod and sent a quick note back that she'd gotten the message and hoped to see everyone alive again soon.

The ship's pilot came over the speaker, tersely ordering everyone to stay in their pods. But Asger and Bjarke hurried to navigation, and Qin followed them. Was Queen Dya firing at them? Or was it the Druckers? Bonita's last message had been ominous.

"What's going on?" Bjarke demanded as they barged into navigation.

Jemadari sat next to the pilot, and they were both focused on the display. Queen Dya's crystal-hulled yacht filled it. The ship fired, missiles streaking toward them.

"Our shields are still at a hundred percent after the first attack," the pilot reported. "Shall we fire back, sir?"

Jemadari, who was gripping his chin, appeared more contemplative than worried.

"*Yes*," Bjarke answered.

"Fire back," Jemadari said slowly, "but don't throw everything we've got at her. In fact, don't try to damage her ship at all. Just make it look like we're putting forth some effort."

Bjarke frowned. "What's going on? Is this a ruse?" He gripped Jemadari's shoulder. "Did you plan something with her?"

Jemadari looked back coolly. "Release me, Sir Knight."

"Answer my question."

"Easy, Father." Asger grabbed Bjarke's arm and pulled him back. "We're guests, remember?"

"We're not guests; we're the combat team, and if there's combat, we should be in charge of it."

The missiles struck and light flared on the display, but the shields remained intact.

"Bonita said we're in trouble," Qin said, not feeling any less confused than Bjarke. "I think she tried to comm Dya and was ignored."

Bjarke's expression grew darker.

Jemadari held up a hand. "I am *guessing* that this is a ruse, yes. Because she's not using full power in her attacks. But we did not plan anything ahead of time, so I'm not positive. We're not that close."

"What, she never invited you in for one of her orgies?" Bjarke growled.

"She invites everyone to those. That doesn't mean you're close."

The pilot gave his boss a weird look, but all he said was, "Firing back, sir."

"She accused us of stealing her slydar detector," Jemadari said, "which, of course, we didn't. If she truly had one and it had been stolen, we would have heard about it on the station. Or directly from her earlier if she believed we were responsible. She wouldn't have waited until we were under the pirates' noses to comm us."

Qin leaned past the pilot to peer at the scanner display and see where those pirates' noses were now. One of their warships was still on course for the station, but the other one was not. She grimaced. It was heading their way.

Dya fired again. A missile slammed into their shields and unleashed more power than the earlier blows. An alert flashed on the console, and the deck shuddered under their feet.

"Maybe it's *not* a ruse," Qin said. "What if someone really did steal from her, and she thinks it's you?"

"She could think you only brought us and the crushers on board so you'd be well-defended if she caught up with you," Asger said.

Jemadari shook his head. "Why wait until now to start all this? She's been following us for half a day. Fire again, Knapp."

"Yes, sir." The pilot sounded uncertain, but he obeyed.

Asger met Qin's eyes.

We're sure there's not *a stolen slydar detector on this ship, right?* he messaged to her chip.

Qin could only spread her arms. It wasn't as if she could smell the difference between one piece of equipment she'd never seen—or smelled—and another.

"The shields are down to forty percent power," the pilot reported quietly. "One more like the last one, and we'll be defenseless."

Jemadari frowned. "Fire back with more power."

"She's comming someone. The Druckers." The pilot's fingers danced across the controls. "It's not encrypted. Let's see if I can catch it…"

Queen Dya's imperious voice came over the speaker. "…offering a reward of five thousand Union dollars if you stop that ship. I will handle boarding and retrieving my stolen belongings. All I need is for you to stop them."

Uncertainty cracked Jemadari's calm facade for the first time.

Qin checked the scanners again. "The Drucker ship that broke off to head our way is increasing its speed."

"Huh." Bjarke leaned back. "This *is* what we wanted."

"Assuming they don't blow us to pieces and *then* search the wreckage for valuables," the pilot muttered.

"That is the risk we all agreed to take with this mission," Bjarke said.

"I didn't agree to take anything. I'm just on the clock." The pilot shot Jemadari a dirty look.

"We'll be fine." Jemadari didn't appear as confident anymore, but he nodded and smiled at his man. "And I'll see to it you get a combat bonus."

"If we survive?"

"Do you want me to arrange to have it sent to your family in the event that we don't?"

"Yes."

"Very well."

Should we be worried, Qin messaged Asger, *that our crew is convinced we're not going to make it?*

It's just one pilot.

That's all right then.

Do you really care? Asger smiled at her. *You're probably eager to go into battle.*

I just hope we get the chance. Qin flexed her hands, her claws trying to extend, but the fingertips of her gauntlets restrained them. When she wore combat armor, she was relegated to using more modern weapons.

We will. Asger sounded certain.

"Queen Dya's ship is slowing down and has stopped firing," the pilot reported.

"Good," Jemadari said.

"The Drucker warship is readying weapons and has us in its sights."

"That could be less good," Jemadari said.

The comm panel flashed.

"This is Groggins," came a man's bored drawl. A familiar drawl that Qin had heard before. "Consider yourself our prisoner. If you fire at us or try to evade us, we'll blast you into the nearest sun. If you put up a fight when we board you, we'll also blast you into the nearest sun. If we don't like the look of you or your women, well, you get the picture."

Memories slammed into Qin at the sound of the man's voice, and she barely heard his words. She remembered Groggins. He'd been with the pirates as long as she had. He was a lowly underling for them, a man who'd often been put in charge of guarding her and her sisters, and he'd come in often to sate his sexual urges on them. He and several others had never seemed to have anything better to do, the assholes.

Qin gripped a nearby handhold, suddenly needing the support, as if the ship were whipping about in high-speed maneuvers that would send them all flying. But it was only her mind that felt that way.

She took a deep breath, struggling to push down the memories. She hadn't realized that he would be there—this hadn't been her ship—or that she would have to deal with anyone she'd interacted with frequently back then. Or that the thought of fighting those people would trouble her. She hated them, but she'd known them for years. Could she truly shoot to kill? Shoot to rescue her sisters?

Are you all right? Asger messaged, peering over at her.

Yes. Qin forced a quick smile. *I just didn't realize I'd recognize some of them. I'm not sure why it didn't occur to me.*

Will you be okay when we come face to face with them?

I'll make sure I am.

He still looked concerned.

The concern touched her, and she warred with wanting his support and not wanting him to have any reason to doubt her capabilities. She *could* handle this. She was sure of it. And yet... *If we run into that one who's talking—Groggins—I wouldn't mind if you poked your pertundo into him for me.*

He hurt you? Asger guessed.

He was... a frequent visitor. Qin couldn't remember how much she'd confided to Asger in the past about how it had been living with the pirates, but he clearly had the gist, for his concern turned into a scowl.

I'll do more than poke him with my pertundo. Trust me. You just point him out. Point any *of them out.*

You're a good man, Asger.

I've got your back, okay?

Okay. Her second smile for him wasn't forced. *And I'll have your back when you need it.*

Such as when there's a hairy old man in a woman's skimpy robe blocking the way to the lav in the middle of the night?

Absolutely.

"We're waiting for an acknowledgment, pretty little yacht," Groggins drawled. "You're to surrender and let us board you, understood?"

Jemadari leaned forward to answer. "*You're* going to board us?" He put a convincing quaver in his voice. "Uhm, didn't Queen Dya say that *she* wanted to handle that?"

"We're going to handle it for her. And charge her an extra fee for the trouble."

"We'd really prefer that she board us," Jemadari said.

"Too bad."

The channel closed, and the pirate ship fired.

The pilot swore. "Trying to reroute more power to the shields, but brace yourselves."

When the blast hit, the force sent Asger tumbling into Qin. She kept her grip on the handhold and managed to keep from tumbling out of navigation. The lights went out, even the indicators on the console darkening. A long moment passed before everything came back on.

"Shields are down," the pilot reported. "And we've taken damage to the engines. We're not going anywhere for a while."

"This isn't quite how I imagined this going," Jemadari muttered.

Thankfully, the pirates didn't fire again. The big warship sauntered closer like a hunter that had already downed its prey and had only to pick it up.

"Start in on repairs," Bjarke said. "When we get done with their boarding party and collect our people, I want to be able to escape, just in case we aren't able to completely take over their ship."

"You're going to try to take over their whole *ship*?" Jemadari gaped back at him. Maybe he hadn't imagined that either.

Bjarke stalked out, yelling to the crushers to ready themselves for combat.

"I have a feeling," Asger said, peering back at the crushers mobilizing and flowing toward the cargo hold and the airlock, "that the pirates aren't going to like the look of our *women* when they come aboard."

"No?" Qin pushed thoughts of Groggins and the others out of her mind and feigned bravado and nonchalance. "I'm kind of sexy."

"Yes, you are," Asger said. "Ready to rescue your sisters?"

Qin didn't allow herself to hesitate before saying, "Absolutely."

CHAPTER 23

THE GREENHOUSE WAS STILL STANDING WHEN OKU, FINN, their mother, and most of the staff, senators, and aides who lived and worked out of Drachen Castle returned to the grounds. Some people, concerned more kamikaze ships would get through the planetary defenses, remained in the Citadel.

Oku had thought about staying behind, but she was eager to get back to her work, and she hadn't yet read Casmir's message, since she hadn't been able to get a minute alone since the news of Jorg's death. Everyone wanted to share their condolences. While she understood and appreciated the sentiment, she wanted some time alone. Her greenhouse was the ideal place—hardly anyone came out to pester her here. Maddie took up a position outside as a deterrent, and not even Chasca came inside. She'd missed the big courtyard and grassy grounds of the castle and was out reacquainting herself with the gophers and squirrels.

Oku made a pretense of unpacking a few things and checking on projects she'd had to abandon, mostly so she would look like she'd come out here for gardening reasons, not secret-reading-of-messages reasons. It made her nervous that she was communicating with someone her father didn't trust and didn't want her to speak with. Further, she was doing so on a new chip that he didn't know she'd gotten. Even though she should have a right to her privacy, it made her feel like a criminal.

Only when she was in a corner and sitting on her favorite garden stool did she allow herself to pull up the message that had been waiting in her inbox all day. Would it be Casmir's response to the proposal that her father had all but promised? Would he have taken the bait? Or would he, as she hoped, see through the sham and respond warily?

Instead of writing, he'd recorded a video message of himself in a cabin with a dark background. No, that was a dark chest. Zee stood behind him.

Casmir smiled and waved. He didn't look quite as wiped out as he had for his previous recording—right after he'd had the Plague—but he hadn't yet returned to his chipper self. His eyes were bloodshot with dark bags under them. Still, the smile was warm and genuine.

"Hullo, Princess. I hope this finds you well and, ah, enjoying privacy, as one would expect someone in the royal family to be able to find." His eyebrow quirk was the only acknowledgment of the last message, of how her father had loomed next to her. "I am recording this before we know when or how the gate will be reopened, so it's likely going to be dated news, but I wanted to check in and let you know that I'm still alive and working on various projects for the Fleet. Prince Jorg ordered me to create a hundred crushers—did you hear about that before the gate went down?"

At the time he'd recorded this, he hadn't known about Jorg's death, she realized.

"I thought it a somewhat impossible task," Casmir said, "but I've actually succeeded."

The black "background" stirred and Zee bent down, his big amorphous head appearing over Casmir's shoulder. "I am seeking a mate from among the new crushers. They are still developing personalities. Casmir Dabrowski assures me that I was also boring when I first acquired consciousness."

Casmir's eyebrows flew up, and he turned to look up at Zee. "I didn't say you were boring."

"You said it took me a while to develop my current sublime personality. I assumed you were being diplomatic—even though strangely few humans are diplomatic with crushers, androids, or robots—and that you meant I was boring."

"You were less quirky."

Zee looked at the camera. "I was boring, Princess Oku, but as you can see, I have developed into a fascinating being. I am certain the others will become more interesting with time. If they do not, I will continue to play network games with the inferior android, Tork, and wait patiently. A mate will come along. I am certain of this. Then I will have someone to interact with while Casmir Dabrowski sleeps. It is unfortunate that humans require such long repair cycles. They are not interesting during this time."

Casmir looked back to the camera, a wrinkle to his brow. "I rehearsed this message before I hit record. This isn't how it was supposed to go."

"I am improving it through interjection and improvisation," Zee said. "The princess will find your personality more interesting by seeing it in contrast to mine."

Oku smiled, wishing she were playing this on her tablet so the video was larger than on her contact display.

"I'm not sure it's my personality she's getting a taste of," Casmir muttered, then made a shooing motion with his hand, and cleared his throat as Zee leaned back, his head disappearing from view. "As I was saying, Your Highness, I have been attempting to comply with the wishes of the Kingdom representatives in this system, though I have admittedly improvised here and there."

"Casmir Dabrowski was responsible for the destruction of Dubashi's moon base and the vile prince's failure to hire a ragtag mercenary fleet to use against the Kingdom," Zee said.

"Ah, yes. Thank you, Zee. Would you mind standing over there by the door? It's possible assassins are on the way and that I'm in danger."

"You are always in danger, Casmir Dabrowski. I sense that you wish me to stop interfering with the composition of your message."

"You are an astute crusher."

"Yes." Zee walked away, leaving a bland gray bulkhead in view behind Casmir.

"I don't actually have a lot to say," Casmir went on alone, "since I don't even know when you'll receive this, but I wanted to let you know that if I make it back to Odin and if I'm allowed to walk freely there again—" why did his face grow wistful and uncertain as he said those words? "—then I would love to join you at a cafe near the university or at some place of your choosing to have an adult beverage together. Kim informs me that fizzop isn't an adult beverage, nor is it anything a princess would drink, so I shall endeavor to order something mature. Like tea." His nose wrinkled. "Maybe that sweet bubble tea that comes with a straw."

His brow furrowed again as he perhaps contemplated whether a drink with a straw would be considered *adult*. Oku would have guessed alcohol would have to be involved for that designation to apply. She wasn't sure she'd ever had a drink with someone who ordered a soda, at least not since she'd been twelve. The knights usually tried to impress her with their knowledge of wine and vineyards. She wouldn't mind sharing a drink with Casmir at the university. Maybe he would show her his robotics lab. She'd been to the greenhouses and botany labs there but hadn't visited the computer science or engineering buildings on campus before.

"But only if you're interested in that," Casmir continued. "I wouldn't want you to think, uhm. Well, I *would* want you to think. And do what you wish to do with whom." He waved as if to acknowledge that had been vague and not well-phrased, but she appreciated that he'd worked it in, that he was letting her know that he didn't expect her to marry him or anything else because her father wished it.

She had no idea *what* her father wished now. He had better not get himself killed while he was out with the Fleet, because she couldn't manage trying to sort things out at home with just Finn. Oh, their mother would help, but as queen consort, it had always been clear that the rule wouldn't fall to her, and her power was limited with the Senate.

Oku knew her own power would be even more limited, and Finn was a fool if he thought things would fall into his lap as if he was the king's only remaining child. More likely, some ambitious distant relative with a lot of resources would assassinate him and try to force the Senate to accept him.

"I'll send another message once the gate is open," Casmir said, and Oku pushed away her bleak thoughts. Just because her brother had died out there didn't mean her father wouldn't make it back home. "Hopefully, one with some good news. Unfortunately, good news hasn't been following me around of late." His mouth twisted wryly. "You might instead get more tales of Zee's quest to find a mate—or to realize that an acceptable one has been within reach all along."

Oku wished they could speak real time so she could ask Casmir what he'd been doing all these months away. Had he truly helped destroy an enemy base? And thwarted plans against the Kingdom? If so, why wasn't he delighted? Surely, her father would reward him for that, not punish him.

"Good night, Your Highness." He bowed, his mop of scruffy brown hair falling into his eyes. Haircuts must not have been a priority out there in space.

HOME FRONT

As she saved the message to play it again later, a rapping came at the greenhouse door.

Maddie stuck her head in, but from her dyspeptic expression, it was obvious she wasn't alone. Or happy to introduce her visitor.

Oku expected Finn, but Maddie said, "Chief Van Dijk from Royal Intelligence here to see you, Your Highness."

Van Dijk strode in without waiting to see if Oku invited her in. Had Oku had more warning, she might have scurried out one of the ventilation windows. She had a hunch what this would be about and braced herself, bringing up the excuses she'd practiced.

"Your Highness." The lean fifty-something intel chief bowed politely, though from her posture and tone, it was clear she would take charge of the conversation. "I came to see you about your chip."

"My chip?" Oku touched her temple and feigned ignorance.

"We believe it's either malfunctioning or that it's been tampered with."

Oku had planned to tell them, when someone from Royal Intelligence inevitably asked, that she'd been having trouble with her chip and had replaced it, but a recalcitrant urge swept through her to say exactly why she'd had the procedure done, and to also say they didn't have the right to monitor her. Why did she have to tiptoe around the castle and everywhere else in the political realm? Would she find herself under guard, a prisoner in her own home, if she refused to cooperate?

"What makes you believe that?" Oku asked, tamping down her urge. "And why is my personal data chip of interest to Royal Intelligence?"

"We keep track of everyone in the royal family for your own safety," Van Dijk said without hesitation. "For the last few days, you haven't registered."

"And yet you found me." Oku smiled and waved to the greenhouse.

"The castle has security cameras. The rest of the city—and the galaxy, should you return to flying to other systems after the war—is less well equipped."

"I'll take my chances."

Van Dijk frowned. "Did you do something to your chip to prevent monitoring?"

"I replaced it. The chip was old and had a few quirks." Such as that it had allowed Intelligence to watch her encrypted messages from Casmir...

A long moment passed. Van Dijk didn't seem to know what to say. Overhead, the greenhouse's automatic lights came on. It was getting dark outside. Oku needed to find Chasca and feed her dinner. Would Van Dijk let her go if she said that?

"For your own safety, I strongly suggest that you come to our office and allow Dr. Tsuji to install a tracker."

"Tracking isn't *all* you do, is it?" Oku lifted her chin and met Van Dijk's pale eyes. "You can see everything I save, everything I research, and read the messages of everyone I communicate with."

Understanding glinted in Van Dijk's eyes. "It wasn't a glitch. You deliberately removed it."

"When I realized my messages were being handed over to my father, as if I'm a troublesome ten-year-old plotting mayhem at school and needing to be stopped? Yes, I did."

"All members of the royal family are monitored for their own safety, Your Highness. You may not believe it, but what you think of as innocent communications could end up being methods for terrorists to gain information. You're known to be the most… approachable of King Jager's children, and you've been targeted for schemes before."

Approachable or the easiest target? And was Van Dijk trying to imply that Casmir was a terrorist? Oku almost spat a defense, but it might be incriminating for both of them if she mentioned his name specifically.

"When I was a teenager, I was targeted by ambitious nobles who wanted to use me against my father and, having more than three IQ points, I saw through their flattery immediately. I didn't need Royal Intelligence to come in and save me then, and I don't need them to step in now."

"Does this mean you won't come to Headquarters and have a tracker installed? For your own safety and the safety of your family?"

"That's what it means, yes. But I'm not going anywhere, if that's what you're worried about. Not until the war has ended, and it's safe for me to go back to meeting with scientists in other systems. For the foreseeable future, I'll be right here with my work." Oku waved toward the worktables she'd filled with projects she meant to restart.

As Van Dijk scanned the soil-dusted surfaces, her mouth set with distaste, Oku imagined her thinking what pointless and unimportant *work* it was. As if helping feed people throughout the systems was some silly hobby barely worth pursuing.

"I will speak to your father when he returns." Van Dijk bowed stiffly and headed for the door.

HOME FRONT

Oku grimaced. Her father was the one person with the power to force her to have her chip monitored—even if she was well past the age of majority, he could make it a royal order. But Van Dijk wasn't pressing the issue now. That was something. It would be weeks before her father returned with the Fleet. Hopefully, Intelligence would get involved in something else and forget about her.

She snorted. "Sure."

No longer in the mood to work, Oku cleaned up and headed out into the approaching night. After the sun set, fog had crept in from the sea, and a soft mist dampened her cheeks.

"Have you seen Chasca?" she asked Maddie, surprised the dog hadn't shown up and been asking for her dinner. The gophers and squirrels should have gone to sleep by now.

"Not since before Chief Van Dijk went in to see you." Maddie frowned as she gazed around the foggy grounds, the yellow glow of the courtyard lights diminished by the fog. "I last saw her in the hedges under the kitchen windows."

As Oku started in that direction, the soft whir of one of the castle's delivery drones came out of the mist. Usually, they sailed from room to room, delivering meals or handwritten messages that required real signatures rather than electronic ones. Oku couldn't remember the last time one had zipped toward her, but this one did.

Maddie dropped a hand to the pistol at her waist and stepped in front of Oku, as if she expected an attack. She glanced toward the guard towers around the castle walls where humans and androids stood guard, a backup to electronic security systems that should have ensured no threats got in from outside.

The drone whirred up to Maddie and tried to get around her to reach Oku. Maddie shifted again to block it from reaching her. Accepting that it wouldn't get through, the drone extended a mechanical arm from its belly, holding out an envelope in its grippers. Oku's name was on the front. Maddie reached for it, but the drone whirred backward out of her grip.

"Persistent thing," she growled.

"It's all right." Oku stepped out from behind her. "I'll get it."

The drone hovered and allowed her to take the envelope, then zipped around a corner of the castle. It didn't look like it had come from over the wall or meant to return that way. Whoever had sent this was here in the castle.

A feeling of foreboding wrapped around Oku, as cold as the mist. Her hands were shaking by the time she reached a lamp and opened the message.

The first thing she pulled out was a photograph with a time stamp in the corner, saying it had been taken less than a half hour ago. It was of Chasca, a chain attached to her collar and wrapped around a boulder formation embedded in the beach. Her tail was clenched, her fur was wet, and she looked bewildered and scared. Tears of fear and worry and anger leaped to Oku's eyes. What the hell?

The accompanying message was typed. *Come to Picnic Point to fetch your dog or she won't survive the next high tide. If you bring anyone with you, she'll be dead before you get to her.*

CHAPTER 24

Outside the porthole in the lounge, the Drucker warship came into view, a great gray spinning arrowhead large enough to have artificial gravity. And large enough to have a *lot* of weapons. But the *Star Mirage* was complying with the pirates' order to slow down and allow a boarding party to come aboard. The only weapons Asger would have to worry about were the ones their troops would be holding.

As his father gave last-minute instructions to Jemadari and the yacht's small crew in navigation, Asger checked his combat armor, pertundo, rifle, and the bandolier of explosives he'd dug out of Bonita's armory. Nearby, Qin also checked her gear. The crushers were gathering in the yacht's cargo hold where an airlock would allow the pirates access.

"Stay in here with that hatch locked," Asger's father's voice floated out.

"Oh, we plan to," Jemadari said. "In case you need any incentive to perform, I'll pay a hundred Union dollars for every pirate you permanently put out of commission."

"I'm a knight, not an assassin," came the cool reply.

"Two hundred? These pirates have been preying on the Miners' Union for decades."

"I'll take the two hundred per pirate," Qin called.

Asger looked at her.

She shrugged. "I'm not a knight. And my sisters won't have any money when they get out. They'll need something to tide them over until they can find work."

"Maybe you should ask for three hundred a head then," Asger suggested.

"Do you think that's greedy?"

"I believe it's called negotiating."

"Greedily?"

"This is your world, not mine. You'll have to decide. But I'll be happy to buy them all dinner on Stardust Palace if we get out of this alive."

"Just keep the door shut," his father told Jemadari, "and we'll handle the rest."

As soon as he left navigation, the hatch shut with a firm clang and a whir.

Qin, Asger, and his father headed to the cargo hold to join the crushers, needing their magnetic boots to stay attached to the deck now that the yacht hung motionless in space. Asger glimpsed the pirate ship through another porthole—it was now all that was visible out there, its immense size blocking the stars.

When they entered the hold, one of the crushers pushed off a wall and landed in front of them. "Sir Asger. Will we take the fight to the enemy ship or should we prepare to ambush them when they come aboard?"

"Let's set up an ambush here," Asger's father said.

The crusher didn't look at him. He waited for orders from Asger. That prompted an exasperated eye roll from his father.

"We'll do the ambush in here. Let their boarding party come on board before you reveal yourselves to them." Asger looked around the hold. There were stacked boxes of supplies strapped to the deck near the walls, but it was relatively open and empty. The three dozen crushers wouldn't fit behind the boxes. "Is there somewhere you can hide?"

"We can hide anywhere," the crusher said.

"You may want to hide too," Qin told Asger. "You and your father are distinctive in that silver armor. The pirates may realize right away it's an ambush if they see Kingdom knights."

"True. And if we hide, we can charge onto their ship while they're distracted here and go find your sisters. Do they know we're coming?" Asger touched his chest.

"They know we're coming, and I mentioned having knight allies, but if the pirates are around, my sisters will have to follow their orders until we can free them. They have embedded chips that can be used to cause pain if they disobey orders, so they won't be able to simply turn on their captors." Qin touched the side of her head and grimaced. She must have also had such a chip once.

"I understand."

HOME FRONT

"Once we get my sisters away from the pirates, I'll make sure they all know you're on our side."

The idea of facing ten or twenty warriors as powerful as Qin alarmed Asger as much as the thought of battling that many crushers. They were deadly, but Qin was ferocious *and* deadly.

"Yes," he said, "also be sure to tell them I'm wonderful, handsome, and good in bed."

Asger's father frowned over at him.

Qin switched to chip-to-chip messaging. *Do your bedroom skills usually keep enemies from attacking you?*

Asger wriggled his eyebrows. *Would* you *attack me now that you know about them?*

I guess not.

That wasn't as rousing an agreement as I would have preferred. He smiled and touched her shoulder.

His father was still frowning in their direction, and Asger frowned back. He remembered Qin's comment about him treating her differently lately and almost said something, but a flashing light on a control panel alerted them that the pirate ship had grabbed them with its maglocker. The yacht lurched as it fell under the influence of the bigger vessel's spin gravity. The pirates would attach its airlock tube and board soon.

"William." His father waved for him to come over.

Feeling wary, Asger joined him. "What?"

His father opened a comm channel straight to his helmet. Speaking quietly, he said, "I know you care for her, but don't let yourself get too attached or do anything foolish over there because you're distracted by feelings."

Hot indignation flushed Asger's cheeks at the implication that he would be foolish because of a woman—because of Qin. "You mean like you're doing by being here, risking yourself to rescue Qin's sisters to make Bonita happy?"

"I'm partially here because of Bonita, but I've also been speaking to Ishii. He agrees that these two warships would be good to take over and add to the Kingdom fleet they're assembling."

"Of course he agrees. He's desperate to get more ships, *any* ships. Did Casmir send you the virus and a way to deploy it?" All Asger wanted to worry about was rescuing Qin's sisters. It seemed hubris to believe they could take two massive warships.

His father hesitated. "He said the crushers would handle it once we're aboard the enemy ship. We just have to give them the opportunity to do so." His father gripped Asger's arm. "Our people need this, William. They need powerful ships to go back and help with the blockade. I aim for us to go back heroes. One way or another."

"I would also rather go back a hero than in disgrace," Asger admitted.

His father let go of him. "Just be aware that even if we go back as heroes with our honor fully restored, our people won't accept someone like her." He tilted his head toward Qin. "The populace would revolt if you tried to bring her home."

"I know that. And she knows it." Asger shook his head, hardly feeling this was the time to discuss this. "She's not angling to be my wife and the mother of your grandchildren." The fact that she never could be that made him angrier than it should have, given that he'd known it all along. He'd even explained it to Qin—not that she hadn't already understood perfectly how the Kingdom viewed her. "I doubt she'd want to get married, even if I proposed. We're just enjoying spending time together."

Asger willed that to be enough for his father. He didn't want to continue discussing it, nor did he want to think about how unfair it was that he was right, that he could never bring home the noble, brave, and beautiful Qin who represented everything knights and the Kingdom held dear. She wasn't *human* enough.

"Okay," his father said. "Good. She's a nice girl and fine for… that. I just wanted to make sure you weren't going to—"

"Embarrass you again?" Asger couldn't help but interrupt. "Yeah, I wouldn't want to disturb your big plans to return a hero with a pirate warship to add to the war museum in the capital. Or maybe you could park it on the estate next to that centuries-old whaling ship that Grandfather got."

His father lifted a hand. "Believe it or not, I wasn't thinking of you embarrassing me. I was thinking of her. You shouldn't take her where she'll be ridiculed if not attacked outright. Your position in the nobility has always protected you, but let's not pretend that our people can't be brutal and ignorant."

"I haven't forgotten that. I'm well aware."

"Good." His father nodded and faced the airlock, as if to say the conversation was over.

That was fine with Asger. He weaved his way back through the crushers to stand at Qin's side.

She gazed at him through her faceplate. She didn't say anything, but he was reminded how keen her ears were.

"You hear all of that?" he murmured in a comm channel to her.

"Yes. It's hard for me not to eavesdrop if I'm in the same room with someone else." She shrugged and waved toward her head, though her helmet hid her pointed ears.

"I'm sorry he's being dumb."

She snorted softly. "It's all right. I'm glad you explained us to him. Maybe that's why he's been weird lately. I didn't think he objected to us sleeping together, but I don't want to come between you."

"Please, there's been a chasm between us for a long time that has nothing to do with you." That there was a slender bridge over that chasm now was a miracle.

Qin smiled and bumped his shoulder. "Does it have to do with the lavender robe?"

"*Yes.*" He smiled back, glad she wasn't upset, though it upset him that everything his father said was true, that his people would never accept Qin as a part of their world.

A soft clank emanated from the hatch.

"Their tube is attached," his father said quietly. "We had better hide."

Asger gripped Qin's shoulder before going to his chosen spot.

Qin nodded back at him. She was ready.

Time to see if Asger's father was delusional to believe they could take over that ship—and if they were all delusional to believe they could get Qin's sisters.

"Any chance we can talk to these mercenaries?" Casmir asked Nalini—or anyone who would listen to him.

Now that he'd finished integrating the slydar detector, he needed another way to help. He felt useless sitting in his pod as their ship whizzed around the asteroid base, firing at the now-revealed mercenary ships. Half of their fleet had gone out to confront the warships on the fringe, and the station itself, despite having lost its shields, was firing frequently. It had damaged several of the attackers, especially those daring to fly close, but the odds seemed against the station unless it could get its shields back up. Had Casmir stayed down there, he might have helped with that.

"They're not here on a contract, right?" he added. "They're just trying to take advantage of the situation?"

"They failed to tell me their exact motivations," Nalini said tightly from the command pod. "You're welcome to open the comm and invite them to dinner, if you wish."

"I am a sexy date, but I was thinking of offering to pay them to go away."

Nalini gave him a flat look—maybe she disagreed with his assessment of his sex appeal. "Do you have money? Because I'm not paying mercenaries to *not* attack our station. That would set an abysmal precedent, and I know my father wouldn't approve." Her mouth twisted. "I know that because he already told me when I brought it up."

"I do not have money, but I've heard that Tristan has a big estate on Odin."

Tristan glanced at him from the weapons station as the ship twisted to chase after another mercenary. "Sir Sebastian tried to leave that to me, but I'm certain the Senate overruled that months ago and gave it to his son."

"But do the *mercenaries* know that?"

"Casmir, you can't give away someone else's land."

"I suppose not. I'm just brainstorming. If we could get them talking, maybe we could trick them into accepting a file download, and I could send my virus over."

"I think everyone in the system has heard about your virus by now and won't fall for your tactics," Nalini said.

Casmir snapped his fingers. "What if, instead of paying them to stop attacking your home, you pay them to go somewhere else? Is anyone, by chance, harassing any of your real-estate holdings right now?"

"Not that I know of." The second look she gave him was less scathing and more thoughtful.

"What about hiring them to go find Dubashi?"

"Unless we give them a slydar detector, they're not any more likely to find him than we are."

HOME FRONT

"They don't have to find him. All we need is for them not to be here." Casmir checked the scanners to see if his request to Ishii was bearing any fruit. Ishii hadn't said anything, but maybe…

Two of the Kingdom warships *were* on the way here. The *Osprey* and the *Eagle*. Good. But unless this turned into a protracted siege, they wouldn't make it in time to help. Bad.

"Damn it." He wished he'd contacted Ishii much earlier.

Casmir noticed one of the Drucker ships had veered off its course toward the station and was attached to Jemadari's yacht. He prayed that his friends would survive that ordeal and come out victorious, and he wished he were able to help. The crushers he'd sent would have to be enough.

"You're welcome to comm the mercenaries, Professor. It's not like talking to them can make anything worse." Nalini's voice lowered to a mutter to add, "Probably."

Before he could send a message, a skirmish on the scanners caught his attention. One of their ships was chasing a visible mercenary ship, which would be fine, but the slydar detector showed two camouflaged mercenary vessels veering in to cut it off.

"Captain of the *Daedalus*," Casmir commed their ally. "You've got two ships coming in from under your belly. Are you getting our scanner transmissions?"

The *Daedalus* fired at their target as one of the hidden mercenary ships fired at *it*. Their shields faltered before establishing themselves. The *Daedalus* veered onto another course, trying to shake its pursuers.

"We're getting them but delayed, Admiral," came a grim female response.

Casmir almost told the officer to call him *Professor* or by name, but his honorific wasn't the priority. "I'm streaming it to the fleet as real-time as possible."

He grimaced. Their ally ships that were farther out were getting the same lag that he'd gotten when relying on the feed from the station.

"I don't suppose you'd like to send a slydar detector over here." She sounded harried.

"Can we get to the *Daedalus* in time to help, Your Highness?" Casmir showed Nalini the scanner display, though this wasn't the only troubling skirmish. Numerous of their fleet were in tight situations, being chased by ships they couldn't detect.

"Do it," Nalini told their helmsman.

The *Daedalus* fired at one of its pursuers, but the blasts streaked through space behind the ship. They couldn't accurately target the camouflaged craft, even with the shared scanner feed. Casmir thumped a fist against his thigh. This wasn't working.

As he watched helplessly, one of their ally ships took too much damage and lost power. The asteroid's surface defenses fired at the camouflaged mercenary, driving it away before it could finish off the ship, but it was still out of the fight. Something needed to change.

Casmir looked up at Zee. "Where's Tork?"

"He is in the cargo bay with the other crushers."

"Tell him to come up here, please. We're the only ones out here with a slydar detector. We're going to have to figure out a way to tag the hidden ships."

"There must be fifty of them," Nalini said, listening in. "What do you propose? Attaching paint buckets to torpedoes? We don't have that many physical weapons in our inventory."

"We may be able to modify one of the DEW-Tek cannons to mark them with a radioactive beacon. If we can catch them with their shields down, and if we're subtle enough that their sensors don't pick up the beam. Let me think on it. In the meantime…" Casmir tapped into the external comm and pinged what appeared to be one of the lead mercenaries, the big ship hanging back and letting the camouflaged ships do the brunt of the work.

"Greetings, Captain," Casmir said and introduced himself. "If you were at that memorable meeting on Dubashi's base, you may remember me—and my accountant. We warned you of the prince's financial challenges."

"Accountant?" Nalini whispered, looking at Tristan. "Is that you?"

"I'm a man of many talents," he told her.

"Remind me to put you to work on my taxes later."

"You have to pay taxes in a system where your own father represents the government?"

"Strange, isn't it?"

"What do you want, Professor?" came the mercenary's response. The man didn't introduce himself, but he sounded smug and confident. "We're in no need of an accountant today."

"I'm offering a warning rather than our services. Stardust Palace Station has acquired a great number of my crushers." All right, he'd only left two down there, but he could take the others back inside if needed. "They're not a problem if you keep your distance, but I assume you're planning to board and loot the station if you succeed in getting through its defenses? You'll find them very difficult to deal with, and they are guarding all the entrances to the station."

"We don't discuss our plans with our enemies," the mercenary said.

"We need not be enemies. We have money and could hire you to find work elsewhere. Such as chasing Prince Dubashi. Do you know where he is these days, by chance?"

Tork came onto the bridge, and Casmir waved him over.

"We also don't give free intelligence to our enemies," the mercenary said and closed the comm.

"Maybe someone actually did hire them for this, rather than suggesting this would be a fun way to spend a weekend." Nalini glanced at him. "Do you want to try some of the other ships? They're not a cohesive fleet. They're—"

Enemy fire blasted into their shields as a mercenary craft flew into view around the curvature of the asteroid.

"There are two of them coming," the helmsman said. "Both gunning for us."

"Gun back," Nalini said.

"I'm on it," Tristan said.

"Tork, do you have any astroshaman knowledge in your memory banks that might be useful for coming up with a way to tag a bunch of slydar-hidden ships so that our fleet can target them?" Casmir explained his current ideas on how to accomplish it.

"I could accomplish this by modifying one of the ship's direct-energy weapons, yes, but we would need to be able to locate the ships first."

"We can." Casmir patted the slydar detector cabled to the open scanner panel under the console. "But we're the only ones out here who have this right now. I want to use it to locate and mark all these mercenary ships."

"This should be possible. I need access to the ship's computers."

Casmir tapped in a few commands and slid out of his pod to give him room. "You've got it."

"I can also be of assistance." Zee sounded like he didn't want to be left out—or allow Tork to be useful while he stood aside.

"Good." Casmir patted him on the back while keeping a firm grip on the console so he wouldn't fly away as the ship maneuvered and returned fire.

A message came in on his chip from Ishii. *Are you on the station or out on one of those ships, Dabrowski?*

On a ship.

Good. That station's defenses are down. It looks like it's in more trouble than it should be given how few ships we see.

It's the ships you can't see that are a problem. We're working on them. Did you get Shayban's slydar detector?

Casmir guessed Grunburg hadn't yet been able to build one for the *Osprey*. Too bad. *I made a second one, and I'll make more.*

Someone's fire hit them square on, and an ominous rumble reverberated through the ship.

If you survive to do so, Ishii replied, probably watching the battle unfold from the scanners on the bridge of the *Osprey*.

That is my goal.

Casmir wondered if they should, if they could get away from their current attackers, head out and harry some of the big mercenary ships hanging back. If they were in charge, damaging them would do more than damaging the cannon fodder being sent in to try to take out the asteroid's defenses. The problem was that he didn't think anyone in particular was in charge of the mercenaries.

The *Moon Dart* flew toward one of the weapons platforms on the asteroid. At the last moment, their pursuers recognized their danger and veered off, but one was too late. The ground-based missile launcher swiveled and fired, having no trouble targeting the camouflaged vessel. One of its thruster housings blew off, and the ship was knocked away from the asteroid, out of control as it spun off into space.

"Thank you, Father," Nalini murmured.

An explosive that one of the mercenary ships must have fired at the asteroid blew up and took out the missile launcher.

Nalini's thanks turned into a vehement curse. "These idiots are destroying my home. The home of thousands of people. And for what? So they can loot my father's art collection?" She turned a plaintive look toward Tristan and Casmir.

"Is his art valuable?" Casmir did wonder how much the mercenaries expected to get out of this once they divvied up whatever loot they found. Or was it all about kidnapping delegates and Miners' Union leaders for ransom?

"No," Nalini said. "His tastes are garish."

"His *ships* are valuable," Tristan said.

Nalini nodded. "We're in one of them, but there are more in his bays. Dubashi tried to get them before to add to his fleet." Her eyes narrowed. "He wouldn't be *here*, would he?"

"Someone did suggest he might be." Casmir didn't cite his source, given everyone's feelings on Rache. "I'm not familiar with the ship he used when he escaped his base, since we couldn't detect slydar at the time, but I assume it would be well armored and fast, and staying out of danger while others do the dirty work." Casmir waved at the scanner console. "So far, all the camouflaged ships have been among those harrying the asteroid. But it's possible he's hanging back out of range."

"How far is the range on the detector?" Nalini asked.

Casmir tapped the controls to shift his scanner data to the forward display so everyone could see it. "It reaches out to where those ships are lurking."

"But not beyond?"

"No. We could go out to visit them so we could see beyond them."

"If we fly out of the range of your father's weapons platforms," Tristan said, "we'll be an easier target."

Nalini gripped her chin. "Let's go *partway* toward them."

Tristan frowned with worry. He probably hadn't come out here expecting to have Nalini's life seriously at risk. Or his own, though Casmir was sure the idea of losing her bothered the former knight more than the idea of dying himself.

Casmir didn't want to lose anybody. "Any progress, Tork?" he asked quietly.

He and Zee were bent over the console, interfacing with the computer as they hung on to keep from flying free whenever the ship shifted directions to avoid more trouble.

"I have uploaded the necessary software to the weapons systems," Tork said. "I will begin tagging the enemy ships."

"Good," Casmir said. "Thank you."

"Where are you flying off to, Princess Nalini?" came a suspicious-sounding comm from one of their ally ships. "We're here to help you, and this is already more than we bargained for."

Casmir had his hand near the comm button, so he answered, not wanting to give the true reason in case the mercenaries were monitoring. "We're going to visit the leaders out there and see how they like my crushers."

"Is that going to work? Because I just saw Denton's ship get blown up. We didn't sign on to sacrifice ourselves here. We're about to—"

"Receive what you're hoping to get," Casmir promised. "Ours is working, and I'll be able to make more."

"*If* we survive," the ship's owner grumbled.

"More camouflaged ships are coming within range," Tristan said, an ominous note in his voice.

Casmir gaped as another dozen vessels showed up on the scanners, almost all of them arranged in a formation to protect a larger central ship, a custom craft like none of the others. It was heavily armored but also appeared fast, and it bristled with weapons like a huffy porcupine.

"I think that's Dubashi," Tristan said.

Casmir sank back into his pod. "I think so too."

And he didn't think their little fleet had the firepower to touch it.

CHAPTER 25

TERROR SENT ADRENALINE SURGING THROUGH OKU'S VEINS AS she read the message again, the promise that Chasca wouldn't make it past high tide if she didn't hurry alone to Picnic Point. She almost sprinted for the back gate to race out of the castle grounds and to the trails leading down to the beach. But she made herself stay rooted, at least until she figured this out. Someone had set a trap, and the stupidest thing she could do was run into it.

She checked the tide schedule on her chip as she envisioned Picnic Point in her mind, a beach she'd visited often in her life. It was two miles to the south of the castle and at the bottom of a cliff. Rock formations rose up out in the water, and boulder piles dotted the beach, boulder piles exactly like the one Chasca was chained to in the photo.

"Your Highness?" Maddie was standing back to give her privacy, but she must have read all the horrified expressions on Oku's face.

Oku hesitated, certain Chasca's kidnapper didn't want her to share this with anyone, but if she went down there alone, she would end up kidnapped. Or worse. She held the note out to Maddie.

"That ass," she growled. "It came from inside the castle, and it had to be someone Chasca knew or she wouldn't have gone along quietly. It had to be Finn."

That thought had crossed Oku's mind. He was enough of a jerk to kidnap her dog. She would like to think he wouldn't *kill* her dog, but if he was worried about his position as heir, maybe he planned to kill her and cared even less about Chasca.

But she shouldn't assume it was he. Jorg's death could have been an impetus for other nefarious people to set plans into motion. Oku had also just irked Chief Van Dijk from Royal Intelligence, though this didn't seem like something people loyal to her father would do.

"Chasca would go with anyone who gave her food. As much as I want to go pummel Finn, that wouldn't do much even if he's responsible. He would have hired someone else to do the dirty work, and it's already been set in motion." Maybe Oku would *still* pummel him to see if he knew anything. "Who do you trust among my other bodyguards not to be bought off?"

Oku would have said she trusted them all, but Maddie was professionally paranoid for a living and more likely to have heard things that people wouldn't say around their princess.

"Gunther and Rokuro. I'll get them and we'll all go down to the beach." Maddie gripped the hilt of her pistol. "We'll find the kidnappers before they can hurt Chasca."

Oku bit her lip. "A sniper could be anywhere on that cliff, or even above it, aiming down from one of the benches lining the walkway up there."

"Not in this visibility." Maddie waved at the fog.

"Ah, good point. They'd have to be close. Maybe in one of the caves in the cliff then. Or out in the open on the beach, but if so, they'd be easier targets themselves."

"We can take care of it, Your Highness."

"Not on foot. They'll be expecting that." There was only one path down to that beach, and they would be watching it. But if Oku flew in… "Can either of those guys pilot a darter?"

"Gunther. I'll tell him to meet us… Where?" Maddie frowned at her. "Under your authority, we can requisition a vehicle from the royal landing pad across the street, but if they've got someone watching for that or watching the exits of the castle to make sure you comply…"

Oku closed her eyes, rethinking childhood memories of winding through the secret tunnels under the castle, of her father showing her and her brothers how to get to the vehicles and air darters stored in the underground hangar in case of an emergency. It had been years since she'd gone down there, but she believed she could still find the way, and she was certain her father maintained the area. She only hoped that Finn or whoever was behind this wouldn't think of that hangar. If someone spotted her not obeying the orders in the note precisely…

She swallowed, trying not to imagine a heartless assassin shooting her best friend.

"Follow me." Oku jogged to the castle, her sandals slapping on the cement sidewalk. If anyone was watching her from one of those guard towers and reporting to the kidnapper, they shouldn't think it odd if she ran inside to grab shoes and a walking stick—or a gun—before running out to the beach. But she couldn't linger long, or that person would report that she hadn't run out the gate as predicted. "Ask the guys to meet us in the Grand Receiving Room."

"To take the secret passage to the air darters under the castle?" Maddie, as Oku's personal bodyguard of twenty years, also knew about the tunnels and the underground hangar.

"Yes. I have one stop I want to make along the way. Just in case."

As she ran to one of the back doors, Oku fought the urge to glare angrily at the guard towers, annoyed that she couldn't trust everyone up there and more annoyed that an innocent animal was being brought into someone's idiotic scheme. What was the point of even targeting her? She didn't want to rule anything or be named as her father's heir.

"Do you have a stunner I can borrow, Maddie?" Oku asked as they slipped inside.

She thought Maddie might object to giving her a weapon, or point out that it was *her* duty to shoot people, but Maddie wordlessly handed her the stunner on her belt, keeping her deadlier pistol for herself.

"Thanks."

Oku kept the weapon close to her side, her finger on the trigger, but she stuck it partway into her pocket so it wouldn't be that noticeable. She ran past staff and distant relatives staying in the castle, not stopping to respond to anyone's questioning looks. The press of time weighed on her, and she second-guessed her decision to detour, but if Finn did have something to do with this, and she could get him to admit it, they might save time.

On the third level of the castle, Finn's bodyguard, Wolfram, lounged against the wall beside the door to his suite.

"He said not to let you in," Wolfram said.

"He was expecting me?" That spoke volumes. Oku hardly ever went to her brothers' quarters.

"Said you might come tonight."

"Maddie." Oku had been leading, but she stepped aside. "Convince Wolfram that I should be let in, please."

As Maddie surged forward, the guard sprang from his lazy pose into a fighting stance to face her. With his attention on Maddie, Oku whipped out the stunner and fired. The blue nimbus caught him full in the chest. He pitched backward as Maddie reached him. She lifted her arms, as if to keep him from crashing down hard and hitting his head, but she stopped herself and let him fall. Maybe they'd had cross words in the past, or maybe Maddie had twigged the same thing that Oku had, that Finn—and at least one of Finn's bodyguards—knew something about the kidnapping.

"That'll be hard to do when he's passed out," she said.

"Will it? Huh." Oku tried the doorknob, but it was locked. She looked down at her stunner but couldn't imagine it would do anything against a mechanical lock.

"Allow me." Maddie dragged the bodyguard out of the way, so she had room to maneuver. Then she turned and threw her whole body into a powerful kick.

The door wasn't that flimsy, but her heel struck like a battering ram. The lock snapped, and Maddie charged in. She surprised Oku by diving to the side and rolling across the hard marble entryway.

A weapon cracked, and a bullet slammed into the wall opposite the now-open door. Oku gaped and jumped farther to the side, glad she hadn't been standing in the open.

"What're you—" That was all Finn got out before the smack of a punch landing sounded.

A clatter followed. His gun hitting the floor? Several thumps followed, and Finn managed to get one angry indignant shout out before his voice broke into a pained yelp.

"Let me know when I should come in," Oku called, feeling silly hiding in the hall. But eyeing the bullet hole in the opposite wall convinced her this was the place for a non-combatant.

Would Finn have shot her if she'd slipped past Wolfram on her own and come into his room? Or did he always keep an old-fashioned firearm close at hand?

"Never," Maddie said, her voice low, as if she was on the floor, "if you don't want to see a horrific mess."

"Uh, like my brother's blood everywhere?"

"Like his dirty underwear everywhere."

HOME FRONT

An angry muffled sound followed her words.

Suspecting the fight was over, Oku peeked around the doorjamb. Maddie had Finn pinned on the floor, his arms behind his back as she kept her knee in his spine. His face was mashed into a rug, his desk chair overturned to the side. The gun he'd fired lay several feet away on the marble tiles. Maddie wasn't exaggerating about the mess.

"Don't you have a cleaning robot, Finn?" Oku walked in, debating how she would get answers out of him.

Would applying pain work? Finn would know that she wouldn't order Maddie to do anything too damaging to him, not even with Chasca's life at stake.

"I don't like spies in my room," he growled, the words muffled and barely audible. The one eye that Oku could see was glaring balefully at her.

"Time, Your Highness," Maddie warned. "What do you want to do?"

"Are you the one who took her, Finn?" Oku asked.

"No," he snarled instead of asking "Her who?" as she might have expected.

"But you know about it."

"You better quit screwing around and go get her." The visible half of his mouth managed an effective sneer. "I heard you don't have much time."

"Heard from whom? The people you paid to kidnap her? Why my *dog*, Finn? You know where I live and have access to the castle. It's not like you couldn't have just come to my room."

It wouldn't have been *that* easy, but Oku was frustrated and wanted answers.

"*I* didn't do it."

"Who did?"

He clammed up and tried to buck Maddie off. She was too good. She only twisted his arms harder and leaned in deeper. He gasped in pain, tears springing to his eyes.

Maddie raised her eyebrows. Asking if she should elicit *more* pain?

Oku bit her lip. It wouldn't take long for someone in security to see the downed bodyguard on a hall camera and send a team up here. And then what? It would be her word against her brother's, whom Father had left in charge of the castle. Or the *planet*, to hear Finn talk. Maybe Father was giving him a chance to prove himself, the same way he had Jorg.

Prove himself an asshole, maybe.

Oku waved at the three computer displays mounted to the wall over the desk, bringing them to life. One showed the blockade, making her believe briefly that her brother cared about the system and what happened, but another was a paused video game. A third—she sucked in a breath—was Chasca in the fog, still chained to those boulders. She was lying in the damp sand, staring toward the waves lapping at the beach, creeping closer. Did she realize her peril yet? Oku hoped not. She didn't want Chasca to be afraid.

"Who's sending you this feed?" she demanded, her voice raspy with anger. "I know it's not one of the public ones."

Finn grunted something unintelligible but unmistakably defiant.

Maddie must have pulled his arms tighter, because he gasped again and snarled, "They didn't give me their *names*."

"You're going along with someone else's plan?" Oku tapped at the computer interface, trying to find the source. The file was unhelpfully called temp_cam1. The sender wasn't listed as a person's name, just a gobbledygook of numbers.

"Someone whose vision aligns with mine," Finn muttered.

"Doubtful."

Voices and footsteps sounded on the nearby stairs. There wasn't much time.

Oku started recording the live feed on her contact camera and got what scant data she could. She had no experience with computer programming—or hacking—but she had friends at the university who were well-connected in that world. She sent off what she got with an urgent request for help to Naruto, who ran one of the computer labs, asking him to track the source and find out who was sending it.

"Let him up," Oku said, backing away. It would be easier to explain her intrusion if they didn't have Finn pinned to the floor.

"Are you sure?" Maddie asked.

"No, but do it anyway. And then open the window."

Maddie gave her a confused look, but she got off Finn. He lunged to his feet and balled his hands into fists, as if he would take a punch at her, but he spun toward Oku instead. Maddie shifted to block him.

"I'm going to have you confined to your room," Finn snarled. "You'll never get that damn dog in time. Why didn't you go right out there after her, you idiot? You could have saved her."

HOME FRONT

"And gotten myself shot or kidnapped?" Oku pointed Maddie toward the window. "Whose interests are aligning with yours, Finn, and for what?"

Maddie kept her eye on him but opened the window onto the foggy night, then came to Oku's side.

"None of your business. Father's *not* going to change his mind and give you the throne. You don't deserve it. Nor is he going to marry you off to some stupid knight who will rule through your name."

This was the last thing Oku cared about right now, but she couldn't help from blurting, "He said he'd do that?"

"Sir Oswald on the Senate is who he mentioned. Not to me. He didn't know I was there."

"When was this?"

"Just yesterday, when he heard about Jorg's death. But it sounded like he had it as a contingency plan all along. If me and Jorg couldn't show we had the chops to rule. Well, *I've* got the chops, and I'll show him that. And *you're* not going to be around to be some knight's trophy wife."

Before the guards appeared in the doorway, Oku pulled out her stunner and shot her brother. He tumbled to the floor, a startled expression frozen on his face. She pocketed the stunner, and she had time to kneel beside him as the first of three burst into the room.

"They went that way," Oku shouted, pointing toward the open window. "Two men were here when I came in, strong-arming him to be a part of a kidnapping attempt on me."

Maddie gave her an incredulous they're-not-going-to-believe-that look. But the guards didn't know what was happening.

One looked at her and started to say, "But she's the one who shot Wolf…" The others burst into motion without stopping to consider if they should doubt her. One ran to the window while the others rushed back into the corridor.

"Ring up an alert," one of them shouted. "Put the castle on lockdown."

For the moment, they were left alone in the room. Oku jerked her head toward the hallway, and Maddie followed her out.

"Are Gunther and Rokuro in the Receiving Room yet?" she whispered.

"Almost."

"Let's go. I still need to get Chasca." And she also had to worry about who'd been pulling her brother's strings to arrange this. Dealing with some plot of Finn's would have been bad enough. But this had turned a lot more dangerous.

Qin stood in the middle of the cargo hold all by herself, or so it would seem to the pirate boarding party. Her faceplate should hide her features at a distance so they would assume she was Jemadari's hired help and nothing more. She held her big Brockinger gun but kept it lowered at her side, as if she knew she was outmatched and intended to surrender.

Asger and Bjarke were hiding behind stacks of crates. The crushers had turned themselves into what looked like black sheets of metal and flattened themselves against the hull to either side of the airlock. That entire side of the hold and part of the ceiling were now black instead of the blue of the ship's interior walls. Hopefully, the pirates wouldn't think anything odd about the quirky paint job until it was too late.

Grinding and wrenching sounds reached Qin's ears as the outer airlock hatch was forced open. She made herself keep her weapon down, though her instincts shouted for her to shoot at the pirates when they barged in.

But when someone entered the airlock chamber and peered through the circular window of the inner hatch, it wasn't the pirate Qin expected. It was a familiar face, one almost identical to her own. The Druckers had sent her sisters to board the ship.

Her first feeling was one of alarm—she'd hoped she wouldn't have to fight them—but then she realized this might work out. If *all* of her sisters were being sent, she could pull them into this ship right away. They might not have to take the battle to the pirate warship at all, unless Asger and Bjarke wanted to sabotage it so they could get away more easily.

More wrenching sounds came as her sisters brought in blowtorches to force open the inner hatch. Qin walked to it—it would be better to ensure Jemadari's ship remained flyable—and held up her hands. Her Brockinger swung on its strap, but she acted as if she would let them in. Which she would.

"Are we going to have to fight them?" Asger murmured quietly over the helmet comm. He was leaning out from behind his stack of crates.

"Let's hope not," she said without moving her lips. "They're good."

"I have no doubt."

HOME FRONT

She resisted the urge to make a shooing motion to send him back out of view. Her sister was watching her. Between the thick window and the faceplates between them, Qin couldn't yet tell which one.

She opened the hatch, revealing numerous familiar faces, then stepped back with her hands raised. As much as she would have liked to hug her sisters, she had no doubt some of the pirates had come along and were behind them in the airlock tube.

Twelve of her sisters tramped in, all wearing combat armor, all pointing their weapons at Qin. All save one.

Mouser stopped in front of her—she'd always favored pale-green bows in her hair, and one dangled into view behind her faceplate—her weapon on a strap rather than in her grip. Her gauntleted hands were clasped behind her back.

Qin was about to say something, but twelve more people strode into the cargo hold, pirates in a hodgepodge of gray, blue, and black armor. One of the Druckers' teams.

"You are alone?" Mouser looked around the hold.

If she hadn't been wearing a helmet, she might have smelled the lingering scents of other people, but the armor would hinder that sense for her as much as it did for Qin.

"There are others on the ship," Qin said.

"Where's this supposed slydar detector?" one pirate asked.

"And any other valuables you've got," another said.

"As long as we get the *valuable* we came for." That was Groggins. He pointed at Qin and grinned.

Her stomach twisted as their eyes met and memories of the past flooded into her mind again.

Several of the men chuckled at Groggins' stupid joke. Qin glanced uneasily at her sisters as she got the first inkling that things weren't going according to plan—the pirates shouldn't have known she was here. They should have been shocked to see her.

"Sorry, Squirt." Mouser removed her hands from behind her back and showed a ball that could expand into an incredibly strong energy net. It looked identical to the one the pirates had used to capture Qin back on Death Knell Station.

She stared instead of reacting, too stunned to accept that instead of setting her own trap, she'd been lured into one by the pirates. By the pirates and her own clone sisters.

"Qin?" Asger's voice came softly over the comm helmet. He didn't seem to quite get what was happening either. Or maybe he didn't know if he should jump out and attack her sisters.

That one is Groggins, she told Asger silently, glaring at the pirate. *And I believe we're betrayed. I'm sorry.*

"They've wanted you back for a long time," Mouser explained as the others spread out around Qin, "and when they learned you were also trapped in this system…"

"There are knights in here," one of the men barked.

Bjarke sprang out from his hiding place, firing toward the pirates. Asger rushed out and targeted Qin's sisters. His DEW-Tek bolts slammed into Mouser's armored back.

Qin recovered from her surprise and was ready when Mouser flung the ball. Qin leaped into the air and over the heads of those gathered around her, hoping the net would unravel and catch one of her sisters instead.

But Mouser was as good as she was and anticipated the maneuver. The ball clipped Qin's boot, and the energy net unfurled with lightning speed, crackling as it wrapped around her lower half.

She landed with a grunt, flopping onto her side since her legs were bound and stuck together. Even with all her strength and the additional strength from her armor, it wasn't enough to break the net, a tool designed to detain even cybernetically enhanced and armored soldiers.

Qin opened fire from the deck, aiming at the damn pirates—aiming at *Groggins*—while avoiding Bjarke and Asger. Bjarke had engaged the pirates, and Asger was trying to fight his way to her, but they were outnumbered. When would the crushers jump in to help?

Two of her sisters dropped atop her, trying to tear away her rifle. Qin snarled as she fought them, hardly believing they were loyal to the pirates—to their slavers and rapists. If she could defeat the men, her sisters would back away and go with her, happy to be rescued. That letter from Mouser couldn't have all been a lie, could it?

Powerful hands gripped her helmet. Trying to tear it off, Qin realized. They wanted to stun her, to knock her out, so they could drag her back to that prison of a life with the Druckers. No. God, no. She thrashed and fought her captor. After the freedom she'd had this last year, she couldn't go back to that life. No way.

She punched backward, connecting with her assailant's faceplate. Her gauntleted fist struck it like a pile driver with a satisfying *crack*. But another foe forced her onto her stomach and wrestled her arms behind her back. Without the use of her legs, she couldn't get any leverage to fight her foes or even jump to her feet.

"What are *they*?" one of her sisters shouted.

Finally, the crushers had removed themselves from the wall and formed into their deadly bipedal forms. Half of them joined Bjarke in battling the pirates. Half of them ran toward Qin's sisters.

Qin had a fleeting hope that she would be saved, but then hands grabbed her helmet again, wrenching it around with such power that it snapped out of its lock. The hands tore it away, and she heard it clunk into one of the approaching crushers.

Asger was being driven farther away from her with two of her sisters battling him at once. Qin caught him glancing at her, his face a mix of anguish and fury, but he couldn't reach her.

A hand with a stunner appeared, and Qin flung herself sideways, rolling into two sets of legs. If she could hold out a few more seconds, her sisters would be too busy fighting the crushers to worry about her.

But the stunner tracked her and fired. A flash of white-blue scorched her retinas, and she lost consciousness.

CHAPTER 26

YAS TREATED RACHE'S ASTROSHAMAN PRISONERS, TRYING TO SMILE often and make them feel at ease, but they put *him* ill-at-ease. The three women had blatant cybernetic upgrades including alterations to their faces, ports in their arms, and chips under the skin on all of their fingertips. They did not speak, at least not out loud or to him, neither answering nor acknowledging his questions. They rarely looked at each other or anyone, instead staring at walls or computer consoles.

He assumed they were speaking chip-to-chip to each other, which almost everyone did, but there was something unhuman about them, more so than with the mercenaries who had cybernetic upgrades. Maybe because the mercenaries only tried to make themselves faster and stronger. They rarely added ports for wiring themselves directly into mainframes.

The astroshamans' injuries were minor, and Yas was relieved to release them to the custody of a couple of sergeants who would take them to the brig. And he hoped eventually back to their ship. He had nothing against these astroshamans and would prefer not to have them gunning for him simply because he was Rache's doctor.

As they departed, Rache walked into sickbay. They glared at him on the way out, but the sergeants shoved them along.

"They'll be returned to their ship shortly," Rache told Yas. "The gate has been reopened and doesn't seem in danger of closing again. I am curious how it was done and undone. As far as I know, High Shaman Moonrazor was responsible, but she never came to the area. Amergin did detect some encrypted data transmissions being beamed at the gate. It's disturbing to think that she has the technology to wave her fingers and disable any of the gates in the system whenever she wishes."

"Perhaps not a good person to make an enemy of," Yas observed, though Rache had done precisely that, irking the astroshaman leader twice. Would that come back to haunt him? Would all those on the ship with Rache be caught in the explosion when it did?

"Perhaps a good person to kill," Rache said bluntly.

"Your problem-solving methods are strange."

"No, they're practical. Amoral and illegal but practical." Rache looked around sickbay. "Pack up, Doctor. We're heading to System Lion to complete my mission."

"And what after that?" Yas asked as Rache turned back toward the exit.

Rache paused. "If we survive, we'll carry on and look for more work."

If they survived? Yas couldn't remember him ever saying that.

"That'll be more difficult as the slydar detectors become more widely available, won't it?" Yas didn't give voice to the rumor that Rache's own clone brother was making more of those slydar detectors now. He didn't want to suggest Casmir was another enemy who should suffer Rache's practical problem-solving methods.

"It will." Rache turned his masked face toward Yas. "What's your point?"

"Maybe you should consider retirement."

"This isn't a job you retire from."

"You just keep doing it until you get killed?"

"What else would I do, Doctor?" Rache asked softly. "War and battle is what I was taught and trained for since childhood. It's all I know."

"Assume another identity, ask Scholar Sato on a date, and fly off to another system to get a gig as a defense contractor. Maybe Tiamat Station would have a use for someone with your unique skill set."

"Are you offering me a job, Peshlakai?" Rache sounded amused.

"I could probably talk someone there into doing so."

"I'll keep that in mind," Rache said, the words of someone who had no intention of giving the offer a further thought.

"At least let your people take some leave after this," Yas called as Rache stepped through the doorway. "Your chief engineer needs surgery and physical therapy."

Rache lifted a hand. In parting? Acknowledgment? Agreement? Yas didn't know.

"That is a difficult man."

HOME FRONT

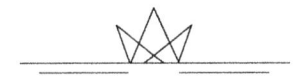

Kim sat in her pod in the guest cabin Casmir had shown her to—her mother had messaged to let her know she and Tork had settled in next door—listening to comm chatter and wondering why she was on the ship. From what she gathered, it wasn't much safer on the station, but she felt useless. She would have liked to pace, but the gravity was erratic as the ship dove and turned and at last, she was fairly certain, spiraled downward in a spin. Her stomach wasn't as sensitive as Casmir's, but even she experienced twinges of queasiness.

Reuben stared blandly at the door, his hand around a grip so he wouldn't tumble away. She wondered if the crusher also felt helpless, stuck down here as her bodyguard. Nobody had even visited her since Casmir left. Not that the other crushers would be doing anything more interesting. If they got boarded or were commanded to board another ship, then they would have more of a purpose. Maybe she would too, though she wore only a galaxy suit with a stunner, not combat armor and a rifle. Rache's suggestion that she hide in a cabinet during any combat wasn't without merit, but she hated being useless.

"The lucky crusher is on this ship, Kim Sato," Reuben stated.

"Uhm, what?"

"Casmir Dabrowski calls the lucky crusher Gad. Perhaps his presence on this ship will keep it from being destroyed. My file on human facial expressions informs me that you may be feeling pensive, either due to the battle or the fact that you are sharing a cabin with an unlucky crusher."

Kim stared at him, wondering if this new crusher was even buggier than Zee. "I'm actually feeling useless because I have no purpose in this battle. I wasn't thinking about luck." Or crushers, but she kept that to herself in case it would hurt his feelings. Normally, she wouldn't think a robot could have feelings, but this one seemed… special. And who knew what capacities Casmir had programmed them with?

"I have a purpose—to protect you—but I also wish I could contribute in a meaningful way."

"It's nice to feel useful."

"Yes."

The ship shifted course hard, and Kim's stomach protested. During a lull in the maneuvers, she ordered the pod to release her and went to the trunk she'd strapped to the deck before takeoff. As she dug through the contents for anti-nausea medicine, she couldn't help but notice the black box with elegant gold embellishments that barely fit in the big trunk. It was long and narrow with some heft, but she wouldn't call it heavy. A ribbon wrapped around the box kept it closed.

She'd been on her way to meet Casmir, so there hadn't been time to open it when it had first arrived, delivered by an enigmatic servant who'd said only that it was a gift from an admirer. Rache, of course. She reached for it now, running a hand along the sleek box. Should she open it? Or wait until the battle was over? Maybe it was something that would be useful in this situation though she couldn't imagine what. Would Rache have sent her some weapon to defend herself against invading mercenaries?

Since the ship was flying straight for the moment, Kim risked untying the ribbon. She was about to lift off the lid when the door chime buzzed.

"I will protect you from assassins, Kim Sato," Reuben stated.

"Thank you, but I don't think they usually ring the doorbell before coming in."

He looked at her. "There was no bell."

"Never mind. Will you open it, please?"

The crusher did so but did not shift aside to allow entry—maybe he thought he might have to block a barrage of weapons fire. Kim's mother scrambled between his legs.

Reuben started to reach for her, but Kim blurted, "It's fine. She can come in."

"Is this the same one from the party?" Her mother's monkey-droid nose wrinkled.

"My bodyguard. Temporarily."

"I didn't realize the ramifications when it was following you around, carrying your trunk earlier. I thought it might be a porter."

"Crushers —" Reuben checked the corridor before closing the door, "—are sophisticated defenders of human beings, not porters."

"What's going on, Mother?" Kim didn't mind the company, but she felt self-conscious about opening Rache's gift with someone besides Reuben in the room. Especially someone she was related to.

HOME FRONT

"I decided to check on you. Tork left to work on something with Casmir."

"Oh." Kim wondered what. Something to do with the slydar detector? "I was just taking some anti-nausea medicine."

"I do not miss that part of being human." Her mother settled on a bunk, using the sleep sack to anchor herself.

"I can imagine not." Kim shifted so that her body blocked what she was doing and untied the ribbon and opened the box. The contents were not made from fungi—or at least she was reasonably sure.

She drew a sword with a long, single-edged curved blade—a katana. It was a real blade to match the wooden bokken she'd been carrying with her when all these space adventures first started and when Rache had first captured her and Casmir. The metalwork was beautiful, and she wished she were somewhere that she could perform a few katas. As it was, it was too dangerous to have out with the ship apt to start up maneuvers again any second.

After carefully tucking it back in the box and securing it with straps, she pulled out a note. It wasn't handwritten—it couldn't have been Rache's writing even if it had been—but it held his words.

Kim, thank you for the gift of the story last time we met. I do not believe you'll find this effective against men in combat armor, but perhaps you'll enjoy an authentic blade with which to practice on your journey home. There is a Kingdom refugee on Stardust Palace who happens to be a smith—he was pleased to have someone to make this for. I understand he usually gets requests for decorative khanjali daggers from the sultan's overly monied children and relatives. Also metal candlesticks and planters.

She snorted softly.

He hadn't signed the note—or had the creator of the gift do it—for obvious reasons. He'd probably used some fake identity and account to purchase it. Understandable, but she found herself wishing for another confession of love. Though maybe it was her turn to say it back. Maybe—

Kim? A message from Casmir popped up on her chip. *We think we've found Dubashi.*

Here?

Here. He's well-protected, so I don't know if there's any chance that we'll be able to get to him—odds are more in favor of us getting blown to bits by these mercenaries—but in case we're extremely lucky and figure out how to board his ship with a few dozen crushers... are you game to hunt for and disarm those rockets?

Yes. Nerves fluttered in Kim's stomach, but she nodded to herself. She had *wanted* to be useful. This was her chance. *I'll rest much easier knowing that virus can never make it home.*

Me too. I'll keep you posted.

Kim chewed on her lip. He hadn't sounded optimistic that they would get a shot at Dubashi. Even though she wasn't up in navigation, she could guess from how much maneuvering they were doing and how often they'd been hit that things weren't going to plan.

Though Kim was almost positive Rache was near the gate and maybe already out of the system, she sent him a message.

David, thank you for the gift. I just had the opportunity to open it. If I get a chance to stab an enemy who isn't wearing combat armor, I will take it.

In case you're still in the system and have been wondering where Dubashi is... he's here. At Stardust Palace, egging on all of these mercenaries. I doubt you're close enough to help, and I know you have your own mission, regardless. Kim didn't let herself add anything that would have condemned his "mission." He already knew how she felt about it. *But if you have any way to help from afar, I am not too proud to ask for that help. If you are already gone from the system, then... my best wishes. If I survive this, I will write another story for you. I trust you will survive long enough to receive it.*

I... She debated on the closing, on adding the logical words. But would they be true? She wasn't sure. Would it be a lie if she added them? She wasn't sure about that either. She lifted the lid of the box to run her hand along the beautiful blade again. A lump formed in her throat and her eyes burned at the thought that she might never get to use his gift. Or see him again to properly thank him for it.

I love you, she flung out, before she could rethink it, then signed the note and sent it off.

Swallowing, she wiped the moisture from her eyes.

A touch to her shoulder startled her.

Her mother had come over. "Are you all right?"

"Yes. I was just... messaging someone. Casmir," she added, not wanting to explain Rache.

HOME FRONT

"Tork said they found Dubashi out there." Her mother pointed to her furry temple, though Kim didn't think her chip was in the same spot as it had been when she'd been human.

"Yeah."

Her mother looked at the box, and Kim had the urge to pull the lid down. She didn't want to explain where the katana had come from, or from whom.

"Your father has some like that," her mother said.

"I know. He uses them at the dojo sometimes."

"Ah. It is strange. You would not think it possible for androids to feel nostalgia, but sometimes, I do." She shook her head and gave her monkey equivalent of a wry smile. "I hope we somehow make it back to System Lion and Odin, though I suppose Jager would see me as an enemy now and forbid me to visit. Especially since…" She twitched her tail.

"Especially since your reason for going would be to help your new people get Jager's gate pieces?" Kim had gotten some of the lowdown on that from Casmir.

"Just the one with the controls in it."

"Maybe you can trade him one of the less useful pieces."

"I'm sure he knows by now what he has."

The ship shuddered, and the lights flashed off for a second. Were the shields still holding? Kim pulled down the lid on the katana box, closed it in her trunk, and maneuvered back to her pod, though she was tempted to run up to navigation and see what was happening.

"I hope we make it out of here," Kim said as her mother returned to the bunk, "and can visit Father together one day."

"I would like that." Judging from her mother's tone, she didn't think it would happen.

CHAPTER 27

WHEN OKU AND MADDIE REACHED THE GRAND RECEIVING Room with its piano, fountain, and seats for hosting formal gatherings, Oku rushed straight to the bust of Admiral Mikita two-thirds of the way down one wall. It was a square-jawed, aquiline-nosed Admiral Mikita bust that she knew, now that she'd met Casmir, couldn't have been based off the real man. She twisted the bust on its pedestal, and a door in the ancient stone opened behind it.

"Wait for Gunther and Rokuro, and follow me down." Oku had lost time stopping at Finn's room and hadn't learned nearly as much as she'd hoped.

Maddie gripped her arm, stopping her. "We'll both wait."

"I know the way. I can get the darter started."

Maddie shook her head. "Someone could have anticipated you would make this move."

Oku stared into the dark tunnel—no automatic lights had come on here—and reluctantly accepted that Maddie was right. She shifted from foot to foot as they waited and had her chip cycle through public parks cameras that overlooked the trails around the city. A few of them showed the foggy beaches, the water rising as the tide came in, but the one from Picnic Point was out, nothing but black on the display.

Gunther and Rokuro came wearing armor, carrying weapons, and they'd stopped to grab flashlights and emergency kits. Oku hoped this wouldn't take long but couldn't fault them for making preparations. Especially after she'd stunned Finn. It was possible this would go to hell, and she wouldn't be able to return to the castle.

"Thank you for coming," Oku whispered.

"An honor to serve, Your Highness." Lean and wiry, Rokuro managed an elegant bow even in combat armor.

"We'll get your girl." The towering Gunther had hands like spatulas and gave her a clumsy shoulder pat.

Oku waved for Maddie to take the lead, then followed her with the men trailing after them. They closed the secret door behind them, and darkness broken only by flashlight beams filled the passage. Dust coated the floor, and cobwebs dangled from the corners, but the route itself was unimpeded.

A message came in on her chip as they wound through ancient passageways behind rooms and under floors. It was from Princess Tambora—she'd been caught by the closed gate and was at Stardust Palace Station. Oku had thought the blockade was the reason she hadn't heard from her acquaintance for so long. It was interesting that she was caught in the same system as Casmir and the small Kingdom fleet, but Oku didn't have time to compose a long reply. She almost set it aside for later, but she did send a quick note asking what had been happening with Dubashi, and if Tambora knew anything about Casmir's involvement.

She was tired of getting reports filtered through Intelligence's eyes. Not even that. Most of what she'd been told about him had come from her father.

The group reached a ladder well that descended into the stone cliff under the castle. Nothing but the clank of boots on rungs and the soft puffs of breaths filled the air as Oku and the others flowed downward. Occasionally, the men's armored shoulders clunked or scraped on the tight walls.

They descended past side openings that led to other tunnels. Oku remembered exploring down here as a girl and finding underground bunkers full of years' worth of emergency rations and supplies. There was also a secret passage to the Royal Intelligence headquarters building and to the dungeons that existed on the lowest official level of the castle. In her youth, she'd been afraid to visit either place, not wanting to chance upon some enemy of the Kingdom being tortured.

Even as a little girl, she'd never had delusions about her father being a kind and noble soul who would never do such things. But she had never gone seeking out evidence of it.

When they reached the bottom of the ladder, Maddie and Oku waited in a tunnel for the men to catch up. It led in only one direction, toward the underground hangar with its secret exit out toward the beach. Oku couldn't make out many details, but there had to be a few pieces of computer equipment with glowing indicators in the hangar, because it wasn't as dark ahead as it had been in the ladder well.

"Gunther," Maddie whispered. "I heard someone. You and your armor go first."

Oku squeezed against the wall with Maddie, her sandaled toes almost being stepped on as the two armored men passed. They strode fearlessly forward. Oku assumed the only one up there would be some bored guard tasked with keeping an eye on the place.

Weapons fire opened up, and Oku jumped.

She leaned out to peer past Maddie toward the hangar. Should she have gone first to identify herself? If it *was* a duty guard, maybe he'd been startled by two armored men striding out.

Before Oku could take a step, Maddie's arm came out and flattened her back to the wall. Maddie shifted to fill the tunnel—and block any shots that might be fired back toward Oku.

Someone shouted, "…wasn't doing anything!" and was cut off.

More weapons fired. Oku bit her lip, confused and worried and wishing she could help. At the least, she wanted to know what was going on. Had people been stationed down here to keep her from escaping? From going out to get Chasca?

As weapons continued to fire, she checked the time and groaned at the seconds ticking past. Before she'd opted for this route, two hours had seemed like plenty of time to grab a darter and fly to the beach, but now she was stuck.

When Oku tried to recheck the tide schedule to make sure Chasca was still all right, she couldn't. This far underground, there wasn't enough reception for her chip to load the data.

Oku groaned in frustration. She almost jumped when a text message made it through on the limited available bandwidth.

It was her programmer acquaintance at the university, Naruto. *Princess Oku, I got your message, and I think I've almost traced the sender. It's someone in the city. By the way, it's great to hear from you. The war has been crazy. You're missed at the university.*

Another burst of weapons fire echoed from the hangar, and she almost laughed at the absurdity that Naruto was sitting in a dorm room with no idea that she and Chasca were in danger.

Is it true that you're dating Professor Dabrowski? the note burbled on. She almost fell over. *What?*

There's a rumor. Because you went and got his parents to stay in the Citadel during the bombing. That's stellar. They're really good people. His mom makes cookies for the teacher-assistant Christmas party at the university every year even though that's not her religion. She says she'll bake any time it'll make people happy. Hang on, almost got it.

Oku was so startled by the aside about Casmir that she almost forgot what she'd asked Naruto for.

"I think it's almost over," Maddie whispered over her shoulder.

The weapons fire had stopped. Lights flared to life in the hangar, and Oku squinted as white brilliance flooded the tunnel.

"All clear, Maddie," Gunther called back.

"Stay here. I'll check." Maddie looked over her shoulder. "You still have that stunner?"

Oku showed it to her.

"Good. Stay here," she repeated, then jogged into the hangar.

Here you go, Princess Oku. That handle belongs to Sir Slayer. Nobody's supposed to know his identity, but there's a lot of data to almost prove he's a Military Intelligence officer. Those guys aren't the best at hiding their footprints. It's not like they have to care that much if they're caught. Yup, Military Intelligence for sure. I've traced it back to the base here in town. Oh, this is hot stuff. I could get in lots of trouble poking around with the military. But you'll rescue me from jail if I'm thrown in right? Princesses can absolutely do that. And I have to finish this semester. I'm super close to graduating.

Military Intelligence? Oku let her shoulder blades thump back against the stone wall.

Try not to get caught, she replied, feeling weak. Why would the military be after her? Of all people who should be loyal to her father's wishes... *But I'll do what I can if you get in trouble. Thank you for the help.*

Welcome! Sorry, I don't know how much more information I can get. Slayer is hiding himself behind some pretty secure firewalls.

It's fine. You were great. Maybe once she made sure Chasca was safe, Oku could try speaking with her brother again. Did he even *know* who had set this all up? Or had he wanted for Oku to disappear so badly that he'd said yes to someone with a hidden identity?

HOME FRONT

"Princess Oku?" Maddie stepped into view, the harsh light of the hangar framing her. "You can come out here. If you want to." There was a weird note to her voice.

"Why wouldn't I want to? This ladder and tunnel are not interesting."

"It's messier than Finn's room," Maddie said without humor, then walked back into the hangar.

Oku trailed her out with the stunner in hand. Two men in black galaxy suits were down, the dark fabric scored from weapons blasts. One man wasn't moving—was he dead?—but the other groaned and twitched as Rokuro stood over him, a deadly rifle pointed downward. Next to them, Gunther knelt, gripping his arm. His armor was split from a barrage of fire that had struck him.

Maddie waved for Oku to follow her past them and toward one of three air darters parked in the hangar. The big sliding doors at the front, an exit she knew led out of the cliff and over the water, were closed. On one side of the hangar, four armored ground vehicles were parked near a small exit. She vaguely remembered that it led into a tunnel that eventually came out under a bridge in the city. She'd been eight the only time her father had taken her that way, not because of an emergency but because he'd been making sure that she, Jorg, and Finn knew how to escape if needed.

"Over here, Your Highness." Maddie stood at the open canopy of the cockpit of a darter and pointed into it, rather than directing her toward the passenger hatch in the back. What did she want Oku to see?

Oku grimaced as she came up to Maddie's side. A man was slumped forward, his torso and head pressed against the console. He wore the blue and silver uniform of the staff, a hole in the back with a blood stain darkening the fabric around it.

"Dead?" Oku stared at him and then toward the men in galaxy suits. "Did our people do it or…?"

Maddie shook her head. "They fired at those intruders out there, but we believe this man was dead when we came in." She gently pulled his head up to show his face. "It's one of your father's pilots."

Oku's stomach twisted as she recognized him. "Hideki. I've flown with him before. He has—had—a sense of humor."

It was an inane thing to say, but it was all that came to mind. The former army captain turned castle pilot Hideki had been easygoing and quick to crack jokes with Oku and her brothers when they'd been younger. So many of her father's staff were humorless—maybe he preferred it that way.

"I'm confused," Oku said. "Why was he down here? And who are they? You think they shot him?"

Maddie nodded. "One of them is still alive. Rokuro will drag him up for questioning once we've made sure you and Chasca are safe."

Oku appreciated that Maddie was keeping her mission ahead of whatever this new problem was, but she felt guilty now that a person had died. It wasn't *her* fault—she couldn't see how—but it made her worry about what was going on here. She still needed to get Chasca, but this had escalated into something scarier.

"Can Gunther still fly?" Oku pointed to the injured bodyguard.

He pushed himself to his feet. "Yes, Your Highness." Pain leaked into his voice, but he strode over, only hesitating when he saw Hideki. "Are we taking this one?"

Maddie looked over the other air darters. "It's the farthest from where the fighting was. It's probably least likely to be damaged."

"Right." Gunther sighed and they worked together to pull out the body, while Oku tried not to get in the way.

When they were done, Oku sat in the co-pilot's seat. Gunther took Hideki's seat and fired up the darter, and Maddie sat behind them in the first row of passenger seats. After the canopy closed, one of the displays lit up with a prompt for a fingerprint—authorization required to open the hangar doors.

Oku, hoping Finn wouldn't have thought of this and figured out a way to revoke her access, pressed her index finger to the screen. Long seconds ticked past.

"Is it possible Finn was planning to leave tonight?" she wondered.

"I can't think of any other reason Hideki would have been down here," Maddie said. "He's your father's personal pilot and only flies him, your mother, and you kids."

You kids, she said, as if they were all still ten.

The display finally recognized Oku's fingerprint and flashed an approval. The rolling doors slowly opened to the dark, foggy night.

"It's possible your mother had some reason to sneak out," Maddie said slowly, "but I can't imagine what it would be. Nobody would stop her if she went to the royal landing pad and ordered a flight. But we know Finn has been up to something shifty."

"I bet he was the one to recommend they use Chasca to get me out of the castle."

Oku wondered if there was any way she could question her brother under one of those military truth drugs. Not likely. Not with him in charge. Not unless she forced her way back into his suite and had Maddie overpower him again. That would be hard to do twice. As it was, he would probably try to convince security to confine her to her room—or arrest her—when she got back.

Would they? She didn't know. She'd never tried to cultivate anyone's loyalty for some insurrection, but she thought—hoped—she was less of an ass than he was and that they might side with her over Finn. Maybe that was naive to believe. After all, Father had put *him* in charge.

"They who?" Maddie sounded as puzzled as Oku had been all night.

Oku almost mentioned the Military Intelligence tie-in, but she would keep Naruto's information to herself until she knew more. And until Chasca was safe. Oku didn't know if the people in black had been lying in wait for her or for Finn—but she worried there would be more than a lone sniper on that beach watching Chasca. Poor girl. She never should have been brought into this.

As the darter sailed out of the hangar and banked to head south along the beach, Oku's reception improved. With fog obscuring the view in all directions, she looked up the tide tables and checked them against the time. Her fingers curled tight around the armrests of her seat. Everything had taken far longer than she'd wanted it to. It was going to be close, and if they had to fight when they got there…

Maddie leaned forward and gripped her shoulder, as if she knew Oku's exact thoughts. Maybe they weren't that hard to guess.

"We'll get her," Maddie said. "It's not far."

All Oku could do was nod and hope she was right.

Asger's heart broke when he saw Qin crumpled unconscious on the deck with her helmet ripped off by her own sisters, but he was fighting for his life, and he couldn't reach her. They wanted her alive—to take back to their awful coven of slaves—but neither the sisters nor the pirates cared about keeping *Asger* alive. They were shooting to kill.

Thankfully, the crushers were as powerful as the genetically modified women, and they outnumbered them. One slammed a fist into the helmet of one of Asger's two opponents. It dented the nearly indestructible material, and his foe tumbled to the side and went down. That only left one facing him.

He growled, using his pertundo against her, lightning crackling over the blade as he alternately swung it like an axe and jabbed at her protected torso with the sharp pointed tip. Already, he'd gotten past her defenses and struck her several times, denting her armor and sending the energy sizzling around her. If he could just connect with a seam. But she defended with speed and power, using her armored forearms or her rifle to block so hard that it jarred his joints and set him back on his heels.

"I'm on the warship," Asger's father reported over the helmet comm.

He'd rushed the pirates and disappeared into the airlock tube with half the crushers, letting them tear open their foes' armor, then coming behind with his pertundo, driving the weapon into exposed flesh and killing them on the spot. He clearly felt no remorse, no need to take prisoners, for the pirates he'd been undercover with for a year.

Knowing they'd tricked Qin, Asger felt no remorse for them either. Nor did he have fond feelings for Qin's sisters. As soon as he spotted an opening in his attacker's defenses, he slammed his pertundo into the seam between her arm and torso. The wicked point pierced armor and flesh, and she stumbled back, gasping in pain. Using his pertundo, he knocked her rifle out of her grip.

"Better get to engineering and see if you can sabotage the ship so we can get away." Asger swung his blade again, hoping to cleave her armor the rest of the way open.

"I'm going to the bridge. The—" A barrage of weapons fire and a snarl of rage interrupted his father's reply. "We're taking over the ship," he panted a second later.

"*Father.*"

"I'm giving the crushers the time they need to upload the virus. Keep—" His father broke off again, and Asger wanted to tell him to focus on fighting. A never-ending stream of rifle fire buzzed over his comm. "Keep the women busy," he finished.

"I'll kill them if I can," Asger growled, still after the one he'd wounded.

She sprang back again, then leaped in, trying to get around his pertundo to slam a punch into his faceplate. He whipped the shaft of his weapon across to deflect the blow, then kicked her in the knee. She tumbled back as a crusher grabbed her from behind. He hefted her into the air and flung her armored form across the hold. She crashed twenty feet up against the wall.

"That's not what Qin wants," his father said.

"These bitches *betrayed* her," Asger shouted, wanting them to hear the words.

Two of them glanced at each other, but he didn't know if it had anything to do with his shout. The crushers were keeping them busy, but they worked together, fighting back to back. A team, a team that Qin had been a part of once, but not today. They were rejecting her. And he would take them down if he could. He yanked up his rifle and fired into the knot of armored women.

"Trust me, boy. They're brainwashed and probably have stim-chips to electrically punish them if they don't comply. Gotta go. Another wave of pirates just showed up. And is that gas? What idiots gas someone in armor with thirty robots?" He snarled and the comm fell silent as he closed the channel.

One of the crushers hurled an armored pirate across the hold, keeping him from escaping back onto his own ship. He skipped off the deck and came to a stop right in front of Asger. Startled eyes looked up at him, and Asger recognized the pirate Qin had pointed out. Groggins. One of the men who'd tormented her.

Fury flushed Asger's face with heat. The pirate tried to scramble to his feet, but Asger lifted his pertundo and drove the point downward too quickly for Groggins to dodge. It drove into the seam between his torso and arm piece, and the pirate screamed, legs bucking on the deck, as energy flowed from the weapon, crackling all around him.

Asger yanked his weapon out. The pirate screamed again.

"Mercy, please!" Groggins blurted.

"You could have had mercy if you'd left her alone—left them *all* alone." This time when Asger drove his pertundo downward, he swung with such force that the point broke through the man's faceplate and drove into his skull. The legs stopped twitching, and the pirate soon lay still.

Weapons fire blasted off Asger's armor, and there wasn't time to feel satisfaction over taking out one of Qin's tormentors. He yanked his pertundo free and spun to face the next threat.

The battle wasn't over, but the crushers had successfully driven the warrior women back. The path to Qin's unconscious form grew clear, save for one of her sisters, kneeling over her with that damn stunner.

Asger growled and rushed at her. "Get away from her!"

He fired at the woman's chest and faceplate, and she leaped to her feet. She started to raise the stunner but saw he wore his full armor and switched to a rifle.

"What does a Kingdom knight care for one of our kind?" she snarled, firing at him.

Alerts lit up on his faceplate display, warning him of hits that would threaten his armor's integrity. He fired back, hardly caring. He could take as much as she could.

"She's *my* Qin. And she came to help you, you ungrateful snots." Aware of the crushers plowing into the other women, breaking up their back-to-back formation and hurling them about the hold, Asger focused on this one enemy. He fired and pushed her back until he stood above Qin, making sure nobody would step on her unprotected head or—worse—shoot her by accident.

Surprisingly, the woman stopped firing. Qin's exact face peered at him, save for a green bow dangling from a clump of hair beside her cheek. She glanced around the hold.

The pirates who'd come aboard had all fallen, and her sisters were losing to the crushers. They lacked the experience that Asger and Qin had with the sturdy killing machines—if they'd expected them, they would have brought explosives. That was the only thing Asger had ever seen knock them to pieces, however temporarily.

HOME FRONT

"We're not ungrateful," the woman with the bow said. "We didn't want to do this, but we had no choice."

"No? You're the only ones in this hold now. You're fighting for them voluntarily. You betrayed *Qin* voluntarily." Asger struggled to get his rage under control. He'd made it through to Qin and was protecting her, and his side had gained the advantage, at least in here.

He expected the woman to say she had no choice or to say that Qin had betrayed *them* by leaving.

Instead, she asked, "You care about her? A knight from the Kingdom? We are—" she kept hold of her rifle, kept it pointed at him, but she jerked one hand down her body, "—freaks. That is what your people say." Her voice lowered. "That is what many people say."

One of the women roared, and a crusher went flying over Asger's head to slam into a stack of shipping containers. The fight wasn't over yet.

He couldn't believe the one he faced was bringing this up now, but maybe it was worth responding to her. If she stopped fighting, would the others? If she was like Qin—*his* Qin—she might genuinely care about the answer, care about being regarded as a freak by the outside universe.

"I've known Qin—Qin Liangyu Three—for months, and we've fought together many times," Asger said. "She's not a freak. She's a loyal friend." Friend? More than that, but he wasn't going to bring up his love life with strangers, even strangers that knew Qin and looked just like her. "Put down your weapons and surrender, and come with us, with Qin. I promise you'll have a place with us."

"In the Kingdom?" the woman asked skeptically.

"Wherever you want to go. Qin works for a bounty hunter on the *Stellar Dragon*. You must have learned about her ship if you were planning this *trap*." Asger couldn't keep the sneer off his lips or the snarl out of his voice. "They'll have a place for you. And if you do come to the Kingdom, you can stay at my father's castle. We'll sic the guard alligators in the moat on anyone who gives you a hard time about visiting."

"You have a castle?" She sounded wistful, as if she'd forgotten they were in the middle of a battle.

"*Seven!*" one of the other ones yelled. She was pinned against the wall by two crushers, the chest plate of her armor torn off. "What are you doing?"

"Nothing!" The woman Asger faced put both hands back on her rifle and pointed it at his chest. "They'll come after us if we leave, if they believe we've betrayed them. That's why we're here now. They wouldn't let even one of us go. They found out Squirt—Three—was here and insisted we get her. They'll come after *all* of us if we try to leave. They paid a fortune for us." Bitterness infused her voice. "As they always remind us, we belong to them. They'll never let us go."

"They will if they're dead." Asger pointed at the crushers, making sure she saw that her side had almost lost. "Our friend made those, and they're helping my father take over your warship right now." He *hoped* that was what was happening.

"There are four other warships," she said.

"We'll take those over too."

She snorted. "Your people are only on board that one because we tricked you."

"Or we tricked you. No, not *you*. We came to get you. We tricked *them*." Asger flung a hand toward the pirate ship and Groggins' unmoving body. "And we *will* take over the other ships." Or the one other ship, at least. He didn't see how they could do anything to the three in System Cerberus from here, but if they took these two ships back to System Lion as war prizes, he truly doubted the Druckers would come after them, not against the Kingdom. As long as the Kingdom came out victorious in the war… "We have a powerful ally who made those crushers, and he can make a lot more."

Never would Asger have thought he'd call Casmir a *powerful ally*, but he *had* made the crushers, and each one was worth a knight. He'd also wrangled that astroshaman computer virus into submission and was using it against Kingdom enemies now. He *was* powerful, in his own way. Funny that it had taken Asger so long to realize that.

At his feet, Qin groaned.

Her sister flinched. She'd been keeping her weapon aimed at Asger but not firing. Asger kept his weapon aimed at her while he bent to help Qin up. An energy net had her legs bound, and her eyes were glassy, so she needed help standing. He wrapped an arm around her to support her and held her as he faced the sister.

The woman's mouth gaped open.

"Seven!" came another protest from the woman the crushers had pinned and now disarmed.

All except two of the other sisters were down on the deck, trapped by crushers and unconscious or groaning at their injuries. Seven looked from Asger to Qin and back to Asger. Different expressions warred for dominance on her face, and he couldn't tell if she would surrender or try one last time to defeat him, maybe to grab Qin and run back to her ship.

"We surrender," she finally whispered.

"Seven?" came her sister's startled and distressed response.

But Seven wasn't looking at her. She was looking at Asger and Qin. "We surrender, and we're all going to go together to this knight's castle."

"Did you get hit in the head?"

"Three or four times, yeah."

"Shit."

"We surrender," Seven said more firmly this time. She tossed her rifle to the deck. "*All* of us."

The remaining conscious women slumped, and those who still had their weapons dropped them. Maybe Seven was their leader.

"Crushers," Asger said. "Take their weapons and…" And what? Lock them up? Give them a guest cabin? Put them in navigation with Jemadari and his crew? "A few of you stay here in the cargo hold and keep an eye on them. Try not to hurt them further. They are our prisoners for the moment, but we're also here to collect them and protect them. The rest of us will go help my father on the warship."

Seven hesitated. "Do you want us to help too?"

She sounded uncertain. Asger doubted she wanted to go up against the Druckers. If Asger's side ended up losing, they would be punished worse for betraying their keepers.

"No." Asger patted Qin on the back—she was still groggy from the stun and staring blearily at him. "I want you to stay here with Qin—my Qin—and keep her safe and let me and my father and the crushers handle the pirates."

"*Your* Qin," Seven mouthed.

Asger couldn't tell if it was a question or a statement of surprise.

"Yes. Get the net off her, will you, please?" Asger wouldn't have trusted any other enemy he'd just been fighting to take care of Qin, but it had been clear they meant from the beginning to capture her, not kill her. The worst he had to worry about was them trying to escape and take Qin to the pirate ship, but if he removed all their weapons and left some of the crushers to guard them, he shouldn't have to worry about that.

"Yes." Seven came forward and took his place holding Qin up. "We will."

"Good. Thank you." Asger backed away, told five crushers to stay—they were already gathering the sisters' weapons—and ordered the others to follow him into the airlock tube.

He hoped his father was doing all right and truly could capture the pirate vessel. Because if they didn't succeed, Qin and all of her sisters would be back in the Druckers' torture chamber of a ship at the end of the day.

CHAPTER 28

"DON'T GET ANY CLOSER," NALINI TOLD HER PILOT, her gaze locked on the forward display showing what they believed was Dubashi's vessel—more a warship than the yacht so many of the Miners' Union leaders had—and the dozen ships protecting it. "We've seen what we needed to see. We can't take them on."

Casmir nodded in reluctant agreement. Their ship wouldn't have the firepower to go up against Dubashi's craft one on one, and if all the other mercenaries piled on, they would be dead in a second. Still, if that vessel held the virus-laden rockets that Dubashi meant to use on Odin, would it be worth a kamikaze run to try to take it out? But even if they meant to sacrifice themselves, which he would prefer not to do, he doubted they could get close before they were mowed down.

"If we could lure that ship close to the asteroid somehow..." Tristan mused.

"What's left of Father's base defenses might have the firepower to destroy that ship," Nalini agreed, "but those weapons platforms are being whittled away even as we sit here." She lifted a finger, as if to give the order to go back to helping fight the mercenaries doing that whittling, but Tork spoke first.

"I have marked several of the slydar-hulled ships. Shall I mark those craft?" He pointed at Dubashi's ships.

Nalini snorted. "That isn't quite what I had in mind as far as luring them back, but maybe they'll be so pissed that they'll chase us. Or—" she looked at Casmir, "—would they notice us doing that?"

"They would notice. The mercenaries might not have realized the ramifications yet, but Dubashi would guess right away, especially since we're using some astroshaman technology." Casmir waved at Tork, then shrugged. "We can be cheeky and do it anyway."

"I'm willing to be cheeky if he'll give chase and we can lure him back to the asteroid."

"Sounds like a way to get ourselves killed," Tristan said.

"We have to do something," Nalini said. "Some of our allies are edging away from the battle. If they've heard that the gate is open, they might give up on us altogether."

"Let's tag them," Casmir said. "Two Kingdom warships are on the way. *They* might have the power to deal with Dubashi and his protectors."

"Aren't they almost a day out?" Nalini asked.

"Yes, but—" Casmir spun toward Tork, realizing this might be the answer. Even if he couldn't save the station, maybe he could protect the Kingdom. "How long will that tracker last?"

"For some time—days at least—if they do not remove it," Tork said.

"Which they might be able to do." Casmir clenched his fist. "It's still worth trying. If the *Osprey* and the *Eagle* get here in time…"

Nalini squinted at him, probably realizing he was prioritizing getting Dubashi over finding a solution for their station. But she nodded to Tork. "Go ahead and do it. He's my father's mortal enemy."

"Proceeding," Tork said.

"I am assisting," Zee said, "until such time as I may go into battle and excel at that which I was made to do."

"Clubbing enemies with those big mallet fists?" Tork asked.

"Defending my people and battling nefarious foes," Zee said.

"Clubbing enemies." Tork nodded.

"Are your robots squabbling, Casmir?" Tristan's eyes were tense—everybody on the bridge was tense—but he managed a quick, bemused smile.

"Yes. They do that. They're kind of like a husband and wife. Or gender-neutral mates, I suppose you could say." Casmir kept waiting for Zee to realize that Tork might be the mate he'd been looking for all this time.

"Tork is an inferior android," Zee said, "not my mate. My mate will be another crusher like myself."

"Another clubber of enemies," Tork said. "I have no wish to have a killing machine for a mate."

Nalini sank deeper into her pod and dropped her face into her hand.

"Maybe you can discuss it later," Casmir told them.

"We are working as we debate," Tork said. "I have tagged six of the twelve ships surrounding Dubashi's. I will finish that task and also tag his vessel."

HOME FRONT

Your obvious tactics will not work a second time, clone, a message appeared on Casmir's contact.

There was no identification, but he quickly traced it to its origin. The large ship they believed belonged to Dubashi.

Are you certain, Prince Dubashi? he replied. *What else would you suggest? I would dearly like to keep you from killing the people who live in this station and also all the people who live on Odin. I'm open to bargaining with you if you're open to not doing those things.*

Jager sealed your planet's fate when he threatened to wipe me and my followers out of the Twelve Systems. I'll give him no leniency now.

Why would he have done that? Is it possible you misunderstood? Casmir remembered that clip of a message he'd pulled up on Dubashi's personal computer. It had practically been his screensaver.

I did not misunderstand. *He came to me in person last year. I am not an idiot, though I suppose you think most people are, given your progenitor's supposed brilliance.* The sneer came through loud and clear, even though it was only a text message.

I believe there's still some controversy over the heritability of IQ, with a poor prenatal environment, childhood hardship, and disease potentially having deleterious effects on one's genetic potential.

I see. And did you have a difficult childhood?

I did crack my head on the floor several times in my youth. Casmir didn't mention that seizures had been the cause. He didn't need to give another enemy that weapon to use against him. *If King Jager has offended you, I apologize, but surely you can agree that it's not fair to punish—or utterly destroy—an entire population because of one man's lack of tact. And to punish those who live on this station is also unfair, don't you agree? To take resources from Sultan Shayban that do not belong to you... Will you not consider—*

Shayban has been a thorn in my side for more than fifty years. He started our feud, no matter what he told you. I am not the criminal here, boy. You are associating with villains.

An interesting accusation from a man who's hired the services of the notoriously villainous Captain Rache. Casmir knew he was doing a bad job of negotiating—he should be trying harder to act as the neutral third party and not cast judgment—but a new idea was brewing in his mind. Besides, he wanted to distract Dubashi while Tork finished his task. He was also curious if Dubashi knew Rache was his clone brother.

One is left to desperate measures when one's base and ships have been destroyed. Besides, he wanted that mission. He practically paid me to give it to him. Your king is the devil incarnate, and that you haven't assassinated him already yourself speaks to your own evilness.

I am evil because I have not murdered a human being? I find your logic faulty and without moral merit, Prince Dubashi. But if you were to come voluntarily with me to testify before the Kingdom Senate that Jager personally threatened you, I would... What? What could he promise that wouldn't be a lie? *I would find a way to share the footage with the planetary media and help you ensure you're heard. Perhaps the Senate would decide that another leader should be chosen.*

Ousting the king would take a unanimous Senate vote, and Jager would have a lot of those senators in his pocket, but it was hard not to daydream about the possibility. Maybe if Jager were out of the picture, Casmir would have a better shot of being allowed to return home. But even suggesting that he would help Dubashi with the Senate was treason, and he could envision the prince saving a log of this message and distributing it later to incriminate him. Maybe it didn't matter. Casmir feared he'd already been thoroughly and indisputably incriminated in the eyes of his people.

You're delusional if you believe your people would listen to me or allow me to step foot on your planet. And I don't believe you're delusional. I do believe you're trying to buy time. To what end, boy?

I thought my tactics were obvious. Casmir had assumed Dubashi had spotted the tagging when he'd contacted him, but maybe he'd been referring to the slydar detectors.

"I have successfully tagged the rest of the ships and Dubashi's ship," Tork stated.

"Good," Casmir said. "Princess Nalini?"

"Yes?"

"I've confirmed that Dubashi is over there on that big ship."

"Through the scanners?"

"Through the fact that he's messaging me," Casmir said. "You didn't seem that willing to send the mercenaries off on a random mission, but how about trying to hire them for a specific one? I am willing to send the tracking information to all of the mercenaries if they're willing to go after Dubashi—it will allow them to find him without a slydar detector."

"If he already hired these people..." Nalini started.

"We don't believe he did. They know he's broke. They may not even be aware that he was the one to spread the information that the talks were taking place on the station and they might all profit." Casmir spread his open palm. "I understand that you don't want to let it be known that people who attack you can be given money to leave you alone—precedents, you mentioned—but would you consider an exception in this case? If I had money, I'd do it myself, but I haven't gotten a paycheck for several months now."

Her lips thinned. Casmir couldn't tell if she was considering it or if she was annoyed that he kept asking her for money. He worried it wouldn't take Dubashi long to figure out that he'd been tagged—and figure out how to get rid of it. They couldn't wait for the Kingdom reinforcements to arrive.

Even so, while he waited for her to decide, Casmir sent the tracking information to Rache and Ishii. He doubted Rache was still in the system or would do anything with it, but on the off chance he was wrong, why not try? Ishii would act on it. If only he were closer.

"There's always Tristan's land to bargain with," Casmir offered to Nalini's silence.

"The land I don't have," Tristan said.

"If you ever decide to press a lawsuit regarding it, I'll send some crushers in with you to the Senate floor to lend the intimidation factor."

"I'm sure *that* will work."

Nalini lifted a hand to stop their conversation. "I'll give it a shot. Does anyone know how much mercenaries expect to be paid? We're outside my realm of expertise."

"Well, they wouldn't have to expend any fuel," Casmir said. "Dubashi is right behind their butts."

"So I should just offer them an exorbitant hourly wage?"

"Maybe throw in one of those short-term rental condos you're developing on Oceanus," Tristan said. "Pasty pale space mercenaries probably enjoy vacations in the tropics."

"Just what I want. Grubby mercenaries on the furniture." Nalini tapped the comm panel on her command chair.

Casmir closed his eyes as she initiated contact, hoping she would have luck enticing them.

While they waited to see if her hail would be answered, Casmir checked on Sultan Shayban. More of the asteroid's weapons platforms had been taken out, and he worried the mercenary ships would believe it safe to head inside and force their way onto the station.

We've apprehended the men who sabotaged the shield generator, Shayban responded. *They are from our own station. Dubashi paid them off. I want that son of a bitch dead.*

Your daughter is currently trying to bribe the mercenaries to turn on him. Maybe you could add some funds to increase the reward. Casmir snapped his fingers. "Wait. Don't just offer to pay them. Make it a reward. A *bounty*. He's been putting bounties on my head for months. He deserves some turnabout. And then you only have to pay whoever brings him in."

"That's… not a bad idea." Nalini nodded and glanced at the comm panel. "Someone's answering now. But maybe I should broadcast my offer to everybody in the area."

Casmir almost suggested that they send it to everybody in the system, but then Dubashi would find out he'd been tagged. "Do pinpoint messages to select ships. Encrypted. Dubashi will figure out a way to nullify our tracker as soon as he realizes it exists."

"Right." She bent over the comm and spoke to whoever she had on the line.

Is he out there? Shayban asked.

Oh, yes. He's probably just outside the range of your slydar detector. He's got twelve ships guarding him.

I will speak to Nalini and add my funds to this reward offer.

Good. And get that shield generator back up, please. Even if we're lucky and this works, I'm sure he won't go down without a fight.

So am I, Casmir. So am I.

Bonita would have paced the *Stellar Dragon's* small navigation cabin if there had been gravity to do so. But she'd slowed to a stop and was watching from a distance as Dya's yacht sped off in another direction and one of the two looming Drucker warships held Jemadari's *Star Mirage* in its clutches.

HOME FRONT

Nobody was updating her, so she had no idea if her team's plan was being carried out or if the Druckers had overpowered and captured—or killed—them all. Qin had sent a brief and belated response to her last warning, and that was the last message she'd received.

"I shouldn't message Bjarke or Qin while it's possible they're in battle." Bonita pushed her floating braid out of the air in front of her face. "It could distract them."

"Do you want *me* to message them?" Viggo asked.

"How would that be less of a distraction?"

"I am discreet and circumspect."

"One of your vacuums is whirring past my ear and up the wall. Non-discreetly."

"The dust rises when there's no gravity," Viggo said. "I discreetly checked in with Casmir earlier. He did not mind."

"He's too polite to say anything if he did mind." Bonita glanced at the long-range scanners. "I wish he and Kim had come along in another ship. My gut tells me this isn't going well."

"They are experiencing difficulties of their own. There are far more mercenaries attacking the station than anyone expected."

"Fantastic. So it's a crap day for all."

"My day is thus far adequate."

A proximity alert went off on the console.

"That has just changed," Viggo said ominously.

"What now?" Bonita leaned over to check, but she needn't have bothered.

A massive gray warship similar to the one attached to the *Star Mirage* appeared on the forward display, so close she could see streaks from the last time someone had washed the hull. She could have almost reached out and touched it.

The ship sailed over the *Dragon*—lining its airlock up with hers?

Bonita swore and pulled the navigation arm up to her chip. "Is that the second Drucker warship? How did it poof over here?"

"It's not the second one. It's a third. With a slydar hull."

Her swearing turned into a groan as she fired up the thrusters to back the *Dragon* away. But it was far too late to avoid being captured.

"I believe," Viggo said cautiously as the hull continued past on the display, "it's just flying past us."

"Nobody flies that close unless they're making a point."

"It's possible both are true. If they don't stop, they're on course to join the ship attached to the *Star Mirage*." A moment later, he added, "Ah. That's not good."

"What now?" Bonita curled her fingers around the armrest in her pod.

"The second Drucker ship—the second *visible* ship—is flying toward the first."

"Qin and Bjarke and Asger must be attacking it successfully." Bonita *hoped* it was a successful attack. "And the Druckers are sending reinforcements."

"It's possible that if a third ship is here and camouflaged… the rest of their fleet is also here, and we never knew it."

The tail end of the ship flew out of view of the display, leaving them looking at stars again. Thanks to the slydar hull, the warship soon disappeared from the scanners, but Viggo was right. The course it had been on was clear. Qin and the others were about to have a lot more trouble.

Bonita commed Queen Dya's ship—none of the pirates were paying attention to *it* as it flew away.

"Did you know about this, lady?" Bonita demanded without preamble, then realized Dya was too far away and wouldn't have seen the hidden ship.

"That the second warship would join the first?" she answered the comm personally. "It seemed likely. Did your friends not anticipate that? I thought I was helping them. Tell Jemadari he owes me."

"You can tell him yourself if he and everyone else on that ship don't get obliterated. There's a *third* Drucker warship. And maybe a fourth and fifth around here somewhere too."

"I know nothing of that. I attempted to help you with your goals, because I wished to see certain nefarious parties snubbed. Don't blame me if you can't pull off your ambush."

Dya closed the comm.

Bonita glowered at the console. "With help like that, we'd all be better off sleeping with our enemies than our friends."

"Another warship is approaching," Viggo said as the stars on the display were once again blotted out.

A ship almost identical to the last, except with a green hull instead of gray, followed the same path as the last one had.

"There's Number Four." Bonita shook her head. "We might as well assume the fifth is here too."

HOME FRONT

She sent a warning to Bjarke. Even if it would distract him, she had to risk it. He needed to know about this. They all did.

How they would deal with so many ships, she didn't know, but maybe if her friends succeeded in capturing the first from within, the Druckers would be hesitant to fire upon their own vessel. Or maybe they would fire upon it twice as hard, preferring to destroy it rather than letting someone else have it. She shook her head bleakly.

"Uh oh," Viggo said. "This one isn't—"

Something jarred the ship, and an alert flashed on the console. The Druckers had deployed a maglocker and taken hold of the *Dragon*.

"—flying past," Viggo finished grimly.

Bonita sagged in her pod. She didn't have an army of crushers to help ward off a boarding party. She didn't even have Qin.

"How are we going to get out of this one, Viggo?"

"I'm afraid I don't know."

CHAPTER 29

QIN HAD TAKEN THE STUNNER BLAST FULL IN the face, and it took her a while to fully recover her awareness. She'd been dimly aware of Asger pulling her up from the deck and holding her against him while he spoke to Mouser, but that conversation had been a blur. She hadn't been coherent enough to protest when he'd left her behind with her sisters and five crushers to charge onto the warship to help his father. He should have known she would want to help. He *needed* her.

At least someone had freed her legs from that damn energy net. She was sitting on the deck, propped against a shipping container with the crushers arrayed around her kin. Some of her sisters were injured and unconscious—even though they'd betrayed her, she dearly hoped none of them were dead—and others sat or stood, their weapons taken from them.

Legs wobbly from the stun—and the blows she'd taken from her own sisters during the fight—Qin stood up. She started toward the nearest comm panel so she could check in with Jemadari and his crew before going to assist Asger and Bjarke, but she glanced down at one of the dead pirates and paused. His faceplate was shattered, the work of a pertundo, but she still recognized the eyes frozen open inside that helmet. Groggins.

He'd still been alive when Bjarke had left the ship, so Qin knew Asger had been the one to deal with him. She wished he were here so she could hug him for that. Even though she wanted to believe she could have handled facing one of her bullies of old, she was glad she hadn't needed to. She was also glad she'd told Asger everything. No, not everything, but enough. He'd understood how she felt, and true to his word, he'd been there for her.

Reminding herself that the battle wasn't over, Qin continued to the comm panel. Voices behind her made her pause.

"I just want to talk to her." That was Mouser. "You've got my weapons. I'm not doing anything."

"All prisoners will remain in that corner until the battle is over and Sir Asger has returned," the crusher stated.

Mouser tried to walk past him. He grabbed her arm with lightning speed. With her fast reflexes, she might have evaded the grab, but she didn't try.

"Squirt?" Mouser looked at her. "Can we talk?"

"This isn't the time." Even though Qin understood why they'd betrayed her, she couldn't keep from feeling stung. It wasn't surprising that her sisters had gone along with the Druckers when they had set this up, but Mouser had been messaging her personally, never slipping in a hint that anything was amiss. Qin couldn't trust her—*shouldn't* have trusted her—not then, and not now.

"In case it doesn't work out for you and your friends... I'd rather say something now."

"Fine." Qin looked at the crusher. "Will you release her, please?"

She half-expected him to ignore her—it had sounded like they were programmed to obey only Asger—but he released Mouser.

Keeping a wary eye toward the crusher, Mouser joined Qin, as if she wanted to have a private conversation. Qin didn't know how private it would be since all of their sisters had enhanced hearing, and she wouldn't be surprised if the crushers also had auditory detectors superior to human hearing.

"I'm sorry," Mouser said quietly. "I—we—didn't want to do it. I meant what I said about being happy you'd gotten away. I didn't want to come after you, but Captain Framer was so obsessed about getting you back, about not letting anyone appear to have gotten the best of him and his brothers..." Mouser spread her hand. "You remember what it's like, I'm sure. We all have those embedded chips with no way to remove them without suffering intense pain. We would have to find a surgeon." Mouser touched the side of her head and grimaced. "And if we disobey..."

"I remember." Qin commed navigation, reluctant to talk to Mouser or any of the others. She remembered, and she understood, but that

HOME FRONT

didn't make any of this feel all right. "Mr. Jemadari, are your people still all right?"

"We're all right."

"The knights have gone over to the warship, and I'm going to help them." Qin didn't know if she should be sharing her plans in front of her sisters, who might be communicating with the pirates even now, but it wasn't as if they wouldn't know as soon as she walked into the airlock tube. If Asger had wanted to keep them in the dark, he should have locked them in a cabin.

"He's going to need more help than you can give," Jemadari said.

"Sir?"

"There are more warships coming."

"The second one is heading this way?" Qin asked. "I believe they anticipated that."

Mouser was shaking her head before Jemadari answered.

"Another ship just grabbed your Captain Lopez's freighter. It's got slydar, so we can't see it, but she commed us."

Qin, a message came in from Bonita. *I have bad news.*

Qin slumped. *I'm hearing about it now.*

You know that all five Drucker ships are in the area?

All five? Qin gaped. She never would have suggested this plan to her friends if she'd known there were more than two. When had the Druckers gotten slydar hulls installed on the other ships? It had happened in the time since she'd left. Less than a year.

We know of four for certain, and it seems likely that if four are here, the fifth is here too. One grabbed the Dragon. *They haven't boarded yet, but I assume they will, and that they'll… take me prisoner.*

That wasn't what she'd been thinking. Qin could tell from that pause. Bonita had irked the Druckers before by helping Qin, and now she worried they would shoot her out of spite. And because her life meant nothing to them.

But it meant something to Qin. A *lot*.

Hide, Captain. Please. Don't try to fight. Don't let them find you. I'll figure out a way to get rid of them, so they leave the Dragon *alone. Somehow, I will.*

She had no idea how, but she had to find the captain and bargain with him, do whatever it took. She couldn't let Bonita be killed because of her.

I'm so sorry, Qin added. *I had no idea about the slydar-hulled ships. That's new. I'm sorry.*

I know. It's not your fault that they're assholes. I'm going to message Bjarke next and see if some of his Kingdom buddies will come help. As far as I can tell, all but the two ships headed to Stardust Palace are hanging out by the gate and scratching the pimples on their asses.

Qin shook her head slowly. Even if the Kingdom would come to help their knights, they would arrive far too late.

We'll take this ship, and then maybe we'll be in a bargaining position. Qin had to believe that. "I'm going over there to help," she said aloud, more for Jemadari's sake—the comm was still open—than Mouser's.

But she was the one to answer. "Let me help you."

"You've already helped enough." Qin turned a baleful glare on their sisters. Some were still unconscious, but some were looking over, listening to the conversation. "Stay here."

Qin grabbed her Brockinger and strode for the airlock.

"Just let me come." Mouser stepped after her, but one of the crushers came over to stop her. "Let me make it up to you. I've seen what your army can do, and I believe you have a shot of taking that ship. Maybe not the others, but… I want to help. I want to blow a hole in Framer's head, even if he does hurt me." She waved to her neck. "I know you have no reason to believe me, but I feel horrible that we did this. I didn't want to. I wanted to warn you, but I was afraid to defy them. Give me a second chance."

Qin stood in the airlock chamber, staring at Mouser, at what seemed to be genuine anguish on her face. *Was* it? If Qin allowed her to come, would she be helpful? Or would she bide her time until she could complete what she'd failed to do here? Capture Qin and drag her back. As her masters wanted.

Qin couldn't imagine *herself* doing such a thing, no matter what the possible ramifications if she didn't obey, but she shouldn't judge her sisters based on her own values. Once, she'd known them better than anyone could imagine, but she'd changed a lot in this last year, and she struggled to remember the person she'd once been. The person these women still were. But… Qin might need all the help she could get to fight her way to Asger and Bjarke.

Hoping she wasn't making a mistake, she said, "Grab your weapon and let's go."

HOME FRONT

Qin pointed to where the crushers had cast aside their rifles. They didn't try to stop Mouser from retrieving one.

"Don't help her," one of the others whispered to Mouser. "Being captured is shameful, but they won't kill us or punish us too much for it. If you attack them…"

"I know what I'm doing," Mouser said.

As Qin led the way past the unconscious or dead pirates and into the warship, she hoped *she* did. She wanted an ally and she wanted to trust her sister, but her shoulder blades itched as they raced into the corridors to find Asger and Bjarke.

"Don't make me regret this," Qin whispered, not glancing back.

Mouser heard. "I won't."

It had been fifteen minutes since any ships had attacked the *Moon Dart* and five minutes since Nalini had finished sending messages to select mercenary ships—the big warships with the power to damage or destroy Dubashi's vessel if the captains could be convinced to do so.

Casmir gnawed on his knuckle and waited impatiently for something to happen. Were the mercenaries thinking about it? Talking amongst each other? Unfortunately, other mercenary ships were still attacking the asteroid, trying to take out the last of Shayban's weapons platforms.

"I don't think it's going to work, Casmir," Nalini said softly, looking over at him from her command pod.

"What kind of mercenaries don't want money?" he asked. "Isn't that why they do what they do?"

"They're probably afraid there will be ramifications from attacking a wealthy and powerful prince," Tristan said.

"But he's not wealthy now. You saw his bank accounts."

"He still has a lot of assets. Maybe he's managed to liquidate them, has more funds, and has paid these people."

A glum thought. Casmir was rifling through his mind for a Plan B—or were they up to Plan C or D by now?—when movement on the scanner display caught his eye.

"One of the big mercenary ships on the outskirts is moving," he reported.

"To join forces against my home?" Nalini asked.

"No..." Casmir didn't want to get anyone's hopes up prematurely, but it was moving in the direction of Dubashi's ships. "Not *yet* anyway. Maybe that's on the agenda for later."

"Thank you so much."

Casmir leaned forward in his pod. "It's opening fire! On Dubashi's ship."

Nalini rushed over, gripping the back of his pod as she leaned over his shoulder.

"I marked that ship." Tork sounded smug.

"I could have marked it," Zee said.

"You could not have. I used astroshaman technology."

"The fact that astroshamans uploaded their programs into your system does not make you superior."

"The fact that you club people with your mallet-hands does not make *you* superior," Tork said.

"Not now, guys." Casmir tried to wave them to silence. "Later, after we all hopefully live, you can let a game of *Stars and Battleships* decide who's the superior being."

They fell silent, and Casmir thought that was that. He held his breath as he watched the mercenary ship, hoping Nalini's entreaty had worked, that she'd managed to entice the big warships to switch sides with the promise of a reward.

"As if a single playing of a network game could sufficiently determine one's worth," Tork said.

"Humans, even the maker Casmir Dabrowski, cannot truly understand our kind."

"No, but he is better than most."

"Yes," Zee agreed.

"Do you find it unnerving when they talk about you?" Nalini asked.

"Only when I wake up in the middle of the night and they're deep in a philosophical discussion that involves me." Casmir pointed. "Look. Another ship is veering toward his cluster."

"Does that happen often?" she asked.

"Them talking about me? Not *often*, but occasionally." Casmir wondered what her definition of *often* was.

HOME FRONT

"Do you sleep with them?"

"Not *with* them. It's not like they need beds. But Zee is my bodyguard. He's sometimes bed-adjacent." Casmir decided not to mention that he'd had up to a dozen crushers in the cabin with him when he slept. That wasn't weird. Space was limited on warships.

"Hm."

He thought Nalini was privately judging him, but she pointed at the scanner display, so maybe she was debating something else. "I didn't comm those two."

"The ones firing at him?" Casmir asked.

If Dubashi had been startled, he'd recovered. His ships were veering away from the mercenaries that had opened fire.

"I tried to hire that one." She pointed to a ship that was turning toward Dubashi now that the others had committed to attacking. "And I tried to entice that one with a reward." The next one she pointed to hadn't yet moved.

"Maybe they shared the news with each other."

Casmir watched in fascination as Dubashi's protector ships opened fire on the larger mercenary warships. More mercenaries, including the one Nalini had pointed to that hadn't been moving earlier, closed on them. If not for the slydar detector, half the battle would have been invisible to Casmir, but he saw it all, and thanks to Tork's trackers, the mercenaries had no problem detecting their camouflaged opponents.

Dubashi's ship sped away from the battle. Casmir leaned forward, about to plead with Nalini to pursue it, but Dubashi wasn't fleeing the area. Instead of winging off into the starry expanse, his ship sped toward the asteroid.

Was the asteroid's shield generator still offline? Casmir checked. Yes.

"We may want to try to intercept him," Casmir told Nalini.

Some of the mercenaries were too engaged with the dozen defenders Dubashi had left behind, but a few veered after Dubashi's ship. What did he intend to do? Ram the asteroid? That wouldn't do anything to destroy it, and Casmir couldn't imagine the prince giving up his life in some futile gesture—or even if he believed he could take out his opponent.

"On it." Nalini rushed back to her pod and gave orders to the helmsman.

"What's he up to?" Tristan wondered from the pod next to Casmir's.

"Nothing good," Casmir said.

You're welcome, came a surprising message from Rache. *I'm about to leave the system, and it's all I could manage, but I've bribed some of those mercenaries to turn on Dubashi. I suppose Dubashi will inevitably find out I haven't been his wholehearted supporter this month, but so be it.*

Rache had paid those mercs? Casmir had sent him the tracking information and briefly mentioned their predicament, but he hadn't truly expected him to do anything. If Nalini hadn't said she hadn't contacted those mercenaries, Casmir wouldn't have believed he had, but he could think of no other explanation for the turnabout.

How come they're willing to take your money and not Princess Nalini's?

I'm a formidable force with a fearsome reputation. Some *people find it wise not to irk me. Nobody worries about irking princesses.*

Since Rache was helping him, Casmir refrained from commenting on his ego. He *would* tell Kim that he claimed to be a formidable force. That was almost as bad as referring to himself as the main event.

Thank you. Did you do this out of brotherly love or because Kim is on board? Casmir hadn't mentioned that in his earlier note, but by now, Rache could guess that Casmir and Kim went most places together, at least when they were stuck in a remote star system at the same time.

Do you really need to ask?

I'm wounded that our shared genetic code wasn't enough to spur you to magnanimous actions.

She sent me a nice letter. Keep her alive, or I'll flay you.

"He's faster than us, Your Highness." The helmsman was giving chase, zipping after Dubashi's ship as it headed toward the asteroid. "But we're following. I'm trying to get the *Spring Thaw* to intercept him."

"We're more likely to get some of the mercenaries to intercept him now," Nalini said.

Casmir wondered how many Rache had paid. Just the two who'd turned on him first?

"Looks like he's heading toward the entrance," Tristan said.

Casmir checked the asteroid on the scanners. "The two big guns protecting the entrance are still online. Wait, he just ejected something. A bomb?"

Nalini swore. "Are we too far away to target it before it hits?"

"Yes," Tristan said. "Also his ship is in the way. We can't see it."

"Well, target *that*."

HOME FRONT

The *Moon Dart* opened fire, blasts streaking across space to hammer into Dubashi's ship's armored backside. More mercenaries swept into the fray. Dubashi's ship fired back—at the *Dart*. Their vessel shuddered as powerful weapons struck it, reminding Casmir that they'd taken earlier damage. Alarms flashed on several consoles.

Hoping the others could deal with it, he focused on the bomb or whatever it was that Dubashi had launched at the asteroid. It wasn't zipping toward its target with the speed of a rail gun blast. Its descent toward the asteroid was almost leisurely.

"We've got an unimpeded view of it now," Casmir said to anyone listening—Nalini was giving terse orders to the helmsman. "I'm going to try to zoom in and get a visual. The scanners show that it's giving off heat."

As he brought the visual up on a display, the unidentified projectile landed on the asteroid. Yes, *landed*. It had slowed its descent even more before it touched down. It was an eight-foot-tall, bullet-shaped device with spider-like legs now resting on—or digging into?—the rock.

It had come down a thousand meters from the entrance tunnel that led into the station. Casmir imagined a map of the interior in his mind and guessed it was above the control room in the palace. But a mile of rock stood between it and the station. Could the device do anything from that far away?

He jumped as the legs spread farther and the bottom of the bullet popped open. A drill shot out and started burrowing into the rock as easily as if it were butter. It was like the much smaller drill weapons he'd seen inside Dubashi's base that had cut into walls—and through Asger's armor.

"This is going to be a problem." Casmir was about to point it out to Nalini and Tristan when the camera view disappeared. He started to blurt a, "What happened?" but realized he'd lost the visual because the *Dart* had flown out of range. "Wait, we have to go back."

Nalini looked over at him. "We're chasing Dubashi. And we've got help." She waved to mercenary ships and their ally ships all racing after the prince's ship with a common goal.

"Let them do it." Casmir brought up the scanner display showing the tiny blip of heat that indicated the drill device. "Dubashi launched this, and it's cutting into the asteroid. It might drill all the way down to the station. And *into* the station."

"Is it a bomb?" Fortunately, Nalini ordered the helmsman to turn them around before waiting for an answer.

"I don't know," Casmir said, "but it can't be anything good."

"No kidding."

As the *Dart* returned to the asteroid, Casmir was able to bring up the visual again. There wasn't much to see. The device had burrowed down into the asteroid. All that was visible was the hole it had left behind, with tiny bits of rock flowing out, the detritus as the device cut deeper. The rocks flew upward in the asteroid's minimal gravity before eventually settling down on the surface.

"It must be a bomb that he's trying to deliver somewhere important," Nalini said grimly. "I'll warn my father. Maybe he can get a crew ready to meet it and clear the area of people. Damn, I wish we'd left Dubashi for the others and had fired on it right away. Who knows how vile it's going to be to deal with? A bomb detonating against the wall of the station—or cutting through the wall to detonate inside—could do a lot of damage."

Casmir stared at the hole, the tiny bits of rock flowing out, and a sinking feeling came over him. "It might be designed to deliver more than damage."

Nalini looked sharply at him. "What do you mean?"

"Dubashi got away from his base with two rockets with containers holding a deadly virus inside. Maybe he took out one of the containers for this attack." Casmir imagined how much easier it would be for the prince to steal Shayban's ships if everyone inside the station were dead or hospitalized.

Kim? he messaged his friend. *I think we're going to need your help.*

CHAPTER 30

ASGER RAN OUT OF THE LIFT AND ONTO the top level of the warship. So far, he'd only had to fight two quick battles against solo pirates who'd charged out of side corridors and into his path. He'd passed dozens—maybe hundreds—of downed men, their armor torn open by the sheer power of the crushers. Bulkheads and doors were dented or completely torn open. In one spot, an unmoving pirate in armor was stuck halfway through one of the doors, his boots dangling above the deck.

Occasionally, Asger spotted a pirate with scorched armor and a pertundo stab through it and knew his father had been this way. Clangs, thumps, and shouts of fighting came from ladder wells and corridors that he passed, but he kept going toward the bridge.

Father, Asger messaged his chip—he'd already tried his comm and hadn't gotten a response. *Did you make it to the bridge yet? I'm on the ship and coming your way.*

A boom came from ahead, and smoke flowed around a bend in the corridor.

We're trying to get in now, his father replied. *Dozens of pirates have locked themselves in, and they've sent robots of their own to try to drive us away. They also tried to gas the corridors, so make sure there aren't any leaks in your helmet if you come up here.*

Understood.

Asger leaped over two bodies and rounded the bend. Through the smoke, the backs of a dozen crushers came into view. Several whirled to face him, poised to spring.

"I'm Sir Asger," he blurted, lifting his pertundo in what he hoped was more of a wave than a threatening gesture. For an instant, he imagined what would happen if someone succeeded in taking over the crushers and turning them against him and his team.

"Sir Asger has arrived," one announced.

The crushers shifted their backs to the bulkheads to make room for him to go through the smoke. But orange and red DEW-Tek bolts blasted through the smoke as well. They bounced off the crushers and the bulkheads, the crushers the more indifferent target. Those bulkheads were blackened, gouged, and dented, and intermittent holes showed burned conduits inside.

Asger spotted his father's silver armor up ahead. The side of his helmet had been crunched in. Maybe that was why his comm wasn't working. He crouched beside the double doors to the bridge—they were warped and half torn open—either from crusher power or explosives. Smoke or gas or both clouded the air and made the armored figures on the bridge indistinct as they crouched behind pods and consoles and fired into the corridor.

As Asger drew close, one pirate leaned into view and fired a grenade launcher. One of the crushers sprang through the mangled doors, shifting his form so he would fit through the gap, and caught the grenade.

"Don't let it destroy any of the equipment," Asger's father barked.

Instead of throwing it back at the pirates, the crusher wrapped his body around the grenade. It exploded, and pieces of black crusher flew everywhere.

Asger halted and gaped.

His father glanced back. "That's why we didn't just charge in. We're trying to take over a working ship, not blow up the bridge, and the pirates are threatening to self-destruct."

"We got one of the bastards!" one of the defenders yelled.

"No, we didn't. It's liquefying and slurping itself back together."

The pirates fired at the blobs of crusher rolling across the deck and back toward the leg stumps that hadn't been blown apart in the blast.

"They're distracted," Asger said. "Go in now."

He meant it as advice, not an order, but he forgot that Casmir's constructs were programmed to obey him first and foremost. The crushers in the corridor rushed past his father and leaped onto the bridge. Weapons fire opened up, but the crushers closed quickly on the pirates, ripping weapons out of their hands and flinging the armored men into each other and against consoles.

HOME FRONT

Asger winced at the sound of equipment smashing. His father shot him a glare, then ran in after the crushers. Another boom sounded, and more smoke filled the bridge.

"Where's the captain?" Asger's father demanded.

Nobody answered. Asger wished they would come face to face with one of the Drucker brothers. He wanted to pound on the men who'd kept Qin as a slave for years and years.

One of the pirates tried to flee off the bridge after the crushers were all in. Asger, still in the corridor, rammed his pertundo into the man's chest, hoping this was one of the cowardly Druckers.

The pirate's armor was already damaged, and the spike of Asger's pertundo found his seam and bored through into flesh. Blue streaks of electricity crackled around his foe, and the man screamed. Asger thrust his weapon and hurled his foe off the tip and back onto the bridge. The pirate struck one of the crushers—he might as well have struck a solid wall.

Asger didn't get a chance to battle a second foe. When he stepped onto the bridge, his father and the crushers had already taken down the dozen-odd men who'd been making their last stand inside.

"Self-destruct is activated," a computer voice announced. "This ship will self-destruct in three minutes."

Asger's father swore. "I was hoping they were bluffing."

"Where is it?" Asger spun, peering through the smoke and looking for alerts on the consoles. So many of them had been damaged beyond repair. What if the terminal where the self-destruct had been set wasn't accessible anymore? There wasn't time to get off the warship, figure out how to detach Jemadari's ship, and fly away.

"I don't know." His father charged around the bridge, pushing unconscious men off consoles and trying to find the right controls.

"I have downloaded the specifications of this model of warship," one of the crushers stated and strode to a corner of the bridge. "This is the station that controls the self-destruct programming." He laid one of his tarry black hands on the console, then started tapping at the keys.

"Do you know what you're doing?" Asger's father charged over, lifting his arms as if he might yank the crusher away.

"Certainly. I am a Z-6000, programmed by Professor Casmir Dabrowski. Navigating computer systems is a simple matter."

"Won't it need a passcode or a retina scan or something?" Asger asked.

His father had stopped short of grabbing the crusher, but he looked back, his eyes as concerned as Asger had ever seen them.

"There are methods of bypassing such security measures," the crusher stated.

Three other crushers went to different computer stations. To help? Or on some other mission? Asger hadn't asked them to do anything—had his father?

"Should we be uneasy that they're taking charge?" Asger's father asked.

"I don't know. Casmir programmed them, and he's on our side, right?"

"I sure hope so."

"Do *you* know any of the Druckers' passcodes?" Asger remembered that his father had spent a year with these people, but he didn't think it had been on this particular ship.

"Not for bridge stuff. I could probably still get into their accounts-receivable files."

"Oh, good. *That's* sure to stop the ship from blowing up."

His father held up a finger. "I've got a message from Bonita. Did you see this?"

"She hasn't sent me anything."

"She says more Drucker warships are here. *More* than the one other we knew about."

"Two minutes until the ship self-destructs," the computer announced.

Asger swallowed down the panic rising into his throat like bile. "We've got to get Jemadari's ship detached. In case this doesn't work."

And maybe they should be charging back down there and trying to escape themselves…

"I am working on releasing the *Star Mirage* currently," a crusher at one of the consoles said.

"Good." Asger tried to keep his voice calm. He was, after all, in command. And then, because Casmir would have done it, he added, "Thank you."

"I've warned Jemadari." His father peered over the arm of the crusher at the self-destruct console. "Making any progress?"

"I have not been able to deactivate the self-destruct," the crusher said.

His father swore.

"As an alternative, I am uploading the virus that Casmir Dabrowski gave me. It should close down the engines and all power on the ship. That should render the self-destruct system inoperable."

HOME FRONT

"*Should?*"

The lights went out, and the bridge fell dark. *Completely* dark.

"The virus has been deployed," the crusher said.

"I succeeded in releasing the *Star Mirage* before the power went out," the other crusher said. "The airlock tube is still attached, but it could be removed manually if necessary."

"I isolated the auxiliary comm system before you deployed the virus," a third crusher said, another of the ones at the controls. "It is operating on limited battery power but should remain usable for several hours."

"Usable for what?" Asger felt like he'd lost control of this mission. He activated his helmet's night vision system so he could see, but that only made the already surreal situation feel more surreal.

"To speak with the leaders of the other pirate ships." The crusher looked toward Asger and his father. "You have a plan to keep them from destroying this vessel, correct?"

Asger managed not to blurt, "Uhhh." But barely. His plan had been to get Qin's sisters and get out of here. That was it.

"I'm refining a plan," his father said, but he was still watching the dark console that had controlled the self-destruct system. Maybe waiting for the computer voice to say they had less than a minute left?

But a minute passed and another, and nothing happened. It seemed the virus had successfully knocked out everything, the self-destruct included. The crushers waited patiently, several facing the exit in case any more pirates charged onto the bridge. The distant sounds of fighting had faded. Asger knew that many more pirates remained, but they might have gone into hiding when the power had gone out.

Asger's father faced him. "Bonita says we're about ten minutes from being surrounded by the rest of the Drucker ships."

"How's your refining going?" Asger didn't mean to be snarky, but he didn't have anything constructive to add.

"Crusher." His father tapped the one closest to him. "Can you—"

"I am called Gad by Casmir Dabrowski," the crusher said.

"Uh, all right. Gad. Is there any chance you can send that virus to the other four ships over that auxiliary comm we supposedly have up?"

"I could send it, but they would be required to download and open the file in order for it to spread. It is likely they have learned that we have taken over their ship and would be wary about any files we send."

Casmir had warned Asger of exactly that. Here, the crusher had been able to upload the file directly, but unless they could send this crusher—Gad—to all the other ships, it wouldn't work again.

A faint beep came from the other side of the bridge. The comm.

"One of the pirate ships is hailing us," the crusher at the station said.

Asger, came a message from Bonita. *I already told your father, but I see that the power went out on that warship. In case you didn't know… you're surrounded. And one of them has the* Dragon. *If you have any brilliance planned, I encourage you to deploy it. Now.*

"They have Bonita," Asger told his father.

"I know." His eyes were bleaker than ever.

"*Do* you have a plan?"

His father hesitated, then nodded and strode to the comm. "Surrender."

Asger lunged and caught his arm. "That's not acceptable."

"They have *Bonita*. And thanks to that virus, we're sitting on a brick that can't do anything. If you have another plan, let's hear it."

Asger scoured his brain, trying to find the brilliance Bonita wanted. And that his father wanted.

"We negotiate," he said.

"Oh, yeah. That'll work great. We're so obviously in a position of power."

"We have one of their ships. They'll want it back. That's something."

His father's face radiated skepticism.

"Let me talk to them," Asger said, hoping inspiration would come. "Trust me."

His father's hesitation was longer this time, emotions warring on his face. There was a hint of hope in his eyes, hope that Asger could pull magic out of his ass, but it was being pummeled by skepticism.

His father spread his hand toward the comm station. "Talk to them. If you can get us out of this, I'll…"

Asger raised his eyebrows. Even though it hardly mattered right now, he was curious how his father would finish the sentence.

"I'll go to the king personally and argue for you to be allowed to bring Qin home and date her or marry her or whatever you wish."

Asger almost snorted—they both knew Jager would never allow that—but the thought that his father would stand up for him to the king touched him. "We might start with dating."

"That seems reasonable."

HOME FRONT

Kim reached the airlock bay of the *Dart* with an oxygen tank fastened to her galaxy suit and all the useful equipment she'd been able to fit in the space-rated kit she'd grabbed from the ship's sickbay. The last she'd heard, their ship had left the battle to the rest of the fleet and was flying into the asteroid. The *Dart* had tried firing directly at the hole the drilling device had created and disappeared into, but it had been like shooting a cannonball into a pinhole.

Casmir clomped into the bay with Zee and several other crushers, though Kim couldn't imagine what they would do against a canister holding a virus. For that matter, she didn't know what *she* could do. The crusher could blow it up as easily as she could.

She assumed Casmir wanted her along to lend her expertise if it was needed, but she would be better off helping the station's medical personnel establish a quarantine and deal with the virus inside if it got through. She refrained from pointing that out, since walking away would mean leaving Casmir to go in alone. He looked more like a goofy teenager than an experienced professor as he shambled toward the airlock in oversized armor, his bangs dangling down into his eyes, and his not-space-rated tool satchel flopping against his hip. Because of his medical vulnerabilities, she'd always felt protective of him. Even if he was taking the crushers, she worried he would get himself into trouble and need a friend to guard his back.

"What are they going to do out there?" Kim pointed at the crushers that crowded behind him. Was one of them Reuben? She thought he'd followed her down, but she couldn't tell him apart now that he was among the others.

"Either lend moral support or stand in front of us if a bomb goes off."

Kim groaned at the thought of a bomb, but if Dubashi had been planning this since he'd left his base, he'd had plenty of time to build an extremely effective virus-delivery device. "Only you would want moral support from a robot."

"I can be morally supportive, Kim Sato," one of the crushers said. She thought it was Zee, but then he added, "Since I cannot lend good luck that I do not have, I am willing to fill other roles."

"Reuben is still dealing with feelings of inadequacy because he never won any currants," Kim told Casmir when he raised his eyebrows. "Next time, you better program them all with a sense of luckiness."

Casmir smiled faintly. "They were programmed with foundational desires in line with their mission, but I think it's interesting that they're developing personalities based on environmental stimuli."

"Environmental stimuli like a currant shortage?"

"Yup. If I ever get back to academia, I look forward to writing a paper on it." Casmir patted Reuben on the shoulder. "Luck can change, my friend. And I know Kim will appreciate your moral support, even if she acts gruff and doesn't admit it."

The crusher turned to Kim, as if to ask if this was true. As if it mattered to him.

What was she supposed to say? Reuben seemed needier than the other crushers. She didn't want him to feel even more unlucky because he'd been stuck guarding someone ungrateful.

"I appreciate all of your support, Reuben. Thank you."

If it was possible for a big crusher with only vague facial features to brighten up, Reuben did. "Excellent." He placed a hand on her shoulder and nodded. "I am prepared to be supportive on this mission."

"Good. Thank you," she repeated, feeling awkward.

But Casmir smiled, and Reuben was happy, so she figured she'd said the right thing.

Casmir tilted his head—checking something on his chip? "The ships chasing Dubashi have knocked out his engines. Several are sending over boarding parties, including the crushers we sent, hopefully to capture him."

Capture him, right. Kim was positive Sultan Shayban's orders were for his nemesis's head to be blown off.

"What happens if he escapes again?" Kim gripped a handhold as the ship tilted and shifted, zipping through the curving tunnel toward the station at top speed. "He must have a lifeboat or some equivalent, and it won't be marked." She'd been listening to the comm chatter on the bridge from her cabin and had kept up with the gist of the battle.

"He probably does. I left the slydar detector running with Tork monitoring it and watching for any new camouflaged ships that come up. He won't be able to mark it from inside the asteroid here, but if he can alert the others, hopefully, they will be close enough to see an escape shuttle and target it."

"I hope so. The last thing we want is for him to speed off to the gate and Odin while we're dealing with this."

Casmir blew out a slow breath. "One problem at a time."

A clank reverberated from the nearest airlock hatch, and the deck lurched, their sense of gravity changing direction as they attached to the station and piggybacked off its spin gravity.

"Nalini?" Casmir asked over his helmet comm. "Are we docking to the station or flying to the spot where the device will come out?"

"Your android analyzed its trajectory," Nalini said, "and there's not a big enough gap between the station and the asteroid at that location for us to fly the ship to it. You'll have to wait for it to burrow into the station and deal with it there."

"That's not ideal," Kim said.

"My father has a team waiting to open up fire and blow it up as soon as it enters. He's also sealed off the area from the rest of the station."

"That may not be good enough," Kim said. "It would be much better to destroy it before it breaches your station. This virus will be highly contagious, with extremely small particles. It's possible your existing filtration systems will not be sufficient to contain it."

"How big is the gap between the station and asteroid? Can we reach it in our suits?" Casmir asked.

"Let me check," Nalini said.

Casmir looked at Kim. "The station is a cylinder that spins around its axis to create artificial gravity, and the asteroid remains in place, so they can't be touching except at the top and bottom poles. Hang on, I'll pull up a map. Yes, there isn't room for the ship, but there is for us. Plenty." He peered out the nearest porthole. "It looks like we're at the nearest bank of airlocks to where the device will burrow through. We're going to have to climb. Or walk. Do you have magnetic boots?" Casmir waved to her galaxy suit footwear.

"No." Kim hadn't planned to board any ships or go into battle. Besides, nobody had offered her combat armor.

"Reuben, will you keep Kim from drifting off into space?" Casmir asked.

"Yes," Reuben said.

"Uh." Kim imagined herself floating behind a crusher like a kite.

"You'll be fine." Casmir patted her on the shoulder. "We've got this. Ready?"

"I guess I have to be." Kim was less daunted by the idea of deactivating a potential bomb and dealing with a deadly virus than she was by walking along the outside of a spinning station, only a crusher keeping her from flying away and smashing into the rock ceiling.

"Maybe we'll be lucky, and it'll *just* be a bomb." Casmir tapped the control panel and opened the inner airlock hatch.

Kim, envisioning a powerful explosive blowing up as she and Casmir walked up to it, couldn't find that thought heartening. Shaking her head, she stepped into the airlock chamber.

As the crushers were about to follow them inside—would they all fit?—someone in armor rushed into the cargo hold. Tristan.

"I can come with you in case you need help," he said.

Casmir held up a hand to keep him from joining them. "The fewer people out there, the better. Just in case."

Tristan stopped in front of the hatch. "I'd be coming for the *just in case*."

"There's nothing you could do except be blown away with us." Casmir glanced at Kim. "Not that that's going to happen. We're going to deactivate it."

"If you were sure of that, you wouldn't be worried about me coming." Tristan frowned through his faceplate at them.

"Thanks for offering, Tristan. You're a good man. If I don't make it, Zee will go back to Odin with you and loom threateningly at the Senate to make them give you your land."

"I don't think that will work, but thanks."

"Zee is very persuasive."

Zee came up behind Tristan and lifted him off his feet, startling him. Before Tristan could decide to pull a weapon or fight the manhandling, Zee set him aside and stepped into the airlock chamber.

"Very persuasive," Casmir repeated.

"I'm sure that'll work on those crusty senators." Tristan handed Casmir a rifle. "Here. In case blowing it to bits is the correct answer."

Casmir hesitated, then accepted it, slinging it across his torso on its strap. He looked like he cared a lot more about having easy access to his tool kit than the rifle.

HOME FRONT

Reuben and four other crushers walked in after Zee, some reforming themselves to ooze around behind Kim and Casmir. Kim found it disconcerting, especially when a black wave of liquid metal spread across the porthole in the exterior hatch behind her. Tristan lifted a hand in parting and closed the interior hatch.

"Here we go," Casmir murmured as the air cycled out of the chamber.

"You know," Kim said quietly, "you don't really need to come either. If all that device is doing is delivering the virus... I can take care of it."

The idea of going alone, or alone with only the crushers, was unappealing, but if something crazy happened, she also hated the idea of Casmir being infected right alongside her.

"I'll be shocked if it's not delivering an explosive along with the virus—it's probably got a way to plug the exterior of the station once it burrows in, then it'll blow through multiple levels inside and ensure no containment methods will work." Casmir shook his head. "You'll need me. Unless you've been engaged in home study courses these last few months, I don't believe you have experience deactivating explosives."

"And you do, robotics professor?" Kim was relieved he insisted on going with her, but she'd felt she should offer to go alone.

"Thanks to this ongoing adventure, I have more than I did when we first left home. But thanks for trying to leave me behind for my own good."

"You're welcome."

"The scanners report activity in the rock above the station," Nalini's voice came over their helmet comms. "We don't have much time until it breaks through."

"We're going out now." Casmir opened the exterior hatch.

Kim took a deep breath. She'd wanted an opportunity to feel useful. This was it.

CHAPTER 31

OKU CHECKED THE CONSOLE'S SIMPLE SCANNERS AS THE air darter flew close to Picnic Point. They were nothing as sophisticated as what spaceships had, and detecting life on a planet's surface was a lot harder than detecting something warm in the icy reaches of space, but if whoever had dragged Chasca out here wasn't wearing combat armor, maybe the scanners could pick up a heat signature.

Her breath caught. The signature that the scanners picked up wasn't a sniper. It was Chasca on the beach. The water was rising all around her, and she was moving—struggling to get free.

Tears pricked Oku's eyes, and she realized she hadn't brought anything to cut that chain.

"The scanners aren't showing anyone out here with her," Gunther said, "but there are a lot of nooks in that cliff."

"Land next to her so you're blocking her from anyone in the cliff, please." Oku was amazed that her voice came out calm and reasonable. Inside, she was panicking. What if they didn't make it in time?

Maddie was looking out a window instead of at the scanner display, and she said, "Someone's leaning out of the cliff!"

The craft accelerated and dropped down between the boulder formation Chasca was chained to and the cliff as someone fired. Orange DEW-Tek bolts blasted through the dark fog. The darter rocked as they struck the hull.

Oku lunged out of her seat and toward the hatch in the passenger area, not caring that Gunther was still trying to land. What if some of those shots had gotten past the darter and hit Chasca?

A bolt slammed into a rear window, shattering it and gouging deeply into the opposite wall.

"Open the hatch." Maddie pushed Oku back so she could go out first.

"You're not in armor," Gunther barked as he struggled to land the darter while shots plowed into the side of it, jolting the entire frame.

"I don't care!"

"I do," he snarled, landing them on the beach with a thumping jolt that sent Oku careening into the back row of seats.

The hatch opened, and both Gunther and Maddie jumped out with their weapons. They ran around the craft and toward the cliff.

Chasca barked and whined, visible from the open hatch, tidal water surging up to her armpits. Oku scrambled to her feet. She wanted to leap straight out and run to her dog, but if she couldn't free her, there was no point. She tore open compartments, looking for something that would break a chain.

Behind a panel in the back, she found two rifles. She snatched one and jumped out, damp sand shifting under her feet. A DEW-Tek blast took out the darter's running lights, plunging the beach into darkness.

Weapons fire buzzed on the other side of the craft, Maddie and Gunther versus however many people were shooting from the cliff. Oku would be in danger if she ran out from behind the darter's cover, but she couldn't wait. She had to trust that Maddie and Gunther would keep their enemies busy—and hope she wouldn't be that noticeable in the dark. Only the energy bolts lit up the night, glimpses of orange and crimson showing the waves breaking around the rocks that Chasca was chained to.

"Stay in the darter," came a concerned call from Maddie.

Was Oku visible to her? If she was, their enemies might see her too. Oku hesitated, trying to tell her thudding heart that she should give her people more time to take care of the threat.

But a huge wave came in, rolling over Chasca's head. Terror drove Oku into the water. The tide tugged at her legs as she pushed out toward the rocks.

The wave receded, leaving the water at her dog's chest level. Chasca coughed hoarsely.

"Coming, coming," Oku whispered as loudly as she dared, not wanting to draw attention to herself.

Chasca barked, but when she saw Oku, she switched from barking to whining. The scared pleas tore at Oku's heart. She plunged deeper, holding the rifle overhead so it wouldn't be damaged by the water.

HOME FRONT

When she reached Chasca, the dog tried to fling all of her eighty pounds into Oku's arms.

Oku patted her awkwardly, trying to see how she was restrained. It was more than a clip to her collar. They'd wrapped the chain around her torso and under her front legs.

"Bastards," Oku swore, trying to find a clasp or way to unhook her. If she couldn't, she would have to break the chain.

Another wave broke and roared toward them. Oku tried to raise the rifle overhead again. Claws scrabbled at her, tearing at her through her clothing as Chasca whined in renewed fear.

The dark, icy water surged over both their heads. The raw power of the sea swept Oku off her feet, and only her grasp on the chained Chasca kept her from being torn away. And that grasp was tenuous. Chasca squirmed in terror, not understanding that Oku could help but needed her to be still to do so.

The water receded, and Oku gasped for air.

"Hold still, girl," she rasped to the struggling dog. "I know it's horrible. Let me just find…"

She gave up on trying to find a clasp and grabbed the chain itself. But it was underwater and tight enough that she couldn't pull it up. It took her a moment to realize she needed to move Chasca closer to the rock formation to gain some slack. Pushing and pulling and coaxing, she drew the dog through the water. Finally, she could pull the chain out of the water so she could see it.

The rifle had gotten wet. She prayed it would still work.

Awkwardly and fighting Chasca as much as the waves, she aimed the weapon at the chain.

"Please, girl. Hold still for a second. I can't risk hitting you." She put her back to Chasca, trying to make sure she couldn't get in the way.

Another wave roared as it formed. Hands shaking, Oku pointed the muzzle of the rifle at the chain. An alert flashed across her contact, and she swore. High blood sugar. No kidding.

She fired, and the force of the impact blew the chain out of her hand. Another wave came in, knocking her over again. She lost the rifle.

Chasca surged away from her, and Oku lunged, grabbing for her. She caught the dog's collar. Chasca hauled her like a sled being pulled at top speed across a northern glacier.

It was only then that Oku realized it had worked. She'd broken the chain.

Chasca dragged her up until the water was only knee deep. As Oku found her feet, keeping a death grip on Chasca's collar lest she take off down the beach, more orange bolts streaked out from the direction of the cliff.

Oku hurried toward the protection of the darter, a dozen holes now blown in it. Before she reached it, a bolt sizzled toward her. There was no time to react, and it would have struck her, but Chasca lunged to the side, pulling her off balance. As it was, the bolt skimmed her shoulder and fiery pain surged through her body.

Chasca almost succeeded in lunging away, but Oku gritted her teeth and kept her hold on the collar. Panting, she hauled the dog up the beach and dropped to her knees beside the darter's open hatch. Her shoulder burned, but it could have been a lot worse.

"Get him, get him!" Maddie yelled from somewhere near the cliff.

Cursing came in response. Gunther. Then he swore in pain.

Oku thought about dragging Chasca inside the darter, but there were so many holes in the hull that she could almost *see* the firefight on the other side. Shards of Glasnax—or maybe these old darters had real glass windows—littered the deck inside. Another reason to avoid it. But what if Maddie and Gunther didn't succeed in driving off the attackers?

Wet and scared, Chasca shivered in Oku's arms. Every time the dog stirred, she bumped Oku's shoulder, and fresh pain stabbed her, but Oku was too afraid she'd run off if she let go of her.

Lights flared in the sky up above as a shuttle soared into view over the cliff. Some new enemy? Kidnappers who had been plotting to get her all along?

Oku leaned against the hull, hoping the darkness hid her. The shuttle flew lower, coming straight toward the battered darter. The weapons fire stopped. Oku squinted as a wide beam of light landed on the beach—on her.

"Inside, girl," she whispered to Chasca, forcing herself to her feet.

Chasca didn't want to go in the darter any more than she would have wanted to go back in the ocean—maybe she feared the tide would keep coming and sweep it away—but Oku lifted her in. Her shoulder protested every movement. She couldn't get the hatch closed, so she left it and pulled Chasca deeper inside. Oku hunkered down between seats, hoping they would provide cover if more shots blasted into the darter.

But it grew silent on the beach. Oku resisted the urge to peer out the hatch. She crept back to the weapons storage compartment she'd found before and pulled out a stunner.

The lighting outside shifted as the shuttle landed. Chasca whined.

"Ssh," Oku whispered. "We're hiding."

Chasca gave her a *look*. One that suggested they should have fled up the beach to the castle and hidden in Oku's room.

A shadow fell across the hatchway. Oku pointed the stunner.

Finn looked in, and she almost fired, but he swore and jerked back during her split-second of indecision. The next person who looked in was their mother. Relief washed over her, though she might still be in trouble. What had Finn told her?

"Oku?" Her mother eyed the stunner, Oku's soggy clothes, and the shaking and wet Chasca. "Are you all right?"

"Chasca was almost murdered, and I was shot." Oku meant the words to come out matter-of-factly, but they sounded panicked, almost a screech in her own ear. She drew in a shuddering breath and groped for calmness. "I wasn't hit badly, but I need a vet for Chasca."

"And a doctor," her mother said, eyeing her. "So does your bodyguard. Come. We're all going to have a long talk in the morning."

She didn't look pleased as she backed out of view. Again, Oku worried that Finn had been filling her ear with lies. She hoped her mother wouldn't believe them. But she *had* stunned his bodyguard and broken into his room...

Oku groaned and leaned her head against Chasca's damp fur. "This has not been a good day, girl."

Chasca whined in agreement.

The crushers walked across the hull of the rotating station, the rocky ceiling of the carved out asteroid passing overhead. Here and there, conduits and knots of electronics ran along the rock or disappeared into holes.

The speed of the station's rotation and the threat of flying off weren't as great as Kim had imagined, but she did feel the pull of centrifugal force as their odd little group trundled along. The crushers could magnetize their soles so they didn't float away, whereas Kim was stuck being pulled along by Reuben with her feet out behind her like the kite she'd envisioned. Casmir, a small form even in his bulky combat armor, led the way across the massive exterior station. Intermittent lights embedded in the hull illuminated their route.

"I'm glad I took motion-sickness tablets earlier." Casmir glanced back, then pressed his satchel down as it tried to float away from his hip.

"Are they proving effective?" Kim asked.

He hesitated. "Mostly. Hopefully. I had to promise not to throw up in this combat armor to get someone to lend it to me. Funny how word has gotten around the entire Twelve Systems—at least three of them—that I have a problem with motion sickness."

As they progressed along the outside of the station, the rock ceiling dropped lower. As promised, there soon wasn't enough space for a ship to fly through, but it wasn't as claustrophobic as Kim had feared. There was plenty of room overhead for them and would have been for small repair vehicles. She even spotted something that looked like a three-foot-tall version of Viggo's robot vacuums roaming along the surface.

"It's breaking through the rock," came an alarmed report over the comm.

"We're almost there," Casmir said with impressive calmness.

He turned on a headlamp integrated into his helmet, and the cone of light brightened the lumpy brown surface in the distance. It took him a few head turns to find the spot where a drill bit was breaking through.

Casmir picked up his pace, as much as he could while relying on the magnetic soles of his boots, but Zee held up a hand and pointed for another of the crushers to rush ahead of Casmir. They were out in the vacuum of space now, so Kim couldn't hear the crushers speak, but he must have communicated wirelessly with all of them, because the others also maneuvered around Casmir and took the lead.

They stopped when they were in line with the drill bit but not yet under it—the station would continue rotating toward that spot. The device was busting through fully now, a few rocks trickling slowly down toward the station as a dusty cloud of regolith formed under the hole. Kim had no idea how much gravity the asteroid had other than it was very little.

The device floated out of the hole, propelled by whatever motor had sent it through the asteroid. It was a bronze-colored bullet-shaped cylinder a little longer than a coffin. Articulating legs that reminded her of squid tentacles trailed behind it, and the huge drill bit protruded from its nose.

"It looks like some metal sculptor's version of a nightmare sea creature," Casmir said.

"Actually, it looks a lot like a giant bacteriophage," Kim said. "Which is disturbingly apt."

"Hm." Casmir glanced at Zee and shook his head. "No, if anything we should back up. The body's big enough to have a big payload in there. A big explosive payload."

"What did he ask?"

"If I should try to blow it up before it lands. But it's too close at this point. If there's a nuke in there, it could blow away half the station—and everybody in it. We need to deactivate it. But first, we need to render the drill inoperable so it can't get inside."

The device sailed down, its articulating legs spreading out and shifting direction to help with the landing. Landing and attaching itself to the hull.

"You're going to send one of the crushers to do all that while you stand safely back, right?" Kim asked.

Casmir hesitated again.

"Use them for your eyes and hands and stay back here," Kim said.

Maybe it was silly—if a huge explosive detonated, fifty feet wouldn't make a difference, but the device could have other defensive measures, attacks that the nearly indestructible crushers might survive.

"I am in armor," Casmir pointed out.

"Use the crushers anyway. Or I'll use Rache's gift on you." An empty threat, since she hadn't brought the katana along.

"I guess it's not psychedelic mushrooms then."

"No. It's pointier."

The device settled on the hull, and hooks on the ends of the metal legs burrowed into it as if they also had the power to drill.

"Right, go check it out, Zee, Joseph, and Levi," Casmir said. "Please be careful. Send close-up photos back to me and see if there are any panels you can open. Also, watch for booby traps. I'm *positive* there will be booby traps." His gauntleted fingers groped in the air, as if he could barely imagine not rushing over there and checking the device himself.

Kim suspected the crushers wouldn't be able to do their jobs for them, but they could at least act as the bomb squad and determine if that thing had defenses. If it was safe, aside from the possibility of the horrific virus inside, then she and Casmir could go in.

Reuben remained at Kim's side with two of the other crushers and continued to keep her from floating away. She wished there had been time to hunt down magnetic boots.

"Can they hear you?" she asked.

"No. I'm sending the message over my chip to them too. I'm just talking out loud for your sake. Ah, good. There's a zoom option in my faceplate." Casmir circled the device until he could see something on the side, then crouched down, observing as the crushers approached the device.

Kim's helmet lacked all the fancy upgrades of combat armor, but she opened her kit and pulled out a scanner to see what it could tell her. In particular, she wanted to know if there was a heated interior chamber where a virus might be kept warm and viable. Freezing it wouldn't kill it, but it would neutralize it until it thawed. Dubashi would have wanted it to be a threat immediately.

The drill extended, and it started burrowing into the hull of the station. That would be stronger than the rock of the asteroid but not nearly as thick. Kim worried they didn't have much time. Judging by the way Casmir shifted his weight around, he was nervous too.

The crushers reached the device and fanned out around it.

"There's a panel right there," Casmir said. "As soon as you check for booby traps, see if you can open it, please, Zee."

"I'm scanning the device," Kim said. "It's putting out an energy signature beyond what I believe is powering the drill, and I believe the interior is hollow. Possibly holding a canister of the virus. Possibly holding explosives. Or both."

"That's what I'm afraid of," he said as the crushers ran their hands over the outer shell.

"You better stay farther back."

"Unfortunately, there's nothing to access, no wireless accessibility. All of its commands seem to be self-contained. We'll need to gain access manually to derail it." Casmir seemed to be talking to himself more than to her, working things through.

One of the crushers formed his fingers into a screwdriver and removed a panel that took up a third of the device. But as soon as he removed it, he flew backward like a cartoon character zapped by electricity.

HOME FRONT

He struck the asteroid ceiling twenty feet above and bounced off. He twisted, trying to grab the rough rock to keep from floating free, but he wasn't quite fast enough. With nothing to grab, the crusher started floating slowly back toward the hull.

"And there are the booby traps." Casmir lifted a hand. "Zee, can you get Levi?"

Zee pushed off, angling himself toward the other crusher. He hooked his cohort and his momentum took them both to the ceiling. They pushed off back toward the station and landed beside Casmir again, locking their soles to the surface.

The panel had slowly tipped downward, leaving the interior exposed. Kim could see some of the complicated electronics in there, but she stayed back, not wanting to get in the way—or be zapped.

"Let me see if I've got…" Casmir rummaged in his satchel, tools threatening to escape, and pulled out something that reminded Kim of her vibrating toothbrush. "Pulse wrench. Let's see if this will allow me the fine manipulation ability I need without actually touching anything."

As he leaned forward, Kim held her breath, afraid he would be zapped even if he didn't physically touch the device himself—and afraid it would kill him.

Meanwhile, the drill drove deeper into the hull. It was sure to bite through any second. At which point the station would be susceptible to the virus if the device truly held a container of it. Did it?

"Hah. Step One complete."

It took Kim a moment to notice that the drill had stopped spinning. "Did it make it through?"

"It doesn't look like the station was breached. We should have more time to figure this out now." Casmir went back to poking about in the interior with his pulse wrench, careful not to touch anything. "Or… perhaps not." He swore and then muttered what Kim guessed was a prayer in Hebrew.

"Do I want to know?"

"Well, we don't have any more time. We have, ah, slightly over four minutes. There's a detonator and a timer ticking down, which I assume leads to…" He leaned to the side, nudging something in the interior carefully with the pulse tool. "I see two things of import. A canister with a biohazard label on the side and… Well. The good news is that the warhead isn't humungous. The bad news is that it's definitely a warhead."

Kim's hands were moist and clammy inside her gloves. "The canister sounds familiar."

Back on Dubashi's base, she'd incinerated several of them.

"I feared it would, but the warhead is the more immediate concern. I'm going to try to disarm it in less than three minutes and fifty-four seconds."

She licked her dry lips. "Do you know how?"

"I've seen this setup quite often."

"When?" she asked suspiciously.

"In comic books. Do you think Dubashi is a fan?"

Kim groaned. "Any chance it's a nuke and the detonation will be underwhelming in space?"

"I don't think so. I'm guessing it's engineered for maximum... whelm. Is that a word?"

"Yes."

"Oh, good."

He was tinkering while he spoke, but Kim wanted to tell him to shut up and concentrate. She refrained. She knew he babbled when he was nervous and that his hands were perfectly capable of working independently of his mouth. But she was afraid and wanted to help. Somehow. If there had been more time, she would have asked him to remove the canister, so she could get rid of that while he worked on the warhead, but she didn't want to distract him.

Reuben patted her on the shoulder, as if to reassure her that it would be all right. Great, she looked so distressed that even a crusher could tell she needed comforting.

Zee and the other two crushers with him stood behind Casmir as he worked. Kim thought about suggesting he leave some instructions and have *them* disarm the bomb, but it wasn't as if there was time to get away. Besides, Casmir was their best bet for disarming it.

As he leaned in close to peer around the edge of the panel, she almost reminded him not to touch it—his helmet was perilously close—but he froze and didn't brush it.

"Ah, I see you. Almost got it, Kim."

But as he shifted his tool to a different angle, light flashed. Kim flinched and looked away as it turned into a series of pulsing flashes, but a second later, she realized what it would do to Casmir. What it had been *designed* to do to him. Damn it, Dubashi had taken a page from Rache's book.

Kim pulled herself forward as the flashes stopped, hoping Casmir had closed his eyes and dimmed his faceplate in time, but she groaned when she spotted him, already in Zee's arms. Already in the middle of a seizure.

She swore. There was nothing she could do for him and no way he would recover before the countdown finished. *She* had to finish disarming the bomb. And how the hell did she do that?

Right away, she spotted the little timer. They were down to a minute. She felt like she was observing all this from outside her own body. The moment was surreal, and she saw her death counting down on that timer.

She was about to reach in and start randomly yanking on things and hoping to get lucky, but Zee startled her by picking her up and moving her aside. He'd handed Casmir to one of the other crushers. He reached inside, hands shifting into something like scissors. Another crusher came forward and held him down. The device's defenses tried to knock Zee away, as it had done the first crusher, but his buddy kept him in place, and if electrical surges were threatening to destroy Zee's innards, he didn't let them stop him. He pulled out the warhead and the detonator, not trying to stop the timer from counting down. It was still attached, still ticking down. Less than thirty seconds now.

"What are you doing?" Kim asked, even though she knew they couldn't hear her.

With one arm wrapped around the warhead, Zee pointed at the ceiling, as if he planned to leap up there. To try to get it away from them?

Kim shook her head. "It's not going to be far enough."

Zee crouched and would have sprung, but one of the other crushers stepped forward. Reuben. He pointed at Zee, pointed at Casmir, and pointed at the warhead.

Zee looked at Casmir. He'd stopped twitching and hung limply in another crusher's grip.

Kim had no idea what they were debating via that wireless link, but there wasn't time for debate. If they had an idea, they needed to do it now. Less than twenty seconds.

Zee handed the warhead to Reuben. With all this manhandling, Kim couldn't believe it hadn't gone off yet. Reuben looked at her, then pointed at his chest and the ceiling again. He crouched to spring.

"Wait," Kim blurted and lunged for the device. A surge of electricity ran up her arm as she reached in and grabbed the biohazard canister. Pain shot through her entire body as she twisted and pulled it out, but she managed to hand it to Reuben. If the bomb went off out here and the hull of the station somehow wasn't breached, the explosion could damn well take the virus with it.

One of the crushers pulled her back. She was gasping for air, her entire body tingling and her heart pounding in her ears.

With the canister and the warhead in his arms, Reuben sprang away from the hull, his legs easily carrying him to the ceiling in the fractional gravity. The station had spun a full rotation and was back to where the device had drilled in. Reuben scrambled along the ceiling toward that hole, creating an extra set of arms to propel himself along the lumpy rock. He wouldn't have time to pull himself out of the mile-thick wall of asteroid around the station, but maybe if he got far enough before it blew…

Zee pointed downward, and he pushed Kim and Casmir down to the hull. The other crushers hurried over and shifted their forms, melding together to create a barrier, a protective dome. As it closed over Kim and Casmir, the last thing she saw was Reuben turning himself into a box—an amorphous container with the bomb and the canister inside—and disappearing up into the hole.

Then all went dark as the crushers-turned-dome blocked out her view of everything. She and Casmir lay on their stomachs with their faceplates pressed to the hull when the explosion went off. The hull quaked, and she squinted her eyes shut, expecting the worst.

But the quaking subsided, and the blast of pain she expected right before the end of her life did not come.

The crushers pulled away from each other and resumed their bipedal shapes. Pieces of rock from the asteroid floated free, and there was a great crater up there now, but the station was still intact. Reuben was gone.

CHAPTER 32

QIN AND MOUSER TROTTED THROUGH THE DARK CORRIDORS of the *Scimitar*, the ship familiar to Qin, though the smoke and scorch marks on the walls and the lack of lighting or power anywhere gave it the strange feel of a derelict. She didn't peer into the faceplates of the broken unmoving bodies they passed, not wanting to see people she recognized. Even if the pirates had been her owners and not her friends, it was hard not to feel something at seeing them dead.

She tried to focus on the mission—getting to the bridge to help Asger and Bjarke—but every turn brought back memories. The sounds of battle drifted to them from side corridors, as well, as they passed through intersections. She glanced warily down them, anticipating ambushes.

If she had been wearing the same armor as her sisters, she might have pretended to be one of them—an ally rather than an enemy—and run past the pirates as if she belonged there. But Bonita had purchased her new armor, armor without the taint of slavery and a hundred past battles where Qin had fought her morals to obey her masters, and she wore it now proudly. She was her own person, and she intended to stay that way.

Clanks came from a side corridor ahead. Footfalls ringing out on the deck. Several sets of them.

A group of crushers? Pirates *avoiding* the crushers?

"Slow down," Mouser whispered. "I think that's—"

A group of four armored men rounded the corner and pointed rifles at them. Qin had her Brockinger in hand and would have fired before any of them could, but she recognized the man in back, for he stared right at her through his faceplate. Gray hair, gray mustache, cold gray eyes.

Captain Framer, one of the five Drucker brothers, one of the men who'd paid for her to be made in a scientist's laboratory twenty years earlier. One of the first men to come down and take sexual pleasure on his wares after Qin and the others had arrived.

Hatred roiled through her, but the conditioning they'd instilled in her over the years rooted her feet to the deck and froze her finger on the trigger of her gun.

If you hurt any of us, you will be punished... If you hurt any of us, you will be punished...

"Why aren't you two fighting?" the lieutenant at Framer's side demanded. "They're taking the bridge."

The captain's eyes narrowed. "That's the escaped slave. Get her!"

Mouser lunged forward.

Framer hit a control fob on the wrist of his armor, and Mouser bent forward, her weapon falling from her fingers with a clatter. She gasped and grabbed her helmet with both hands.

Qin recovered from her shock and the barrage of memories. She roared in anger and charged the men. She wanted to get to Framer, since he was the one with the controller that was hurting Mouser, but the three others were in front of him. They fired at her armor, and alerts flashed on her helmet display. She jumped and fired over one man's head, the explosive round of her Brockinger clipping the captain in the shoulder and exploding.

In the confined space, the shockwave rocked into the others, and they tottered off balance. Qin experienced it too, but she recovered more quickly. Almost on top of the pirates, she tackled them instead of reloading, rage and years of pent-up frustration giving her extra speed and strength. She hurled the pirates against the bulkheads and pounded them into each other. A piece of one man's armor snapped, and he screamed as she dislocated his shoulder.

A kick flew in from the side and knocked her Brockinger out of her hand. Qin barely noticed. She grabbed the nearest pirate and mashed him against the bulkhead, faceplate cracking as it struck like a boulder dropped from a mountaintop.

"Get her off me!" he screamed.

She smashed his faceplate against the wall again, then threw him toward the captain. Framer's armor was dented and covered in soot from her explosive, and his arm hung limply at his side, but he was still on his feet and still armed. He twisted, sidestepping the human projectile coming at him.

The lieutenant grabbed Qin from behind and gripped her helmet, trying to pull it off. She threw an elbow backward, catching him in the armored chest. He grunted, but didn't let go, instead wrapping an arm around her neck. She'd knocked two of the pirates down, but she couldn't get the leverage she needed to escape this one's vise-like grip.

Captain Framer had backed away and pulled out a Brockinger of his own. "Throw her this way, and then get back," he snarled to his man.

"I thought we wanted to recapture her." The lieutenant twisted, forcing her to face Framer.

"The doc'll put her back together and we can keep using her. *After* she's properly punished for running away."

Qin roared and tried to twist free, but the lieutenant had cybernetic upgrades as well as his armor and was far stronger than the average man. Framer sneered and raised his weapon toward her eyes. What would there be left to put back together if an explosive detonated in her face?

She jerked her head back, smashing her helmet into the lieutenant's faceplate. He staggered, and this time, she managed to twist in his grip so that her chest wasn't toward the captain. But she feared it wouldn't be enough, that he would still incapacitate her with his fire.

Then another roar filled the corridor. It was Mouser. She'd found her feet. Still hunched with pain, she sprang at Framer.

He jerked his big gun to the side to aim at her, but she bowled into him first. Qin managed to slip her leg between the lieutenant's legs and jam her hip against him. Gripping his arm, she twisted and threw him over her shoulder. He smashed into the bulkhead.

Mouser screamed, utter agony tearing from her throat. Qin snatched the lieutenant's rifle off his back, the strap snapping, and grabbed her own weapon off the deck. As she whirled to help her sister, she halted short of shooting. Mouser was on the captain's back, her legs wrapped around his chest, her hands gripping the sides of his helmet. The wrist control for the pain implants lay in pieces on the deck.

The captain struggled to shove her off, stumbling into the bulkhead. He'd already dropped his weapon. Mouser tore his helmet off and threw it down the corridor.

"I've had enough from you!" She grabbed his head, and Qin realized she would tear that off too.

"Wait!" she blurted, though she wasn't sure she should. "We may need him as a hostage. To negotiate with the other captains to get out of here."

Mouser, her hands gripping the sides of Framer's head, looked back at Qin. Eyes identical to her own stared at her with frustration and anger.

"If it doesn't work out," Qin offered, "we can space him later."

Without releasing her grip on his head, Mouser jumped down.

"You're going to die for this insurrection, you bitches," Framer snarled, triumph rising above the pain in his eyes. Did he think he'd won? "And you'll never get away from my brothers, no matter what you do to me and my ship."

As Qin came forward and collected his weapon, Mouser shoved Framer sideways, his unprotected head smashing against the bulkhead. He crumpled to the deck.

"Are you sure we can't space him now?" Mouser asked.

"Let's see if we can use him first." Qin hugged her, relieved she hadn't made a mistake in bringing Mouser along.

Her sister hugged her back. "We're going to get out of this and away from all of them, right?" Mouser sounded like she needed to believe that, that she wouldn't end up back in that communal pen, back serving the Druckers.

"Damn straight, we are." Qin released her—they still had work to do. "Let's carry him with us to the bridge."

She'd intended to help, but Mouser grabbed the unconscious pirate by the hair and dragged him down the corridor by herself. Smiling, Qin followed, watching her sister's back.

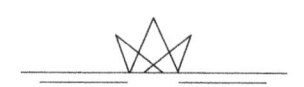

Asger gaped when Qin walked onto the bridge with her sister, who was dragging an unconscious pirate by the hair. The gape turned to a proud grin when Qin explained that their prisoner was the ship's captain.

"*Now* we have a bargaining chip." Asger pointed to the comm panel. He, his father, and their band of crushers were currently on hold.

HOME FRONT

Some underling had commed them, demanding their surrender. Asger had stated that they'd taken over the ship and demanded the *Druckers* surrender. The last he'd heard, the underling was getting the captain.

Qin came over to stand next to Asger, leaning her hip against the smashed console. He rested a hand on her shoulder. Though he didn't know if their situation had improved vastly, he felt better having her on the bridge with him. And he hoped it meant something that she'd acquired the most valuable possible prisoner on the ship. Would the captain's brothers care enough to save his life?

The prisoner groaned. Qin's sister hefted him to his feet and pinned his arms behind his back.

"This is Captain Khan," a tight voice said. "I'll have the name of whoever thought it was a bright idea to take over my brother's ship."

"I'm Sir William Asger." He shifted the camera to make sure the pirate would see his knight's armor and pertundo. "And he deserved having his ship taken over. He stopped and boarded my transport ship and attempted to kidnap one of my crew."

Asger thought the pirate captain would pretend he didn't know what he was talking about, but he snapped, "Qin Three is ours, not a member of some Kingdom crew of one. What are knights even doing here? Your system is at war."

"Gathering allies. Such as genetically engineered warrior women who are well past their majority and cannot legally be kept as slaves."

"We ordered them created twenty years ago and paid for them fair and square. In System Cerberus. As I'm sure you know, it's legal to own clones there."

"We're not in System Cerberus. It's not legal here. Regardless, we are hiring the Qins for our war effort, and we're also taking your ships back to System Lion to help break the blockade. You can surrender them to us now, or you can lose them the hard way, the way your brother here did."

This is your idea of negotiating? Bjarke gave him an incredulous look as he sent the message via his chip.

Asger held up a finger toward him. "Captain Framer, do you want to say hello so your brother knows you're still alive? For the moment." Asger shifted the camera so it would take in their captive.

"Screw you," Framer said.

"I trust you heard that, Captain," Asger said. "Framer, would you also like to tell your brother how dark and powerless your ship is?"

The pirate captain glowered at him and said nothing.

"We can see that it has no power," Khan said neutrally.

"Because we deployed the virus made by Professor Casmir Dabrowski," Asger said. "You may have heard of how it was used in System Hydra on several pirate ships there. Or you may not have, since they were utterly destroyed and none of the crew survived. But I invite you to check the news while we finish preparing to beam the virus over to your ships." Asger knew it needed to be voluntarily downloaded, but he was crossing his fingers that the pirates didn't know that. "Contact us if you wish to surrender before we knock out power to the rest of the ships in your fleet. At which point, that little freighter you're harassing will be able to destroy all of you with its one rail gun."

Asger hurried to close the channel, worried one of the helpful crushers would point out that the virus didn't work like that. But they remained silent. Now that they'd done their duties with the computer systems, they seemed content to let the humans handle the negotiations.

His father came over, putting his back toward Framer on the other side of the bridge, and stood shoulder to shoulder with him. He removed his helmet and rubbed his forehead.

"You think Dabrowski's name is going to drive fear into their hearts?" he murmured.

"You know what happened at Tiamat Station," Asger said back, equally quietly. "I'm hoping they do too."

"I doubt most people know that was a computer virus."

"Don't be too sure. He's used it more than once now, and I'd be surprised if all of the Twelve Systems hadn't heard about the crushers." Asger had been sure to pan around the smoking bridge to show how many of them they had. "I'm hoping they don't know exactly how the virus works. It's not like they're astroshamans."

I'm sending this to all three of you, came a message from Bonita. *One of the Drucker captains is comming me and asking if you have the means to knock them all out with the same virus that took down the pirate fleet in System Hydra.*

Tell them yes, Asger messaged back promptly.

I did. They also wanted to know if you're really friends with Casmir Dabrowski and how many of those crushers you have. If we weren't all in the clutches of angry pirates right now, I would take the time to be

HOME FRONT

highly amused—maybe bemused—that the kid with the rumpled robot T-shirt who pukes in zero-g has become someone who pirates are afraid of. I alluded to the dinner we all had with Rache. I figured it couldn't hurt if they believed that you're best friends with him too.

"Bonita," Asger's father murmured, rubbing his forehead again.

Asger hoped Bonita hadn't overplayed it and had simply corroborated their story.

Their comm beeped again.

"Yes?" Asger asked politely, as if he wasn't worried about a thing.

"We are willing to consider surrender, but we are countering your draconian conditions," Captain Khan said.

Asger was so surprised that he almost fell over. Was this a *trick*?

"What is your counter?" he managed to ask.

"No more of our people will be killed." Khan must have gotten reports from the men on this ship about the crushers relentlessly mowing down all the pirates in their path. "Including my brother. We will give you the Qins, but you will not take our ships. You will pile into that floating turd of a freighter with them and leave."

A part of Asger wanted to leap for joy at the idea that his Qin and all her sisters might be released from the pirates' claims of ownership, but he was immediately suspicious. From the way his father shook his head, Asger knew he wasn't the only one.

"Oh sure," he said. "We'll all jump into that freighter, so you can shoot us down as we leave. The only way we'll consider that acceptable is if we deploy the virus to all of your ships first. Leaving you powerless in space until you run out of air and die. Or some enterprising ships come by and board you themselves."

"What do *you* propose then?" Khan asked angrily. "We're not *giving* you all five of our ships. If you take them and leave me alive, then I'll spend the rest of my life hunting you down and anyone you care about, including those girls. Have you screwed them yet, Knight? They're a good lay, aren't they?"

Asger snapped his fingers into fists, fury making him speechless. Which was good because he would have said something stupid and ruined any chance at a positive outcome to this negotiation.

Qin, no doubt reading his emotions, clasped his hand and shook her head.

Asger had to remind himself that he couldn't back up his threat with the virus. He had to keep his cool and bluff convincingly.

Besides, what was it Casmir had said about getting what one wanted by helping others get what they wanted? What could he give to these murderous assholes without thrashing his morals the way these crushers had thrashed the pirates?

"I care nothing about *lays*," Asger said calmly. "I am merely recruiting individuals and ships with the power to rid my system of its intruders. It would be a shame to destroy five warships when they could be used by my people. My counter is that your ships, under the command of Kingdom Fleet officers, each with a dozen crushers to act as bodyguards and enforcers of their rule, will accompany us to the Kingdom to end the blockade there. Once that problem is resolved, which it inevitably will be, given the allies we've secured here, you will be free to return to your own system, under the condition that your ships will never again enter System Lion. You will release the Qins, never bothering any of them again, and accept that they are free human beings, allowed to choose their own fates and work for whomever they please."

The captain started to say something—it sounded like more of an objection than agreement—but Asger interrupted him and pressed on. If the pirates didn't get something out of it, they would still be trouble.

"*Furthermore*," Asger said, "since we are depriving you of some of your best warriors—"

"*Some?*" Qin mouthed, genuinely appearing offended.

"—my friend, Professor Dabrowski, will give you a personal crusher, one for you and one for each of your brothers. One per Drucker warship. I trust you've been receiving reports from your men about how deadly they are."

Captain Khan fell silent. Well, at least it wasn't a protest.

Those aren't your crushers to trade, Asger's father messaged, though his expression was more contemplative than objecting.

They were Jorg's technically. They probably belong to the Fleet now. I'm guessing the Fleet—Ambassador Romano or Ishii or whoever is in charge—will agree that five crushers are a fair trade for the use of five warships.

I wouldn't assume Ambassador Romano will agree to anything reasonable.

We'll have Casmir glare at him if he gives us trouble. Apparently, the systems now believe him a force to be reckoned with. Asger meant it as a joke, and his father snorted, but he didn't disagree.

HOME FRONT

"We agree to lend our assistance and accompany you to System Lion under the command of your officers," Khan said, "but we insist on being at the back of the attack formation. Your war is not our war, and we care little about who wins. Our intelligence suggests that even a modest display of power should clear that blockade, given that Dubashi failed to hire his mercenary army. You don't need to use us for cannon fodder."

"Agreed," Asger said, though he expected more stipulations.

"And we will trade one Qin for one crusher. We have twenty-one of the girls left. We want twenty-one crushers in exchange. No, twenty-two, because you have Qin Three as well, and she belonged to us."

"We are not trading human beings as if they are chattel," Asger growled, though he wondered if Casmir would make the same objection on behalf of his crushers, especially since Asger was offering them to pirates. "You will let the women go free. We will receive nothing, unless they wish to work for us, as I'm hoping they will during the war. The offer is one crusher per ship. Besides, one crusher is worth far more than any single warrior woman." He mouthed, "Sorry," to Qin when her eyebrows flew up. "That is my final offer, Captain. My team is ready to deploy the virus if you do not find this deal acceptable."

Another long silence followed. Asger held his breath, afraid he'd pushed his bluff too far. All it would take was Khan saying, "Prove it," about the virus, and then what?

"We accept," Khan finally said. "We see your Kingdom warships on the way. We will allow their officers on board without a fight." The captain's voice suggested his mouth was twisted into a sneer of distaste. "You will inform them to leave one crusher when they go."

"You'll receive your crusher, but I will ask Professor Dabrowski to reprogram them first. Currently, they have orders to obey me and only me. You may find that displeasing."

"Agreed. But one more thing, *Sir* Asger."

"Yes?"

"For the sake of your health, I suggest that neither you nor any of the Qins fly into System Cerberus ever again."

"I'll keep your suggestion in mind." Asger closed the comm and pointed to one of the crushers next to Qin's sister—she was still holding Framer. "Would you and some of your buddies put him in the brig? And find a way to contain the rest of the pirates on the ship, please. Do a search. We need to round up everyone so they don't make trouble while we wait for the Kingdom Fleet ships to arrive and lend us assistance."

"We will secure the ship, Sir Asger."

Qin's sister hesitantly let the crusher take her prisoner from her. "I'll show them where the brig is."

She walked out trailed by crushers.

"I'm beginning to like those guys," Asger said.

"Are you going to ask Casmir to program the ones that go to the pirates to be dumb?" his father asked.

"I hadn't thought of that. Maybe it's a good idea."

"Don't make them dumb," Qin said, smiling at Asger. "Make them good."

"Good?"

"Morally upright individuals who object to pirating and murdering and who will only accept orders to help people."

"Well, I'm sure Casmir would go for that."

"I'm sure he would too. Will you take off your helmet?" Qin made a lifting motion with her fingers.

"Why?" Asger looked around to make sure all the threats were gone, then tapped the button to make his helmet retract.

"So I can do this." Qin faced him, rested her hands on his shoulders, and kissed him.

Asger's father made a disgruntled noise, said, "I'll help with the roundup," and walked out.

Asger barely noticed.

Qin broke the kiss long enough to whisper, "You've given us our freedom," and gazed into his eyes, her face only inches from his.

"I couldn't have done it without you. And Casmir's new reputation."

"I'll kiss him too. But not like this." Qin pulled him close for one of the more memorable kisses he'd had in his life, and he suddenly didn't mind that it would take hours for the Kingdom Fleet ships to arrive.

CHAPTER 33

CASMIR WOKE UP GROGGY AND CONFUSED—AND STARING AT a rocky wall. No, wait. That was a rocky ceiling. Or at least it was above him. He was... floating? No, lying on the hull of some ship, a hint of gravity pressing his back to it.

The confusion was slow to clear from his seizure-muddled mind, and he tried to rub his watering eyes twice, knuckles clunking against his faceplate, before he realized he was in combat armor. Someone leaned over and peered down at him.

"Kim?" he croaked.

Her features lay in shadow behind a faceplate.

"Bomb," he blurted, memories slowly returning, and he jerked his head up to look around. The device. The explosive. That damn series of flashing lights that had taken him down. How had Dubashi learned about his seizure disorder? Was that out on the public networks now? Or in some downloadable file freely traded around by villains who wanted to take him out?

"It's all right." Kim pressed her hand against his chest, keeping him from scrambling to his feet. "It's gone. And I'm sorry, but so is Reuben." She looked up toward the dark ceiling. "I don't know if he was unlucky or lucky. He chose that fate."

Casmir swallowed, his throat tight. Was it his imagination that tiny black bits were floating about up there? Pieces of the crusher that had been too completely destroyed to reassemble himself?

Yes, it was his imagination, he realized, since the station had continued its inexorable spin. He could no longer see the spot where the device had drilled in, nor evidence of the explosion except on the scorched melted hull all around them. All around them save for a circular undamaged spot where the other crushers must have protected them.

Sadness crept past the worry still making his heart pound in his chest. He'd known the crushers weren't completely indestructible—if that warhead had gone off, it was amazing that any of them were still alive—but this was the first one he'd lost. "What happened?"

Kim described the moments he'd lost, Zee's attempt to sacrifice himself and Reuben's successful sacrifice. She'd never been expressive, but he thought he caught sadness from her when she spoke of his death. She'd never warmed up to Zee, but maybe she'd bonded a little with Reuben. If so, that made him sadder.

"I'm not a hundred percent certain we weren't contaminated by the virus at some point in this, so we're waiting for Shayban to send a medical ship out with a proper decontamination chamber to douse us and your crushers." Kim moved her hand off his chest. "Can you stand? We have to move back down to where there's more room so the ship can reach us."

"I think so." Casmir had a monstrous headache, his thoughts were processing at half-speed, and his eyelid was twitching like a frog in a science lab, but maybe after the decontamination bath, he could take a nice nap. Sleep sounded very appealing.

He wobbled as he tried to stand, but Zee, who'd been poised nearby as his silent guardian steadied him, then picked him up. Casmir slumped, too tired to worry about his pride. If Zee was willing to carry him, he would happily accept.

"Have you gotten any updates on Dubashi?" Casmir's seizures usually only lasted a few minutes, at most, so he doubted he'd been out for long, but it was possible he had missed important reports before his brain had been working well enough again to grasp them.

"Nalini said they got him."

"Got him? Captured him?"

Kim looked back at him. Was that a pitying look? Maybe he would never stop being naive.

"They disabled his ship and when he tried to escape in a shuttle, three mercenary ships flew in and blew it to pieces. They wanted to make sure they could collect the bounty, so they sent men out in armor to look for the body. One group got the torso, another the head. Shayban and Nalini will have to decide who they want to give the reward to."

HOME FRONT

Imagining the grisly collection of body parts made Casmir queasy—as did the fact that he'd more or less come up with the idea that had resulted in this fate for the nemesis he'd never wanted. He tried to tell himself that he should be relieved. Kim and the crushers had saved the station from the bomb, and neither Casmir nor the Kingdom would have to worry about Dubashi again. But he was too tired to feel relief, and he doubted he would ever feel jubilant, not when he suspected Jager had, for his own reasons, engineered this enemy. If Jager hadn't decided to piss off Dubashi, it was unlikely the prince ever would have heard of Casmir, ever would have targeted him.

Kim stopped and pointed toward a medical shuttle flying slowly toward them, hugging the hull of the station.

"I know you well enough," she said, "to be certain you're not happy about anybody's death, but you've done all we set out to do in this system—and then some. If there's any fairness in the universe—and in the Kingdom—you'll be rewarded when we return home."

"I'd just like to go back to my job, teaching and leading a lab full of bright university students who love tinkering with robotics."

Was that true? He felt an intense nostalgia for his old life—for when his universe had been very small and he'd thought his highest calling was to teach a few dozen students a semester—but he wasn't sure if he could go back to that life. Not now that he knew about the injustices in the systems—including those stemming from his own monarchy. He would love to teach again, but he would also love a chance to make a difference on a larger stage.

"I'd like for you to be able to do that. And for me to be able to go back to my lab." Kim sighed wistfully as the shuttle settled onto the hull next to them.

"Do you think that'll happen?"

"No. I know the early reports that made it back to Royal Intelligence and King Jager about us weren't flattering. I doubt anything has changed. I have a feeling someone else will get credit for defeating Dubashi, and we'll be forced to leave our homes."

"I'm afraid of that too," Casmir said quietly as the hatch opened.

"I don't suppose you would entertain the idea of not going back at all?" Kim looked at him. "Tiamat Station is a possibility for both of us. Or you've also been offered a job here."

"There's still the blockade in our system. It's possible it'll peter out and disappear when the captains hear about Dubashi's death, but it's also possible they won't believe it and that our people will still have to fight. I think the fleet we've cobbled together here will go back with us, especially if each ship is promised a slydar detector, but I don't think they'll go without us. Or without me, at least. You could probably slip off. I wouldn't stop you."

Kim looked toward the shuttle for a long moment before speaking again. "No. I'll go back with you in case it makes a difference. We've been in this together since the beginning. We'll go home together to face our fates."

Casmir smiled, glad to have a friend to stand with him. "And if that fate is abysmal, *then* we'll run away to another system."

"Damn straight."

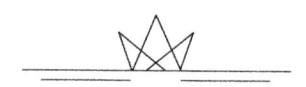

Bonita had been getting updates from Bjarke, Asger, and Qin, but she didn't allow herself to believe she would get out of this alive until the Drucker warship released its grip on the *Dragon*.

Two Kingdom warships, along with several ally vessels the Kingdom had rounded up, had arrived in the area a couple of hours earlier and had been ferrying passengers over to the Drucker ships. The one that had been looming above her like a giant wart was the last to receive a shuttle.

"Will the pirates actually comply with the Kingdom officers who are taking charge?" Viggo wondered. "It sounds like there'll only be a few of their officers on board each warship."

"And a few crushers."

"Crushers are not indestructible. Those other four warships haven't suffered any casualties and should still have their crews of hundreds."

"You have as many details as I do," Bonita said. "I gather the Druckers believe any one of those crushers can twitch a finger and afflict them with that virus."

The comm beeped, and when she answered it, Bjarke's face appeared on the display. His hair was tousled, his beard needed a trim, and soot smeared one side of his face, but he still managed to appear appealing.

HOME FRONT

"Good evening, Captain Laser," Bjarke drawled, his eyelashes drooping and reminding her of him naked, pretending to be the bear that was his namesake as he prowled to her bed.

"Good evening, *osito*. It looks like you got your head caught in a chimney." Bonita spotted Asger and Qin leaning against each other in the background. For support, she thought at first, but they kept gazing at each other with goofy smiles on their faces. Maybe they were simply enjoying sharing the same floor tile.

"Just a few explosions. I'm still fit and hale and capable of fulfilling all of your womanly needs in bed."

Apparently, she wasn't the only one who had randy thoughts after surviving a near miss with pirates.

"That's disgusting," Viggo said.

"Nobody asked you to listen," Bonita said.

"I thought he might have mission-critical data to share with us."

"This is *bedroom*-critical data. What are you wearing under your armor, Bjarke?"

"Nothing. With a press of a button, my full magnificence can be on display for you."

"*Truly* disgusting," Viggo said. "Make sure he washes himself before he presses anything. He's filthy."

"Yes. Yes, he is." Bonita smiled at Bjarke, pleased he'd made it and that he had, from what she'd heard, risked his life leading those crushers against an entire warship of pirates. All to help Qin. Oh sure, he'd probably planned from the beginning to get the pirate ships for his people, but she knew he'd also wanted to help Qin for Qin's sake. And maybe Bonita's sake, since Bonita cared about Qin. "Will you be visiting me here, Bjarke?" she added. "Or going home with your fleet?"

"I must go home with my fleet to ensure the blockade is broken and my people are safe, but there's no stipulation on which ship I ride in." Bjarke wriggled his eyebrows.

"I imagine they'd prefer it was one heading to your system."

"Allow me to invite you to head to my system—and transport me and my son William."

"As fond as I am of you and your son William, I don't have a cargo or any desire to fly into a war zone. *This*—" Bonita waved in the direction of the pirate ships, "—was bad enough."

"I don't think you'll be in any danger if you have your fine ship carry us into System Lion. Between the allies Ishii has gathered, the pirate ships we've temporarily acquired, and the groupies Dabrowski has gathered, the blockade ships should flee without much of a fight."

"Casmir has groupies?" Bonita asked. "Like a bunch of geeky roboticists eager to hold his tools?"

"A bunch of leading scientists and government leaders eager to hold his tools."

"That would explain the fleet of private ships now leaving Stardust Palace Station and heading to the gate," Viggo said. "I hope Casmir stops to chat with us along the way. I am certain he knows how to keep his clothes on when visiting another person's ship."

"Thankfully," Bonita murmured, looking at the long-range scanners. There *was* a large fleet of ships heading in this general direction, a hodgepodge from all over the systems, if she recognized the models correctly. Yachts, mining ships, armored transports, and private defenders. "If Casmir is leading that, the kid has come a long way since we met him. Or people have gotten crazy. Who would follow him anywhere?"

"He's making them all slydar detectors," Bjarke said dryly.

"What? He is? Can I get one if I join his little fleet?"

"If you also give us a ride to System Lion, yes. I can have my boy put in a good word for you. He's already promised crushers to the pirate captains, so William and Dabrowski *must* be close."

"Is this the way to win over the universe? Not by war and conquering but by giving people things?"

"By giving them *epic* things." Bjarke patted a nearby crusher with unexpected fondness. Maybe they'd bonded during their battle.

"Well, maybe someone should tell your king. His current methodology leaves a lot to be desired." Bonita swung the navigation arm toward her temple. "I'm setting in a course to come pick up Qin, and I'll allow you and Asger to tag along."

"You'll extend that invitation to her twenty-one sisters, I trust. They're eager to leave the Druckers behind."

"Er, I'll have to make up the guest cabins. *All* of them." And then some. Would Qin's sisters mind sleeping in the cargo hold?

"How domestic of you." Bjarke's eyes crinkled at the corners. "What will you wear while you perform these housekeeping duties?"

"The same outfit you're wearing under your armor."

HOME FRONT

"Sexy."

"Trust me. It will be." Bonita closed the comm.

"I find your new romance disturbing," Viggo said, "and not at all the sort of thing alluded to in Qin's books of fairy tales."

"You've been around in one way or another for over a century. You can't possibly believe that any romances are like what's in those books."

"Qin and Asger's might be."

"Asger goes to the lav naked in the middle of the night. No way is that fairy tale material."

"As opposed to borrowing your skimpy purple robe for the purpose? I find these knights all quite disappointing when it comes to romance. And getting along nicely with each other. You don't think there will be more door slamming if they're both back on board together again, do you?"

"They're getting along better now."

"I hope so. I also hope you purchased Bjarke his own robe on the station."

"I didn't think of it."

"Just smear petroleum jelly over my cameras now."

"Your vacuums would slurp that off in under three seconds."

"Curse their efficiency."

CHAPTER 34

"Y OU LOOK REMARKABLY WELL FOR SOMEONE WHO WAS in close proximity to a warhead detonating," Stardust Palace's doctor said, scrutinizing Kim's vitals on a medical scanner.

Kim and Casmir had spent an hour going through extensive decontamination procedures before being brought back on the station. Fortunately, even though the surface of the asteroid outside had hundreds of new craters and dozens of wrecked weapons platforms, the inside had survived unscathed. The lights and computers were all on in sickbay, and last she'd heard, power had been restored to the shield generator protecting the asteroid.

"I had a shield of crushers around me. *Two* shields." Kim grimaced, thinking of Reuben's sacrifice, and looked toward Casmir.

He was lying on the sickbay bed next to hers and should have been sleeping, given that she didn't think he'd gotten so much as a nap since they'd first arrived, but his eyes were open. Glassy, but open. He returned her grimace, probably knowing exactly what she was thinking.

A week ago, Kim wouldn't have guessed that the destruction—the *death*—of any of the crushers would bother her that much. Even though she'd been glad to have Zee as an ally numerous times, she'd seen him as one of Casmir's dozens of pet projects—and a somewhat buggy one at that—not as a friend. She wasn't sure she'd had time to start to consider Reuben as a friend exactly, but his laments about being unlucky had made him seem… human. And now that he'd sacrificed himself for them, she wished she'd spent more time talking to him, maybe losing some games of chance to him so he would have felt luckier.

"Very fortunate," the doctor said. "You appear fine and fit for travel, Scholar Sato."

"Am I fine and fit?" Casmir asked.

"Not at all. Your blood pressure is elevated, you're showing signs of intense stress and fatigue, and you have postictal cerebral edema."

"If that means I have a headache, I know. But I can travel, right?"

"I'm going to highly recommend at least three days of rest, including long and undisturbed periods of sleep."

Casmir made a mulish face.

Kim pointed to Zee, who was looming on the other side of Casmir's bed. "You should give those instructions to Zee, Doctor. Zee is strong enough to keep Casmir pinned to a bed for three days."

"I should think a sturdy feather could keep him pinned to his bed right now." The doctor sniffed and walked off to check on other patients who'd been brought in from ships that had suffered damage during the battle.

"I don't like him," Casmir whispered to Kim.

"I am currently engaged in network games with the inferior android Tork," Zee said, "but I am capable of enforcing a rest period at the same time. Crushers are excellent multi-taskers. It is quite delightful playing games without lag between moves caused by distance."

"You can rest on a ship heading home," Kim told Casmir, ignoring Zee's chatter. "If that's still where you think you should go."

Casmir opened his mouth, but before he could answer, Sultan Shayban walked in with Nalini.

Worry furrowed Casmir's brow. "You left the *Moon Dart*, Your Highness? Are you still willing to go with us to System Lion to help with the blockade?"

Kim wanted to tell him that he should let Ishii and the rest of the Kingdom ships handle that. Hadn't they done enough?

"We're willing, Casmir," Nalini said. "And you've promised all the delegates and Miners' Union leaders slydar detectors in exchange for their assistance, so their ships are sticking around too."

"As my daughter said, my ships will go with you under your command," Shayban said, "as Dubashi's death has been verified, and we owe you for assisting us in this matter, but are you *sure* you want to go back there, Professor? The Kingdom cannot be trusted as long as that family is in charge."

HOME FRONT

Kim's thoughts exactly. She wanted to go home, and wanted to see her family—she had finally received an update from her father, letting her know that he and her brothers were safe—but she couldn't help but think things might blow over if she and Casmir stayed away for a year or so. If they showed up now, she didn't know what would happen. It would be safer for both of them to find work here or on Tiamat Station for a while.

"The latest news reports that the blockade is still there and still a threat to our people." Casmir touched his temple. "If it's in my power to bring ships to help… I *have* to do that."

"Was it not Dubashi's money that financed that blockade?" Shayban asked. "If so, it should fall apart on its own as soon as word of his death arrives."

"I hope it does. But I'll go with those who will deliver that word. Besides, I'm hoping that some of the help I've done here will be taken into consideration and that King Jager will realize I'm not his enemy. And not an enemy to the Kingdom at all."

Shayban's mouth twisted. "I'd prefer it if you were."

"Casmir doesn't like to make enemies," Kim said. "That's why he gives everyone presents."

"What will you give Jager? Schematics to the slydar detector?" Shayban's bushy white eyebrows lifted. "I assume you made detailed ones when you were copying our prototype."

"Uhm." Casmir didn't look like he knew the safe answer to that question.

"If his past is any indication," Kim said, "he'll give Jager underwear or a purse made out of mushrooms."

Shayban snorted, then blinked and laughed. "That purse is in our gift shop, isn't it?"

Casmir rolled his eyes at Kim, but he also appeared relieved that Shayban had been distracted. "I didn't buy anyone the purse, just the interesting edibles package."

"*Interesting* is right."

"But you did give an enemy underwear?" Shayban asked.

"He wasn't a *complete* enemy by that point," Casmir said. "More of an uncertain entity."

"That still describes him," Kim murmured.

"Hm." Shayban stepped up to Casmir's bedside and rested a hand on his shoulder in a fatherly manner. "Go if you must to help your people, but know that a job opening is still available here for you. I'll throw in a free apartment overlooking the promenade."

Casmir looked a touch wistful, but all he said was, "Thank you, Sultan."

"Thank you. And thank you, as well, for your assistance, Scholar Sato." Shayban inclined his head toward her before heading out.

"We'll be ready to depart when you are," Nalini told Casmir, then looked at Kim. "Your mother and Tork are still on my ship and oddly eager to go to the Kingdom and, as your mother said, observe King Jager's gate piece."

Kim snorted. She'd almost forgotten about that. All these ships weren't going along *just* for slydar detectors. Some of those leaders and delegates had ulterior motives.

When they left, Kim shook her head at Casmir. "Are you sure about this?"

"No, but I'm afraid for my family if I just disappear. If it turns out that I need to do that, I'd prefer to take them with me. But I'm hoping the king will realize how wonderful I've been in this time of crisis for our people and that I should be welcomed home as a hero." He smiled wistfully.

Kim missed when he'd been cheerfully scheming about the future instead of being wistful. "A hero, huh? Are you going to ask for a parade and everything? Maybe a statue outside your lab at the university?"

"I'd settle for not being shot."

"You dream big."

"Yeah."

The next morning, Oku sat in what her mother called the tatami room and her father called the parlor, waiting while Finn, Chief Van Dijk, and the head of castle security spoke in the adjacent office. She didn't know if her father had been briefed on the night's chaos yet. He was with the Fleet on the way to the blockade.

Nervous about her upcoming meeting—or would it be an interrogation?—she squirmed on her cushion on the grass floor mat. Her shoulder twinged, and she grimaced. She'd spent an hour with a doctor

HOME FRONT

the night before—the wound had been deeper than she'd realized—and he'd injected nanites, but they were still at work, and her shoulder alternated between throbbing and itching. During the late-night medical attention, her mother had watched on tight-lipped and unspeaking. The castle vet had also stayed up late to treat Chasca, but she'd only been a little dehydrated and stressed after the ordeal. She was faring better today than Oku—nobody interrogated dogs.

Maddie and Finn's bodyguard had already been questioned. Oku hadn't been allowed to sit in. Her mother, Royal Intelligence, and castle security seemed to be trying to piece together the truth—or a cohesive story that might pass as the truth—from all the parties by questioning them independently.

Normally, since Oku had done nothing wrong, she wouldn't be worried, but she'd snubbed Van Dijk right before all this started, Finn told lies for a living, and what evidence she'd seen the night before had been confusing rather than enlightening. She had no idea who'd killed her father's pilot, and she didn't even know if the people who'd shot her and chained up Chasca had been captured.

While she twiddled her thumbs, Chasca walked into the parlor carrying a big bone with gristly meat bits stuck to it. Chasca was getting a lot of sympathy—and special treats—from the castle staff.

She wagged her tail and flopped onto the mat to work on the bone.

"I'm sure my mother will be pleased to have you leaving nasty pieces of meat and tendon on her grass mats," Oku said.

Chasca swished her tail enthusiastically.

The office door opened, and Finn walked out, a glassy expression replacing his usual smug one. Oku stared. Had he been *drugged* for the questioning? Would they also drug her?

Finn's bodyguard accompanied him—supported him as they walked out—and he leveled a cool stare in Oku's direction. Chasca ignored their passing in favor of working on her bone. That was probably best for one's sanity.

"Come in, Oku," came her mother's voice from the office.

"I guess you're not invited, girl." Oku pushed herself to her feet and left Chasca, trusting nothing else bad would befall her today.

Her own fate was more in question, though she felt a little heartened that Finn had been drugged. With a truth drug, she hoped. Even if they did the same to her, she had no fear of telling the truth.

Chief Van Dijk gave Oku a baleful stare as she waved her into a chair. "If they'd succeeded in kidnapping you, we wouldn't have been able to track you since you replaced your chip."

"Maddie was with me. You could have tracked her."

"*Maddie* almost got herself shot."

Oku looked at her mother instead of Van Dijk. "Do they know who was responsible? Finn said it wasn't him, that he just went along with it."

Her mother held up a hand. "We don't know yet. Intelligence is looking into it. Wait until the doctor has applied the eslevoamytal, please, before explaining your version of the events of last night."

Oku looked at the doctor preparing the jet injector. She hoped they'd gotten the *real* version out of Finn. And that she wouldn't somehow manage to say something to incriminate herself. She hadn't *done* anything wrong. But that didn't put her mind hugely at ease.

"You're questioning me?" Oku asked the obvious question as the doctor approached to test her for an allergic reaction. "With a truth drug?"

"I've just lost one son," her mother said. "I don't intend to lose more children to ambition and stupidity."

"That seems reasonable." Oku watched in morbid fascination as the doctor pricked her, then waited to gauge her reaction. As long as Finn had been questioned the same way, it didn't seem too unfair.

When nothing happened, the doctor gave her the injection. It wasn't until Chief Van Dijk sat athwart a backward-facing chair in front of her that Oku realized she might be in trouble. What if the woman took the opportunity to ask her about her chip?

She did. She started with that, damn it.

"Why did you have your chip replaced, Your Highness?"

Oku clenched her jaw, but it soon grew slack under the influence of the drug. A strange mellow state came over her, and she found herself patiently explaining that it wasn't right for her father to dangle her as a prize to Casmir nor for the Intelligence agents to spy on their conversations. Her mother's eyebrows flew up at one point, but Oku couldn't quite imagine what surprised her. Had Casmir's parents made it safely back to their home? She hoped so. They were nice people. They'd baked Chasca dog treats.

Van Dijk must have heard what she wanted, for she directed Oku's rambling to the previous night's events. With no hesitation, Oku explained everything, though she felt sheepish mentioning that she'd stunned Finn's bodyguard. And Finn. And who was this Sir Slayer who'd been sending him a feed?

Van Dijk murmured a few notes to her recorder at that. Fortunately, there weren't too many more questions, and Mother's eyebrows remained in a neutral position for the rest of the interview. When it was over, Mother walked Oku out herself. Oku wobbled a bit when Chasca bounded over and leaned against her legs.

"What happens next?" she asked, her mind still muzzy, but her sense of self-awareness slowly returning. "With Finn and, uhm, everything."

Her mother sighed. "I'm sending the recordings of these interviews to your father. He can figure it out on his way to derail that blockade, or afterward. I don't care when, but I refuse to have more plotting under my own roof. I'm sending Finn up to orbit to survey what Fleet ships were left to protect the planet and the moon base. Hopefully, it'll give him something to do besides become a target for schemes."

"Isn't he ruling the planet in Father's stead? Won't he object to being *sent*?"

"He can do whatever ruling he wants from a spaceship headed into orbit. He may believe he's in charge of something because your father gave him vague directions to keep an eye on things while he's gone, but he has little support among the Senate, Jager's aides, or even the staff. Jager may change something when he returns, but for now at least, Finn should be out of your hair."

Oku patted Chasca's head. "I'm glad to hear that." She was also glad that her mother had cared enough to step in. Perhaps still loopy with the drug, Oku hugged her mother.

"Don't let your guard down, Oku." Her mother patted her. "I'm not sure this will change anything long term, but at least your father and I know where you two truly stand now."

Chasca dropped her bone on the floor.

"We've *always* known where you stood," Mother told the dog.

Chasca wagged her tail.

"If there's nothing else," Oku said, backing up, "I have work to do in the greenhouse."

"Oku?" Her mother's tone turned to one of warning. "Van Dijk will push to have tracking software put in your new chip, and I think your father will agree to force the issue after what just happened."

Oku grimaced.

"And for your sake, I don't think you should send any more messages to Casmir Dabrowski."

Her grimace deepened.

"I don't know what's going on out there, and the reports filtering back have been patchy, but I know your father isn't pleased with him. You had best avoid speaking with him and his family until…" Her mother's bleak expression suggested she wanted to say *forever*. But as diplomatic as always, she said, "Until everything is settled and figured out."

Whenever that would be.

Oku wondered if Casmir could find a way to clear his name or at least avoid her father's wrath. It seemed like the deck was stacked against him, that her father wanted to believe him some nefarious plotter. She thought of the last message she'd gotten from him and shook her head. She couldn't believe it. But she could believe that he was idealistic enough, and so focused on what he believed was important, that he wouldn't invest the necessary time in defending himself and clearing his name.

Maybe he needed someone who cared to do that *for* him. After her mother left, Van Dijk walked out of the office with the doctor.

"Chief?" Oku held up a finger to stop her, while waving for the doctor to continue on.

"Yes, Your Highness?" Van Dijk approached warily.

Expecting some outrage at having been drugged? No. Oku didn't think she'd incriminated herself—and she hoped that Finn *had* incriminated himself—so she wasn't upset. Besides, the drug hadn't fully left her system, and she felt mellow rather than angry. Mellow and determined.

"I've been considering our talk yesterday." Sort of. She was considering it now and if she might have a bargaining chip.

Another wary, "Yes?" came out.

"Given the unpleasant events I experienced last night, I realize I may have been rash in not wanting you to be able to track me."

Van Dijk's eyebrows rose. "If you'd gone missing and we hadn't been able to find you, it would have been our responsibility." She touched her chest. "Royal Intelligence would have taken the blame. *I* would have taken it."

Whether she adored Oku personally or not, Van Dijk wouldn't want that. Yes, Oku had a bargaining chip.

HOME FRONT

"I'm not quite ready to put a tracker in my head again—I still need to consider this, as it disturbs me that nobody ever told me I was being monitored before." She frowned, though she'd gotten over it already. Van Dijk didn't need to know that.

"It would have been your father's choice to tell you, Your Highness."

"Of course. If you do me a favor, I'll consider coming in to have my chip altered." Oku realized that was a vague offer, not a promise, and might not entice Van Dijk. "I'll also send you what a computer hacker friend of mine learned about the person who tried to rope Finn in on my kidnapping scheme. I trust Finn didn't know the person's identity?"

Van Dijk's face was hard to read—she'd spent her career perfecting the art of not giving away information for free—but she nodded in agreement. "He didn't know. He was so eager for the opportunity to get rid of you without having to lift a finger, he went along with it foolishly. I trust your father, when he returns, will talk some sense into the boy. If Finn would betray you, he might also betray Jager." She lifted her chin. "I've put this in my report to him."

Oku hadn't expected Van Dijk to admit that much to her. Maybe it was naive, but she hoped that meant the woman liked her—or would at least prefer to work with her—more than Finn.

"I would like whatever information you acquired to see if it's in addition to or different from what we've discovered," Van Dijk added.

"I'll give you what I learned if you give me everything that's come back from the Fleet in System Stymphalia, from Ambassador Romano, from your agents and spies around the system and from Stardust Palace Station, if you have an agent there."

"We don't."

"No? Hm, I have a friend who's there now who would probably send me a detailed report. I'll share it with you if you share everything you have with me."

"Princess Tambora?" Van Dijk guessed, reminding Oku how much Royal Intelligence knew about all her trips and who she made friends with in other systems.

"Yes." Oku lifted her chin, expecting an argument that Tambora was too young to be reliable. Oku still had to deal with that prejudice herself when speaking with all the crusty old senators and people in control of her life.

"I'll accept that report," Van Dijk surprised her by saying. "And I'll send over what I have that isn't too sensitive for—"

"All of it."

"Pardon?"

"Send everything. If anyone has clearance, surely I do." Oku lowered her voice. "Especially now."

She didn't want to claim her older brother's vacated position—and she highly doubted her father would ever name her his heir—but Van Dijk was someone who considered all the possibilities, and there *was* a remote possibility it would come to pass. If so, she would have to deal with Oku in an official capacity for a long time to come.

"Very well, Your Highness. All my reports from the system. Unfiltered." Van Dijk's eyebrows twitched. "I hope you can read quickly."

"You've seen my academic records."

"I have. Stay safe, Your Highness." Van Dijk bowed and left.

Oku dared hope she had a new ally, or at least someone who would send her what she wanted. She also hoped that while delving into the reports, she would find what she wanted to be there, proof that Casmir had been working for the good of the Kingdom all along, not against it.

CHAPTER 35

CASMIR'S HEART WAS POUNDING WHEN HE REGAINED AWARENESS after coming out of the wormhole.

His first thought was that something had happened, that they were already under attack, but the voices of Nalini's crew were calm and quiet as they reported in. The Kingdom warships and their allies, the five Drucker vessels, and most of the fleet Casmir had temporarily acquired had gone through ahead of the *Dart*, so even if the blockaders had been prepared to jump on anyone coming through the gate, they would have been too busy to attack this ship.

His second thought was that he would have a seizure or some other medical event, and he freed an arm from his pod so he could rest it on his chest. He could *feel* his heart pounding under his fingers. It wasn't his imagination. But he didn't experience any of the telltale symptoms of an impending seizure.

"Maybe your body just knows that you've come home," he muttered to himself, "and that home is a dangerous place for you now."

Zee leaned around the side of his pod and peered at him. "Are you well, Casmir Dabrowski?"

"I hope so."

"Your heart rate is accelerated."

"I'm nervous." Casmir smiled, hoping that was all it was.

After all he'd been through, it would be mortifying if he developed some terrible new illness as he flew back into his home system. He bit his lip. The home system where he didn't know if he would be welcome...

"Maybe we will be if we can take care of this blockade," he muttered.

The words were for himself, but Nalini looked over at him from the command pod. On the journey to the gate, she'd kept offering the seat to him, pointing out that he was in charge of this hodgepodge fleet, but he kept refusing, saying he was more comfortable at the scanner station. And it was true. He kept tinkering with and refining the slydar detector.

"I think that's going to happen whether we lift a finger or not," she said. "Have you checked the scanners yet?"

No, he'd been busy checking his heartbeats.

Feeling sheepish, Casmir focused on his station. There were a *lot* of ships out there. His mouth dropped as he worried that they all represented the invasion force that Dubashi had put together, but no… Many of those were Kingdom Fleet ships, and not only the warships Casmir had been working with for months now. There were at least twenty warships in an array facing the gate and firing at the blockaders. Ishii was leading his own fleet to flank those same blockaders, careful to stay out of the crossfire.

Nalini murmured an order to her helmsman to do the same.

"It doesn't look like they even needed our help," she pointed out.

A chip message popped up from Ishii. *Dabrowski, this slydar detector Grunburg and Hodges put together with your schematics is fantastic. But is it correct? We're only reading about twenty hidden ships, and nothing as large as our warships. Is that what you get?*

Yes. Casmir sent over the results from his scan of the area around the gate so Ishii could compare.

This is excellent. We'll focus on those. Have your princess help us, since we're the only two ships with slydar detectors.

If anything, she's Tristan's princess. Casmir didn't have a princess, alas, though he still dreamed of a coffee date with Oku. Maybe this would work out for him somehow and that could happen. Ishii knew that he'd helped the Kingdom. Could one captain make a difference? He was a noble. Maybe the king and the Senate would listen to him if he spoke on Casmir's behalf.

I don't care. Just get that pretty Miners' Union ship over here to blow up hidden stragglers.

"Captain Ishii of the *Osprey* humbly requests that we assist him in targeting the ships with slydar hulls," Casmir said.

Nalini gave him such a flat look that Casmir wondered if his message had somehow been intercepted. "Your people are abysmal at being humble Casmir. All except you and Tristan. It's no wonder you fled."

HOME FRONT

"I believe Tristan was ostracized," Casmir murmured, "and it's possible the same will happen to me."

She gave orders to the helmsman and the weapons officer, then turned a gentler look toward Casmir. "You have a home on Stardust Palace if you want it, though I understand you're wanted many places now. You can build slydar detectors and crushers and bring pirate fleets to their knees with viruses. Wherever you end up, you can expect monthly kidnapping attempts as people risk life and wealth to acquire your brain."

Casmir touched his seizure-prone skull and would have laughed, except he thought of poor Scholar Sunflyer, who'd been kidnapped for *his* brain. The idea of something similar happening to him was more horrifying than funny.

"No kidnappers would succeed in obtaining Casmir Dabrowski," Zee stated. "I will always be his bodyguard and protect him."

"Thank you, Zee." Casmir patted his solid arm.

Zee ruffled his hair.

"If the one you made for my father ever ruffles his hair," Nalini said, "I want to be there to see it."

"Doesn't he wear that turban most of the time?"

"Yes. Would that stop your crusher? Your Zee?"

"No," Zee stated.

Casmir looked up at him. "I believe you patted my head when I was wearing my kippah for prayer."

"This is true. I did not wish to dislodge it."

"Crushers are considerate," Casmir told Nalini.

"Who would have imagined?" she murmured and smiled.

"We're going in after two armored yachts," the helmsman said. "One of the Kingdom ships and two of our allies are following us to fire where we fire."

"Let's do this," Nalini said.

"She's only determined," someone said, "so she can visit the planet and find real-estate deals."

"I'm also interested in deals on their moon," Nalini said.

The sense of gravity shifted, Casmir's pod protecting him from the various g-forces as the *Dart* tore after Kingdom enemies, and his stomach protested. He'd taken an anti-nausea pill, but it didn't seem to matter today. His whole body was on edge.

Fortunately, the battle was over in less than an hour, with little damage done to the allies he'd gathered. He had the feeling the large and impressive Kingdom Fleet had been in the process of mopping up the blockade when they'd arrived and that all they'd done was help. So, why had that fleet taken so many weeks to get organized and get out here?

Casmir was about to start scanning the local news, now that they were in the system and finally had close to real-time access to it, when Kim walked onto the bridge. The *Dart* wasn't in active pursuit of any ships then, and it was relatively safe to move about. Casmir's stomach was also less queasy than it had been earlier, thankfully.

Heard from anyone who might have beaten us here? Casmir messaged her silently as she sat down in a nearby pod. He knew the *Dragon* carrying Bonita, Asger, Bjarke, and Qin had slid in at the rear of the formation and was, probably to the knights' disgruntlement, avoiding the battlefield. But that wasn't who he had in mind.

Rache?

Who else? I was wondering—worrying—if he was already halfway to Odin and plotting Jager's assassination. Casmir's slydar detector would only detect the *Fedallah* if it was nearby.

I haven't heard from him since he left System Stymphalia, no. I'm not sure I want to check in to find out how his plans are going.

Understandable.

I came up here when I realized how easy this blockade breach is turning out to be. Between our ships and all those Kingdom Fleet ships, they're pulverizing the invaders.

Yes. I noticed.

*Is Nalini planning to take her ship to Odin? Or will she and all of Shayban's allies—*your *new allies—return to their system after they've finished giving the help they promised?*

I'm not sure. They may consider me an ally because I promised them slydar detectors, but there's also the gate piece that Jager has that's apparently key. I think Nalini will fly us to Odin, if that's what we want. Casmir raised his eyebrows, wondering if Kim was thinking of going with her mother to Tiamat Station. He wasn't delusional enough to think that all of his—their—transgressions would be forgiven because they'd come to help with the blockade.

"That's unexpected," Tristan murmured from the communications station.

HOME FRONT

Nalini looked over at him. "Your fellow knights have learned you're here, realized what a mistake they made to boot you out, and are begging for you to return?"

"No. Asger messaged me—he and Sir Bjarke were located and briefed shortly after they arrived. King Jager is out here personally. On the *Starhawk*. It's his flagship, and it was at the head of the battle."

"Where is the *Starhawk* now?" Casmir had been uneasy before, but now that he knew Jager was here instead of a week's travel away on Odin, his insides tied themselves into knots. He was at the scanner station and could have answered his own question, but he was afraid to look.

"Uhm." Tristan paused. "Maybe it's a coincidence, but it's left the Fleet formation and is heading this way."

"Oy." Casmir slumped deeper into his pod.

"Maybe he's learned that Princess Nalini is on this ship and wants to thank her for coming to help." Kim didn't sound like she believed that.

"Given that we kicked Jorg off our station, I highly doubt that," Nalini said. "He deserved it, but what are the odds that his father will agree?"

"Especially now that he's dead," Tristan murmured.

"Any chance they were estranged and his father didn't like Jorg?" Nalini asked.

"No," Tristan said, then sighed. "A second warship is flying after the *Starhawk*. And a third. The *Kestrel* and the *Raven*. That's one high-powered escort, if that's what it is. All three ships are on course for our position. And now, we have an incoming comm. It's the *Starhawk*."

Casmir wanted to disappear completely into his pod. Maybe he was being self-centered to believe this had to do with him, but…

I'm giving you a heads-up, came a message from Ishii, *even though I risk my career to do so.*

King Jager is heading for me and wants me dead?

Well, he's heading for you. I don't know if he plans to kill you, but he at least plans to collect you.

Thanks for the warning.

Here's one more: he requested our slydar detector, and we gave it to him. The Starhawk *has it now. In case you have any allies using slydar… they had better stay out of the way. He's got a lot of firepower with him out here.*

Where was all his firepower during the weeks and weeks that the gate was blockaded? Casmir asked, though he'd long since suspected Jager of feigning ineptness to get what he wanted. More power? A citizenship too scared to do anything but give it to him? Permission to go to war? Maybe all of those. At the expense of their home world being bombed and thousands of people being killed.

Ishii's pause was long, but in the end, all he said was, *It's not my place to question the king. I just commed to say that if you have a way to get out of the system before he reaches you, now would be a good time.*

Casmir could tell from the ships barreling toward them that it was already too late, but he appreciated the message. *I'm glad I got to know you again as a man, Sora. Best wishes for your future and a career your father will be proud of.*

Shit, Dabrowski. Don't get yourself killed.

I'll try.

"I'm putting them on the forward display. They want video." Tristan peered apologetically over the side of Casmir's pod. "And to talk to you."

"Is it too late to flee back through the gate?" Since Casmir hadn't managed to disappear, he reluctantly rotated his pod to face the display.

"Trust me," Nalini said. "It crossed my mind."

"They're faster than us," Tristan said.

The star field on the display faded and was replaced by King Jager's craggy face. Casmir didn't think he'd seen him since they'd faced each other outside of the clinic in Zamek City. His mind summoned a dozen perky and silly greetings that he could have babbled out with false cheer, but no amount of cheer or feigning ignorance would work on the king now. Instead, he bowed his head—all he could manage from the pod—and attempted to look calm and competent. At least not terrified.

"Casmir Dabrowski," Jager stated without preamble, "you are suspected of playing a role in the murder of my son Prince Jorg."

Casmir blinked. Of all the accusations Jager could have made, that wasn't one he'd expected. "I did not."

"My reports say that your virus was used on ships chasing him and possibly on his ship."

What? It wasn't *his* virus.

"You've been at odds with the Kingdom since before you left this system," Jager continued. "You had opportunities to right your wrongs by obeying, and you hared off to pursue your own schemes. Now—" his already cold voice grew even colder, "—you have arrived in my system with an invasion fleet."

HOME FRONT

"We came to help Captain Ishii and the Kingdom with the blockade," Casmir managed to say. "That's all. Your Highness, you instructed us to raise a fleet."

"I instructed *Jorg* to raise a fleet. You were instructed to build crushers and obey his commands, not to collude to *kill* him."

"I did no such thing. Someone else attacked and boarded his ship." Casmir didn't look at Kim and didn't bring up Rache—did he truly need to? Surely, Ambassador Romano or Lieutenant Meister on Ishii's ship hadn't missed the fact that the *Fedallah* had been there and responsible for that. How could they have?

"My Intelligence reports also inform me that this ragtag fleet from half a dozen other systems wants the meager few gate pieces that we managed to acquire. Meager few when it should have been the complete gate, but you thwarted us there too. You've been working against the Kingdom—against *me*—from the beginning."

Casmir clenched his fists in frustration. How did he respond to that? He had been trying to distribute the gate fairly, not help Jager stash it away only for the Kingdom. He focused on the one thing that absolutely had no shred of truth to it.

"I didn't kill Prince Jorg, Your Highness, nor did I ever plot against him in any way."

"Captain Hammerstein of the *Kestrel* is going to take over the mop-up duty. I am personally going to arrest you and take you back to Zamek City for interrogation before your ultimate fate is decided." Jager's eyes narrowed. "If you resist the men I send over, or if you try to bring any allies along, including those crushers, your family will *also* be arrested, and their ultimate fate will become something we will decide pending yours."

"I am Zee, Casmir Dabrowski's bodyguard. I must accompany him wherever he travels."

"*No* crushers," Jager repeated.

Casmir was so numb, he didn't know how to respond.

His family. This had been his fear all along. That his actions would put his parents in trouble. Why had he even come back? He could have sent whatever ships would help with Ishii and... and what? Stayed on Stardust Palace until some assassin came for him? Spent the rest of his life looking over his shoulder? He had to clear his name. But how?

Next to him, Kim's fists were also clenched, fury stamped on her usually calm face. She looked like she was about to explode.

Don't get involved, Casmir urged her via his chip. *So far, he only wants me.* He forced a quick smile. *Let's not remind him that you're here too.*

It's ludicrous that anyone could think you had anything to do with Jorg's death. If you hadn't given Rache that virus, Dubashi's ships would have gotten him anyway. That idiot sealed his own fate by pissing off everyone in that system.

"My flagship is sending a shuttle full of armored soldiers for you," Jager said. "I repeat, since you're so poor at following directions, you will enter it unarmed and *alone*. No friends, no bags of tools, and *no* crushers. You will order all of the crushers you created to obey me and my Fleet captains. If you don't, they will be melted down and destroyed." Jager glanced at some readout to the side. "The shuttle is on the way."

The display went dark.

"Can you even do that?" Tristan asked. "Change who they obey with a snap of your fingers?"

"*No*," Zee said firmly.

Casmir sighed again. "I could give them all temporary orders, but I'd have to reprogram them for what he wants. It's in their base programming to defend themselves, so he will not have good luck if he tries to melt them or destroy them."

"I will defend myself, and I will defend Casmir Dabrowski." Zee put a hand on Casmir's shoulder and frowned down at him inasmuch as his vague mouth had been designed to frown. "I will not allow you to be taken prisoner. This ship must fly out of this system and escape."

"Thank you, Zee." His heart ached that his robotic defender cared and wanted to keep him from going off to some horrible fate, very possibly death. "But I have to cooperate."

"Casmir," Kim said sharply. "You can't hand yourself over to him without a way to escape or protect yourself."

"I can't do anything—anything *else*—that will put my family at risk." He blinked away moisture trying to form in his eyes as he wondered what his parents had been told and what they believed about his actions these past months. All he'd ever wanted to do was make the Kingdom a better place—without sticking it to the rest of humanity in the process.

"You cannot go alone without a crusher," Zee said. "Without *me*."

"I have to." Casmir hugged Zee, expecting the crusher to do nothing or maybe pat him on the head.

HOME FRONT

Zee hesitated, as if figuring out the proper human response, then hugged him back. The moisture forming in Casmir's eyes turned to tears that ran down his cheeks. He didn't care.

Next, he hugged Kim. She was just as frustrated about letting him go as Zee, and that touched him, but he couldn't disobey Jager. Not this time.

She didn't hesitate to hug him back, but he sensed that she also wanted to punch him for getting himself into this mess. He couldn't blame her for the sentiment.

Lastly, he shook Tristan's and Nalini's hands, then headed off the bridge to wait for the shuttle.

EPILOGUE

"W E'RE GETTING ANOTHER COMM MESSAGE." TRISTAN'S VOICE HAD an odd note to it. "Encrypted. Tight-beam."

Kim was sitting in her pod, kicking the underside of a console. She would have been pacing, or maybe taking out her aggressions in a sparring match with Zee, but the *Dart* was stationary in space and had no gravity. That made pacing difficult.

"Who is it?" Even Nalini, who barely knew Casmir, sounded glum and sad.

The Kingdom shuttle had arrived, and he'd gone with them without a fight, and without her or Zee, as he'd promised. It had disappeared back into the belly of the Kingdom warship, and he was now King Jager's prisoner. Would he even make it back to Odin alive?

Nalini had been forbidden from following Jager's warship and ordered to take her hodgepodge fleet out of the system within twenty-four hours or there would be "repercussions." The ungrateful bastards.

Kim had heard that Bonita and everybody else who wasn't flying a Kingdom military vessel had been given the same order, all save the Drucker warships, since they were being commanded by some of Ishii's officers. Someone must have forgotten that there were numerous crushers aboard the *Dart* and the *Dragon*. Jager had mentioned that he wanted Casmir to reprogram them, but his people hadn't wanted any to come in the shuttle with Casmir, so they were still here. Kim wished she knew how that could help.

"Captain Rache from the *Fedallah*," Tristan said.

"Is he nearby?" That surprised Kim—she'd assumed he had arrived days earlier and was halfway to Odin—but then she realized it made sense. *Jager* was out here by the gate. Where *else* would Rache be?

"I can't pinpoint the exact source of the transmission, but it seems to be coming from behind the gate." Tristan pulled himself over to the scanner station where Casmir had been sitting. "His ship doesn't show up even with the slydar detector activated, but it's possible he knows its precise range and is just outside of it."

"Is there any reason why we would want to talk to him?" Nalini asked.

"I don't," Tristan said.

Kim wanted to talk to him. Maybe he would be willing to help one last time and retrieve Casmir.

She sent him a message via her chip. *I'm on board the* Moon Dart, *but maybe you already knew that.*

Yes. I know much, he replied, no lag in the response. He was close.

Another time, she would have poked fun at his cockiness, but she wasn't in the mood. *What do you want? Tristan and Nalini aren't interested in talking to you.*

How rude. I was going to invite Tristan to join his fellow knights on my ship and give them a ride to Odin, if they wish it. I understand my chatty brother is headed that way on a warship turned prison transport.

Hope blossomed in her heart. *What other knights? Are you talking about staging a rescue?*

The two Asgers and a bunch of furry women. I suppose we can't call them knights. *When the* Dragon *gets close enough to my ship lurking back here and nobody is paying attention—we may need to wait a few hours—I'll send a shuttle to retrieve them. Captain Lopez, like everyone else here who isn't in the Kingdom Fleet, has been ordered to leave the system. Her passengers, having learned of Dabrowski's capture, wish to rescue him.*

And you're willing to help? I assume you know Jager is out here.

Jager is out here on the most armored warship in the Fleet, and as I've learned, it now carries the slydar detector that Casmir built the schematics for. Ironic, don't you think, that he has given the Kingdom the device that will preclude me from getting close enough to rescue him?

Then what's your plan?

Follow at a distance. Bide our time. Find an opportunity.

Asger and Bjarke are willing to go with you to do that? Kim asked. *They aren't your biggest fans.*

It seems the knights have had a falling out with their chain of command and none of their own people were authorized to go pick them up and take them home. They are, in effect, in exile. And desperate. In desperate times, old enemies can become allies.

Kim rubbed her face. *I would love to come with you, Rache. David. I am slightly suspicious of your motives. I'd like to believe you care enough to want to get Casmir before they interrogate and kill him, but I know you have another mission.* She had no trouble imagining him using the knights' rescuing Casmir as a distraction while he went after Jager.

I'll be happy to tell you all about my motives over a glass of wine as we sail off for Odin together.

Kim lowered her hand. What choice did she have? He had the only ship that could go after Casmir, at least from a distance.

Am I going to regret this? she asked.

Certainly not. I purchase only the finest vintages of wine, and I have a special refrigerator unit that uses the marvel of modern technology to keep the bottles from being disturbed by fluctuations in our gravity.

She shook her head.

"Scholar Sato?" Tristan asked. "Is everything all right? They're still comming us. Is there a reason we should answer?"

"You and I, and I suppose all of the crushers on board, are being offered a ride to Odin to rescue Casmir. Asger, Bjarke, Qin, and her newly rescued sisters are all coming."

"A ride by… Rache?" Tristan's face twisted with distaste.

"A ride by Rache. Maybe you'll like his ship more if you're not stuffed in a locker inside a shuttle in his bay."

"I doubt it," Tristan said glumly.

"Do you want to go?" Nalini asked him curiously.

"I… think we owe Casmir one." Tristan spread his hand. "Stardust Palace would be a lot worse off if not for him. Him and Scholar Sato." He shifted his hand toward her.

Kim said nothing, not wanting any of the credit. She hadn't done anything except go along.

"How do we meet up with him?" Nalini asked Kim, apparently more interested in letting *her* talk to the nefarious Rache than in answering his comm.

"Head toward the gate as if we're going to comply with Jager's order to leave the system. I believe he'll find us."

"Fantastic," Tristan muttered.

Tristan and I would be delighted to join you and our allies to rescue Casmir, Kim messaged Rache.

Tristan will be delighted? Interesting. You must have told him about my wine.

I told him he wouldn't have to hide in a locker this time.

Of course not. He can share a cabin with some of the furry women.

Funny.

I moonlight as a comedian.

As the *Dart* accelerated toward the gate to rendezvous with Rache, Kim sent a message to Casmir. She kept it vague with no promise of rescue—she had to assume that Fleet Intelligence on that warship was the best and could intercept it—but she tried to give him a shred of hope without detailing anything definitive.

Unfortunately, she didn't receive an answer. The warship wasn't so far away that there should have been noticeable lag. They must have stuck him in a cell with shielding so he couldn't access the network. By the time he reached Odin, he would be going crazy, whether they tortured him or not.

We're coming for you, Casmir, she thought but did not send, hoping he somehow knew. *We're coming for you.*

THE END

Printed in Great Britain
by Amazon